BEWITCHED

*The Ghostly Tales of
Edith Wharton*

BEWITCHED

The Ghostly Tales of Edith Wharton

Edited by

MIKE ASHLEY

THE BRITISH LIBRARY

This collection first published in 2025 by
The British Library
96 Euston Road
London NW1 2DB
bl.uk

Selection and introduction © 2025 Mike Ashley
Volume copyright © 2025 The British Library Board

Cataloguing in Publication Data
A catalogue record for this publication is available from the British Library

ISBN 978 0 7123 5587 2
eISBN 978 0 7123 6888 9

Cover design by Mauricio Villamayor with illustration by Mag Ruhig.
Original interior ornaments by Mag Ruhig.
Frontispiece photographic print from the Library of
Congress Archives: LC-USZ62-29408.
Text design and typesetting by Tetragon, London
Printed in Glasgow by Bell and Bain Ltd

CONTENTS

Introduction: Behind the Façade	vii
Story Sources	xii
A Note from the Publisher	xiii
The Lady's Maid's Bell	1
The House of the Dead Hand	25
Afterward	55
The Eyes	89
The Triumph of Night	111
Bewitched	139
Miss Mary Pask	163
The Moving Finger	179
Mr. Jones	197
Pomegranate Seed	227
The Fullness of Life	261

INTRODUCTION
Behind the Façade

Edith Wharton (1862–1937) was rich—very rich. But that did not make her happy. She was quite a solitary child—despite having two elder brothers—and was happiest in her father's library where she loved to turn the pages of books, even before she could read, just imagining where they might transport her. Her whole childhood seemed to be one of trying to hide or escape, coming to a head when at seventeen she had to face the debutante's ball—coming out into society. She never regarded herself as pretty—not helped by her parents reminding her of her looks—and she remembered that evening as "one long cold agony of shyness." It made her even more desperate to seek solace in books and to yearn to be a writer. She began a long story, "Fast and Loose", when she was only fourteen, though it was never published. But she did write poetry and her mother financed the publication of her first book, *Verses*, in 1878. In the same year of her society debut, 1879, she had her first poem published professionally, "Only a Child", about a child who commits suicide in prison. Perhaps she was trying to tell people something, if only they would listen.

She was highly strung and impressionable. Her parents tried to stop her reading what they called "silly books", but once, when she was nine and recovering from typhoid fever, she was given a book by "nice" children which turned out to be a gothic horror novella about robbers and ghosts. It frightened her to the core and for years she was afraid that something

INTRODUCTION

was following her or hiding behind a door. She later confessed that until her late twenties she could not sleep in a room if she knew it contained a book with a ghost story and would even burn such books to be rid of them. Yet this girl grew up to be, in the words of horror authority Jack Sullivan, "one of America's finest writers of ghost stories." There is little doubt that because she had known fear, lived and breathed it, she could also evoke it, and the stories collected here include her most atmospheric. Situations where you find yourself watched by a pair of eyes at the end of the bed, or enter a house saturated with the presence of past occupants, or—a frequent theme in many of her stories—places where the past will not let go.

*

Edith Wharton was born Edith Newbold Jones in New York City on 24 January 1862. Her family were among the New York elite, regarded as aristocracy. Her father, George Frederic Jones (1821–1882), was heir to the fortune of his cousins who owned the Chemical Bank of New York, still one of the largest banks in the United States. It so happened her father died before his cousin, so it was Edith who received $120,000—roughly $4 million today—on her cousin's death in 1888. This was in addition to a $20,000 trust fund set up on her father's death in 1882.

It has been said that the phrase "keeping up with the Jones's", meaning trying to give oneself the appearance of being as rich as the richest, applied to Edith's family. Although this has been disputed, it is still very apt. The Jones's spent money like there was no tomorrow. Edith's aunt, Elizabeth, had financed the construction of a gothic mansion called Wyndcliffe in the Hudson Valley in the 1850s and this apparently set off a chain of such projects by the wealthy socialites. However, Edith's father had trouble keeping up with the rest of the Jones's. He ran into financial problems and in 1868 took his family to Europe, settling first in France and later Germany and Italy, where his spending was rather more limited. It was in Germany that Edith caught typhoid and very nearly died.

INTRODUCTION

The family returned to New York in 1872 where Edith received a home education. The family continued to travel and her father died in France in 1882. Soon after, Edith was engaged to Henry Leyden Stevens (1859–1885), from another aristocratic New York family, who spent his time playing sports and was woefully ill-matched to the studious and intellectual young Edith. The engagement lasted barely two months. A year later Edith met Edward, or Teddy, Wharton (1850–1928), a banker. They married in April 1885. Like Stevens, he was also a sportsman, but older and more socially aware. They loved to travel and shared a passion for dogs. Moreover, Teddy encouraged Edith to write, introducing her to a friend, Egerton Winthrop, who became her literary advisor.

She began selling poetry to *Atlantic Monthly* and *Scribner's* from 1889 onwards and her first story, "Mrs. Manstey's View", appeared in the July 1891 edition of *Scribner's*. Unlike her later stories, which were peopled with the New York elite, this portrays an elderly widow, alone in her home, who fears that the view she enjoys from her window will be spoiled by new buildings. Once again, Edith was revealing her mood. Her marriage had not been as happy as she had hoped. Teddy had bouts of mental illness—what we call bipolar today, but known as melancholia or manic depression back then. His father also suffered from it and committed suicide in May 1891, which further aggravated Teddy's depression. Edith had hoped that her marriage would allow her to escape from the burden of life at home. She had become convinced that her parents—especially her mother—were disappointed in her. She had not become the society belle they had expected and instead was reclusive and studious. Alas her marriage became another trap. Teddy sought solace in a mistress, leaving Edith increasingly alone.

The couple kept up appearances, however, travelling extensively and establishing comfortable homes for themselves. Her primary home became The Mount in Lenox, Massachusetts, which they had built and moved into in 1902. Her mother had died the previous year, leaving her another legacy.

It has been estimated that Edith's income from her various trust funds amounted to at least $22,000 a year, in addition to her writing income which was becoming substantial.

Her first weird tale, "The Fullness of Life", appeared in *Scribner's* for December 1893. It is unlike her later tales and again reflects her own state of mind at that time. She confessed to her editor at *Scribner's* that the story was written "in one long shriek." Because it concerns an after-life experience, I have placed it at the end of this collection, where it feels more suitable.

Edith now buried herself in her writing. She had first-hand experience of New York society and would reveal all for what it was. For her first novel, *The Valley of Decision* (1902), however, she distanced herself from New York and set it in eighteenth-century Italy. It nevertheless follows the rise to power of a young boy raised in poverty though of noble birth, and explores the conflict between individuality and the expectations of authority. It served as a dry run for her first socialite novel, *The House of Mirth* (1905), which again explores the vicissitudes of a young woman who has fallen from grace and struggles to survive in what is portrayed as a restricting and corrupt upper-class society. The book became a bestseller and established Wharton's reputation which would continue to grow, culminating in *The Age of Innocence* (1920), her best-known novel for which she would become the first woman to win the Pulitzer Prize for Fiction.

Throughout this period Wharton would occasionally return to writing ghost stories and weird tales. Her earliest fully-fledged ghost story is also her best known, "The Lady's Maid's Bell" (1902), in which the supernatural element is crucial to the protection of an ill wife from her cruel husband. The relationship between husbands and wives in Wharton's stories clearly relate to her own situation. Although she had continued to live with Teddy, any feelings between them had diluted and they would eventually divorce in 1913. You will find in many of these stories patriarchal figures who dominate wives or children and whose coercive control lives on after them, as in "The House of the Dead Hand" (1904). Sometimes it works the other way round.

INTRODUCTION

In "Pomegranate Seed" (1931) it seems that a man continues to receive letters from his dead wife advising him what he should do.

But I shall reveal no further spoilers. Wharton continued to write ghostly tales for the rest of her life, assembling the majority of them in *Ghosts*, published just after her death in 1937. She had continued to travel, spending much of her time in Europe, including England. She was nominated three times for the Nobel Prize for Literature (in 1927, 1928 and 1930), but was not selected.

She died in France of a stroke, aged 75, and was buried at Les Gonards Cemetery in Versailles.

Edith Wharton is a fine example of a remarkable talent unsuited to the world in which she was born and who sought escape in her imagination. The fact that she wrote so many ghost stories, despite originally being horrified by them, says much about her character. Rather than escape her fears, she faced them, and in so doing produced some of the most memorable literature of her day.

MIKE ASHLEY, 2025

Mike Ashley is an award-winning author, anthologist and genre encyclopaedia editor with a specialism for seeking out rare stories from the periodicals and magazines of the nineteenth and twentieth centuries. He has edited multiple collections of lost stories for the Tales of the Weird series—including *Queens of the Abyss, From the Depths, Glimpses of the Unknown* and *The Ghost Slayers*—along with hardback volumes of stories by Algernon Blackwood, Arthur Conan Doyle and Margaret Oliphant.

STORY SOURCES

"The Fullness of Life", first published in *Scribner's Magazine*, December 1893. First collected in volume one of *The Collected Short Stories of Edith Wharton*, edited by R.W.B. Lewis (Scribner's, 1968).

"The Moving Finger", first published in *Harper's Monthly Magazine*, March 1901 and collected in *Crucial Instances* (Scribner's, 1901).

"The Lady's Maid's Bell", first published in *Scribner's Magazine*, November 1902 and collected in *The Descent of Man and Other Stories* (Scribner's, 1904).

"The House of the Dead Hand", first published in *Atlantic Monthly*, August 1904 and collected in *The Descent of Man and Other Stories*, English edition only (Macmillan, 1904).

"Afterward", first published in *Century Magazine*, January 1910 and collected in *Tales of Men and Ghosts* (Scribner's, 1910).

"The Eyes", first published in *Scribner's Magazine*, June 1910 and collected in *Tales of Men and Ghosts* (Scribner's, 1910).

"The Triumph of Night", first published in *Scribner's Magazine*, August 1914 and collected in *Xingu and Other Stories* (Scribner's, 1916).

"Bewitched", first published in *Pictorial Review*, March 1925 and collected in *Here and Beyond* (Appleton, 1926).

"Miss Mary Pask", first published in *Pictorial Review*, April 1925 and collected in *Here and Beyond* (Appleton, 1926).

"Mr. Jones", first published in *Ladies Home Journal*, April 1928 and collected in *Certain People* (Appleton, 1930).

"Pomegranate Seed", first published in *Saturday Evening Post*, 25 April 1931 and collected in *The World Over* (Appleton-Century, 1936).

A NOTE FROM THE PUBLISHER

The original short stories reprinted in the British Library's classic fiction series were written and published in a period ranging across the nineteenth and twentieth centuries. There are many elements of these stories which continue to entertain modern readers; however, in some cases there are also uses of language, instances of stereotyping and some attitudes expressed by narrators or characters which may not be endorsed by the publishing standards of today. We acknowledge therefore that some elements in the stories selected for reprinting may continue to make uncomfortable reading for some of our audience. With this series British Library Publishing aims to offer a new readership a chance to read some of the rare material of the British Library's collections in an affordable format, to enjoy their merits and to look back into the worlds of the past two centuries as portrayed by their writers. It is not possible to separate these stories from the history of their writing and therefore the following stories are presented as they were originally published with the inclusion of minor edits made for consistency of style and sense. We welcome feedback from our readers, which can be sent to the following address:

British Library Publishing
The British Library
96 Euston Road
London, NW1 2DB
United Kingdom

THE LADY'S MAID'S BELL

I

It was the autumn after I had the typhoid. I'd been three months in hospital, and when I came out I looked so weak and tottery that the two or three ladies I applied to were afraid to engage me. Most of my money was gone, and after I'd boarded for two months, hanging about the employment-agencies, and answering any advertisement that looked any way respectable, I pretty nearly lost heart, for fretting hadn't made me fatter, and I didn't see why my luck should ever turn. It did though—or I thought so at the time. A Mrs. Railton, a friend of the lady that first brought me out to the States, met me one day and stopped to speak to me: she was one that had always a friendly way with her. She asked me what ailed me to look so white, and when I told her, "Why, Hartley," says she, "I believe I've got the very place for you. Come in tomorrow and we'll talk about it."

The next day, when I called, she told me the lady she'd in mind was a niece of hers, a Mrs. Brympton, a youngish lady, but something of an invalid, who lived all the year round at her country-place on the Hudson, owing to not being able to stand the fatigue of town life.

"Now, Hartley," Mrs. Railton said, in that cheery way that always made me feel things must be going to take a turn for the better—"now understand me; it's not a cheerful place I'm sending you to. The house is big and gloomy; my niece is nervous, vapourish; her husband—well, he's generally away; and the two children are dead. A year ago, I would as soon have thought of shutting a rosy active girl like you into a vault; but you're not particularly brisk yourself just now, are you? and a quiet place, with country air and wholesome food and early hours, ought to be the very thing for you. Don't mistake me," she added, for I suppose I looked a trifle downcast; "you may find it dull, but you won't be unhappy. My niece is an angel. Her former maid, who died last spring, had been with her twenty years and worshipped the ground she walked on. She's a kind mistress to all, and where the mistress is kind, as you know, the servants are generally good-humoured, so you'll probably get on well enough with the rest of the household. And you're the very woman I want for my niece: quiet, well-mannered, and educated above your station. You read aloud well, I think? That's a good thing; my niece likes to be read to. She wants a maid that can be something of a companion: her last was, and I can't say how she misses her. It's a lonely life… Well, have you decided?"

"Why, ma'am," I said, "I'm not afraid of solitude."

"Well, then, go; my niece will take you on my recommendation. I'll telegraph her at once and you can take the afternoon train. She has no one to wait on her at present, and I don't want you to lose any time."

I was ready enough to start, yet something in me hung back; and to gain time I asked, "And the gentleman, ma'am?"

"The gentleman's almost always away, I tell you," said Mrs. Railton, quick-like—"and when he's there," says she suddenly, "you've only to keep out of his way."

I took the afternoon train and got out at D—— station at about four o'clock. A groom in a dog-cart was waiting, and we drove off at a smart pace. It was a dull October day, with rain hanging close overhead, and by the time we turned into the Brympton Place woods the daylight was almost gone. The drive wound through the woods for a mile or two, and came out on a gravel court shut in with thickets of tall black-looking shrubs. There were no lights in the windows, and the house *did* look a bit gloomy.

I had asked no questions of the groom, for I never was one to get my notion of new masters from their other servants: I prefer to wait and see for myself. But I could tell by the look of everything that I had got into the right kind of house, and that things were done handsomely. A pleasant-faced cook met me at the back door and called the housemaid to show me up to my room. "You'll see madam later," she said. "Mrs. Brympton has a visitor."

I hadn't fancied Mrs. Brympton was a lady to have many visitors, and somehow the words cheered me. I followed the housemaid upstairs, and saw, through a door on the upper landing, that the main part of the house seemed well-furnished, with dark panelling and a number of old portraits. Another flight of stairs led us up to the servants' wing. It was almost dark now, and the housemaid excused herself for not having brought a light. "But there's matches in your room," she said, "and if you go careful you'll be all right. Mind the step at the end of the passage. Your room is just beyond."

I looked ahead as she spoke, and halfway down the passage, I saw a woman standing. She drew back into a doorway as we passed, and the housemaid didn't appear to notice her. She was a thin woman with a white face, and a darkish stuff gown and apron. I took her for the housekeeper and thought it odd that she didn't speak, but just gave me a long look as she went by. My room opened into a square hall at the end of the passage. Facing my door was another which stood open: the housemaid exclaimed when she saw it.

"There—Mrs. Blinder's left that door open again!" said she, closing it.

"Is Mrs. Blinder the housekeeper?"

"There's no housekeeper: Mrs. Blinder's the cook."

"And is that her room?"

"Laws, no," said the housemaid, cross-like. "That's nobody's room. It's empty, I mean, and the door hadn't ought to be open. Mrs. Brympton wants it kept locked."

She opened my door and led me into a neat room, nicely furnished, with a picture or two on the walls; and having lit a candle she took leave, telling me that the servants'-hall tea was at six, and that Mrs. Brympton would see me afterward.

I found them a pleasant-spoken set in the servants' hall, and by what they let fall I gathered that, as Mrs. Railton had said, Mrs. Brympton was the kindest of ladies; but I didn't take much notice of their talk, for I was watching to see the pale woman in the dark gown come in. She didn't show herself, however, and I wondered if she ate apart; but if she wasn't the housekeeper, why should she? Suddenly it struck me that she might be a trained nurse, and in that case her meals would of course be served in her room. If Mrs. Brympton was an invalid it was likely enough she had a nurse. The idea annoyed me, I own, for they're not always the easiest to get on with, and if I'd known, I shouldn't have taken the place. But there I was, and there was no use pulling a long face over it; and not being one to ask questions, I waited to see what would turn up.

When tea was over, the housemaid said to the footman: "Has Mr. Ranford gone?" and when he said yes, she told me to come up with her to Mrs. Brympton.

Mrs. Brympton was lying down in her bedroom. Her lounge stood near the fire and beside it was a shaded lamp. She was a delicate-looking lady, but when she smiled I felt there was nothing I wouldn't do for her. She spoke very pleasantly, in a low voice, asking me my name and age and so on, and if I had everything I wanted, and if I wasn't afraid of feeling lonely in the country.

"Not with you I wouldn't be, madam," I said, and the words surprised me when I'd spoken them, for I'm not an impulsive person; but it was just as if I'd thought aloud.

She seemed pleased at that, and said she hoped I'd continue in the same mind; then she gave me a few directions about her toilet, and said Agnes the housemaid would show me next morning where things were kept.

"I am tired tonight, and shall dine upstairs," she said. "Agnes will bring me my tray, that you may have time to unpack and settle yourself; and later you may come and undress me."

"Very well, ma'am," I said. "You'll ring, I suppose?"

I thought she looked odd.

"No—Agnes will fetch you," says she quickly, and took up her book again.

Well—that was certainly strange: a lady's-maid having to be fetched by the housemaid whenever her lady wanted her! I wondered if there were no bells in the house; but the next day I satisfied myself that there was one in every room, and a special one ringing from my mistress's room to mine; and after that it did strike me as queer that, whenever Mrs. Brympton wanted anything, she rang for Agnes, who had to walk the whole length of the servants' wing to call me.

But that wasn't the only queer thing in the house. The very next day I found out that Mrs. Brympton had no nurse; and then I asked Agnes about the woman I had seen in the passage the afternoon before. Agnes said she had seen no one, and I saw that she thought I was dreaming. To be sure, it was dusk when we went down the passage, and she had excused herself for not bringing a light; but I had seen the woman plain enough to know her again if we should meet. I decided that she must have been a friend of the cook's, or of one of the other women-servants: perhaps she had come down from town for a night's visit, and the servants wanted it kept secret. Some ladies are very stiff about having their servants' friends in the house overnight. At any rate, I made up my mind to ask no more questions.

In a day or two, another odd thing happened. I was chatting one afternoon with Mrs. Blinder, who was a friendly disposed woman, and had been longer in the house than the other servants, and she asked me if I was quite comfortable and had everything I needed. I said I had no fault to find with my place or with my mistress, but I thought it odd that in so large a house there was no sewing-room for the lady's maid.

"Why," says she, "there *is* one: the room you're in is the old sewing-room."

"Oh," said I; "and where did the other lady's maid sleep?"

At that she grew confused, and said hurriedly that the servants' rooms had all been changed about last year, and she didn't rightly remember.

That struck me as peculiar, but I went on as if I hadn't noticed: "Well, there's a vacant room opposite mine, and I mean to ask Mrs. Brympton if I mayn't use that as a sewing-room."

To my astonishment, Mrs. Blinder went white, and gave my hand a kind of squeeze. "Don't do that, my dear," said she, trembling-like. "To tell you the truth, that was Emma Saxon's room, and my mistress has kept it closed ever since her death."

"And who was Emma Saxon?"

"Mrs. Brympton's former maid."

"The one that was with her so many years?" said I, remembering what Mrs. Railton had told me.

Mrs. Blinder nodded.

"What sort of woman was she?"

"No better walked the earth," said Mrs. Blinder. "My mistress loved her like a sister."

"But I mean—what did she look like?"

Mrs. Blinder got up and gave me a kind of angry stare. "I'm no great hand at describing," she said; "and I believe my pastry's rising." And she walked off into the kitchen and shut the door after her.

II

I had been near a week at Brympton before I saw my master. Word came that he was arriving one afternoon, and a change passed over the whole household. It was plain that nobody loved him below stairs. Mrs. Blinder took uncommon care with the dinner that night, but she snapped at the kitchen-maid in a way quite unusual with her; and Mr. Wace, the butler, a serious, slow-spoken man, went about his duties as if he'd been getting ready for a funeral. He was a great Bible-reader, Mr. Wace was, and had a beautiful assortment of texts at his command; but that day he used such dreadful language that I was about to leave the table, when he assured me it was all out of Isaiah; and I noticed that whenever the master came Mr. Wace took to the prophets.

About seven, Agnes called me to my mistress's room; and there I found Mr. Brympton. He was standing on the hearth; a big fair bull-necked man, with a red face and little bad-tempered blue eyes: the kind of man a young simpleton might have thought handsome, and would have been like to pay dear for thinking it.

He swung about when I came in, and looked me over in a trice. I knew what the look meant, from having experienced it once or twice in my former places. Then he turned his back on me, and went on talking to his wife; and I knew what *that* meant, too. I was not the kind of morsel he was after. The typhoid had served me well enough in one way: it kept that kind of gentleman at arm's-length.

"This is my new maid, Hartley," says Mrs. Brympton in her kind voice; and he nodded and went on with what he was saying.

In a minute or two he went off, and left my mistress to dress for dinner, and I noticed as I waited on her that she was white, and chill to the touch.

Mr. Brympton took himself off the next morning, and the whole house drew a long breath when he drove away. As for my mistress, she put on her hat and furs (for it was a fine winter morning) and went out for a walk in the gardens, coming back quite fresh and rosy, so that for a minute, before her colour faded, I could guess what a pretty young lady she must have been, and not so long ago, either.

She had met Mr. Ranford in the grounds, and the two came back together, I remember, smiling and talking as they walked along the terrace under my window. That was the first time I saw Mr. Ranford, though I had often heard his name mentioned in the hall. He was a neighbour, it appeared, living a mile or two beyond Brympton, at the end of the village; and as he was in the habit of spending his winters in the country he was almost the only company my mistress had at that season. He was a slight tall gentleman of about thirty, and I thought him rather melancholy-looking till I saw his smile, which had a kind of surprise in it, like the first warm day in spring. He was a great reader, I heard, like my mistress, and the two were forever borrowing books of one another, and sometimes (Mr. Wace told me) he would read aloud to Mrs. Brympton by the hour, in the big dark library where she sat in the winter afternoons. The servants all liked him, and perhaps that's more of a compliment than the masters suspect. He had a friendly word for every one of us, and we were all glad to think that Mrs. Brympton had a pleasant companionable gentleman like that to keep her company when the master was away. Mr. Ranford seemed on excellent terms with Mr. Brympton too; though I couldn't but wonder that two gentlemen so unlike each other should be so friendly. But then I knew how the real quality can keep their feelings to themselves.

As for Mr. Brympton, he came and went, never staying more than a day or two, cursing the dulness and the solitude, grumbling at everything, and (as I soon found out) drinking a deal more than was good for him. After Mrs. Brympton left the table he would sit half the night over the old Brympton port and madeira, and once, as I was leaving my mistress's room rather later than usual, I met him coming up the stairs in such a state that I turned sick to think of what some ladies have to endure and hold their tongues about.

The servants said very little about their master; but from what they let drop I could see it had been an unhappy match from the beginning. Mr. Brympton was coarse, loud and pleasure-loving; my mistress quiet, retiring, and perhaps a trifle cold. Not that she was not always pleasant-spoken to him: I thought her wonderfully forbearing; but to a gentleman as free as Mr. Brympton I daresay she seemed a little offish.

Well, things went on quietly for several weeks. My mistress was kind, my duties were light, and I got on well with the other servants. In short, I had nothing to complain of; yet there was always a weight on me. I can't say why it was so, but I know it was not the loneliness that I felt. I soon got used to that; and being still languid from the fever, I was thankful for the quiet and the good country air. Nevertheless, I was never quite easy in my mind. My mistress, knowing I had been ill, insisted that I should take my walk regular, and often invented errands for me:—a yard of ribbon to be fetched from the village, a letter posted, or a book returned to Mr. Ranford. As soon as I was out of doors my spirits rose, and I looked forward to my walks through the bare moist-smelling woods; but the moment I caught sight of the house again my heart dropped down like a stone in a well. It was not a gloomy house exactly, yet I never entered it but a feeling of gloom came over me.

Mrs. Brympton seldom went out in winter; only on the finest days did she walk an hour at noon on the south terrace. Excepting Mr. Ranford, we had no visitors but the doctor, who drove over from D—— about once a week. He sent for me once or twice to give me some trifling direction about my mistress, and though he never told me what her illness was, I thought, from a waxy look she had now and then of a morning, that it might be the heart that ailed her. The season was soft and unwholesome, and in January we had a long spell of rain. That was a sore trial to me, I own, for I couldn't go out, and sitting over my sewing all day, listening to the drip, drip of the eaves, I grew so nervous that the least sound made me jump. Somehow, the thought of that locked room across the passage began to weigh on me. Once or twice, in the long rainy nights, I fancied I heard noises there; but that was nonsense, of course, and the daylight drove such notions out of my head. Well, one morning Mrs. Brympton gave me quite a start of pleasure by telling me she wished me to go to town for some shopping. I hadn't known till then how low my spirits had fallen. I set off in high glee, and my first sight of the crowded streets and the cheerful-looking shops quite took me out of myself. Toward afternoon, however, the noise and confusion began to tire me, and I was actually looking forward to the quiet of Brympton, and thinking how I should enjoy the drive home through the dark woods, when I ran across an old acquaintance, a maid I had once been in service with. We had lost sight of each other for a number of years, and I had to stop and tell her what had happened to me in the interval. When I mentioned where I was living she rolled up her eyes and pulled a long face.

"What! The Mrs. Brympton that lives all the year at her place on the Hudson? My dear, you won't stay there three months."

"Oh, but I don't mind the country," says I, offended somehow at her tone. "Since the fever I'm glad to be quiet."

She shook her head. "It's not the country I'm thinking of. All I know is she's had four maids in the last six months, and the last one, who was a friend of mine, told me nobody could stay in the house."

"Did she say why?" I asked.

"No—she wouldn't give me her reason. But she says to me, *Mrs. Ansey,* she says, *if ever a young woman as you know of thinks of going there, you tell her it's not worth while to unpack her boxes.*"

"Is she young and handsome?" said I, thinking of Mr. Brympton.

"Not her! She's the kind that mothers engage when they've gay young gentlemen at college."

Well, though I knew the woman was an idle gossip, the words stuck in my head, and my heart sank lower than ever as I drove up to Brympton in the dusk. There *was* something about the house—I was sure of it now…

When I went in to tea I heard that Mr. Brympton had arrived, and I saw at a glance that there had been a disturbance of some kind. Mrs. Blinder's hand shook so that she could hardly pour the tea, and Mr. Wace quoted the most dreadful texts full of brimstone. Nobody said a word to me then, but when I went up to my room Mrs. Blinder followed me.

"Oh, my dear," says she, taking my hand, "I'm so glad and thankful you've come back to us!"

That struck me, as you may imagine. "Why," said I, "did you think I was leaving for good?"

"No, no, to be sure," said she, a little confused, "but I can't a-bear to have madam left alone for a day even." She pressed my hand hard, and, "Oh, Miss Hartley," says she, "be good to your mistress, as you're a Christian woman." And with that she hurried away, and left me staring.

A moment later Agnes called me to Mrs. Brympton. Hearing Mr. Brympton's voice in her room, I went round by the dressing-room, thinking I would lay out her dinner-gown before going in. The dressing-room is a large room with a window over the portico that looks toward the gardens. Mr. Brympton's apartments are beyond. When I went in, the door into the bedroom was ajar, and I heard Mr. Brympton saying angrily:—"One would suppose he was the only person fit for you to talk to."

"I don't have many visitors in winter," Mrs. Brympton answered quietly.

"You have *me!*" he flung at her, sneering.

"You are here so seldom," said she.

"Well—whose fault is that? You make the place about as lively as a family vault—"

With that I rattled the toilet-things, to give my mistress warning and she rose and called me in.

The two dined alone, as usual, and I knew by Mr. Wace's manner at supper that things must be going badly. He quoted the prophets something terrible, and worked on the kitchen-maid so that she declared she wouldn't go down alone to put the cold meat in the ice-box. I felt nervous myself, and after I had put my mistress to bed I was half-tempted to go down again and persuade Mrs. Blinder to sit up awhile over a game of cards. But I heard her door closing for the night, and so I went on to my own room. The rain had begun again, and the drip, drip, drip seemed to be dropping into my brain. I lay awake listening to it, and turning over what my friend in town had said. What puzzled me was that it was always the maids who left…

After a while I slept; but suddenly a loud noise wakened me. My bell had rung. I sat up, terrified by the unusual sound, which seemed to go on jangling through the darkness. My hands shook so that I couldn't find the matches. At length I struck a light and jumped out of bed. I began to think I must have been dreaming; but I looked at the bell against the wall, and there was the little hammer still quivering.

I was just beginning to huddle on my clothes when I heard another sound. This time it was the door of the locked room opposite mine softly opening and closing. I heard the sound distinctly, and it frightened me so that I stood stock still. Then I heard a footstep hurrying down the passage toward the main house. The floor being carpeted, the sound was very faint, but I was quite sure it was a woman's step. I turned cold with the thought of it, and for a minute or two I dursn't breathe or move. Then I came to my senses.

"Alice Hartley," says I to myself, "someone left that room just now and ran down the passage ahead of you. The idea isn't pleasant, but you may as well face it. Your mistress has rung for you, and to answer her bell you've got to go the way that other woman has gone."

Well—I did it. I never walked faster in my life, yet I thought I should never get to the end of the passage or reach Mrs. Brympton's room. On the way I heard nothing and saw nothing: all was dark and quiet as the grave. When I reached my mistress's door the silence was so deep that I began to think I must be dreaming, and was half-minded to turn back. Then a panic seized me, and I knocked.

There was no answer, and I knocked again, loudly. To my astonishment the door was opened by Mr. Brympton. He started back when he saw me, and in the light of my candle his face looked red and savage.

"*You?*" he said, in a queer voice. "*How many of you are there, in God's name?*"

At that I felt the ground give under me; but I said to myself that he had been drinking, and answered as steadily as I could: "May I go in, sir? Mrs. Brympton has rung for me."

"You may all go in, for what I care," says he, and, pushing by me, walked down the hall to his own bedroom. I looked after him as he went, and to my surprise I saw that he walked as straight as a sober man.

I found my mistress lying very weak and still, but she forced a smile when she saw me, and signed to me to pour out some drops for her. After that she lay without speaking, her breath coming quick, and her eyes closed. Suddenly she groped out with her hand, and "*Emma,*" says she, faintly.

"It's Hartley, madam," I said. "Do you want anything?"

She opened her eyes wide and gave me a startled look.

"I was dreaming," she said. "You may go, now, Hartley, and thank you kindly. I'm quite well again, you see." And she turned her face away from me.

III

There was no more sleep for me that night, and I was thankful when daylight came.

Soon afterward, Agnes called me to Mrs. Brympton. I was afraid she was ill again, for she seldom sent for me before nine, but I found her sitting up in bed, pale and drawn-looking, but quite herself.

"Hartley," says she quickly, "will you put on your things at once and go down to the village for me? I want this prescription made up—" here she hesitated a minute and blushed—"and I should like you to be back again before Mr. Brympton is up."

"Certainly, madam," I said.

"And—stay a moment—" she called me back as if an idea had just struck her—"while you're waiting for the mixture, you'll have time to go on to Mr. Ranford's with this note."

It was a two-mile walk to the village, and on my way I had time to turn things over in my mind. It struck me as peculiar that my mistress should wish the prescription made up without Mr. Brympton's knowledge; and, putting this together with the scene of the night before, and with much else that I had noticed and suspected, I began to wonder if the poor lady was weary of her life, and had come to the mad resolve of ending it. The idea took such hold on me that I reached the village on a run, and dropped breathless into a chair before the chemist's counter. The good man, who was just taking down his shutters, stared at me so hard that it brought me to myself.

"Mr. Limmel," I says, trying to speak indifferent, "will you run your eye over this, and tell me if it's quite right?"

He put on his spectacles and studied the prescription.

"Why, it's one of Dr. Walton's," says he. "What should be wrong with it?"

"Well—is it dangerous to take?"

"Dangerous—how do you mean?"

I could have shaken the man for his stupidity.

"I mean—if a person was to take too much of it—by mistake of course—" says I, my heart in my throat.

"Lord bless you, no. It's only lime-water. You might feed it to a baby by the bottleful."

I gave a great sigh of relief, and hurried on to Mr. Ranford's. But on the way another thought struck me. If there was nothing to conceal about my visit to the chemist's, was it my other errand that Mrs. Brympton wished me to keep private? Somehow, that thought frightened me worse than the other. Yet the two gentlemen seemed fast friends, and I would have staked my head on my mistress's goodness. I felt ashamed of my suspicions, and concluded that I was still disturbed by the strange events of the night. I left the note at Mr. Ranford's—and, hurrying back to Brympton, slipped in by a side door without being seen, as I thought.

An hour later, however, as I was carrying in my mistress's breakfast, I was stopped in the hall by Mr. Brympton.

"What were you doing out so early?" he says, looking hard at me.

"Early—me, sir?" I said, in a tremble.

"Come, come," he says, an angry red spot coming out on his forehead, "didn't I see you scuttling home through the shrubbery an hour or more ago?"

I'm a truthful woman by nature, but at that a lie popped out ready-made. "No, sir, you didn't," said I, and looked straight back at him.

He shrugged his shoulders and gave a sullen laugh. "I suppose you think I was drunk last night?" he asked suddenly.

"No, sir, I don't," I answered, this time truthfully enough.

He turned away with another shrug. "A pretty notion my servants have of me!" I heard him mutter as he walked off.

Not till I had settled down to my afternoon's sewing did I realise how the events of the night had shaken me. I couldn't pass that locked door without a shiver. I knew I had heard someone come out of it, and walk down the passage ahead of me. I thought of speaking to Mrs. Blinder or to Mr. Wace, the only two in the house who appeared to have an inkling of what was going on, but I had a feeling that if I questioned them they would deny everything, and that I might learn more by holding my tongue and keeping my eyes open. The idea of spending another night opposite the locked room sickened me, and once I was seized with the notion of packing my trunk and taking the first train to town; but it wasn't in me to throw over a kind mistress in that manner, and I tried to go on with my sewing as if nothing had happened.

I hadn't worked ten minutes before the sewing-machine broke down. It was one I had found in the house, a good machine, but a trifle out of order: Mrs. Blinder said it had never been used since Emma Saxon's death. I stopped to see what was wrong, and as I was working at the machine a drawer which I had never been able to open slid forward and a photograph fell out. I picked it up and sat looking at it in a maze. It was a woman's likeness, and I knew I had seen the face somewhere—the eyes had an asking look that I had felt on me before. And suddenly I remembered the pale woman in the passage.

I stood up, cold all over, and ran out of the room. My heart seemed to be thumping in the top of my head, and I felt as if I should never get away from the look in those eyes. I went straight to Mrs. Blinder. She was taking her afternoon nap, and sat up with a jump when I came in.

"Mrs. Blinder," said I, "who is that?" And I held out the photograph.

She rubbed her eyes and stared.

"Why, Emma Saxon," says she. "Where did you find it?"

I looked hard at her for a minute. "Mrs. Blinder," I said, "I've seen that face before."

Mrs. Blinder got up and walked over to the looking-glass. "Dear me! I must have been asleep," she says. "My front is all over one ear. And now do run along, Miss Hartley, dear, for I hear the clock striking four, and I must go down this very minute and put on the Virginia ham for Mr. Brympton's dinner."

IV

To all appearances, things went on as usual for a week or two. The only difference was that Mr. Brympton stayed on, instead of going off as he usually did, and that Mr. Ranford never showed himself. I heard Mr. Brympton remark on this one afternoon when he was sitting in my mistress's room before dinner.

"Where's Ranford?" says he. "He hasn't been near the house for a week. Does he keep away because I'm here?"

Mrs. Brympton spoke so low that I couldn't catch her answer.

"Well," he went on, "two's company and three's trumpery; I'm sorry to be in Ranford's way, and I suppose I shall have to take myself off again in a day or two and give him a show." And he laughed at his own joke.

The very next day, as it happened, Mr. Ranford called. The footman said the three were very merry over their tea in the library, and Mr. Brympton strolled down to the gate with Mr. Ranford when he left.

I have said that things went on as usual; and so they did with the rest of the household; but as for myself, I had never been the same since the night my bell had rung. Night after night I used to lie awake, listening for it to ring again, and for the door of the locked room to open stealthily. But the bell never rang, and I heard no sound across the passage. At last the silence began to be more dreadful to me than the most mysterious sounds. I felt that *someone* were cowering there, behind the locked door, watching and listening as I watched and listened, and I could almost have cried out, "Whoever you are, come out and let me see you face to face, but don't lurk there and spy on me in the darkness!"

Feeling as I did, you may wonder I didn't give warning. Once I very nearly did so; but at the last moment something held me back. Whether it was compassion for my mistress, who had grown more and more dependent on me, or unwillingness to try a new place, or some other feeling that I couldn't put a name to, I lingered on as if spellbound, though every night was dreadful to me, and the days but little better.

For one thing, I didn't like Mrs. Brympton's looks. She had never been the same since that night, no more than I had. I thought she would brighten up after Mr. Brympton left, but though she seemed easier in her mind, her spirits didn't revive, nor her strength either. She had grown attached to me, and seemed to like to have me about; and Agnes told me one day that, since Emma Saxon's death, I was the only maid her mistress had taken to. This gave me a warm feeling for the poor lady, though after all there was little I could do to help her.

After Mr. Brympton's departure, Mr. Ranford took to coming again, though less often than formerly. I met him once or twice in the grounds, or in the village, and I couldn't but think there was a change in him too; but I set it down to my disordered fancy.

The weeks passed, and Mr. Brympton had now been a month absent. We heard he was cruising with a friend in the West Indies, and Mr. Wace said that was a long way off, but though you had the wings of a dove and went to the uttermost parts of the earth, you couldn't get away from the Almighty. Agnes said that as long as he stayed away from Brympton, the Almighty might have him and welcome; and this raised a laugh, though Mrs. Blinder tried to look shocked, and Mr. Wace said the bears would eat us.

We were all glad to hear that the West Indies were a long way off, and I remember that, in spite of Mr. Wace's solemn looks, we had a very merry dinner that day in the hall. I don't know if it was because of my being in better spirits, but I fancied Mrs. Brympton looked better too, and seemed more cheerful in her manner. She had been for a walk in the morning, and after luncheon she lay down in her room, and I read aloud to her. When she dismissed me I went to my own room feeling quite bright and happy, and for the first time in weeks walked past the locked door without thinking of it. As I sat down to my work I looked out and saw a few snowflakes falling. The sight was pleasanter than the eternal rain, and I pictured to myself how pretty the bare gardens would look in their white mantle. It seemed to me as if the snow would cover up all the dreariness, indoors as well as out.

The fancy had hardly crossed my mind when I heard a step at my side. I looked up, thinking it was Agnes.

"Well, Agnes—" said I, and the words froze on my tongue; for there, in the door, stood Emma Saxon.

I don't know how long she stood there. I only know I couldn't stir or take my eyes from her. Afterward I was terribly frightened, but at the time it wasn't fear I felt, but something deeper and quieter. She looked at me long and long, and her face was just one dumb prayer to me—but how in the world was I to help her? Suddenly she turned, and I heard her walk down the passage. This time I wasn't afraid to follow—I felt that I must know what she wanted. I sprang up and ran out. She was at the other end of the passage, and I expected her to take the turn toward my mistress's room; but instead of that she pushed open the door that led to the backstairs. I followed her down the stairs, and across the passageway to the back door. The kitchen and hall were empty at that hour, the servants being off duty, except for the footman, who was in the pantry. At the door she stood still a moment, with another look at me; then she turned the handle, and stepped out. For a minute I hesitated. Where was she leading me to? The door had closed softly after her, and I opened it and looked out, half-expecting to find that she had disappeared. But I saw her a few yards off, hurrying across the court-yard to the path through the woods. Her figure looked black and lonely in the snow, and for a second my heart failed me and I thought of turning back. But all the while she was drawing me after her; and catching up an old shawl of Mrs. Blinder's I ran out into the open.

Emma Saxon was in the wood-path now. She walked on steadily, and I followed at the same pace, till we passed out of the gates and reached the high-road. Then she struck across the open fields to the village. By this time the ground was white, and as she climbed the slope of a bare hill ahead of me I noticed that she left no foot-prints behind her. At sight of that, my heart shrivelled up within me, and my knees were water. Somehow, it was worse here than indoors. She made the whole countryside seem lonely as the grave, with none but us two in it, and no help in the wide world.

Once I tried to go back; but she turned and looked at me, and it was as if she had dragged me with ropes. After that I followed her like a dog. We came to the village, and she led me through it, past the church and the blacksmith's shop, and down the lane to Mr. Ranford's. Mr. Ranford's house stands close to the road: a plain old-fashioned building, with a flagged path leading to the door between box-borders. The lane was deserted, and as I turned into it I saw Emma Saxon pause under the old elm by the gate. And now another fear came over me. I saw that we had reached the end of our journey, and that it was my turn to act. All the way from Brympton I had been asking myself what she wanted of me, but I had followed in a trance, as it were, and not till I saw her stop at Mr. Ranford's gate did my brain begin to clear itself. I stood a little way off in the snow, my heart beating fit to strangle me, and my feet frozen to the ground; and she stood under the elm and watched me.

I knew well enough that she hadn't led me there for nothing. I felt there was something I ought to say or do—but how was I to guess what it was? I had never thought harm of my mistress and Mr. Ranford, but I was sure now that, from one cause or another, some dreadful thing hung over them. *She* knew what it was; she would tell me if she could; perhaps she would answer if I questioned her.

It turned me faint to think of speaking to her; but I plucked up heart and dragged myself across the few yards between us. As I did so, I heard the house-door open, and saw Mr. Ranford approaching. He looked handsome and cheerful, as my mistress had looked that morning, and at sight of him the blood began to flow again in my veins.

"Why, Hartley," said he, "what's the matter? I saw you coming down the lane just now, and came out to see if you had taken root in the snow." He stopped and stared at me. "What are you looking at?" he says.

I turned toward the elm as he spoke, and his eyes followed me; but there was no one there. The lane was empty as far as the eye could reach.

A sense of helplessness came over me. She was gone, and I had not been able to guess what she wanted. Her last look had pierced me to the marrow; and yet it had not told me! All at once, I felt more desolate than when she had stood there watching me. It seemed as if she had left me all alone to carry the weight of the secret I couldn't guess. The snow went round me in great circles, and the ground fell away from me...

A drop of brandy and the warmth of Mr. Ranford's fire soon brought me to, and I insisted on being driven back at once to Brympton. It was nearly dark, and I was afraid my mistress might be wanting me. I explained to Mr. Ranford that I had been out for a walk and had been taken with a fit of giddiness as I passed his gate. This was true enough; yet I never felt more like a liar than when I said it.

When I dressed Mrs. Brympton for dinner she remarked on my pale looks and asked what ailed me. I told her I had a headache, and she said she would not require me again that evening, and advised me to go to bed.

It was a fact that I could scarcely keep on my feet; yet I had no fancy to spend a solitary evening in my room. I sat downstairs in the hall as long as I could hold my head up; but by nine I crept upstairs, too weary to care what happened if I could but get my head on a pillow. The rest of the household went to bed soon afterward; they kept early hours when the master was away, and before ten I heard Mrs. Blinder's door close, and Mr. Wace's soon after.

It was a very still night, earth and air all muffled in snow. Once in bed I felt easier, and lay quiet, listening to the strange noises that come out in a house after dark. Once I thought I heard a door open and close again below: it might have been the glass door that led to the gardens. I got up and peered out of the window; but it was in the dark of the moon, and nothing visible outside but the streaking of snow against the panes.

I went back to bed and must have dozed, for I jumped awake to the furious ringing of my bell. Before my head was clear I had sprung out of bed, and was dragging on my clothes. *It is going to happen now*, I heard myself saying; but what I meant I had no notion. My hands seemed to be covered with glue—I thought I should never get into my clothes. At last I opened my door and peered down the passage. As far as my candle-flame carried, I could see nothing unusual ahead of me. I hurried on, breathless; but as I pushed open the baize door leading to the main hall my heart stood still, for there at the head of the stairs was Emma Saxon, peering dreadfully down into the darkness.

For a second I couldn't stir; but my hand slipped from the door, and as it swung shut the figure vanished. At the same instant there came another sound from below stairs—a stealthy mysterious sound, as of a latchkey turning in the house-door. I ran to Mrs. Brympton's room and knocked.

There was no answer, and I knocked again. This time I heard some one moving in the room; the bolt slipped back and my mistress stood before me. To my surprise I saw that she had not undressed for the night. She gave me a startled look.

"What is this, Hartley?" she says in a whisper. "Are you ill? What are you doing here at this hour?"

"I am not ill, madam; but my bell rang."

At that she turned pale, and seemed about to fall.

"You are mistaken," she said harshly; "I didn't ring. You must have been dreaming." I had never heard her speak in such a tone. "Go back to bed," she said, closing the door on me.

But as she spoke I heard sounds again in the hall below: a man's step this time; and the truth leaped out on me.

"Madam," I said, pushing past her, "there is someone in the house—"

"Someone—?"

"Mr. Brympton, I think—I hear his step below—"

A dreadful look came over her, and without a word, she dropped flat at my feet. I fell on my knees and tried to lift her: by the way she breathed I saw it was no common faint. But as I raised her head there came quick steps on the stairs and across the hall: the door was flung open, and there stood Mr. Brympton, in his travelling-clothes, the snow dripping from him. He drew back with a start as he saw me kneeling by my mistress.

"What the devil is this?" he shouted. He was less high-coloured than usual, and the red spot came out on his forehead.

"Mrs. Brympton has fainted, sir," said I.

He laughed unsteadily and pushed by me. "It's a pity she didn't choose a more convenient moment. I'm sorry to disturb her, but—"

I raised myself up, aghast at the man's action.

"Sir," said I, "are you mad? What are you doing?"

"Going to meet a friend," said he, and seemed to make for the dressing-room.

At that my heart turned over. I don't know what I thought or feared; but I sprang up and caught him by the sleeve.

"Sir, sir," said I, "for pity's sake look at your wife!"

He shook me off furiously.

"It seems that's done for me," says he, and caught hold of the dressing-room door.

At that moment I heard a slight noise inside. Slight as it was, he heard it too, and tore the door open; but as he did so he dropped back. On the threshold stood Emma Saxon. All was dark behind her, but I saw her plainly, and so did he. He threw up his hands as if to hide his face from her; and when I looked again she was gone.

He stood motionless, as if the strength had run out of him; and in the stillness my mistress suddenly raised herself, and opening her eyes fixed a look on him. Then she fell back, and I saw the death-flutter pass over her…

*

We buried her on the third day, in a driving snow-storm. There were few people in the church, for it was bad weather to come from town, and I've a notion my mistress was one that hadn't many near friends. Mr. Ranford was among the last to come, just before they carried her up the aisle. He was in black, of course, being such a friend of the family, and I never saw a gentleman so pale. As he passed me, I noticed that he leaned a trifle on a stick he carried; and I fancy Mr. Brympton noticed it too, for the red spot came out sharp on his forehead, and all through the service he kept staring across the church at Mr. Ranford, instead of following the prayers as a mourner should.

When it was over and we went out to the graveyard, Mr. Ranford had disappeared, and as soon as my poor mistress's body was underground, Mr. Brympton jumped into the carriage nearest the gate and drove off without a word to any of us. I heard him call out, "To the station," and we servants went back alone to the house.

THE HOUSE OF THE DEAD HAND

I

"Above all," the letter ended, "don't leave Siena without seeing Doctor Lombard's Leonardo. Lombard is a queer old Englishman, a mystic or a madman (if the two are not synonymous), and a devout student of the Italian Renaissance. He has lived for years in Italy, exploring its remotest corners, and has lately picked up an undoubted Leonardo, which came to light in a farmhouse near Bergamo. It is believed to be one of the missing pictures mentioned by Vasari, and is at any rate, according to the most competent authorities, a genuine and almost untouched example of the best period.

"Lombard is a queer stick, and jealous of showing his treasures; but we struck up a friendship when I was working on the Sodomas in Siena three years ago, and if you will give him the enclosed line you may get a peep at the Leonardo. Probably not more than a peep, though, for I hear he refuses to have it reproduced. I want badly to use it in my monograph on the Windsor drawings, so please see what you can do for me, and if you can't persuade him to let you take a photograph or make a sketch, at least jot down a detailed description of the picture and get from him all the facts you can. I hear that the French and Italian governments have offered him a large advance on his purchase, but that he refuses to sell at any price, though he certainly can't afford such luxuries; in fact, I don't see where he got enough money to buy the picture. He lives in the Via Papa Giulio."

Wyant sat at the table d'hôte of his hotel, re-reading his friend's letter over a late luncheon. He had been five days in Siena without having found time to call on Doctor Lombard; not from any indifference to the opportunity presented, but because it was his first visit to the strange red city and he was still under the spell of its more conspicuous wonders—the brick palaces flinging out their wrought-iron torch-holders with a gesture of arrogant suzerainty; the great council-chamber emblazoned with civic allegories; the pageant of Pope Julius on the Library walls; the Sodomas smiling balefully through the dusk of mouldering chapels—and it was only when his first hunger was appeased that he remembered that one course in the banquet was still untasted.

He put the letter in his pocket and turned to leave the room, with a nod to its only other occupant, an olive-skinned young man with lustrous eyes and a low collar, who sat on the other side of the table, perusing the *Fanfulla di Domenica*. This gentleman, his daily vis-à-vis, returned the nod with a Latin eloquence of gesture, and Wyant passed on to the ante-chamber, where he paused to light a cigarette. He was just restoring the case to his pocket when he heard a hurried step behind him, and the lustrous-eyed young man advanced through the glass doors of the dining-room.

"Pardon me, sir," he said in measured English, and with an intonation of exquisite politeness; "you have let this letter fall."

Wyant, recognising his friend's note of introduction to Doctor Lombard, took it with a word of thanks, and was about to turn away when he perceived that the eyes of his fellow diner remained fixed on him with a gaze of melancholy interrogation.

"Again pardon me," the young man at length ventured, "but are you by chance the friend of the illustrious Doctor Lombard?"

"No," returned Wyant, with the instinctive Anglo-Saxon distrust of foreign advances. Then, fearing to appear rude, he said with a guarded politeness: "Perhaps, by the way, you can tell me the number of his house. I see it is not given here."

The young man brightened perceptibly. "The number of the house is thirteen; but any one can indicate it to you—it is well known in Siena. It is called," he continued after a moment, "the House of the Dead Hand."

Wyant stared. "What a queer name!" he said.

"The name comes from an antique hand of marble which for many hundred years has been above the door."

Wyant was turning away with a gesture of thanks, when the other added: "If you would have the kindness to ring twice."

"To ring twice?"

"At the doctor's." The young man smiled. "It is the custom."

It was a dazzling March afternoon, with a shower of sun from the mid-blue, and a marshalling of slaty clouds behind the umber-coloured hills. For nearly an hour Wyant loitered on the Lizza, watching the shadows race across the naked landscape and the thunder blacken in the west; then he decided to set out for the House of the Dead Hand. The map in his guidebook showed him that the Via Papa Giulio was one of the streets which radiate from the Piazza, and thither he bent his course, pausing at every other step to fill his eye with some fresh image of weather-beaten beauty. The clouds had rolled upward, obscuring the sunshine and hanging like a funereal baldachin above the projecting cornices of Doctor Lombard's street, and Wyant walked for some distance in the shade of the beetling palace fronts before his eye fell on a doorway surmounted by a sallow marble hand. He stood for a moment staring up at the strange emblem. The hand was a woman's—a dead drooping hand, which hung there convulsed and helpless, as though it had been thrust forth in denunciation of some evil mystery within the house, and had sunk struggling into death.

A girl who was drawing water from the well in the court said that the English doctor lived on the first floor, and Wyant, passing through a glazed door, mounted the damp degrees of a vaulted stairway with a plaster Æsculapius mouldering in a niche on the landing. Facing the Æsculapius was another door, and as Wyant put his hand on the bell-rope he remembered his unknown friend's injunction, and rang twice.

His ring was answered by a peasant woman with a low forehead and small close-set eyes, who, after a prolonged scrutiny of himself, his card, and his letter of introduction, left him standing in a high, cold antechamber floored with brick. He heard her wooden pattens click down an interminable corridor, and after some delay she returned and told him to follow her.

They passed through a long saloon, bare as the ante-chamber, but loftily vaulted, and frescoed with a seventeenth-century Triumph of Scipio or Alexander—martial figures following Wyant with the filmed melancholy gaze of shades in limbo. At the end of this apartment he was admitted to a smaller room, with the same atmosphere of mortal cold, but showing more obvious signs of occupancy. The walls were covered with tapestry which had faded to the grey-brown tints of decaying vegetation, so that the young man felt as though he were entering a sunless autumn wood. Against these hangings stood a few tall cabinets on heavy gilt feet, and at a table in the window three persons were seated: an elderly lady who was warming her hands over a brazier, a girl bent above a strip of needlework, and an old man.

As the latter advanced toward Wyant, the young man was conscious of staring with unseemly intentness at his small round-backed figure, dressed with shabby disorder and surmounted by a wonderful head, lean, vulpine, eagle-beaked as that of some art-loving despot of the Renaissance: a head combining the venerable hair and large prominent eyes of the humanist with the greedy profile of the adventurer. Wyant, in musing on the Italian portrait-medals of the fifteenth century, had often fancied that only in that period of fierce individualism could types so paradoxical have been produced; yet the subtle craftsmen who committed them to the bronze had never drawn a face more strangely stamped with contradictory passions than that of Doctor Lombard.

"I am glad to see you," he said to Wyant, extending a hand which seemed a mere framework held together by knotted veins. "We lead a quiet life here and receive few visitors, but any friend of Professor Clyde's is welcome." Then, with a gesture which included the two women, he added dryly: "My wife and daughter often talk of Professor Clyde."

"Oh yes—he used to make me such nice toast; they don't understand toast in Italy," said Mrs. Lombard in a high plaintive voice.

It would have been difficult, from Doctor Lombard's manner and appearance, to guess his nationality; but his wife was so inconsciently and ineradicably English that even the silhouette of her cap seemed a protest against Continental laxities. She was a stout fair woman, with pale cheeks netted with red lines. A brooch with a miniature portrait sustained a bogwood watch-chain upon her bosom, and at her elbow lay a heap of knitting and an old copy of *The Queen*.

The young girl, who had remained standing, was a slim replica of her mother, with an apple-cheeked face and opaque blue eyes. Her small head was prodigally laden with braids of dull fair hair, and she might have had a kind of transient prettiness but for the sullen droop of her round mouth. It was hard to say whether her expression implied ill-temper or apathy; but Wyant was struck by the contrast between the fierce vitality of the doctor's age and the inanimateness of his daughter's youth.

Seating himself in the chair which his host advanced, the young man tried to open the conversation by addressing to Mrs. Lombard some random remark on the beauties of Siena. The lady murmured a resigned assent, and Doctor Lombard interposed with a smile: "My dear sir, my wife considers Siena a most salubrious spot, and is favourably impressed by the cheapness of the marketing; but she deplores the total absence of muffins and cannel coal, and cannot resign herself to the Italian method of dusting furniture."

"But they don't, you know—they don't dust it!" Mrs. Lombard protested, without showing any resentment of her husband's manner.

"Precisely—they don't dust it. Since we have lived in Siena we have not once seen the cobwebs removed from the battlements of the Mangia. Can you conceive of such housekeeping? My wife has never yet dared to write it home to her aunts at Bonchurch."

Mrs. Lombard accepted in silence this remarkable statement of her views, and her husband, with a malicious smile at Wyant's embarrassment, planted himself suddenly before the young man.

"And now," said he, "do you want to see my Leonardo?"

"*Do I?*" cried Wyant, on his feet in a flash.

The doctor chuckled. "Ah," he said, with a kind of crooning deliberation, "that's the way they all behave—that's what they all come for." He turned to his daughter with another variation of mockery in his smile. "Don't fancy it's for your *beaux yeux*, my dear; or for the mature charms of Mrs. Lombard," he added, glaring suddenly at his wife, who had taken up her knitting and was softly murmuring over the number of her stitches.

Neither lady appeared to notice his pleasantries, and he continued, addressing himself to Wyant: "They all come—they all come; but many are called and few are chosen." His voice sank to solemnity. "While I live," he said, "no unworthy eye shall desecrate that picture. But I will not do my friend Clyde the injustice to suppose that he would send an unworthy representative. He tells me he wishes a description of the picture for his book; and you shall describe it to him—if you can."

Wyant hesitated, not knowing whether it was a propitious moment to put in his appeal for a photograph.

"Well, sir," he said, "you know Clyde wants me to take away all I can of it."

Doctor Lombard eyed him sardonically. "You're welcome to take away all you can carry," he replied; adding, as he turned to his daughter: "That is, if he has your permission, Sybilla."

The girl rose without a word, and laying aside her work, took a key from a secret drawer in one of the cabinets, while the doctor continued in the same note of grim jocularity: "For you must know that the picture is not mine—it is my daughter's."

He followed with evident amusement the surprised glance which Wyant turned on the young girl's impassive figure.

"Sybilla," he pursued, "is a votary of the arts; she has inherited her fond father's passion for the unattainable. Luckily, however, she also recently inherited a tidy legacy from her grandmother; and having seen the Leonardo, on which its discoverer had placed a price far beyond my reach, she took a step which deserves to go down to history: she invested her whole inheritance in the purchase of the picture, thus enabling me to spend my closing years in communion with one of the world's masterpieces. My dear sir, could Antigone do more?"

The object of this strange eulogy had meanwhile drawn aside one of the tapestry hangings, and fitted her key into a concealed door.

"Come," said Doctor Lombard, "let us go before the light fails us."

Wyant glanced at Mrs. Lombard, who continued to knit impassively.

"No, no," said his host, "my wife will not come with us. You might not suspect it from her conversation, but my wife has no feeling for art—Italian art, that is; for no one is fonder of our early Victorian school."

"Frith's *Railway Station*, you know," said Mrs. Lombard, smiling. "I like an animated picture."

Miss Lombard, who had unlocked the door, held back the tapestry to let her father and Wyant pass out; then she followed them down a narrow stone passage with another door at its end. This door was iron-barred, and Wyant noticed that it had a complicated patent lock. The girl fitted another key into the lock, and Doctor Lombard led the way into a small room. The dark panelling of this apartment was irradiated by streams of yellow light slanting through the disbanded thunder clouds, and in the central brightness hung a picture concealed by a curtain of faded velvet.

"A little too bright, Sybilla," said Doctor Lombard. His face had grown solemn, and his mouth twitched nervously as his daughter drew a linen drapery across the upper part of the window.

"That will do—that will do." He turned impressively to Wyant. "Do you see the pomegranate bud in this rug? Place yourself there—keep your left foot on it, please. And now, Sybilla, draw the cord."

Miss Lombard advanced and placed her hand on a cord hidden behind the velvet curtain.

"Ah," said the doctor, "one moment: I should like you, while looking at the picture, to have in mind a few lines of verse. Sybilla—"

Without the slightest change of countenance, and with a promptness which proved her to be prepared for the request, Miss Lombard began to recite, in a full round voice like her mother's, St. Bernard's invocation to the Virgin, in the thirty-third canto of the *Paradise*.

"Thank you, my dear," said her father, drawing a deep breath as she ended. "That unapproachable combination of vowel sounds prepares one better than anything I know for the contemplation of the picture."

As he spoke the folds of velvet slowly parted, and the Leonardo appeared in its frame of tarnished gold.

From the nature of Miss Lombard's recitation Wyant had expected a sacred subject, and his surprise was therefore great as the composition was gradually revealed by the widening division of the curtain.

In the background a steel-coloured river wound through a pale calcareous landscape; while to the left, on a lonely peak, a crucified Christ hung livid against indigo clouds. The central figure of the foreground, however, was that of a woman seated in an antique chair of marble with bas-reliefs of dancing mænads. Her feet rested on a meadow sprinkled with minute wildflowers, and her attitude of smiling majesty recalled that of Dosso Dossi's Circe. She wore a red robe, flowing in closely fluted lines from under a fancifully embroidered cloak. Above her high forehead the crinkled golden hair flowed sideways beneath a veil; one hand drooped on the arm of her chair;

the other held up an inverted human skull, into which a young Dionysus, smooth, brown and sidelong as the St. John of the Louvre, poured a stream of wine from a high-poised flagon. At the lady's feet lay the symbols of art and luxury: a flute and a roll of music, a platter heaped with grapes and roses, the torso of a Greek statuette, and a bowl overflowing with coins and jewels; behind her, on the chalky hilltop, hung the crucified Christ. A scroll in a corner of the foreground bore the legend: *Lux Mundi.*

Wyant, emerging from the first plunge of wonder, turned inquiringly toward his companions. Neither had moved. Miss Lombard stood with her hand on the cord, her lids lowered, her mouth drooping; the doctor, his strange Thoth-like profile turned toward his guest, was still lost in rapt contemplation of his treasure.

Wyant addressed the young girl.

"You are fortunate," he said, "to be the possessor of anything so perfect."

"It is considered very beautiful," she said coldly.

"Beautiful—*beautiful!*" the doctor burst out. "Ah, the poor, worn out, overworked word! There are no adjectives in the language fresh enough to describe such pristine brilliancy: all their brightness has been worn off by misuse. Think of the things that have been called beautiful, and then look at *that!*"

"It is worthy of a new vocabulary," Wyant agreed.

"Yes," Doctor Lombard continued, "my daughter is indeed fortunate. She has chosen what Catholics call the higher life—the counsel of perfection. What other private person enjoys the same opportunity of understanding the master? Who else lives under the same roof with an untouched masterpiece of Leonardo's? Think of the happiness of being always under the influence of such a creation; of living *into* it; of partaking of it in daily and hourly communion! This room is a chapel; the sight of that picture is a sacrament. What an atmosphere for a young life to unfold itself in! My daughter is singularly blessed. Sybilla, point out some of the details to Mr. Wyant: I see that he will appreciate them."

The girl turned her dense blue eyes toward Wyant; then, glancing away from him, she pointed to the canvas.

"Notice the modelling of the left hand," she began in a monotonous voice; "it recalls the hand of the Mona Lisa. The head of the naked genius will remind you of that of the St. John of the Louvre, but it is more purely pagan and is turned a little less to the right. The embroidery on the cloak is symbolic: you will see that the roots of this plant have burst through the vase. This recalls the famous definition of Hamlet's character in *Wilhelm Meister*. Here are the mystic rose, the flame, and the serpent, emblem of eternity. Some of the other symbols we have not yet been able to decipher."

Wyant watched her curiously: she seemed to be reciting a lesson.

"And the picture itself?" he said. "How do you explain that? *Lux Mundi*—what a curious device to connect with such a subject! What can it mean?"

Miss Lombard dropped her eyes: the answer was evidently not included in her lesson.

"What, indeed?" the doctor interposed. "What does life mean? As one may define it in a hundred different ways, so one may find a hundred different meanings in this picture. Its symbolism is as many-faceted as a well-cut diamond. Who, for instance, is that divine lady? Is it she who is the true *Lux Mundi*—the light reflected from jewels and young eyes, from polished marble and clear waters and statues of bronze? Or is that the Light of the World, extinguished on yonder stormy hill, and is this lady the Pride of Life, feasting blindly on the wine of iniquity, with her back turned to the light which has shone for her in vain? Something of both these meanings may be traced in the picture; but to me it symbolises rather the central truth of existence: that all that is raised in incorruption is sown in corruption; art, beauty, love, religion; that all our wine is drunk out of skulls, and poured for us by the mysterious genius of a remote and cruel past."

The doctor's face blazed: his bent figure seemed to straighten itself and become taller.

"Ah," he cried, growing more dithyrambic, "how lightly you ask what it means! How confidently you expect an answer! Yet here am I who have given my life to the study of the Renaissance; who have violated its tomb, laid open its dead body, and traced the course of every muscle, bone and artery; who have sucked its very soul from the pages of poets and humanists; who have wept and believed with Joachim of Flora, smiled and doubted with Æneas Sylvius Piccolomini; who have patiently followed to its source the least inspiration of the masters, and groped in neolithic caverns and Babylonian ruins for the first unfolding tendrils of the arabesques of Mantegna and Crivelli; and I tell you that I stand abashed and ignorant before the mystery of this picture. It means nothing—it means all things. It may represent the period which saw its creation; it may represent all ages past and to come. There are volumes of meaning in the tiniest emblem on the lady's cloak; the blossoms of its border are rooted in the deepest soil of myth and tradition. Don't ask what it means, young man, but bow your head in thankfulness for having seen it!"

Miss Lombard laid her hand on his arm.

"Don't excite yourself, father," she said in the detached tone of a professional nurse.

He answered with a despairing gesture. "Ah, it's easy for you to talk. You have years and years to spend with it; I am an old man, and every moment counts!"

"It's bad for you," she repeated with gentle obstinacy.

The doctor's sacred fury had in fact burnt itself out. He dropped into a seat with dull eyes and slackening lips, and his daughter drew the curtain across the picture.

Wyant turned away reluctantly. He felt that his opportunity was slipping from him, yet he dared not refer to Clyde's wish for a photograph. He now understood the meaning of the laugh with which Doctor Lombard had given him leave to carry away all the details he could remember. The picture was so dazzling, so unexpected, so crossed with elusive and contradictory suggestions, that the most alert observer, when placed suddenly before it, must lose his coordinating faculty in a sense of confused wonder. Yet how valuable to Clyde the record of such a work would be! In some ways it seemed to be the summing up of the master's thought, the key to his enigmatic philosophy.

The doctor had risen and was walking slowly toward the door. His daughter unlocked it, and Wyant followed them back in silence to the room in which they had left Mrs. Lombard. That lady was no longer there, and he could think of no excuse for lingering.

He thanked the doctor, and turned to Miss Lombard, who stood in the middle of the room as though awaiting farther orders.

"It is very good of you," he said, "to allow one even a glimpse of such a treasure."

She looked at him with her odd directness. "You will come again?" she said quickly; and turning to her father she added: "You know what Professor Clyde asked. This gentleman cannot give him any account of the picture without seeing it again."

Doctor Lombard glanced at her vaguely; he was still like a person in a trance.

"Eh?" he said, rousing himself with an effort.

"I said, father, that Mr. Wyant must see the picture again if he is to tell Professor Clyde about it," Miss Lombard repeated with extraordinary precision of tone.

Wyant was silent. He had the puzzled sense that his wishes were being divined and gratified for reasons with which he was in no way connected.

"Well, well," the doctor muttered, "I don't say no—I don't say no. I know what Clyde wants—I don't refuse to help him." He turned to Wyant. "You may come again—you may make notes," he added with a sudden effort. "Jot down what occurs to you. I'm willing to concede that."

Wyant again caught the girl's eye, but its emphatic message perplexed him.

"You're very good," he said tentatively, "but the fact is the picture is so mysterious—so full of complicated detail—that I'm afraid no notes I could make would serve Clyde's purpose as well as—as a photograph, say. If you would allow me—"

Miss Lombard's brow darkened, and her father raised his head furiously.

"A photograph? A photograph, did you say? Good God, man, not ten people have been allowed to set foot in that room! A *photograph?*"

Wyant saw his mistake, but saw also that he had gone too far to retreat.

"I know, sir, from what Clyde has told me, that you object to having any reproduction of the picture published; but he hoped you might let me take a photograph for his personal use—not to be reproduced in his book, but simply to give him something to work by. I should take the photograph myself, and the negative would of course be yours. If you wished it, only one impression would be struck off, and that one Clyde could return to you when he had done with it."

Doctor Lombard interrupted him with a snarl. "When he had done with it? Just so: I thank thee for that word! When it had been re-photographed, drawn, traced, autotyped, passed about from hand to hand, defiled by every ignorant eye in England, vulgarised by the blundering praise of every art-scribbler in Europe! Pah! I'd as soon give you the picture itself: why don't you ask for that?"

"Well, sir," said Wyant calmly, "if you will trust me with it, I'll engage to take it safely to England and back, and to let no eye but Clyde's see it while it is out of your keeping."

The doctor received this remarkable proposal in silence; then he burst into a laugh.

"Upon my soul!" he said with sardonic good humour.

It was Miss Lombard's turn to look perplexedly at Wyant. His last words and her father's unexpected reply had evidently carried her beyond her depth.

"Well, sir, am I to take the picture?" Wyant smilingly pursued.

"No, young man; nor a photograph of it. Nor a sketch, either; mind that,—nothing that can be reproduced. Sybilla," he cried with sudden passion, "swear to me that the picture shall never be reproduced! No photograph, no sketch—now or afterward. Do you hear me?"

"Yes, father," said the girl quietly.

"The vandals," he muttered, "the desecrators of beauty; if I thought it would ever get into their hands I'd burn it first, by God!" He turned to Wyant, speaking more quietly. "I said you might come back—I never retract what I say. But you must give me your word that no one but Clyde shall see the notes you make."

Wyant was growing warm.

"If you won't trust me with a photograph I wonder you trust me not to show my notes!" he exclaimed.

The doctor looked at him with a malicious smile.

"Humph!" he said; "would they be of much use to anybody?"

Wyant saw that he was losing ground and controlled his impatience.

"To Clyde, I hope, at any rate," he answered, holding out his hand. The doctor shook it without a trace of resentment, and Wyant added: "When shall I come, sir?"

"Tomorrow—tomorrow morning," cried Miss Lombard, speaking suddenly.

She looked fixedly at her father, and he shrugged his shoulders.

"The picture is hers," he said to Wyant.

In the ante-chamber the young man was met by the woman who had admitted him. She handed him his hat and stick, and turned to unbar the door. As the bolt slipped back he felt a touch on his arm.

"You have a letter?" she said in a low tone.

"A letter?" He stared. "What letter?"

She shrugged her shoulders, and drew back to let him pass.

THE HOUSE OF THE DEAD HAND

II

As Wyant emerged from the house he paused once more to glance up at its scarred brick façade. The marble hand drooped tragically above the entrance: in the waning light it seemed to have relaxed into the passiveness of despair, and Wyant stood musing on its hidden meaning. But the Dead Hand was not the only mysterious thing about Doctor Lombard's house. What were the relations between Miss Lombard and her father? Above all, between Miss Lombard and her picture? She did not look like a person capable of a disinterested passion for the arts: and there had been moments when it struck Wyant that she hated the picture.

The sky at the end of the street was flooded with turbulent yellow light, and the young man turned his steps toward the church of San Domenico, in the hope of catching the lingering brightness on Sodoma's St. Catherine.

The great bare aisles were almost dark when he entered, and he had to grope his way to the chapel steps. Under the momentary evocation of the sunset, the saint's figure emerged pale and swooning from the dusk, and the warm light gave a sensual tinge to her ecstasy. The flesh seemed to glow and heave, the eyelids to tremble; Wyant stood fascinated by the accidental collaboration of light and colour.

Suddenly he noticed that something white had fluttered to the ground at his feet. He stooped and picked up a small thin sheet of note-paper, folded and sealed like an old-fashioned letter, and bearing the superscription:—

To the Count Ottaviano Celsi.

Wyant stared at this mysterious document. Where had it come from? He was distinctly conscious of having seen it fall through the air, close to his feet. He glanced up at the dark ceiling of the chapel; then he turned and looked about the church. There was only one figure in it, that of a man who knelt near the high altar.

Suddenly Wyant recalled the question of Doctor Lombard's maid-servant. Was this the letter she had asked for? Had he been unconsciously carrying it about with him all the afternoon? Who was Count Ottaviano Celsi, and how came Wyant to have been chosen to act as that nobleman's ambulant letter-box?

Wyant laid his hat and stick on the chapel steps and began to explore his pockets, in the irrational hope of finding there some clue to the mystery; but they held nothing which he had not himself put there, and he was reduced to wondering how the letter, supposing some unknown hand to have bestowed it on him, had happened to fall out while he stood motionless before the picture.

At this point he was disturbed by a step on the floor of the aisle, and turning, he saw his lustrous-eyed neighbour of the table d'hôte.

The young man bowed and waved an apologetic hand.

"I do not intrude?" he inquired suavely.

Without waiting for a reply, he mounted the steps of the chapel, glancing about him with the affable air of an afternoon caller.

"I see," he remarked with a smile, "that you know the hour at which our saint should be visited."

Wyant agreed that the hour was indeed felicitous.

The stranger stood beamingly before the picture.

"What grace! What poetry!" he murmured, apostrophising the St. Catherine, but letting his glance slip rapidly about the chapel as he spoke.

Wyant, detecting the manœuvre, murmured a brief assent.

"But it is cold here—mortally cold; you do not find it so?" The intruder put on his hat. "It is permitted at this hour—when the church is empty. And you, my dear sir—do you not feel the dampness? You are an artist, are you not? And to artists it is permitted to cover the head when they are engaged in the study of the paintings."

He darted suddenly toward the steps and bent over Wyant's hat.

"Permit me—cover yourself!" he said a moment later, holding out the hat with an ingratiating gesture.

A light flashed on Wyant.

"Perhaps," he said, looking straight at the young man, "you will tell me your name. My own is Wyant."

The stranger, surprised, but not disconcerted, drew forth a coroneted card, which he offered with a low bow. On the card was engraved:—

Il Conte Ottaviano Celsi.

"I am much obliged to you," said Wyant; "and I may as well tell you that the letter which you apparently expected to find in the lining of my hat is not there, but in my pocket."

He drew it out and handed it to its owner, who had grown very pale.

"And now," Wyant continued, "you will perhaps be good enough to tell me what all this means."

There was no mistaking the effect produced on Count Ottaviano by this request. His lips moved, but he achieved only an ineffectual smile.

"I suppose you know," Wyant went on, his anger rising at the sight of the other's discomfiture, "that you have taken an unwarrantable liberty. I don't yet understand what part I have been made to play, but it's evident that you have made use of me to serve some purpose of your own, and I propose to know the reason why."

Count Ottaviano advanced with an imploring gesture.

"Sir," he pleaded, "you permit me to speak?"

"I expect you to," cried Wyant. "But not here," he added, hearing the clank of the verger's keys. "It is growing dark, and we shall be turned out in a few minutes."

He walked across the church, and Count Ottaviano followed him out into the deserted square.

"Now," said Wyant, pausing on the steps.

The Count, who had regained some measure of self-possession, began to speak in a high key, with an accompaniment of conciliatory gesture.

"My dear sir—my dear Mr. Wyant—you find me in an abominable position—that, as a man of honour, I immediately confess. I have taken advantage of you—yes! I have counted on your amiability, your chivalry—too far, perhaps? I confess it! But what could I do? It was to oblige a lady"—he laid a hand on his heart—"a lady whom I would die to serve!" He went on with increasing volubility, his deliberate English swept away by a torrent of Italian, through which Wyant, with some difficulty, struggled to a comprehension of the case.

Count Ottaviano, according to his own statement, had come to Siena some months previously, on business connected with his mother's property; the paternal estate being near Orvieto, of which ancient city his father was syndic. Soon after his arrival in Siena the young Count had met the incomparable daughter of Doctor Lombard, and falling deeply in love with her, had prevailed on his parents to ask her hand in marriage. Doctor Lombard had not opposed his suit, but when the question of settlements arose it became known that Miss Lombard, who was possessed of a small property in her own right, had a short time before invested the whole amount in the purchase of the Bergamo Leonardo. Thereupon Count Ottaviano's parents had politely suggested that she should sell the picture and thus recover her independence; and this proposal being met by a curt refusal from Doctor Lombard, they had withdrawn their consent to their son's marriage. The young lady's attitude had hitherto been one of passive submission; she was horribly afraid of her father, and would never venture openly to oppose him; but she had made known to Ottaviano her intention of not giving him up, of waiting patiently till events should take a more favourable turn. She seemed hardly aware, the Count said with a sigh, that the means of escape lay in her own hands; that she was of age, and had a right to sell the picture, and to marry without asking her father's consent. Meanwhile her suitor spared no pains to keep himself before her, to remind her that he, too, was waiting and would never give her up.

Doctor Lombard, who suspected the young man of trying to persuade Sybilla to sell the picture, had forbidden the lovers to meet or to correspond; they were thus driven to clandestine communication, and had several times, the Count ingenuously avowed, made use of the doctor's visitors as a means of exchanging letters.

"And you told the visitors to ring twice?" Wyant interposed.

The young man extended his hands in a deprecating gesture. Could Mr. Wyant blame him? He was young, he was ardent, he was enamoured! The young lady had done him the supreme honour of avowing her attachment, of pledging her unalterable fidelity; should he suffer his devotion to be outdone? But his purpose in writing to her, he admitted, was not merely to reiterate his fidelity; he was trying by every means in his power to induce her to sell the picture. He had organised a plan of action; every detail was complete; if she would but have the courage to carry out his instructions he would answer for the result. His idea was that she should secretly retire to a convent of which his aunt was the Mother Superior, and from that stronghold should transact the sale of the Leonardo. He had a purchaser ready, who was willing to pay a large sum; a sum, Count Ottaviano whispered, considerably in excess of the young lady's original inheritance; once the picture sold, it could, if necessary, be removed by force from Doctor Lombard's house, and his daughter, being safely in the convent, would be spared the painful scenes incidental to the removal. Finally, if Doctor Lombard were vindictive enough to refuse his consent to her marriage, she had only to make a *sommation respectueuse*, and at the end of the prescribed delay no power on earth could prevent her becoming the wife of Count Ottaviano.

Wyant's anger had fallen at the recital of this simple romance. It was absurd to be angry with a young man who confided his secrets to the first stranger he met in the streets, and placed his hand on his heart whenever he mentioned the name of his betrothed. The easiest way out of the business was to take it as a joke. Wyant had played the wall to this new Pyramus and Thisbe, and was philosophic enough to laugh at the part he had unwittingly performed.

He held out his hand with a smile to Count Ottaviano.

"I won't deprive you any longer," he said, "of the pleasure of reading your letter."

"Oh, sir, a thousand thanks! And when you return to the casa Lombard, you will take a message from me—the letter she expected this afternoon?"

"The letter she expected?" Wyant paused. "No, thank you. I thought you understood that where I come from we don't do that kind of thing—knowingly."

"But, sir, to serve a young lady!"

"I'm sorry for the young lady, if what you tell me is true"—the Count's expressive hands resented the doubt—"but remember that if I am under obligations to any one in this matter, it is to her father, who has admitted me to his house and has allowed me to see his picture."

"*His* picture? Hers!"

"Well, the house is his, at all events."

"Unhappily—since to her it is a dungeon!"

"Why doesn't she leave it, then?" exclaimed Wyant impatiently.

The Count clasped his hands. "Ah, how you say that—with what force, with what virility! If you would but say it to *her* in that tone—you, her countryman! She has no one to advise her; the mother is an idiot; the father is terrible; she is in his power; it is my belief that he would kill her if she resisted him. Mr. Wyant, I tremble for her life while she remains in that house!"

"Oh, come," said Wyant lightly, "they seem to understand each other well enough. But in any case, you must see that I can't interfere—at least you would if you were an Englishman," he added with an escape of contempt.

III

Wyant's affiliations in Siena being restricted to an acquaintance with his landlady, he was forced to apply to her for the verification of Count Ottaviano's story.

The young nobleman had, it appeared, given a perfectly correct account of his situation. His father, Count Celsi-Mongirone, was a man of distinguished family and some wealth. He was syndic of Orvieto, and lived either in that town or on his neighbouring estate of Mongirone. His wife owned a large property near Siena, and Count Ottaviano, who was the second son, came there from time to time to look into its management. The eldest son was in the army, the youngest in the Church; and an aunt of Count Ottaviano's was Mother Superior of the Visitandine convent in Siena. At one time it had been said that Count Ottaviano, who was a most amiable and accomplished young man, was to marry the daughter of the strange Englishman, Doctor Lombard, but difficulties having arisen as to the adjustment of the young lady's dower, Count Celsi-Mongirone had very properly broken off the match. It was sad for the young man, however, who was said to be deeply in love, and to find frequent excuses for coming to Siena to inspect his mother's estate.

Viewed in the light of Count Ottaviano's personality the story had a tinge of opera bouffe; but the next morning, as Wyant mounted the stairs of the House of the Dead Hand, the situation insensibly assumed another aspect. It was impossible to take Doctor Lombard lightly; and there was a suggestion of fatality in the appearance of his gaunt dwelling. Who could tell amid what tragic records of domestic tyranny and fluttering broken purposes the little drama of Miss Lombard's fate was being played out? Might not the accumulated influences of such a house modify the lives within it in a manner unguessed by the inmates of a suburban villa with sanitary plumbing and a telephone?

One person, at least, remained unperturbed by such fanciful problems; and that was Mrs. Lombard, who, at Wyant's entrance, raised a placidly wrinkled brow from her knitting. The morning was mild, and her chair had been wheeled into a bar of sunshine near the window, so that she made a cheerful spot of prose in the poetic gloom of her surroundings.

"What a nice morning!" she said; "it must be delightful weather at Bonchurch."

Her dull blue glance wandered across the narrow street with its threatening house fronts, and fluttered back baffled, like a bird with clipped wings. It was evident, poor lady, that she had never seen beyond the opposite houses.

Wyant was not sorry to find her alone. Seeing that she was surprised at his reappearance he said at once: "I have come back to study Miss Lombard's picture."

"Oh, the picture—" Mrs. Lombard's face expressed a gentle disappointment, which might have been boredom in a person of acuter sensibilities. "It's an original Leonardo, you know," she said mechanically.

"And Miss Lombard is very proud of it, I suppose? She seems to have inherited her father's love for art."

Mrs. Lombard counted her stitches, and he went on: "It's unusual in so young a girl. Such tastes generally develop later."

Mrs. Lombard looked up eagerly. "That's what I say! I was quite different at her age, you know. I liked dancing, and doing a pretty bit of fancy-work. Not that I couldn't sketch, too; I had a master down from London. My aunts have some of my crayons hung up in their drawing-room now—I did a view of Kenilworth which was thought pleasing. But I liked a picnic, too, or a pretty walk through the woods with young people of my own age. I say it's more natural, Mr. Wyant; one may have a feeling for art, and do crayons that are worth framing, and yet not give up everything else. I was taught that there were other things."

Wyant, half-ashamed of provoking these innocent confidences, could not resist another question. "And Miss Lombard cares for nothing else?"

Her mother looked troubled.

"Sybilla is so clever—she says I don't understand. You know how self-confident young people are! My husband never said that of me, now—he knows I had an excellent education. My aunts were very particular; I was brought up to have opinions, and my husband has always respected them. He says himself that he wouldn't for the world miss hearing my opinion on any subject; you may have noticed that he often refers to my tastes. He has always respected my preference for living in England; he likes to hear me give my reasons for it. He is so much interested in my ideas that he often says he knows just what I am going to say before I speak. But Sybilla does not care for what I think—"

At this point Doctor Lombard entered. He glanced sharply at Wyant. "The servant is a fool; she didn't tell me you were here." His eye turned to his wife. "Well, my dear, what have you been telling Mr. Wyant? About the aunts at Bonchurch, I'll be bound!"

Mrs. Lombard looked triumphantly at Wyant, and her husband rubbed his hooked fingers, with a smile.

"Mrs. Lombard's aunts are very superior women. They subscribe to the circulating library, and borrow *Good Words* and the *Monthly Packet* from the curate's wife across the way. They have the rector to tea twice a year, and keep a page-boy, and are visited by two baronets' wives. They devoted themselves to the education of their orphan niece, and I think I may say without boasting that Mrs. Lombard's conversation shows marked traces of the advantages she enjoyed."

Mrs. Lombard coloured with pleasure.

"I was telling Mr. Wyant that my aunts were very particular."

"Quite so, my dear; and did you mention that they never sleep in anything but linen, and that Miss Sophia puts away the furs and blankets every spring with her own hands? Both those facts are interesting to the student of human nature." Doctor Lombard glanced at his watch. "But we are missing an incomparable moment; the light is perfect at this hour."

Wyant rose, and the doctor led him through the tapestried door and down the passageway.

The light was, in fact, perfect, and the picture shone with an inner radiancy, as though a lamp burned behind the soft screen of the lady's flesh. Every detail of the foreground detached itself with jewel-like precision. Wyant noticed a dozen accessories which had escaped him on the previous day.

He drew out his notebook, and the doctor, who had dropped his sardonic grin for a look of devout contemplation, pushed a chair forward, and seated himself on a carved settle against the wall.

"Now, then," he said, "tell Clyde what you can; but the letter killeth."

He sank down, his hands hanging on the arm of the settle like the claws of a dead bird, his eyes fixed on Wyant's notebook with the obvious intention of detecting any attempt at a surreptitious sketch.

Wyant, nettled at this surveillance, and disturbed by the speculations which Doctor Lombard's strange household excited, sat motionless for a few minutes, staring first at the picture and then at the blank pages of the notebook. The thought that Doctor Lombard was enjoying his discomfiture at length roused him, and he began to write.

He was interrupted by a knock on the iron door. Doctor Lombard rose to unlock it, and his daughter entered.

She bowed hurriedly to Wyant, without looking at him.

"Father, had you forgotten that the man from Monte Amiato was to come back this morning with an answer about the bas-relief? He is here now; he says he can't wait."

"The devil!" cried her father impatiently. "Didn't you tell him—"

"Yes; but he says he can't come back. If you want to see him you must come now."

"Then you think there's a chance?—"

She nodded.

He turned and looked at Wyant, who was writing assiduously.

"You will stay here, Sybilla; I shall be back in a moment."

He hurried out, locking the door behind him.

Wyant had looked up, wondering if Miss Lombard would show any surprise at being locked in with him; but it was his turn to be surprised, for hardly had they heard the key withdrawn when she moved close to him, her small face pale and tumultuous.

"I arranged it—I must speak to you," she gasped. "He'll be back in five minutes."

Her courage seemed to fail, and she looked at him helplessly.

Wyant had a sense of stepping among explosives. He glanced about him at the dusky vaulted room, at the haunting smile of the strange picture overhead, and at the pink-and-white girl whispering of conspiracies in a voice meant to exchange platitudes with a curate.

"How can I help you?" he said with a rush of compassion.

"Oh, if you would! I never have a chance to speak to any one; it's so difficult—he watches me—he'll be back immediately."

"Try to tell me what I can do."

"I don't dare; I feel as if he were behind me." She turned away, fixing her eyes on the picture. A sound startled her. "There he comes, and I haven't spoken! It was my only chance; but it bewilders me so to be hurried."

"I don't hear any one," said Wyant, listening. "Try to tell me."

"How can I make you understand? It would take so long to explain." She drew a deep breath, and then with a plunge—"Will you come here again this afternoon—at about five?" she whispered.

"Come here again?"

"Yes—you can ask to see the picture,—make some excuse. He will come with you, of course; I will open the door for you—and—and lock you both in"—she gasped.

"Lock us in?"

"You see? You understand? It's the only way for me to leave the house—if I am ever to do it"—She drew another difficult breath. "The key will be returned—by a safe person—in half an hour,—perhaps sooner—"

She trembled so much that she was obliged to lean against the settle for support.

Wyant looked at her steadily; he was very sorry for her.

"I can't, Miss Lombard," he said at length.

"You can't?"

"I'm sorry; I must seem cruel; but consider—"

He was stopped by the futility of the word: as well ask a hunted rabbit to pause in its dash for a hole!

Wyant took her hand; it was cold and nerveless.

"I will serve you in any way I can; but you must see that this way is impossible. Can't I talk to you again? Perhaps—"

"Oh," she cried, starting up, "there he comes!"

Doctor Lombard's step sounded in the passage.

Wyant held her fast. "Tell me one thing: he won't let you sell the picture?"

"No—hush!"

"Make no pledges for the future, then; promise me that."

"The future?"

"In case he should die: your father is an old man. You haven't promised?"

She shook her head.

"Don't, then; remember that."

She made no answer, and the key turned in the lock.

As he passed out of the house, its scowling cornice and façade of ravaged brick looked down on him with the startling-ness of a strange face, seen momentarily in a crowd, and impressing itself on the brain as part of an inevitable future. Above the doorway, the marble hand reached out like the cry of an imprisoned anguish.

Wyant turned away impatiently.

"Rubbish!" he said to himself. "*She* isn't walled in; she can get out if she wants to."

IV

Wyant had any number of plans for coming to Miss Lombard's aid: he was elaborating the twentieth when, on the same afternoon, he stepped into the express train for Florence. By the time the train reached Certaldo he was convinced that, in thus hastening his departure, he had followed the only reasonable course; at Empoli, he began to reflect that the priest and the Levite had probably justified themselves in much the same manner.

A month later, after his return to England, he was unexpectedly relieved from these alternatives of extenuation and approval. A paragraph in the morning paper announced the sudden death of Doctor Lombard, the distinguished English dilettante who had long resided in Siena. Wyant's justification was complete. Our blindest impulses become evidence of perspicacity when they fall in with the course of events.

Wyant could now comfortably speculate on the particular complications from which his foresight had probably saved him. The climax was unexpectedly dramatic. Miss Lombard, on the brink of a step which, whatever its issue, would have burdened her with retrospective compunction, had been set free before her suitor's ardour could have had time to cool, and was now doubtless planning a life of domestic felicity on the proceeds of the Leonardo. One thing, however, struck Wyant as odd—he saw no mention of the sale of the picture. He had scanned the papers for an immediate announcement of its transfer to one of the great museums; but presently concluding that Miss Lombard, out of filial piety, had wished to avoid an appearance of unseemly haste in the disposal of her treasure, he dismissed the matter from his mind. Other affairs happened to engage him; the months slipped by, and gradually the lady and the picture dwelt less vividly in his mind.

It was not till five or six years later, when chance took him again to Siena, that the recollection started from some inner fold of memory. He found himself, as it happened, at the head of Doctor Lombard's street, and glancing down that grim thoroughfare, caught an oblique glimpse of the doctor's house front, with the Dead Hand projecting above its threshold.

The sight revived his interest, and that evening, over an admirable *frittata*, he questioned his landlady about Miss Lombard's marriage.

"The daughter of the English doctor? But she has never married, signore."

"Never married? What, then, became of Count Ottaviano?"

"For a long time he waited; but last year he married a noble lady of the Maremma."

"But what happened—why was the marriage broken?"

The landlady enacted a pantomime of baffled interrogation.

"And Miss Lombard still lives in her father's house?"

"Yes, signore; she is still there."

"And the Leonardo—"

"The Leonardo, also, is still there."

The next day, as Wyant entered the House of the Dead Hand, he remembered Count Ottaviano's injunction to ring twice, and smiled mournfully to think that so much subtlety had been vain. But what could have prevented the marriage? If Doctor Lombard's death had been long delayed, time might have acted as a dissolvent, or the young lady's resolve have failed; but it seemed impossible that the white heat of ardour in which Wyant had left the lovers should have cooled in a few short weeks.

As he ascended the vaulted stairway the atmosphere of the place seemed a reply to his conjectures. The same numbing air fell on him, like an emanation from some persistent will-power, a something fierce and imminent which might reduce to impotence every impulse within its range. Wyant could almost fancy a hand on his shoulder, guiding him upward with the ironical intent of confronting him with the evidence of its work.

A strange servant opened the door, and he was presently introduced to the tapestried room, where, from their usual seats in the window, Mrs. Lombard and her daughter advanced to welcome him with faint ejaculations of surprise.

Both had grown oddly old, but in a dry, smooth way, as fruits might shrivel on a shelf instead of ripening on the tree. Mrs. Lombard was still knitting, and pausing now and then to warm her swollen hands above the brazier; and Miss Lombard, in rising, had laid aside a strip of needlework which might have been the same on which Wyant had first seen her engaged.

Their visitor inquired discreetly how they had fared in the interval, and learned that they had thought of returning to England, but had somehow never done so.

"I am sorry not to see my aunts again," Mrs. Lombard said resignedly; "but Sybilla thinks it best that we should not go this year."

"Next year, perhaps," murmured Miss Lombard, in a voice which seemed to suggest that they had a great waste of time to fill.

She had returned to her seat, and sat bending over her work. Her hair enveloped her head in the same thick braids, but the rose colour of her cheeks had turned to blotches of dull red, like some pigment which has darkened in drying.

"And Professor Clyde—is he well?" Mrs. Lombard asked affably; continuing, as her daughter raised a startled eye: "Surely, Sybilla, Mr. Wyant was the gentleman who was sent by Professor Clyde to see the Leonardo?"

Miss Lombard was silent, but Wyant hastened to assure the elder lady of his friend's well-being.

"Ah—perhaps, then, he will come back some day to Siena," she said, sighing. Wyant declared that it was more than likely; and there ensued a pause, which he presently broke by saying to Miss Lombard: "And you still have the picture?"

She raised her eyes and looked at him. "Should you like to see it?" she asked.

On his assenting, she rose, and extracting the same key from the same secret drawer, unlocked the door beneath the tapestry. They walked down the passage in silence, and she stood aside with a grave gesture, making Wyant pass before her into the room. Then she crossed over and drew the curtain back from the picture.

The light of the early afternoon poured full on it: its surface appeared to ripple and heave with a fluid splendour. The colours had lost none of their warmth, the outlines none of their pure precision; it seemed to Wyant like some magical flower which had burst suddenly from the mould of darkness and oblivion.

He turned to Miss Lombard with a movement of comprehension.

"Ah, I understand—you couldn't part with it, after all!" he cried.

"No—I couldn't part with it," she answered.

"It's too beautiful,—too beautiful,"—he assented.

"Too beautiful?" She turned on him with a curious stare. "I have never thought it beautiful, you know."

He gave back the stare. "You have never—"

She shook her head. "It's not that. I hate it; I've always hated it. But he wouldn't let me—he will never let me now."

Wyant was startled by her use of the present tense. Her look surprised him, too: there was a strange fixity of resentment in her innocuous eye. Was it possible that she was labouring under some delusion? Or did the pronoun not refer to her father?

"You mean that Doctor Lombard did not wish you to part with the picture?"

"No—he prevented me; he will always prevent me."

There was another pause. "You promised him, then, before his death—"

"No; I promised nothing. He died too suddenly to make me." Her voice sank to a whisper. "I was free—perfectly free—or I thought I was till I tried."

"Till you tried?"

"To disobey him—to sell the picture. Then I found it was impossible. I tried again and again; but he was always in the room with me."

She glanced over her shoulder as though she had heard a step; and to Wyant, too, for a moment, the room seemed full of a third presence.

"And you can't"—he faltered, unconsciously dropping his voice to the pitch of hers.

She shook her head, gazing at him mystically. "I can't lock him out; I can never lock him out now. I told you I should never have another chance."

Wyant felt the chill of her words like a cold breath in his hair.

"Oh"—he groaned; but she cut him off with a grave gesture.

"It is too late," she said; "but you ought to have helped me that day."

AFTERWARD

I

"OH, there *is* one, of course, but you'll never know it."

The assertion, laughingly flung out six months earlier in a bright June garden, came back to Mary Boyne with a new perception of its significance as she stood, in the December dusk, waiting for the lamps to be brought into the library.

The words had been spoken by their friend Alida Stair, as they sat at tea on her lawn at Pangbourne, in reference to the very house of which the library in question was the central, the pivotal "feature." Mary Boyne and her husband, in quest of a country place in one of the southern or southwestern counties, had, on their arrival in England, carried their problem straight to Alida Stair, who had successfully solved it in her own case; but it was not until they had rejected, almost capriciously, several practical and judicious suggestions that she threw out: "Well, there's Lyng, in Dorsetshire. It belongs to Hugo's cousins, and you can get it for a song."

The reason she gave for its being obtainable on these terms—its remoteness from a station, its lack of electric light, hot-water pipes, and other vulgar necessities—were exactly those pleading in its favour with two romantic Americans perversely in search of the economic drawbacks which were associated, in their tradition, with unusual architectural felicities.

"I should never believe I was living in an old house unless I was thoroughly uncomfortable," Ned Boyne, the more extravagant of the two, had jocosely insisted; "the least hint of 'convenience' would make me think it had been bought out of an exhibition, with the pieces numbered, and set up again." And they had proceeded to enumerate, with humorous precision, their various doubts and demands, refusing to believe that the house their cousin recommended was *really* Tudor till they learned it had no heating system, or that the village church was literally in the grounds till she assured them of the deplorable uncertainty of the water-supply.

"It's too uncomfortable to be true!" Edward Boyne had continued to exult as the avowal of each disadvantage was successively wrung from her; but he had cut short his rhapsody to ask, with a relapse to distrust: "And the ghost? You've been concealing from us the fact that there is no ghost!"

Mary, at the moment, had laughed with him, yet almost with her laugh, being possessed of several sets of independent perceptions, had been struck by a note of flatness in Alida's answering hilarity.

"Oh, Dorsetshire's full of ghosts, you know."

"Yes, yes; but that won't do. I don't want to have to drive ten miles to see somebody else's ghost. I want one of my own on the premises. *Is* there a ghost at Lyng?"

His rejoinder had made Alida laugh again, and it was then that she had flung back tantalisingly: "Oh, there *is* one, of course, but you'll never know it."

"Never know it?" Boyne pulled her up. "But what in the world constitutes a ghost except the fact of its being known for one?"

"I can't say. But that's the story."

"That there's a ghost, but that nobody knows it's a ghost?"

"Well—not till afterward, at any rate."

"Till afterward?"

"Not till long long afterward."

"But if it's once been identified as an unearthly visitant, why hasn't its *signalement* been handed down in the family? How has it managed to preserve its incognito?"

Alida could only shake her head. "Don't ask me. But it has."

"And then suddenly—" Mary spoke up as if from cavernous depths of divination—"suddenly, long afterward, one says to one's self *That was it?*"

She was startled at the sepulchral sound with which her question fell on the banter of the other two, and she saw the shadow of the same surprise flit across Alida's pupils. "I suppose so. One just has to wait."

"Oh, hang waiting!" Ned broke in. "Life's too short for a ghost who can only be enjoyed in retrospect. Can't we do better than that, Mary?"

But it turned out that in the event they were not destined to, for within three months of their conversation with Mrs. Stair they were settled at Lyng, and the life they had yearned for, to the point of planning it in advance in all its daily details, had actually begun for them.

It was to sit, in the thick December dusk, by just such a wide-hooded fireplace, under just such black oak rafters, with the sense that beyond the mullioned panes the downs were darkened to a deeper solitude: it was for the ultimate indulgence of such sensations that Mary Boyne, abruptly exiled from New York by her husband's business, had endured for nearly fourteen years the soul-deadening ugliness of a Middle Western town, and that Boyne had ground on doggedly at his engineering till, with a suddenness that still made her blink, the prodigious windfall of the Blue Star Mine had put them at a stroke in possession of life and the leisure to taste it. They had never for a moment meant their new state to be one of idleness; but they meant to give themselves only to harmonious activities. She had her vision of painting and gardening (against a background of grey walls), he dreamed of the production of his long-planned book on the "Economic Basis of Culture"; and with such absorbing work ahead no existence could be too sequestered: they could not get far enough from the world, or plunge deep enough into the past.

Dorsetshire had attracted them from the first by an air of remoteness out of all proportion to its geographical position. But to the Boynes it was one of the ever-recurring wonders of the whole incredibly compressed island—a nest of counties, as they put it—that for the production of its effects so little of a given quality went so far: that so few miles made a distance, and so short a distance a difference.

"It's that," Ned had once enthusiastically explained, "that gives such depth to their effects, such relief to their contrasts. They've been able to lay the butter so thick on every delicious mouthful."

The butter had certainly been laid on thick at Lyng: the old house hidden under a shoulder of the downs had almost all the finer marks of commerce with a protracted past. The mere fact that it was neither large nor exceptional made it, to the Boynes, abound the more completely in its special charm—the charm of having been for centuries a deep dim reservoir of life. The life had probably not been of the most vivid order: for long periods, no doubt, it had fallen as noiselessly into the past as the quiet drizzle of autumn fell, hour after hour, into the fish-pond between the yews; but these back-waters of existence sometimes breed, in their sluggish depths, strange acuities of emotion, and Mary Boyne had felt from the first the mysterious stir of intenser memories.

The feeling had never been stronger than on this particular afternoon when, waiting in the library for the lamps to come, she rose from her seat and stood among the shadows of the hearth. Her husband had gone off, after luncheon, for one of his long tramps on the downs. She had noticed of late that he preferred to go alone; and, in the tried security of their personal relations, had been driven to conclude that his book was bothering him, and that he needed the afternoons to turn over in solitude the problems left from the morning's work. Certainly the book was not going as smoothly as she had thought it would, and there were lines of perplexity between his eyes such as had never been there in his engineering days. He had often, then, looked fagged to the verge of illness, but the native demon of "worry" had never branded his brow. Yet the few pages he had so far read to her—the introduction, and a summary of the opening chapter—showed a firm hold on his subject, and an increasing confidence in his powers.

The fact threw her into deeper perplexity, since, now that he had done with "business" and its disturbing contingencies, the one other possible source of anxiety was eliminated. Unless it were his health, then? But physically he had gained since they had come to Dorsetshire, grown robuster, ruddier and fresher-eyed. It was only within the last week that she had felt in him the undefinable change which made her restless in his absence, and as tongue-tied in his presence as though it were *she* who had a secret to keep from him!

The thought that there *was* a secret somewhere between them struck her with a sudden rap of wonder, and she looked about her down the long room.

"Can it be the house?" she mused.

The room itself might have been full of secrets. They seemed to be piling themselves up, as evening fell, like the layers and layers of velvet shadow dropping from the low ceiling, the rows of books, the smoke-blurred sculpture of the hearth.

"Why, of course—the house is haunted!" she reflected.

The ghost—Alicia's imperceptible ghost—after figuring largely in the banter of their first month or two at Lyng, had been gradually left aside as too ineffectual for imaginative use. Mary had, indeed, as became the tenant of a haunted house, made the customary inquiries among her rural neighbours, but, beyond a vague "They dü say so, Ma'am," the villagers had nothing to impart. The elusive spectre had apparently never had sufficient identity for a legend to crystallise about it, and after a time the Boynes had set the matter down to their profit-and-loss account, agreeing that Lyng was one of the few houses good enough in itself to dispense with supernatural enhancements.

"And I suppose, poor ineffectual demon, that's why it beats its beautiful wings in vain in the void," Mary had laughingly concluded.

"Or, rather," Ned answered in the same strain, "why, amid so much that's ghostly, it can never affirm its separate existence as *the* ghost." And thereupon their invisible housemate had finally dropped out of their references, which were numerous enough to make them soon unaware of the loss.

Now, as she stood on the hearth, the subject of their earlier curiosity revived in her with a new sense of its meaning—a sense gradually acquired through daily contact with the scene of the lurking mystery. It was the house itself, of course, that possessed the ghost-seeing faculty, that communed visually but secretly with its own past; if one could only get into close enough communion with the house, one might surprise its secret, and acquire the ghost-sight on one's own account. Perhaps, in his long hours in this very room, where she never trespassed till the afternoon, her husband *had* acquired it already, and was silently carrying about the weight of whatever it had revealed to him. Mary was too well versed in the code of the spectral world not to know that one could not talk about the ghosts one saw: to do so was almost as great a breach of taste as to name a lady in a club. But this explanation did not really satisfy her. "What, after all, except for the fun of the shudder," she reflected, "would he really care for any of their old ghosts?" And thence she was thrown back once more on the fundamental dilemma: the fact that one's greater or less susceptibility to spectral influences had no particular bearing on the case, since, when one *did* see a ghost at Lyng, one did not know it.

"Not till long afterward," Alida Stair had said. Well, supposing Ned *had* seen one when they first came, and had known only within the last week what had happened to him? More and more under the spell of the hour, she threw back her thoughts to the early days of their tenancy, but at first only to recall a lively confusion of unpacking, settling, arranging of books, and calling to each other from remote corners of the house as, treasure after treasure, it revealed itself to them. It was in this particular connection that she presently recalled a certain soft afternoon of the previous October, when, passing from the first rapturous flurry of exploration to a detailed inspection of the old house, she had pressed (like a novel heroine) a panel that opened on a flight of corkscrew stairs leading to a flat ledge of the roof—the roof which, from below, seemed to slope away on all sides too abruptly for any but practised feet to scale.

The view from this hidden coign was enchanting, and she had flown down to snatch Ned from his papers and give him the freedom of her discovery. She remembered still how, standing at her side, he had passed his arm about her while their gaze flew to the long tossed horizon-line of the downs, and then dropped contentedly back to trace the arabesque of yew hedges about the fish-pond, and the shadow of the cedar on the lawn.

"And now the other way," he had said, turning her about within his arm; and closely pressed to him, she had absorbed, like some long satisfying draught, the picture of the grey-walled court, the squat lions on the gates, and the lime-avenue reaching up to the high-road under the downs.

It was just then, while they gazed and held each other, that she had felt his arm relax, and heard a sharp "Hullo!" that made her turn to glance at him.

Distinctly, yes, she now recalled that she had seen, as she glanced, a shadow of anxiety, of perplexity, rather, fall across his face; and, following his eyes, had beheld the figure of a man—a man in loose greyish clothes, as it appeared to her—who was sauntering down the lime-avenue to the court with the doubtful gait of a stranger who seeks his way. Her short-sighted eyes had given her but a blurred impression of slightness and greyishness, with something foreign, or at least unlocal, in the cut of the figure or its dress; but her husband had apparently seen more—seen enough to make him push past her with a hasty "Wait!" and dash down the stairs without pausing to give her a hand.

A slight tendency to dizziness obliged her, after a provisional clutch at the chimney against which they had been leaning, to follow him first more cautiously; and when she had reached the landing she paused again, for a less definite reason, leaning over the banister to strain her eyes through the silence of the brown sun-flecked depths. She lingered there till, somewhere in those depths, she heard the closing of a door; then, mechanically impelled, she went down the shallow flights of steps till she reached the lower hall.

The front door stood open on the sunlight of the court, and hall and court were empty. The library door was open, too, and after listening in vain for any sound of voices within, she crossed the threshold, and found her husband alone, vaguely fingering the papers on his desk.

He looked up, as if surprised at her entrance, but the shadow of anxiety had passed from his face, leaving it even, as she fancied, a little brighter and clearer than usual.

"What was it? Who was it?" she asked.

"Who?" he repeated, with the surprise still all on his side.

"The man we saw coming toward the house."

He seemed to reflect. "The man? Why, I thought I saw Peters; I dashed after him to say a word about the stable drains, but he had disappeared before I could get down."

"Disappeared? But he seemed to be walking so slowly when we saw him."

Boyne shrugged his shoulders. "So I thought; but he must have got up steam in the interval. What do you say to our trying a scramble up Meldon Steep before sunset?"

That was all. At the time the occurrence had been less than nothing, had, indeed, been immediately obliterated by the magic of their first vision from Meldon Steep, a height which they had dreamed of climbing ever since they had first seen its bare spine rising above the roof of Lyng. Doubtless it was the mere fact of the other incident's having occurred on the very day of their ascent to Meldon that had kept it stored away in the fold of memory from which it now emerged; for in itself it had no mark of the portentous. At the moment there could have been nothing more natural than that Ned should dash himself from the roof in the pursuit of dilatory tradesmen. It was the period when they were always on the watch for one or the other of the specialists employed about the place; always lying in wait for them, and rushing out at them with questions, reproaches or reminders. And certainly in the distance the grey figure had looked like Peters.

Yet now, as she reviewed the scene, she felt her husband's explanation of it to have been invalidated by the look of anxiety on his face. Why had the familiar appearance of Peters made him anxious? Why, above all, if it was of such prime necessity to confer with him on the subject of the stable drains, had the failure to find him produced such a look of relief? Mary could not say that any one of these questions had occurred to her at the time, yet, from the promptness with which they now marshalled themselves at her summons, she had a sense that they must all along have been there, waiting their hour.

II

Weary with her thoughts, she moved to the window. The library was now quite dark, and she was surprised to see how much faint light the outer world still held.

As she peered out into it across the court, a figure shaped itself far down the perspective of bare limes: it looked a mere blot of deeper grey in the greyness, and for an instant, as it moved toward her, her heart thumped to the thought "It's the ghost!"

She had time, in that long instant, to feel suddenly that the man of whom, two months earlier, she had had a distant vision from the roof, was now, at his predestined hour, about to reveal himself as *not* having been Peters; and her spirit sank under the impending fear of the disclosure. But almost with the next tick of the clock the figure, gaining substance and character, showed itself even to her weak sight as her husband's; and she turned to meet him, as he entered, with the confession of her folly.

"It's really too absurd," she laughed out, "but I never *can* remember!"

"Remember what?" Boyne questioned as they drew together.

"That when one sees the Lyng ghost one never knows it."

Her hand was on his sleeve, and he kept it there, but with no response in his gesture or in the lines of his preoccupied face.

"Did you think you'd seen it?" he asked, after an appreciable interval.

"Why, I actually took *you* for it, my dear, in my mad determination to spot it!"

"Me—just now?" His arm dropped away, and he turned from her with a faint echo of her laugh. "Really, dearest, you'd better give it up, if that's the best you can do."

"Oh, yes, I give it up. Have *you?*" she asked, turning round on him abruptly.

The parlour-maid had entered with letters and a lamp, and the light struck up into Boyne's face as he bent above the tray she presented.

"Have *you?*" Mary perversely insisted, when the servant had disappeared on her errand of illumination.

"Have I what?" he rejoined absently, the light bringing out the sharp stamp of worry between his brows as he turned over the letters.

"Given up trying to see the ghost." Her heart beat a little at the experiment she was making.

Her husband, laying his letters aside, moved away into the shadow of the hearth.

"I never tried," he said, tearing open the wrapper of a newspaper.

"Well, of course," Mary persisted, "the exasperating thing is that there's no use trying, since one can't be sure till so long afterward."

He was unfolding the paper as if he had hardly heard her; but after a pause, during which the sheets rustled spasmodically between his hands, he looked up to ask, "Have you any idea *how long?*"

Mary had sunk into a low chair beside the fireplace. From her seat she glanced over, startled, at her husband's profile, which was projected against the circle of lamplight.

"No; none. Have *you*?" she retorted, repeating her former phrase with an added stress of intention.

Boyne crumpled the paper into a bunch, and then, inconsequently, turned back with it toward the lamp.

"Lord, no! I only meant," he explained, with a faint tinge of impatience, "is there any legend, any tradition, as to that?"

"Not that I know of," she answered; but the impulse to add "What makes you ask?" was checked by the reappearance of the parlour-maid, with tea and a second lamp.

With the dispersal of shadows, and the repetition of the daily domestic office, Mary Boyne felt herself less oppressed by that sense of something mutely imminent which had darkened her afternoon. For a few moments she gave herself to the details of her task, and when she looked up from it she was struck to the point of bewilderment by the change in her husband's face. He had seated himself near the farther lamp, and was absorbed in the perusal of his letters; but was it something he had found in them, or merely the shifting of her own point of view, that had restored his features to their normal aspect? The longer she looked the more definitely the change affirmed itself. The lines of tension had vanished, and such traces of fatigue as lingered were of the kind easily attributable to steady mental effort. He glanced up, as if drawn by her gaze, and met her eyes with a smile.

"I'm dying for my tea, you know; and here's a letter for you," he said.

She took the letter he held out in exchange for the cup she proffered him, and, returning to her seat, broke the seal with the languid gesture of the reader whose interests are all enclosed in the circle of one cherished presence.

Her next conscious motion was that of starting to her feet, the letter falling to them as she rose, while she held out to her husband a newspaper clipping.

"Ned! What's this? What does it mean?"

He had risen at the same instant, almost as if hearing her cry before she uttered it; and for a perceptible space of time he and she studied each other, like adversaries watching for an advantage, across the space between her chair and his desk.

"What's what? You fairly made me jump!" Boyne said at length, moving toward her with a sudden half-exasperated laugh. The shadow of apprehension was on his face again, not now a look of fixed foreboding, but a shifting vigilance of lips and eyes that gave her the sense of his feeling himself invisibly surrounded.

Her hand shook so that she could hardly give him the clipping.

"This article—from the *Waukesha Sentinel*—that a man named Elwell has brought suit against you—that there was something wrong about the Blue Star Mine. I can't understand more than half."

They continued to face each other as she spoke, and to her astonishment she saw that her words had the almost immediate effect of dissipating the strained watchfulness of his look.

"Oh, *that!*" He glanced down the printed slip, and then folded it with the gesture of one who handles something harmless and familiar. "What's the matter with you this afternoon, Mary? I thought you'd got bad news."

She stood before him with her undefinable terror subsiding slowly under the reassurance of his tone.

"You knew about this, then—it's all right?"

"Certainly I knew about it; and it's all right."

"But what *is* it? I don't understand. What does this man accuse you of?"

"Pretty nearly every crime in the calendar." Boyne had tossed the clipping down, and thrown himself into an armchair near the fire. "Do you want to hear the story? It's not particularly interesting—just a squabble over interests in the Blue Star."

"But who is this Elwell? I don't know the name."

"Oh, he's a fellow I put into it—gave him a hand up. I told you all about him at the time."

"I daresay. I must have forgotten." Vainly she strained back among her memories. "But if you helped him, why does he make this return?"

"Probably some shyster lawyer got hold of him and talked him over. It's all rather technical and complicated. I thought that kind of thing bored you."

His wife felt a sting of compunction. Theoretically, she deprecated the American wife's detachment from her husband's professional interests, but in practice she had always found it difficult to fix her attention on Boyne's report of the transactions in which his varied interests involved him. Besides, she had felt during their years of exile, that, in a community where the amenities of living could be obtained only at the cost of efforts as arduous as her husband's professional labours, such brief leisure as he and she could command should be used as an escape from immediate preoccupations, a flight to the life they always dreamed of living. Once or twice, now that this new life had actually drawn its magic circle about them, she had asked herself if she had done right; but hitherto such conjectures had been no more than the retrospective excursions of an active fancy. Now, for the first time, it startled her a little to find how little she knew of the material foundation on which her happiness was built.

She glanced at her husband, and was again reassured by the composure of his face; yet she felt the need of more definite grounds for her reassurance.

"But doesn't this suit worry you? Why have you never spoken to me about it?"

He answered both questions at once. "I didn't speak of it at first because it *did* worry me—annoyed me, rather. But it's all ancient history now. Your correspondent must have got hold of a back number of the *Sentinel*."

She felt a quick thrill of relief. "You mean it's over? He's lost his case?"

There was a just perceptible delay in Boyne's reply. "The suit's been withdrawn—that's all."

But she persisted, as if to exonerate herself from the inward charge of being too easily put off. "Withdrawn it because he saw he had no chance?"

"Oh, he had no chance," Boyne answered.

She was still struggling with a dimly felt perplexity at the back of her thoughts.

"How long ago was it withdrawn?"

He paused, as if with a slight return of his former uncertainty. "I've just had the news now; but I've been expecting it."

"Just now—in one of your letters?"

"Yes; in one of my letters."

She made no answer, and was aware only, after a short interval of waiting, that he had risen, and, strolling across the room, had placed himself on the sofa at her side. She felt him, as he did so, pass an arm about her, she felt his hand seek hers and clasp it, and turning slowly, drawn by the warmth of his cheek, she met his smiling eyes.

"It's all right—it's all right?" she questioned, through the flood of her dissolving doubts; and "I give you my word it was never righter!" he laughed back at her, holding her close.

III

One of the strangest things she was afterward to recall out of all the next day's strangeness was the sudden and complete recovery of her sense of security.

It was in the air when she woke in her low-ceiled, dusky room; it went with her downstairs to the breakfast-table, flashed out at her from the fire, and reduplicated itself from the flanks of the urn and the sturdy flutings of the Georgian teapot. It was as if, in some roundabout way, all her diffused fears of the previous day, with their moment of sharp concentration about the newspaper article—as if this dim questioning of the future, and startled return upon the past, had between them liquidated the arrears of some haunting moral obligation. If she had indeed been careless of her husband's affairs, it was, her new state seemed to prove, because her faith in him instinctively justified such carelessness; and his right to her faith had now affirmed itself in the very face of menace and suspicion. She had never seen him more untroubled, more naturally and unconsciously himself, than after the cross-examination to which she had subjected him: it was almost as if he had been aware of her doubts, and had wanted the air cleared as much as she did.

It was as clear, thank Heaven! as the bright outer light that surprised her almost with a touch of summer when she issued from the house for her daily round of the gardens. She had left Boyne at his desk, indulging herself, as she passed the library door, by a last peep at his quiet face, where he bent, pipe in mouth, above his papers; and now she had her own morning's task to perform. The task involved, on such charmed winter days, almost as much happy loitering about the different quarters of her demesne as if spring were already at work there. There were such endless possibilities still before her, such opportunities to bring out the latent graces of the old place, without a single irreverent touch of alteration, that the winter was all too short to plan what spring and autumn executed. And her recovered sense of safety gave, on this particular morning, a peculiar zest to her progress through the sweet still place. She went first to the kitchen-garden, where the espaliered pear-trees drew complicated patterns on the walls, and pigeons were fluttering and preening about the silvery-slated roof of their cot. There was something wrong about the piping of the hot-house, and she was expecting an authority from Dorchester, who was to drive out between trains and make a diagnosis of the boiler. But when she dipped into the damp heat of the greenhouses, among the spiced scents and waxy pinks and reds of old-fashioned exotics—even the flora of Lyng was in the note!—she learned that the great man had not arrived, and, the day being too rare to waste in an artificial atmosphere, she came out again and paced along the springy turf of the bowling-green to the gardens behind the house. At their farther end rose a grass terrace, looking across the fish-pond and yew hedges to the long house-front with its twisted chimney-stacks and blue roof angles all drenched in the pale gold moisture of the air.

Seen thus, across the level tracery of the gardens, it sent her, from open windows and hospitably smoking chimneys, the look of some warm human presence, of a mind slowly ripened on a sunny wall of experience. She had never before had such a sense of her intimacy with it, such a conviction that its secrets were all beneficent, kept, as they said to children, "for one's good", such a trust in its power to gather up her life and Ned's into the harmonious pattern of the long, long story it sat there weaving in the sun.

She heard steps behind her, and turned, expecting to see the gardener accompanied by the engineer from Dorchester. But only one figure was in sight, that of a youngish, slightly built man, who, for reasons she could not on the spot have given, did not remotely resemble her notion of an authority on hot-house boilers. The newcomer, on seeing her, lifted his hat, and paused with the air of a gentleman—perhaps a traveller—who wishes to make it known that his intrusion is involuntary. Lyng occasionally attracted the more cultivated traveller, and Mary half-expected to see the stranger dissemble a camera, or justify his presence by producing it. But he made no gesture of any sort, and after a moment she asked, in a tone responding to the courteous hesitation of his attitude: "Is there any one you wish to see?"

"I came to see Mr. Boyne," he answered. His intonation, rather than his accent, was faintly American, and Mary, at the note, looked at him more closely. The brim of his soft felt hat cast a shade on his face, which, thus obscured, wore to her short-sighted gaze a look of seriousness, as of a person arriving "on business," and civilly but firmly aware of his rights.

Past experience had made her equally sensible to such claims; but she was jealous of her husband's morning hours, and doubtful of his having given any one the right to intrude on them.

"Have you an appointment with my husband?" she asked.

The visitor hesitated, as if unprepared for the question.

"I think he expects me," he replied.

It was Mary's turn to hesitate. "You see this is his time for work: he never sees any one in the morning."

He looked at her a moment without answering; then, as if accepting her decision, he began to move away. As he turned, Mary saw him pause and glance up at the peaceful house-front. Something in his air suggested weariness and disappointment, the dejection of the traveller who has come from far off and whose hours are limited by the time-table. It occurred to her that if this were the case her refusal might have made his errand vain, and a sense of compunction caused her to hasten after him.

"May I ask if you have come a long way?"

He gave her the same grave look. "Yes—I have come a long way."

"Then, if you'll go to the house, no doubt my husband will see you now. You'll find him in the library."

She did not know why she had added the last phrase, except from a vague impulse to atone for her previous inhospitality. The visitor seemed about to express his thanks, but her attention was distracted by the approach of the gardener with a companion who bore all the marks of being the expert from Dorchester.

"This way," she said, waving the stranger to the house; and an instant later she had forgotten him in the absorption of her meeting with the boiler-maker.

The encounter led to such far-reaching results that the engineer ended by finding it expedient to ignore his train, and Mary was beguiled into spending the remainder of the morning in absorbed confabulation among the flower-pots. When the colloquy ended, she was surprised to find that it was nearly luncheon-time, and she half expected, as she hurried back to the house, to see her husband coming out to meet her. But she found no one in the court but an under-gardener raking the gravel, and the hall, when she entered it, was so silent that she guessed Boyne to be still at work.

Not wishing to disturb him, she turned into the drawing-room, and there, at her writing-table, lost herself in renewed calculations of the outlay to which the morning's conference had pledged her. The fact that she could permit herself such follies had not yet lost its novelty; and somehow, in contrast to the vague fears of the previous days, it now seemed an element of her recovered security, of the sense that, as Ned had said, things in general had never been "righter."

She was still luxuriating in a lavish play of figures when the parlour-maid, from the threshold, roused her with an enquiry as to the expediency of serving luncheon. It was one of their jokes that Trimmle announced luncheon as if she were divulging a state secret, and Mary, intent upon her papers, merely murmured an absent-minded assent.

She felt Trimmle wavering doubtfully on the threshold, as if in rebuke of such unconsidered assent; then her retreating steps sounded down the passage, and Mary, pushing away her papers, crossed the hall and went to the library door. It was still closed, and she wavered in her turn, disliking to disturb her husband, yet anxious that he should not exceed his usual measure of work. As she stood there, balancing her impulses, Trimmle returned with the announcement of luncheon, and Mary, thus impelled, opened the library door.

Boyne was not at his desk, and she peered about her, expecting to discover him before the book-shelves, somewhere down the length of the room; but her call brought no response, and gradually it became clear to her that he was not there.

She turned back to the parlour-maid.

"Mr. Boyne must be upstairs. Please tell him that luncheon is ready."

Trimmle appeared to hesitate between the obvious duty of obedience and an equally obvious conviction of the foolishness of the injunction laid on her. The struggle resulted in her saying: "If you please, Madam, Mr. Boyne's not upstairs."

"Not in his room? Are you sure?"

"I'm sure, Madam."

Mary consulted the clock. "Where is he, then?"

"He's gone out," Trimmle announced, with the superior air of one who has respectfully waited for the question that a well-ordered mind would have put first.

Mary's conjecture had been right, then. Boyne must have gone to the gardens to meet her, and since she had missed him, it was clear that he had taken the shorter way by the south door, instead of going round to the court. She crossed the hall to the French window opening directly on the yew garden, but the parlour-maid, after another moment of inner conflict, decided to bring out: "Please, Madam, Mr. Boyne didn't go that way."

Mary turned back. "Where *did* he go? And when?"

"He went out of the front door, up the drive, Madam." It was a matter of principle with Trimmle never to answer more than one question at a time.

"Up the drive? At this hour?" Mary went to the door herself, and glanced across the court through the tunnel of bare limes. But its perspective was as empty as when she had scanned it on entering.

"Did Mr. Boyne leave no message?"

Trimmle seemed to surrender herself to a last struggle with the forces of chaos.

"No, Madam. He just went out with the gentleman."

"The gentleman? What gentleman?" Mary wheeled about, as if to front this new factor.

"The gentleman who called, Madam," said Trimmle resignedly.

"When did a gentleman call? Do explain yourself, Trimmle!"

Only the fact that Mary was very hungry, and that she wanted to consult her husband about the greenhouses, would have caused her to lay so unusual an injunction on her attendant; and even now she was detached enough to note in Trimmle's eye the dawning defiance of the respectful subordinate who has been pressed too hard.

"I couldn't exactly say the hour, Madam, because I didn't let the gentleman in," she replied, with an air of discreetly ignoring the irregularity of her mistress's course.

"You didn't let him in?"

"No, Madam. When the bell rang I was dressing, and Agnes—"

"Go and ask Agnes, then," said Mary.

Trimmle still wore her look of patient magnanimity. "Agnes would not know, Madam, for she had unfortunately burnt her hand in trimming the wick of the new lamp from town"—Trimmle, as Mary was aware, had always been opposed to the new lamp—"and so Mrs. Dockett sent the kitchen-maid instead."

Mary looked again at the clock. "It's after two! Go and ask the kitchen-maid if Mr. Boyne left any word."

She went into luncheon without waiting, and Trimmle presently brought her there the kitchen-maid's statement that the gentleman had called about eleven o'clock, and that Mr. Boyne had gone out with him without leaving any message. The kitchen-maid did not even know the caller's name, for he had written it on a slip of paper, which he had folded and handed to her, with the injunction to deliver it at once to Mr. Boyne.

Mary finished her luncheon, still wondering, and when it was over, and Trimmle had brought the coffee to the drawing-room, her wonder had deepened to a first faint tinge of disquietude. It was unlike Boyne to absent himself without explanation at so unwonted an hour, and the difficulty of identifying the visitor whose summons he had apparently obeyed made his disappearance the more unaccountable. Mary Boyne's experience as the wife of a busy engineer, subject to sudden calls and compelled to keep irregular hours, had trained her to the philosophic acceptance of surprises; but since Boyne's withdrawal from business he had adopted a Benedictine regularity of life. As if to make up for the dispersed and agitated years, with their "stand-up" lunches, and dinners rattled down to the joltings of the dining-cars, he cultivated the last refinements of punctuality and monotony, discouraging his wife's fancy for the unexpected, and declaring that to a delicate taste there were infinite gradations of pleasure in the recurrences of habit.

Still, since no life can completely defend itself from the unforeseen, it was evident that all Boyne's precautions would sooner or later prove unavailable, and Mary concluded that he had cut short a tiresome visit by walking with his caller to the station, or at least accompanying him for part of the way.

This conclusion relieved her from farther preoccupation, and she went out herself to take up her conference with the gardener. Thence she walked to the village post-office, a mile or so away; and when she turned toward home the early twilight was setting in.

She had taken a foot-path across the downs, and as Boyne, meanwhile, had probably returned from the station by the high-road, there was little likelihood of their meeting. She felt sure, however, of his having reached the house before her; so sure that, when she entered it herself, without even pausing to inquire of Trimmle, she made directly for the library. But the library was still empty, and with an unwonted exactness of visual memory she observed that the papers on her husband's desk lay precisely as they had lain when she had gone in to call him to luncheon.

Then of a sudden she was seized by a vague dread of the unknown. She had closed the door behind her on entering, and as she stood alone in the long silent room, her dread seemed to take shape and sound, to be there breathing and lurking among the shadows. Her short-sighted eyes strained through them, half-discerning an actual presence, something aloof, that watched and knew; and in the recoil from that intangible presence she threw herself on the bell-rope and gave it a sharp pull.

The sharp summons brought Trimmle in precipitately with a lamp, and Mary breathed again at this sobering reappearance of the usual.

"You may bring tea if Mr. Boyne is in," she said, to justify her ring.

"Very well, Madam. But Mr. Boyne is not in," said Trimmle, putting down the lamp.

"Not in? You mean he's come back and gone out again?"

"No, Madam. He's never been back."

The dread stirred again, and Mary knew that now it had her fast.

"Not since he went out with—the gentleman?"

"Not since he went out with the gentleman."

"But who *was* the gentleman?" Mary insisted, with the shrill note of some one trying to be heard through a confusion of noises.

"That I couldn't say, Madam." Trimmle, standing there by the lamp, seemed suddenly to grow less round and rosy, as though eclipsed by the same creeping shade of apprehension.

"But the kitchen-maid knows—wasn't it the kitchen-maid who let him in?"

"She doesn't know either, Madam, for he wrote his name on a folded paper."

Mary, through her agitation, was aware that they were both designating the unknown visitor by a vague pronoun, instead of the conventional formula which, till then, had kept their allusions within the bounds of conformity. And at the same moment her mind caught at the suggestion of the folded paper.

"But he must have a name! Where's the paper?"

She moved to the desk, and began to turn over the documents that littered it. The first that caught her eye was an unfinished letter in her husband's hand, with his pen lying across it, as though dropped there at a sudden summons.

"My dear Parvis"—who was Parvis?—"I have just received your letter announcing Elwell's death, and while I suppose there is now no farther risk of trouble, it might be safer—"

She tossed the sheet aside, and continued her search; but no folded paper was discoverable among the letters and pages of manuscript which had been swept together in a heap, as if by a hurried or a startled gesture.

"But the kitchen-maid *saw* him. Send her here," she commanded, wondering at her dulness in not thinking sooner of so simple a solution.

Trimmle vanished in a flash, as if thankful to be out of the room, and when she reappeared, conducting the agitated underling, Mary had regained her self-possession, and had her questions ready.

The gentleman was a stranger, yes—that she understood. But what had he said? And, above all, what had he looked like? The first question was easily enough answered, for the disconcerting reason that he had said so little—had merely asked for Mr. Boyne, and, scribbling something on a bit of paper, had requested that it should at once be carried in to him.

"Then you don't know what he wrote? You're not sure it *was* his name?"

The kitchen-maid was not sure, but supposed it was, since he had written it in answer to her inquiry as to whom she should announce.

"And when you carried the paper in to Mr. Boyne, what did he say?"

The kitchen-maid did not think that Mr. Boyne had said anything, but she could not be sure, for just as she had handed him the paper and he was opening it, she had become aware that the visitor had followed her into the library, and she had slipped out, leaving the two gentlemen together.

"But then, if you left them in the library, how do you know that they went out of the house?"

This question plunged the witness into a momentary inarticulateness, from which she was rescued by Trimmle, who, by means of ingenious circumlocutions, elicited the statement that before she could cross the hall to the back passage she had heard the two gentlemen behind her, and had seen them go out of the front door together.

"Then, if you saw the strange gentleman twice, you must be able to tell me what he looked like."

But with this final challenge to her powers of expression it became clear that the limit of the kitchen-maid's endurance had been reached. The obligation of going to the front door to "show in" a visitor was in itself so subversive of the fundamental order of things that it had thrown her faculties into hopeless disarray, and she could only stammer out, after various panting efforts: "His hat, mum, was different-like, as you might say—"

"Different? How different?" Mary flashed out, her own mind, in the same instant, leaping back to an image left on it that morning, and then lost under layers of subsequent impressions.

"His hat had a wide brim, you mean? and his face was pale—a youngish face?" Mary pressed her, with a white-lipped intensity of interrogation. But if the kitchen-maid found any adequate answer to this challenge, it was swept away for her listener down the rushing current of her own convictions. The stranger—the stranger in the garden! Why had Mary not thought of him before? She needed no one now to tell her that it was he who had called for her husband and gone away with him. But who was he, and why had Boyne obeyed him?

IV

It leaped out at her suddenly, like a grin out of the dark, that they had often called England so little—"such a confoundedly hard place to get lost in."

A confoundedly hard place to get lost in! That had been her husband's phrase. And now, with the whole machinery of official investigation sweeping its flashlights from shore to shore, and across the dividing straits; now, with Boyne's name blazing from the walls of every town and village, his portrait (how that wrung her!) hawked up and down the country like the image of a hunted criminal; now the little compact populous island, so policed, surveyed and administered, revealed itself as a Sphinx-like guardian of abysmal mysteries, staring back into his wife's anguished eyes as if with the wicked joy of knowing something they would never know!

In the fortnight since Boyne's disappearance there had been no word of him, no trace of his movements. Even the usual misleading reports that raise expectancy in tortured bosoms had been few and fleeting. No one but the kitchen-maid had seen Boyne leave the house, and no one else had seen "the gentleman" who accompanied him. All enquiries in the neighbourhood failed to elicit the memory of a stranger's presence that day in the neighbourhood of Lyng. And no one had met Edward Boyne, either alone or in company, in any of the neighbouring villages, or on the road across the downs, or at either of the local railway-stations. The sunny English noon had swallowed him as completely as if he had gone out into Cimmerian night.

Mary, while every official means of investigation was working at its highest pressure, had ransacked her husband's papers for any trace of antecedent complications, of entanglements or obligations unknown to her, that might throw a ray into the darkness. But if any such had existed in the background of Boyne's life, they had vanished like the slip of paper on which the visitor had written his name. There remained no possible thread of guidance except—if it were indeed an exception—the letter which Boyne had apparently been in the act of writing when he received his mysterious summons. That letter, read and reread by his wife, and submitted by her to the police, yielded little enough to feed conjecture.

"I have just heard of Elwell's death, and while I suppose there is now no farther risk of trouble, it might be safer—" That was all. The "risk of trouble" was easily explained by the newspaper clipping which had apprised Mary of the suit brought against her husband by one of his associates in the Blue Star enterprise. The only new information conveyed by the letter was the fact of its showing Boyne, when he wrote it, to be still apprehensive of the results of the suit, though he had told his wife that it had been withdrawn, and though the letter itself proved that the plaintiff was dead. It took several days of cabling to fix the identity of the "Parvis" to whom the fragment was addressed, but even after these enquiries had shown him to be a Waukesha lawyer, no new facts concerning the Elwell suit were elicited. He appeared to have had no direct concern in it, but to have been conversant with the facts merely as an acquaintance, and possible intermediary; and he declared himself unable to guess with what object Boyne intended to seek his assistance.

This negative information, sole fruit of the first fortnight's search, was not increased by a jot during the slow weeks that followed. Mary knew that the investigations were still being carried on, but she had a vague sense of their gradually slackening, as the actual march of time seemed to slacken. It was as though the days, flying horror-struck from the shrouded image of the one inscrutable day, gained assurance as the distance lengthened, till at last they fell back into their normal gait. And so with the human imaginations at work on the dark event. No doubt it occupied them still, but week by week and hour by hour it grew less absorbing, took up less space, was slowly but inevitably crowded out of the foreground of consciousness by the new problems perpetually bubbling up from the cloudy caldron of human experience.

Even Mary Boyne's consciousness gradually felt the same lowering of velocity. It still swayed with the incessant oscillations of conjecture; but they were slower, more rhythmical in their beat. There were even moments of weariness when, like the victim of some poison which leaves the brain clear, but holds the body motionless, she saw herself domesticated with the Horror, accepting its perpetual presence as one of the fixed conditions of life.

These moments lengthened into hours and days, till she passed into a phase of stolid acquiescence. She watched the routine of daily life with the incurious eye of a savage on whom the meaningless processes of civilisation make but the faintest impression. She had come to regard herself as part of the routine, a spoke of the wheel, revolving with its motion; she felt almost like the furniture of the room in which she sat, an insensate object to be dusted and pushed about with the chairs and tables. And this deepening apathy held her fast at Lyng, in spite of the entreaties of friends and the usual medical recommendation of "change." Her friends supposed that her refusal to move was inspired by the belief that her husband would one day return to the spot from which he had vanished, and a beautiful legend grew up about this imaginary state of waiting. But in reality she had no such belief: the depths of anguish enclosing her were no longer lighted by flashes of hope. She was sure that Boyne would never come back, that he had gone out of her sight as completely as if Death itself had waited that day on the threshold. She had even renounced, one by one, the various theories as to his disappearance which had been advanced by the press, the police, and her own agonised imagination. In sheer lassitude her mind turned from these alternatives of horror, and sank back into the blank fact that he was gone.

No, she would never know what had become of him—no one would ever know. But the house *knew;* the library in which she spent her long lonely evenings knew. For it was here that the last scene had been enacted, here that the stranger had come, and spoken the word which had caused Boyne to rise and follow him. The floor she trod had felt his tread; the books on the shelves had seen his face; and there were moments when the intense consciousness of the old dusky walls seemed about to break out into some audible revelation of their secret. But the revelation never came, and she knew it would never come. Lyng was not one of the garrulous old houses that betray the secrets entrusted to them. Its very legend proved that it had always been the mute accomplice, the incorruptible custodian, of the mysteries it had surprised. And Mary Boyne, sitting face to face with its silence, felt the futility of seeking to break it by any human means.

v

"I don't say it wasn't straight, and yet I don't say it was straight. It was business."

Mary, at the words, lifted her head with a start, and looked intently at the speaker.

When, half an hour before, a card with "Mr. Parvis" on it had been brought up to her, she had been immediately aware that the name had been a part of her consciousness ever since she had read it at the head of Boyne's unfinished letter. In the library she had found awaiting her a small sallow man with a bald head and gold eyeglasses, and it sent a tremor through her to know that this was the person to whom her husband's last known thought had been directed.

Parvis, civilly, but without vain preamble—in the manner of a man who has his watch in his hand—had set forth the object of his visit. He had "run over" to England on business, and finding himself in the neighbourhood of Dorchester, had not wished to leave it without paying his respects to Mrs.

Boyne; and without asking her, if the occasion offered, what she meant to do about Bob Elwell's family.

The words touched the spring of some obscure dread in Mary's bosom. Did her visitor, after all, know what Boyne had meant by his unfinished phrase? She asked for an elucidation of his question, and noticed at once that he seemed surprised at her continued ignorance of the subject. Was it possible that she really knew as little as she said?

"I know nothing—you must tell me," she faltered out; and her visitor thereupon proceeded to unfold his story. It threw, even to her confused perceptions and imperfectly initiated vision, a lurid glare on the whole hazy episode of the Blue Star Mine. Her husband had made his money in that brilliant speculation at the cost of "getting ahead" of some one less alert to seize the chance; and the victim of his ingenuity was young Robert Elwell, who had "put him on" to the Blue Star scheme.

Parvis, at Mary's first cry, had thrown her a sobering glance through his impartial glasses.

"Bob Elwell wasn't smart enough, that's all; if he had been, he might have turned round and served Boyne the same way. It's the kind of thing that happens every day in business. I guess it's what the scientists call the survival of the fittest—see?" said Mr. Parvis, evidently pleased with the aptness of his analogy.

Mary felt a physical shrinking from the next question she tried to frame: it was as though the words on her lips had a taste that nauseated her.

"But then—you accuse my husband of doing something dishonourable?"

Mr. Parvis surveyed the question dispassionately. "Oh, no, I don't. I don't even say it wasn't straight." He glanced up and down the long lines of books, as if one of them might have supplied him with the definition he sought. "I don't say it *wasn't* straight, and yet I don't say it *was* straight. It was business." After all, no definition in his category could be more comprehensive than that.

Mary sat staring at him with a look of terror. He seemed to her like the indifferent emissary of some evil power.

"But Mr. Elwell's lawyers apparently did not take your view, since I suppose the suit was withdrawn by their advice."

"Oh, yes; they knew he hadn't a leg to stand on, technically. It was when they advised him to withdraw the suit that he got desperate. You see, he'd borrowed most of the money he lost in the Blue Star, and he was up a tree. That's why he shot himself when they told him he had no show."

The horror was sweeping over Mary in great deafening waves.

"He shot himself? He killed himself because of *that*?"

"Well, he didn't kill himself, exactly. He dragged on two months before he died." Parvis emitted the statement as unemotionally as a gramophone grinding out its "record."

"You mean that he tried to kill himself, and failed? And tried again?"

"Oh, he didn't have to *try* again," said Parvis grimly.

They sat opposite each other in silence, he swinging his eyeglasses thoughtfully about his finger, she, motionless, her arms stretched along her knees in an attitude of rigid tension.

"But if you knew all this," she began at length, hardly able to force her voice above a whisper, "how is it that when I wrote you at the time of my husband's disappearance you said you didn't understand his letter?"

Parvis received this without perceptible embarrassment: "Why, I didn't understand it—strictly speaking. And it wasn't the time to talk about it, if I had. The Elwell business was settled when the suit was withdrawn. Nothing I could have told you would have helped you to find your husband."

Mary continued to scrutinise him. "Then why are you telling me now?"

Still Parvis did not hesitate. "Well, to begin with, I supposed you knew more than you appear to—I mean about the circumstances of Elwell's death. And then people are talking of it now; the whole matter's been raked up again. And I thought if you didn't know you ought to."

She remained silent, and he continued: "You see, it's only come out lately what a bad state Elwell's affairs were in. His wife's a proud woman, and she fought on as long as she could, going out to work, and taking sewing at home when she got too sick—something with the heart, I believe. But she had his mother to look after, and the children, and she broke down under it, and finally had to ask for help. That called attention to the case, and the papers took it up, and a subscription was started. Everybody out there liked Bob Elwell, and most of the prominent names in the place are down on the list, and people began to wonder why—"

Parvis broke off to fumble in an inner pocket. "Here," he continued, "here's an account of the whole thing from the *Sentinel*—a little sensational, of course. But I guess you'd better look it over."

He held out a newspaper to Mary, who unfolded it slowly, remembering, as she did so, the evening when, in that same room, the perusal of a clipping from the *Sentinel* had first shaken the depths of her security.

As she opened the paper, her eyes, shrinking from the glaring headlines, "Widow of Boyne's Victim Forced to Appeal for Aid," ran down the column of text to two portraits inserted in it. The first was her husband's, taken from a photograph made the year they had come to England. It was the picture of him that she liked best, the one that stood on the writing-table upstairs in her bedroom. As the eyes in the photograph met hers, she felt it would be impossible to read what was said of him, and closed her lids with the sharpness of the pain.

"I thought if you felt disposed to put your name down—" she heard Parvis continue.

She opened her eyes with an effort, and they fell on the other portrait. It was that of a youngish man, slightly built, with features somewhat blurred by the shadow of a projecting hat-brim. Where had she seen that outline before? She stared at it confusedly, her heart hammering in her ears. Then she gave a cry.

"This is the man—the man who came for my husband!"

She heard Parvis start to his feet, and was dimly aware that she had slipped backward into the corner of the sofa, and that he was bending above her in alarm. She straightened herself, and reached out for the paper, which she had dropped.

"It's the man! I should know him anywhere!" she persisted in a voice that sounded to her own ears like a scream.

Parvis's answer seemed to come to her from far off, down endless fog-muffled windings.

"Mrs. Boyne, you're not very well. Shall I call somebody? Shall I get a glass of water?"

"No, no, no!" She threw herself toward him, her hand frantically clutching the newspaper. "I tell you, it's the man! I *know* him! He spoke to me in the garden!"

Parvis took the journal from her, directing his glasses to the portrait. "It can't be, Mrs. Boyne. It's Robert Elwell."

"Robert Elwell?" Her white stare seemed to travel into space. "Then it was Robert Elwell who came for him."

"Came for Boyne? The day he went away from here." Parvis's voice dropped as hers rose. He bent over, laying a fraternal hand on her, as if to coax her gently back into her seat. "Why, Elwell was dead! Don't you remember?"

Mary sat with her eyes fixed on the picture, unconscious of what he was saying.

"Don't you remember Boyne's unfinished letter to me—the one you found on his desk that day? It was written just after he'd heard of Elwell's death." She noticed an odd shake in Parvis's unemotional voice. "Surely you remember!" he urged her.

Yes, she remembered: that was the profoundest horror of it. Elwell had died the day before her husband's disappearance; and this was Elwell's portrait; and it was the portrait of the man who had spoken to her in the garden. She lifted her head and looked slowly about the library. The library could have borne witness that it was also the portrait of the man who had come in that day to call Boyne from his unfinished letter. Through the misty surgings of her brain she heard the faint boom of half-forgotten words—words spoken by Alida Stair on the lawn at Pangbourne before Boyne and his wife had ever seen the house at Lyng, or had imagined that they might one day live there.

"This was the man who spoke to me," she repeated.

She looked again at Parvis. He was trying to conceal his disturbance under what he probably imagined to be an expression of indulgent commiseration; but the edges of his lips were blue. "He thinks me mad; but I'm not mad," she reflected; and suddenly there flashed upon her a way of justifying her strange affirmation.

She sat quiet, controlling the quiver of her lips, and waiting till she could trust her voice; then she said, looking straight at Parvis: "Will you answer me one question, please? When was it that Robert Elwell tried to kill himself?"

"When—when?" Parvis stammered.

"Yes; the date. Please try to remember."

She saw that he was growing still more afraid of her. "I have a reason," she insisted.

"Yes, yes. Only I can't remember. About two months before, I should say."

"I want the date," she repeated.

Parvis picked up the newspaper. "We might see here," he said, still humouring her. He ran his eyes down the page. "Here it is. Last October—the—"

She caught the words from him. "The 20th, wasn't it?" With a sharp look at her, he verified. "Yes, the 20th. Then you *did* know?"

"I know now." Her gaze continued to travel past him. "Sunday, the 20th—that was the day he came first."

Parvis's voice was almost inaudible. "Came *here* first?"

"Yes."

"You saw him twice, then?"

"Yes, twice." She just breathed it at him. "He came first on the 20th of October. I remember the date because it was the day we went up Meldon

Steep for the first time." She felt a faint gasp of inward laughter at the thought that but for that she might have forgotten.

Parvis continued to scrutinise her, as if trying to intercept her gaze.

"We saw him from the roof," she went on. "He came down the lime-avenue toward the house. He was dressed just as he is in that picture. My husband saw him first. He was frightened, and ran down ahead of me; but there was no one there. He had vanished."

"Elwell had vanished?" Parvis faltered.

"Yes." Their two whispers seemed to grope for each other. "I couldn't think what had happened. I see now. He *tried* to come then; but he wasn't dead enough—he couldn't reach us. He had to wait for two months to die; and then he came back again—and Ned went with him."

She nodded at Parvis with the look of triumph of a child who has worked out a difficult puzzle. But suddenly she lifted her hands with a desperate gesture, pressing them to her temples.

"Oh, my God! I sent him to Ned—I told him where to go! I sent him to this room!" she screamed.

She felt the walls of books rush toward her, like inward falling ruins; and she heard Parvis, a long way off, through the ruins, crying to her, and struggling to get at her. But she was numb to his touch, she did not know what he was saying. Through the tumult she heard but one clear note, the voice of Alida Stair, speaking on the lawn at Pangbourne.

"You won't know till afterward," it said. "You won't know till long, long afterward."

THE EYES

I

WE had been put in the mood for ghosts, that evening, after an excellent dinner at our old friend Culwin's, by a tale of Fred Murchard's—the narrative of a strange personal visitation.

Seen through the haze of our cigars, and by the drowsy gleam of a coal fire, Culwin's library, with its oak walls and dark old bindings, made a good setting for such evocations; and ghostly experiences at first hand being, after Murchard's opening, the only kind acceptable to us, we proceeded to take stock of our group and tax each member for a contribution. There were eight of us, and seven contrived, in a manner more or less adequate, to fulfil the condition imposed. It surprised us all to find that we could muster such a show of supernatural impressions, for none of us, excepting Murchard himself and young Phil Frenham—whose story was the slightest of the lot—had the habit of sending our souls into the invisible. So that, on the whole, we had every reason to be proud of our seven "exhibits," and none of us would have dreamed of expecting an eighth from our host.

Our old friend, Mr. Andrew Culwin, who had sat back in his armchair, listening and blinking through the smoke circles with the cheerful tolerance of a wise old idol, was not the kind of man likely to be favoured with such contacts, though he had imagination enough to enjoy, without envying, the superior privileges of his guests. By age and by education he belonged to the stout Positivist tradition, and his habit of thought had been formed in the days of the epic struggle between physics and metaphysics. But he had been, then and always, essentially a spectator, a humorous detached observer of the immense muddled variety show of life, slipping out of his seat now and then for a brief dip into the convivialities at the back of the house, but never, as far as one knew, showing the least desire to jump on the stage and do a "turn."

Among his contemporaries there lingered a vague tradition of his having, at a remote period, and in a romantic clime, been wounded in a duel; but this legend no more tallied with what we younger men knew of his character than my mother's assertion that he had once been "a charming little man with nice eyes" corresponded to any possible reconstitution of his physiognomy.

"He never can have looked like anything but a bundle of sticks," Murchard had once said of him. "Or a phosphorescent log, rather," some one else amended; and we recognised the happiness of this description of his small squat trunk, with the red blink of the eyes in a face like mottled bark. He had always been possessed of a leisure which he had nursed and protected, instead of squandering it in vain activities. His carefully guarded hours had been devoted to the cultivation of a fine intelligence and a few judiciously chosen habits; and none of the disturbances common to human experience seemed to have crossed his sky. Nevertheless, his dispassionate survey of the universe had not raised his opinion of that costly experiment, and his study of the human race seemed to have resulted in the conclusion that all men were superfluous, and women necessary only because some one had to do the cooking. On the importance of this point his convictions were absolute, and gastronomy was the only science which he revered as a dogma. It must be owned that his little dinners were a strong argument in favour of this view, besides being a reason—though not the main one—for the fidelity of his friends.

Mentally he exercised a hospitality less seductive but no less stimulating. His mind was like a forum, or some open meeting-place for the exchange of ideas: somewhat cold and draughty, but light, spacious and orderly—a kind of academic grove from which all the leaves have fallen. In this privileged area a dozen of us were wont to stretch our muscles and expand our lungs; and, as if to prolong as much as possible the tradition of what we felt to be a vanishing institution, one or two neophytes were now and then added to our band.

Young Phil Frenham was the last, and the most interesting, of these recruits, and a good example of Murchard's somewhat morbid assertion that our old friend "liked 'em juicy." It was indeed a fact that Culwin, for all his dryness, specially tasted the lyric qualities in youth. As he was far too good an Epicurean to nip the flowers of soul which he gathered for his garden, his friendship was not a disintegrating influence: on the contrary, it forced the young idea to robuster bloom. And in Phil Frenham he had a good subject for experimentation. The boy was really intelligent, and the soundness of his nature was like the pure paste under a fine glaze. Culwin had fished him out of a fog of family dulness, and pulled him up to a peak in Darien; and the adventure hadn't hurt him a bit. Indeed, the skill with which Culwin had contrived to stimulate his curiosities without robbing them of their bloom of awe seemed to me a sufficient answer to Murchard's ogreish metaphor. There was nothing hectic in Frenham's efflorescence, and his old friend had not laid even a finger-tip on the sacred stupidities. One wanted no better proof of that than the fact that Frenham still reverenced them in Culwin.

"There's a side of him you fellows don't see. *I* believe that story about the duel!" he declared; and it was of the very essence of this belief that it should impel him—just as our little party was dispersing—to turn back to our host with the joking demand: "And now you've got to tell us about *your* ghost!"

The outer door had closed on Murchard and the others; only Frenham and I remained; and the devoted servant who presided over Culwin's destinies, having brought a fresh supply of soda-water, had been laconically ordered to bed.

Culwin's sociability was a night-blooming flower, and we knew that he expected the nucleus of his group to tighten around him after midnight. But Frenham's appeal seemed to disconcert him comically, and he rose from the chair in which he had just reseated himself after his farewells in the hall.

"*My* ghost? Do you suppose I'm fool enough to go to the expense of keeping one of my own, when there are so many charming ones in my friends' closets?—Take another cigar," he said, revolving toward me with a laugh.

Frenham laughed too, pulling up his slender height before the chimney-piece as he turned to face his short bristling friend.

"Oh," he said, "you'd never be content to share if you met one you really liked."

Culwin had dropped back into his armchair, his shock head embedded in the hollow of worn leather, his little eyes glimmering over a fresh cigar.

"Liked—*liked?* Good Lord!" he growled.

"Ah, you *have*, then!" Frenham pounced on him in the same instant, with a side-glance of victory at me; but Culwin cowered gnomelike among his cushions, dissembling himself in a protective cloud of smoke.

"What's the use of denying it? You've seen everything, so of course you've seen a ghost!" his young friend persisted, talking intrepidly into the cloud. "Or, if you haven't seen one, it's only because you've seen two!"

The form of the challenge seemed to strike our host. He shot his head out of the mist with a queer tortoise-like motion he sometimes had, and blinked approvingly at Frenham.

"That's it," he flung at us on a shrill jerk of laughter; "it's only because I've seen two!"

The words were so unexpected that they dropped down and down into a deep silence, while we continued to stare at each other over Culwin's head, and Culwin stared at his ghosts. At length Frenham, without speaking, threw himself into the chair on the other side of the hearth, and leaned forward with his listening smile…

II

"Oh, of course they're not show ghosts—a collector wouldn't think anything of them… Don't let me raise your hopes… their one merit is their numerical strength: the exceptional fact of their being *two*. But, as against this, I'm bound to admit that at any moment I could probably have exorcised them both by asking my doctor for a prescription, or my oculist for a pair of spectacles. Only, as I never could make up my mind whether to go to the doctor or the oculist—whether I was afflicted by an optical or a digestive delusion—I left them to pursue their interesting double life, though at times they made mine exceedingly uncomfortable…

"Yes—uncomfortable; and you know how I hate to be uncomfortable! But it was part of my stupid pride, when the thing began, not to admit that I could be disturbed by the trifling matter of seeing two—

"And then I'd no reason, really, to suppose I was ill. As far as I knew I was simply bored—horribly bored. But it was part of my boredom—I remember—that I was feeling so uncommonly well, and didn't know how on earth to work off my surplus energy. I had come back from a long journey—down in South America and Mexico—and had settled down for the winter near New York, with an old aunt who had known Washington Irving and corresponded with N. P. Willis. She lived, not far from Irvington, in a damp Gothic villa, overhung by Norway spruces, and looking exactly like a memorial emblem done in hair. Her personal appearance was in keeping with this image, and her own hair—of which there was little left—might have been sacrificed to the manufacture of the emblem.

"I had just reached the end of an agitated year, with considerable arrears to make up in money and emotion; and theoretically it seemed as though my aunt's mild hospitality would be as beneficial to my nerves as to my purse. But the deuce of it was that as soon as I felt myself safe and sheltered my energy began to revive; and how was I to work it off inside of a memorial emblem? I had, at that time, the illusion that sustained intellectual effort could engage a man's whole activity; and I decided to write a great book—I forget about what. My aunt, impressed by my plan, gave up to me her Gothic library, filled with classics bound in black cloth and daguerreotypes of faded celebrities; and I sat down at my desk to win myself a place among their number. And to facilitate my task she lent me a cousin to copy my manuscript.

"The cousin was a nice girl, and I had an idea that a nice girl was just what I needed to restore my faith in human nature, and principally in myself. She was neither beautiful nor intelligent—poor Alice Nowell!—but it interested me to see any woman content to be so uninteresting, and I wanted to find out the secret of her content. In doing this I handled it rather rashly, and put it out of joint—oh, just for a moment! There's no fatuity in telling you this, for the poor girl had never seen any one but cousins…

"Well, I was sorry for what I'd done, of course, and confoundedly bothered as to how I should put it straight. She was staying in the house, and one evening, after my aunt had gone to bed, she came down to the library to fetch a book she'd mislaid, like any artless heroine on the shelves behind us. She was pink-nosed and flustered, and it suddenly occurred to me that her hair, though it was fairly thick and pretty, would look exactly like my aunt's when she grew older. I was glad I had noticed this, for it made it easier for me to decide to do what was right; and when I had found the book she hadn't lost I told her I was leaving for Europe that week.

"Europe was terribly far off in those days, and Alice knew at once what I meant. She didn't take it in the least as I'd expected—it would have been easier if she had. She held her book very tight, and turned away a moment to wind up the lamp on my desk—it had a ground glass shade with vine leaves, and glass drops around the edge, I remember. Then she came back, held out her hand, and said: 'Goodbye.' And as she said it she looked straight at me and kissed me. I had never felt anything as fresh and shy and brave as her kiss. It was worse than any reproach, and it made me ashamed to deserve a reproach from her. I said to myself: 'I'll marry her, and when my aunt dies she'll leave us this house, and I'll sit here at the desk and go on with my book; and Alice will sit over there with her embroidery and look at me as she's looking now. And life will go on like that for any number of years.' The prospect frightened me a little, but at the time it didn't frighten me as much as doing anything to hurt her; and ten minutes later she had my seal ring on her finger, and my promise that when I went abroad she should go with me.

"You'll wonder why I'm enlarging on this incident. It's because the evening on which it took place was the very evening on which I first saw the queer sight I've spoken of. Being at that time an ardent believer in a necessary sequence between cause and effect I naturally tried to trace some kind of link between what had just happened to me in my aunt's library, and what was to happen a few hours later on the same night; and so the coincidence between the two events always remained in my mind.

"I went up to bed with rather a heavy heart, for I was bowed under the weight of the first good action I had ever consciously committed; and young as I was, I saw the gravity of my situation. Don't imagine from this that I had hitherto been an instrument of destruction. I had been merely a harmless young man, who had followed his bent and declined all collaboration with Providence. Now I had suddenly undertaken to promote the moral order of the world, and I felt a good deal like the trustful spectator who has given his gold watch to the conjurer, and doesn't know in what shape he'll get it back when the trick is over… Still, a glow of self-righteousness tempered my fears, and I said to myself as I undressed that when I'd got used to being good it probably wouldn't make me as nervous as it did at the start. And by the time I was in bed, and had blown out my candle, I felt that I really *was* getting used to it, and that, as far as I'd got, it was not unlike sinking down into one of my aunt's very softest wool mattresses.

"I closed my eyes on this image, and when I opened them it must have been a good deal later, for my room had grown cold, and intensely still. I was waked by the queer feeling we all know—the feeling that there was something in the room that hadn't been there when I fell asleep. I sat up and strained my eyes into the darkness. The room was pitch black, and at first I saw nothing; but gradually a vague glimmer at the foot of the bed turned into two eyes staring back at me. I couldn't distinguish the features attached to them, but as I looked the eyes grew more and more distinct: they gave out a light of their own.

"The sensation of being thus gazed at was far from pleasant, and you might suppose that my first impulse would have been to jump out of bed and hurl myself on the invisible figure attached to the eyes. But it wasn't—my impulse was simply to lie still… I can't say whether this was due to an immediate sense of the uncanny nature of the apparition—to the certainty that if I did jump out of bed I should hurl myself on nothing—or merely to the benumbing effect of the eyes themselves. They were the very worst eyes I've ever seen: a man's eyes—but what a man! My first thought was that he must be frightfully old. The orbits were sunk, and the thick red-lined lids hung over the eyeballs like blinds of which the cords are broken. One lid drooped a little lower than the other, with the effect of a crooked leer; and between these folds of flesh, with their scant bristle of lashes, the eyes themselves, small glassy disks with an agate-like rim, looked like sea-pebbles in the grip of a star-fish.

"But the age of the eyes was not the most unpleasant thing about them. What turned me sick was their expression of vicious security. I don't know how else to describe the fact that they seemed to belong to a man who had done a lot of harm in his life, but had always kept just inside the danger lines. They were not the eyes of a coward, but of some one much too clever to take risks; and my gorge rose at their look of base astuteness. Yet even that wasn't the worst; for as we continued to scan each other I saw in them a tinge of derision, and felt myself to be its object.

"At that I was seized by an impulse of rage that jerked me to my feet and pitched me straight at the unseen figure. But of course there wasn't any figure there, and my fists struck at emptiness. Ashamed and cold, I groped about for a match and lit the candles. The room looked just as usual—as I had known it would; and I crawled back to bed, and blew out the lights.

"As soon as the room was dark again the eyes reappeared; and I now applied myself to explaining them on scientific principles. At first I thought the illusion might have been caused by the glow of the last embers in the chimney; but the fireplace was on the other side of my bed, and so placed that the fire could not be reflected in my toilet glass, which was the only mirror in the room. Then it struck me that I might have been tricked by the reflection of the embers in some polished bit of wood or metal; and though I couldn't discover any object of the sort in my line of vision, I got up again, groped my way to the hearth, and covered what was left of the fire. But as soon as I was back in bed the eyes were back at its foot.

"They were an hallucination, then: that was plain. But the fact that they were not due to any external dupery didn't make them a bit pleasanter. For if they were a projection of my inner consciousness, what the deuce was the matter with that organ? I had gone deeply enough into the mystery of morbid pathological states to picture the conditions under which an exploring mind might lay itself open to such a midnight admonition; but I couldn't fit it to my present case. I had never felt more normal, mentally and physically; and the only unusual fact in my situation—that of having assured the happiness of an amiable girl—did not seem of a kind to summon unclean spirits about my pillow. But there were the eyes still looking at me…

"I shut mine, and tried to evoke a vision of Alice Nowell's. They were not remarkable eyes, but they were as wholesome as fresh water, and if she had had more imagination—or longer lashes—their expression might have been interesting. As it was, they did not prove very efficacious, and in a few moments I perceived that they had mysteriously changed into the eyes at the foot of the bed. It exasperated me more to feel these glaring at me through my shut lids than to see them, and I opened my eyes again and looked straight into their hateful stare…

"And so it went on all night. I can't tell you what that night was like, nor how long it lasted. Have you ever lain in bed, hopelessly wide awake, and tried to keep your eyes shut, knowing that if you opened 'em you'd see something you dreaded and loathed? It sounds easy, but it's devilish hard. Those eyes hung there and drew me. I had the *vertige de l'abîme*, and their red lids were the edge of my abyss… I had known nervous hours before: hours when I'd felt the wind of danger in my neck; but never this kind of strain. It wasn't that the eyes were awful; they hadn't the majesty of the powers of darkness. But they had—how shall I say?—a physical effect that was the equivalent of a bad smell: their look left a smear like a snail's. And I didn't see what business they had with me, anyhow—and I stared and stared, trying to find out…

"I don't know what effect they were trying to produce; but the effect they *did* produce was that of making me pack my portmanteau and bolt to town early the next morning. I left a note for my aunt, explaining that I was ill and had gone to see my doctor; and as a matter of fact I did feel uncommonly ill—the night seemed to have pumped all the blood out of me. But when I reached town I didn't go to the doctor's. I went to a friend's rooms, and threw myself on a bed, and slept for ten heavenly hours. When I woke it was the middle of the night, and I turned cold at the thought of what might be waiting for me. I sat up, shaking, and stared into the darkness; but there wasn't a break in its blessed surface, and when I saw that the eyes were not there I dropped back into another long sleep.

"I had left no word for Alice when I fled, because I meant to go back the next morning. But the next morning I was too exhausted to stir. As the day went on the exhaustion increased, instead of wearing off like the fatigue left by an ordinary night of insomnia: the effect of the eyes seemed to be cumulative, and the thought of seeing them again grew intolerable. For two days I fought my dread; and on the third evening I pulled myself together and decided to go back the next morning. I felt a good deal happier as soon as I'd decided, for I knew that my abrupt disappearance, and the strangeness of my not writing, must have been very distressing to poor Alice. I went to bed with an easy mind, and fell asleep at once; but in the middle of the night I woke, and there were the eyes...

"Well, I simply couldn't face them; and instead of going back to my aunt's I bundled a few things into a trunk and jumped aboard the first steamer for England. I was so dead tired when I got on board that I crawled straight into my berth, and slept most of the way over; and I can't tell you the bliss it was to wake from those long dreamless stretches and look fearlessly into the dark, *knowing* that I shouldn't see the eyes...

"I stayed abroad for a year, and then I stayed for another; and during that time I never had a glimpse of them. That was enough reason for prolonging my stay if I'd been on a desert island. Another was, of course, that I had perfectly come to see, on the voyage over, the complete impossibility of my marrying Alice Nowell. The fact that I had been so slow in making this discovery annoyed me, and made me want to avoid explanations. The bliss of escaping at one stroke from the eyes, and from this other embarrassment, gave my freedom an extraordinary zest; and the longer I savoured it the better I liked its taste.

"The eyes had burned such a hole in my consciousness that for a long time I went on puzzling over the nature of the apparition, and wondering if it would ever come back. But as time passed I lost this dread, and retained only the precision of the image. Then that faded in its turn.

"The second year found me settled in Rome, where I was planning, I believe, to write another great book—a definitive work on Etruscan influences in Italian art. At any rate, I'd found some pretext of the kind for taking a sunny apartment in the Piazza di Spagna and dabbling about in the Forum; and there, one morning, a charming youth came to me. As he stood there in the warm light, slender and smooth and hyacinthine, he might have stepped from a ruined altar—one to Antinous, say; but he'd come instead from New York, with a letter (of all people) from Alice Nowell. The letter—the first I'd had from her since our break—was simply a line introducing her young cousin, Gilbert Noyes, and appealing to me to befriend him. It appeared, poor lad, that he 'had talent,' and 'wanted to write'; and, an obdurate family having insisted that his calligraphy should take the form of double entry, Alice had intervened to win him six months' respite, during which he was to travel abroad on a meagre pittance, and somehow prove his ability to increase it by his pen. The quaint conditions of the test struck me first: it seemed about as conclusive as a mediæval 'ordeal.' Then I was touched by her having sent him to me. I had always wanted to do her some service, to justify myself in my own eyes rather than hers; and here was a beautiful occasion.

"I imagine it's safe to lay down the general principle that predestined geniuses don't, as a rule, appear before one in the spring sunshine of the Forum looking like one of its banished gods. At any rate, poor Noyes wasn't a predestined genius. But he *was* beautiful to see, and charming as a comrade. It was only when he began to talk literature that my heart failed me. I knew all the symptoms so well—the things he had 'in him,' and the things outside him that impinged! There's the real test, after all. It was always— punctually, inevitably, with the inexorableness of a mechanical law—it was *always* the wrong thing that struck him. I grew to find a certain fascination in deciding in advance exactly which wrong thing he'd select; and I acquired an astonishing skill at the game...

"The worst of it was that his *bêtise* wasn't of the too obvious sort. Ladies who met him at picnics thought him intellectual; and even at dinners he passed for clever. I, who had him under the microscope, fancied now and then that he might develop some kind of a slim talent, something that he could make 'do' and be happy on; and wasn't that, after all, what I was concerned with? He was so charming—he continued to be so charming—that he called forth all my charity in support of this argument; and for the first few months I really believed there was a chance for him...

"Those months were delightful. Noyes was constantly with me, and the more I saw of him the better I liked him. His stupidity was a natural grace—it was as beautiful, really, as his eyelashes. And he was so gay, so affectionate, and so happy with me, that telling him the truth would have been about as pleasant as slitting the throat of some gentle animal. At first I used to wonder what had put into that radiant head the detestable delusion that it held a brain. Then I began to see that it was simply protective mimicry—an instinctive ruse to get away from family life and an office desk. Not that Gilbert didn't—dear lad!—believe in himself. There wasn't a trace of hypocrisy in him. He was sure that his 'call' was irresistible, while to me it was the saving grace of his situation that it *wasn't*, and that a little money, a little leisure, a little pleasure would have turned him into an inoffensive idler. Unluckily, however, there was no hope of money, and with the alternative of the office desk before him he couldn't postpone his attempt at literature. The stuff he turned out was deplorable, and I see now that I knew it from the first. Still, the absurdity of deciding a man's whole future on a first trial seemed to justify me in withholding my verdict, and perhaps even in encouraging him a little, on the ground that the human plant generally needs warmth to flower.

"At any rate, I proceeded on that principle, and carried it to the point of getting his term of probation extended. When I left Rome he went with me, and we idled away a delicious summer between Capri and Venice. I said to myself: 'If he has anything in him, it will come out now,' and it *did*. He was never more enchanting and enchanted. There were moments of our pilgrimage when beauty born of murmuring sound seemed actually to pass into his face—but only to issue forth in a flood of the palest ink…

"Well, the time came to turn off the tap; and I knew there was no hand but mine to do it. We were back in Rome, and I had taken him to stay with me, not wanting him to be alone in his *pension* when he had to face the necessity of renouncing his ambition. I hadn't, of course, relied solely on my own judgment in deciding to advise him to drop literature. I had sent his stuff to various people—editors and critics—and they had always sent it back with the same chilling lack of comment. Really there was nothing on earth to say—

"I confess I never felt more shabbily than I did on the day when I decided to have it out with Gilbert. It was well enough to tell myself that it was my duty to knock the poor boy's hopes into splinters—but I'd like to know what act of gratuitous cruelty hasn't been justified on that plea? I've always shrunk from usurping the functions of Providence, and when I have to exercise them I decidedly prefer that it shouldn't be on an errand of destruction. Besides, in the last issue, who was I to decide, even after a year's trial, if poor Gilbert had it in him or not?

"The more I looked at the part I'd resolved to play, the less I liked it; and I liked it still less when Gilbert sat opposite me, with his head thrown back in the lamplight, just as Phil's is now... I'd been going over his last manuscript, and he knew it, and he knew that his future hung on my verdict—we'd tacitly agreed to that. The manuscript lay between us, on my table—a novel, his first novel, if you please!—and he reached over and laid his hand on it, and looked up at me with all his life in the look.

"I stood up and cleared my throat, trying to keep my eyes away from his face and on and the manuscript.

"'The fact is, my dear Gilbert,' I began—

"I saw him turn pale, but he was up and facing me in an instant.

"'Oh, look here, don't take on so, my dear fellow! I'm not so awfully cut up as all that!' His hands were on my shoulders, and he was laughing down on me from his full height, with a kind of mortally-stricken gaiety that drove the knife into my side.

"He was too beautifully brave for me to keep up any humbug about my duty. And it came over me suddenly how I should hurt others in hurting him: myself first, since sending him home meant losing him; but more particularly poor Alice Nowell, to whom I had so longed to prove my good faith and my desire to serve her. It really seemed like failing her twice to fail Gilbert—

"But my intuition was like one of those lightning flashes that encircle the whole horizon, and in the same instant I saw what I might be letting myself in for if I didn't tell the truth. I said to myself: 'I shall have him for life'—and I'd never yet seen any one, man or woman, whom I was quite sure of wanting on those terms. Well, this impulse of egotism decided me. I was ashamed of it, and to get away from it I took a leap that landed me straight in Gilbert's arms.

"'The thing's all right, and you're all wrong!' I shouted up at him; and as he hugged me, and I laughed and shook in his clutch, I had for a minute the sense of self-complacency that is supposed to attend the footsteps of the just. Hang it all, making people happy *has* its charms—

"Gilbert, of course, was for celebrating his emancipation in some spectacular manner; but I sent him away alone to explode his emotions, and went to bed to sleep off mine. As I undressed I began to wonder what their after-taste would be—so many of the finest don't keep! Still, I wasn't sorry, and I meant to empty the bottle, even if it *did* turn a trifle flat.

"After I got into bed I lay for a long time smiling at the memory of his eyes—his blissful eyes... Then I fell asleep, and when I woke the room was deathly cold, and I sat up with a jerk—and there were the *other eyes*...

"It was three years since I'd seen them, but I'd thought of them so often that I fancied they could never take me unawares again. Now, with their red sneer on me, I knew that I had never really believed they would come back, and that I was as defenceless as ever against them... As before, it was the insane irrelevance of their coming that made it so horrible. What the deuce were they after, to leap out at me at such a time? I had lived more or less carelessly in the years since I'd seen them, though my worst indiscretions were not dark enough to invite the searchings of their infernal glare; but at this particular moment I was really in what might have been called a state of grace; and I can't tell you how the fact added to their horror...

"But it's not enough to say they were as bad as before: they were worse. Worse by just so much as I'd learned of life in the interval; by all the damnable implications my wider experience read into them. I saw now what I hadn't seen before: that they were eyes which had grown hideous gradually, which had built up their baseness coral-wise, bit by bit, out of a series of small turpitudes slowly accumulated through the industrious years. Yes—it came to me that what made them so bad was that they'd grown bad so slowly…

"There they hung in the darkness, their swollen lids dropped across the little watery bulbs rolling loose in the orbits, and the puff of flesh making a muddy shadow underneath—and as their stare moved with my movements, there came over me a sense of their tacit complicity, of a deep hidden understanding between us that was worse than the first shock of their strangeness. Not that I understood them; but that they made it so clear that some day I should… Yes, that was the worst part of it, decidedly; and it was the feeling that became stronger each time they came back…

"For they got into the damnable habit of coming back. They reminded me of vampires with a taste for young flesh, they seemed so to gloat over the taste of a good conscience. Every night for a month they came to claim their morsel of mine: since I'd made Gilbert happy they simply wouldn't loosen their fangs. The coincidence almost made me hate him, poor lad, fortuitous as I felt it to be. I puzzled over it a good deal, but couldn't find any hint of an explanation except in the chance of his association with Alice Nowell. But then the eyes had let up on me the moment I had abandoned her, so they could hardly be the emissaries of a woman scorned, even if one could have pictured poor Alice charging such spirits to avenge her. That set me thinking, and I began to wonder if they would let up on me if I abandoned Gilbert. The temptation was insidious, and I had to stiffen myself against it; but really, dear boy! he was too charming to be sacrificed to such demons. And so, after all, I never found out what they wanted…"

III

The fire crumbled, sending up a flash which threw into relief the narrator's gnarled face under its grey-black stubble. Pressed into the hollow of the chair-back, it stood out an instant like an intaglio of yellowish red-veined stone, with spots of enamel for the eyes; then the fire sank and it became once more a dim Rembrandtish blur.

Phil Frenham, sitting in a low chair on the opposite side of the hearth, one long arm propped on the table behind him, one hand supporting his thrown-back head, and his eyes fixed on his old friend's face, had not moved since the tale began. He continued to maintain his silent immobility after Culwin had ceased to speak, and it was I who, with a vague sense of disappointment at the sudden drop of the story, finally asked: "But how long did you keep on seeing them?"

Culwin, so sunk into his chair that he seemed like a heap of his own empty clothes, stirred a little, as if in surprise at my question. He appeared to have half-forgotten what he had been telling us.

"How long? Oh, off and on all that winter. It was infernal. I never got used to them. I grew really ill."

Frenham shifted his attitude, and as he did so his elbow struck against a small mirror in a bronze frame standing on the table behind him. He turned and changed its angle slightly; then he resumed his former attitude, his dark head thrown back on his lifted palm, his eyes intent on Culwin's face. Something in his silent gaze embarrassed me, and as if to divert attention from it I pressed on with another question:

"And you never tried sacrificing Noyes?"

"Oh, no. The fact is I didn't have to. He did it for me, poor boy!"

"Did it for you? How do you mean?"

"He wore me out—wore everybody out. He kept on pouring out his lamentable twaddle, and hawking it up and down the place till he became a thing of terror. I tried to wean him from writing—oh, ever so gently, you understand, by throwing him with agreeable people, giving him a chance to make himself felt, to come to a sense of what he *really* had to give. I'd foreseen this solution from the beginning—felt sure that, once the first ardour of authorship was quenched, he'd drop into his place as a charming parasitic thing, the kind of chronic Cherubino for whom, in old societies, there's always a seat at table, and a shelter behind the ladies' skirts. I saw him take his place as 'the poet': the poet who doesn't write. One knows the type in every drawing-room. Living in that way doesn't cost much—I'd worked it all out in my mind, and felt sure that, with a little help, he could manage it for the next few years; and meanwhile he'd be sure to marry. I saw him married to a widow, rather older, with a good cook and a well-run house. And I actually had my eye on the widow... Meanwhile I did everything to help the transition—lent him money to ease his conscience, introduced him to pretty women to make him forget his vows. But nothing would do him: he had but one idea in his beautiful obstinate head. He wanted the laurel and not the rose, and he kept on repeating Gautier's axiom, and battering and filing at his limp prose till he'd spread it out over Lord knows how many hundred pages. Now and then he would send a barrelful to a publisher, and of course it would always come back.

"At first it didn't matter—he thought he was 'misunderstood.' He took the attitudes of genius, and whenever an opus came home he wrote another to keep it company. Then he had a reaction of despair, and accused me of deceiving him, and Lord knows what. I got angry at that, and told him it was he who had deceived himself. He'd come to me determined to write, and I'd done my best to help him. That was the extent of my offence, and I'd done it for his cousin's sake, not his.

"That seemed to strike home, and he didn't answer for a minute. Then he said: 'My time's up and my money's up. What do you think I'd better do?'

"'I think you'd better not be an ass,' I said.

"'What do you mean by being an ass?' he asked.

"I took a letter from my desk and held it out to him.

"'I mean refusing this offer of Mrs. Ellinger's: to be her secretary at a salary of five thousand dollars. There may be a lot more in it than that.'

"He flung out his hand with a violence that struck the letter from mine. 'Oh, I know well enough what's in it!' he said, red to the roots of his hair.

"'And what's the answer, if you know?' I asked.

"He made none at the minute, but turned away slowly to the door. There, with his hand on the threshold, he stopped to say, almost under his breath: 'Then you really think my stuff's no good?'

"I was tired and exasperated, and I laughed. I don't defend my laugh—it was in wretched taste. But I must plead in extenuation that the boy was a fool, and that I'd done my best for him—I really had.

"He went out of the room, shutting the door quietly after him. That afternoon I left for Frascati, where I'd promised to spend the Sunday with some friends. I was glad to escape from Gilbert, and by the same token, as I learned that night, I had also escaped from the eyes. I dropped into the same lethargic sleep that had come to me before when I left off seeing them; and when I woke the next morning, in my peaceful room above the ilexes, I felt the utter weariness and deep relief that always followed on that sleep. I put in two blessed nights at Frascati, and when I got back to my rooms in Rome I found that Gilbert had gone… Oh, nothing tragic had happened—the episode never rose to *that*. He'd simply packed his manuscripts and left for America—for his family and the Wall Street desk. He left a decent enough note to tell me of his decision, and behaved altogether, in the circumstances, as little like a fool as it's possible for a fool to behave…"

IV

Culwin paused again, and Frenham still sat motionless, the dusky contour of his young head reflected in the mirror at his back.

"And what became of Noyes afterward?" I finally asked, still disquieted by a sense of incompleteness, by the need of some connecting thread between the parallel lines of the tale.

Culwin twitched his shoulders. "Oh, nothing became of him—because he became nothing. There could be no question of 'becoming' about it. He vegetated in an office, I believe, and finally got a clerkship in a consulate, and married drearily in China. I saw him once in Hong Kong, years afterward. He was fat and hadn't shaved. I was told he drank. He didn't recognise me."

"And the eyes?" I asked, after another pause which Frenham's continued silence made oppressive.

Culwin, stroking his chin, blinked at me meditatively through the shadows. "I never saw them after my last talk with Gilbert. Put two and two together if you can. For my part, I haven't found the link."

He rose, his hands in his pockets, and walked stiffly over to the table on which reviving drinks had been set out.

"You must be parched after this dry tale. Here, help yourself, my dear fellow. Here, Phil—" He turned back to the hearth.

Frenham made no response to his host's hospitable summons. He still sat in his low chair without moving, but as Culwin advanced toward him, their eyes met in a long look; after which the young man, turning suddenly, flung his arms across the table behind him, and dropped his face upon them.

Culwin, at the unexpected gesture, stopped short, a flush on his face.

"Phil—what the deuce? Why, have the eyes scared *you*? My dear boy—my dear fellow—I never had such a tribute to my literary ability, never!"

He broke into a chuckle at the thought, and halted on the hearth-rug, his hands still in his pockets, gazing down at the youth's bowed head. Then, as Frenham still made no answer, he moved a step or two nearer.

"Cheer up, my dear Phil! It's years since I've seen them—apparently I've done nothing lately bad enough to call them out of chaos. Unless my present evocation of them has made *you* see them; which would be their worst stroke yet!"

His bantering appeal quivered off into an uneasy laugh, and he moved still nearer, bending over Frenham, and laying his gouty hands on the lad's shoulders.

"Phil, my dear boy, really—what's the matter? Why don't you answer? *Have* you seen the eyes?"

Frenham's face was still hidden, and from where I stood behind Culwin I saw the latter, as if under the rebuff of this unaccountable attitude, draw back slowly from his friend. As he did so, the light of the lamp on the table fell full on his congested face, and I caught its reflection in the mirror behind Frenham's head.

Culwin saw the reflection also. He paused, his face level with the mirror, as if scarcely recognising the countenance in it as his own. But as he looked his expression gradually changed, and for an appreciable space of time he and the image in the glass confronted each other with a glare of slowly gathering hate. Then Culwin let go on Frenham's shoulders, and drew back a step...

Frenham, his face still hidden, did not stir.

THE TRIUMPH OF NIGHT

I

It was clear that the sleigh from Weymore had not come; and the shivering young traveller from Boston, who had counted on jumping into it when he left the train at Northridge Junction, found himself standing alone on the open platform, exposed to the full assault of night-fall and winter.

The blast that swept him came off New Hampshire snow-fields and ice-hung forests. It seemed to have traversed interminable leagues of frozen silence, filling them with the same cold roar and sharpening its edge against the same bitter black-and-white landscape. Dark, searching and sword-like, it alternately muffled and harried its victim, like a bull-fighter now whirling his cloak and now planting his darts. This analogy brought home to the young man the fact that he himself had no cloak, and that the overcoat in which he had faced the relatively temperate air of Boston seemed no thicker than a sheet of paper on the bleak heights of Northridge. George Faxon said to himself that the place was uncommonly well-named. It clung to an exposed ledge over the valley from which the train had lifted him, and the wind combed it with teeth of steel that he seemed actually to hear scraping against the wooden sides of the station. Other building there was none: the village lay far down the road, and thither—since the Weymore sleigh had not come—Faxon saw himself under the necessity of plodding through several feet of snow.

He understood well enough what had happened: his hostess had forgotten that he was coming. Young as Faxon was, this sad lucidity of soul had been acquired as the result of long experience, and he knew that the visitors who can least afford to hire a carriage are almost always those whom their hosts forget to send for. Yet to say that Mrs. Culme had forgotten him was too crude a way of putting it. Similar incidents led him to think that she had probably told her maid to tell the butler to telephone the coachman to tell one of the grooms (if no one else needed him) to drive over to Northridge to fetch the new secretary; but on a night like this, what groom who respected his rights would fail to forget the order?

Faxon's obvious course was to struggle through the drifts to the village, and there rout out a sleigh to convey him to Weymore; but what if, on his arrival at Mrs. Culme's, no one remembered to ask him what this devotion to duty had cost? That, again, was one of the contingencies he had expensively learned to look out for, and the perspicacity so acquired told him it would be cheaper to spend the night at the Northridge inn, and advise Mrs. Culme of his presence there by telephone. He had reached this decision, and was about to entrust his luggage to a vague man with a lantern, when his hopes were raised by the sound of bells.

Two sleighs were just dashing up to the station, and from the foremost there sprang a young man muffled in furs.

"Weymore?—No, these are not the Weymore sleighs."

The voice was that of the youth who had jumped to the platform—a voice so agreeable that, in spite of the words, it fell consolingly on Faxon's ears. At the same moment the wandering station-lantern, casting a transient light on the speaker, showed his features to be in the pleasantest harmony with his voice. He was very fair and very young—hardly in the twenties, Faxon thought—but his face, though full of a morning freshness, was a trifle too thin and fine-drawn, as though a vivid spirit contended in him with a strain of physical weakness. Faxon was perhaps the quicker to notice such delicacies of balance because his own temperament hung on lightly quivering nerves, which yet, as he believed, would never quite swing him beyond a normal sensibility.

"You expected a sleigh from Weymore?" the newcomer continued, standing beside Faxon like a slender column of fur.

Mrs. Culme's secretary explained his difficulty, and the other brushed it aside with a contemptuous "Oh, *Mrs. Culme!*" that carried both speakers a long way toward reciprocal understanding.

"But then you must be—" The youth broke off with a smile of interrogation.

"The new secretary? Yes. But apparently there are no notes to be answered this evening." Faxon's laugh deepened the sense of solidarity which had so promptly established itself between the two.

His friend laughed also. "Mrs. Culme," he explained, "was lunching at my uncle's today, and she said you were due this evening. But seven hours is a long time for Mrs. Culme to remember anything."

"Well," said Faxon philosophically, "I suppose that's one of the reasons why she needs a secretary. And I've always the inn at Northridge," he concluded.

"Oh, but you haven't, though! It burned down last week."

"The deuce it did!" said Faxon; but the humour of the situation struck him before its inconvenience. His life, for years past, had been mainly a succession of resigned adaptations, and he had learned, before dealing practically with his embarrassments, to extract from most of them a small tribute of amusement.

"Oh, well, there's sure to be somebody in the place who can put me up."

"No one *you* could put up with. Besides, Northridge is three miles off, and our place—in the opposite direction—is a little nearer." Through the darkness, Faxon saw his friend sketch a gesture of self-introduction. "My name's Frank Rainer, and I'm staying with my uncle at Overdale. I've driven over to meet two friends of his, who are due in a few minutes from New York. If you don't mind waiting till they arrive I'm sure Overdale can do you better than Northridge. We're only down from town for a few days, but the house is always ready for a lot of people."

"But your uncle—?" Faxon could only object, with the odd sense, through his embarrassment, that it would be magically dispelled by his invisible friend's next words.

"Oh, my uncle—you'll see! I answer for *him*! I daresay you've heard of him—John Lavington?"

John Lavington! There was a certain irony in asking if one had heard of John Lavington! Even from a post of observation as obscure as that of Mrs. Culme's secretary the rumour of John Lavington's money, of his pictures, his politics, his charities and his hospitality, was as difficult to escape as the roar of a cataract in a mountain solitude. It might almost have been said that the one place in which one would not have expected to come upon him was in just such a solitude as now surrounded the speakers—at least in this deepest hour of its desertedness. But it was just like Lavington's brilliant ubiquity to put one in the wrong even there.

"Oh, yes, I've heard of your uncle."

"Then you *will* come, won't you? We've only five minutes to wait," young Rainer urged, in the tone that dispels scruples by ignoring them; and Faxon found himself accepting the invitation as simply as it was offered.

A delay in the arrival of the New York train lengthened their five minutes to fifteen; and as they paced the icy platform Faxon began to see why it had seemed the most natural thing in the world to accede to his new acquaintance's suggestion. It was because Frank Rainer was one of the privileged beings who simplify human intercourse by the atmosphere of confidence and good humour they diffuse. He produced this effect, Faxon noted, by the exercise of no gift but his youth, and of no art but his sincerity; and these qualities were revealed in a smile of such sweetness that Faxon felt, as never before, what Nature can achieve when she deigns to match the face with the mind.

He learned that the young man was the ward, and the only nephew, of John Lavington, with whom he had made his home since the death of his mother, the great man's sister. Mr. Lavington, Rainer said, had been "a regular brick" to him—"But then he is to every one, you know"—and the young fellow's situation seemed in fact to be perfectly in keeping with his person. Apparently the only shade that had ever rested on him was cast by the physical weakness which Faxon had already detected. Young Rainer had been threatened with tuberculosis, and the disease was so far advanced that, according to the highest authorities, banishment to Arizona or New Mexico was inevitable. "But luckily my uncle didn't pack me off, as most people would have done, without getting another opinion. Whose? Oh, an awfully clever chap, a young doctor with a lot of new ideas, who simply laughed at my being sent away, and said I'd do perfectly well in New York if I didn't dine out too much, and if I dashed off occasionally to Northridge for a little fresh air. So it's really my uncle's doing that I'm not in exile—and I feel no end better since the new chap told me I needn't bother." Young Rainer went on to confess that he was extremely fond of dining out, dancing and similar distractions; and Faxon, listening to him, was inclined to think that the physician who had refused to cut him off altogether from these pleasures was probably a better psychologist than his seniors.

"All the same you ought to be careful, you know." The sense of elder-brotherly concern that forced the words from Faxon made him, as he spoke, slip his arm through Frank Rainer's.

The latter met the movement with a responsive pressure. "Oh, I *am*: awfully, awfully. And then my uncle has such an eye on me!"

"But if your uncle has such an eye on you, what does he say to your swallowing knives out here in this Siberian wild?"

Rainer raised his fur collar with a careless gesture. "It's not that that does it—the cold's good for me."

"And it's not the dinners and dances? What is it, then?" Faxon good-humouredly insisted; to which his companion answered with a laugh: "Well, my uncle says it's being bored; and I rather think he's right!"

His laugh ended in a spasm of coughing and a struggle for breath that made Faxon, still holding his arm, guide him hastily into the shelter of the fireless waiting-room.

Young Rainer had dropped down on the bench against the wall and pulled off one of his fur gloves to grope for a handkerchief. He tossed aside his cap and drew the handkerchief across his forehead, which was intensely white, and beaded with moisture, though his face retained a healthy glow. But Faxon's gaze remained fastened to the hand he had uncovered: it was so long, so colourless, so wasted, so much older than the brow he passed it over.

"It's queer—a healthy face but dying hands," the secretary mused: he somehow wished young Rainer had kept on his glove.

The whistle of the express drew the young men to their feet, and the next moment two heavily-furred gentlemen had descended to the platform and were breasting the rigour of the night. Frank Rainer introduced them as Mr. Grisben and Mr. Balch, and Faxon, while their luggage was being lifted into the second sleigh, discerned them, by the roving lantern-gleam, to be an elderly grey-headed pair, of the average prosperous business cut.

They saluted their host's nephew with friendly familiarity, and Mr. Grisben, who seemed the spokesman of the two, ended his greeting with a genial—"and many many more of them, dear boy!" which suggested to Faxon that their arrival coincided with an anniversary. But he could not press the enquiry, for the seat allotted him was at the coachman's side, while Frank Rainer joined his uncle's guests inside the sleigh.

A swift flight (behind such horses as one could be sure of John Lavington's having) brought them to tall gateposts, an illuminated lodge, and an avenue on which the snow had been levelled to the smoothness of marble. At the end of the avenue the long house loomed up, its principal bulk dark, but one wing sending out a ray of welcome; and the next moment Faxon was receiving a violent impression of warmth and light, of hot-house plants, hurrying servants, a vast spectacular oak hall like a stage-setting, and, in its unreal middle distance, a small figure, correctly dressed, conventionally featured, and utterly unlike his rather florid conception of the great John Lavington.

The surprise of the contrast remained with him through his hurried dressing in the large luxurious bedroom to which he had been shown. "I don't see where he comes in," was the only way he could put it, so difficult was it to fit the exuberance of Lavington's public personality into his host's contracted frame and manner. Mr. Lavington, to whom Faxon's case had been rapidly explained by young Rainer, had welcomed him with a sort of dry and stilted cordiality that exactly matched his narrow face, his stiff hand, and the whiff of scent on his evening handkerchief. "Make yourself at home—at home!" he had repeated, in a tone that suggested, on his own part, a complete inability to perform the feat he urged on his visitor. "Any friend of Frank's… delighted… make yourself thoroughly at home!"

II

In spite of the balmy temperature and complicated conveniences of Faxon's bedroom, the injunction was not easy to obey. It was wonderful luck to have found a night's shelter under the opulent roof of Overdale, and he tasted the physical satisfaction to the full. But the place, for all its ingenuities of comfort, was oddly cold and unwelcoming. He couldn't have said why, and could only suppose that Mr. Lavington's intense personality—intensely negative, but intense all the same—must, in some occult way, have penetrated every corner of his dwelling. Perhaps, though, it was merely that Faxon himself was tired and hungry, more deeply chilled than he had known till he came in from the cold, and unutterably sick of all strange houses, and of the prospect of perpetually treading other people's stairs.

"I hope you're not famished?" Rainer's slim figure was in the doorway. "My uncle has a little business to attend to with Mr. Grisben, and we don't dine for half an hour. Shall I fetch you, or can you find your way down?

Come straight to the dining-room—the second door on the left of the long gallery."

He disappeared, leaving a ray of warmth behind him, and Faxon, relieved, lit a cigarette and sat down by the fire.

Looking about with less haste, he was struck by a detail that had escaped him. The room was full of flowers—a mere "bachelor's room," in the wing of a house opened only for a few days, in the dead middle of a New Hampshire winter! Flowers were everywhere, not in senseless profusion, but placed with the same conscious art that he had remarked in the grouping of the blossoming shrubs in the hall. A vase of arums stood on the writing-table, a cluster of strange-hued carnations on the stand at his elbow, and from bowls of glass and porcelain clumps of freesia-bulbs diffused their melting fragrance. The fact implied acres of glass—but that was the least interesting part of it. The flowers themselves, their quality, selection and arrangement, attested on some one's part—and on whose but John Lavington's?—a solicitous and sensitive passion for that particular form of beauty. Well, it simply made the man, as he had appeared to Faxon, all the harder to understand!

The half-hour elapsed, and Faxon, rejoicing at the prospect of food, set out to make his way to the dining-room. He had not noticed the direction he had followed in going to his room, and was puzzled, when he left it, to find that two staircases, of apparently equal importance, invited him. He chose the one to his right, and reached, at its foot, a long gallery such as Rainer had described. The gallery was empty, the doors down its length were closed; but Rainer had said: "The second to the left," and Faxon, after pausing for some chance enlightenment which did not come, laid his hand on the second knob to the left.

The room he entered was square, with dusky picture-hung walls. In its centre, about a table lit by veiled lamps, he fancied Mr. Lavington and his guests to be already seated at dinner; then he perceived that the table was covered not with viands but with papers, and that he had blundered into what seemed to be his host's study. As he paused Frank Rainer looked up.

"Oh, here's Mr. Faxon. Why not ask him—?"

Mr. Lavington, from the end of the table, reflected his nephew's smile in a glance of impartial benevolence.

"Certainly. Come in, Mr. Faxon. If you won't think it a liberty—"

Mr. Grisben, who sat opposite his host, turned his head toward the door. "Of course Mr. Faxon's an American citizen?"

Frank Rainer laughed. "That's all right!... Oh, no, not one of your pin-pointed pens, Uncle Jack! Haven't you got a quill somewhere?"

Mr. Balch, who spoke slowly and as if reluctantly, in a muffled voice of which there seemed to be very little left, raised his hand to say: "One moment: you acknowledge this to be—?"

"My last will and testament?" Rainer's laugh redoubled. "Well, I won't answer for the 'last.' It's the first, anyway."

"It's a mere formula," Mr. Balch explained.

"Well, here goes." Rainer dipped his quill in the inkstand his uncle had pushed in his direction, and dashed a gallant signature across the document.

Faxon, understanding what was expected of him, and conjecturing that the young man was signing his will on the attainment of his majority, had placed himself behind Mr. Grisben, and stood awaiting his turn to affix his name to the instrument. Rainer, having signed, was about to push the paper across the table to Mr. Balch; but the latter, again raising his hand, said in his sad imprisoned voice: "The seal—?"

"Oh, does there have to be a seal?"

Faxon, looking over Mr. Grisben at John Lavington, saw a faint frown between his impassive eyes. "Really, Frank!" He seemed, Faxon thought, slightly irritated by his nephew's frivolity.

"Who's got a seal?" Frank Rainer continued, glancing about the table. "There doesn't seem to be one here."

Mr. Grisben interposed. "A wafer will do. Lavington, you have a wafer?"

Mr. Lavington had recovered his serenity. "There must be some in one of the drawers. But I'm ashamed to say I don't know where my secretary keeps these things. He ought to have seen to it that a wafer was sent with the document."

"Oh, hang it—" Frank Rainer pushed the paper aside: "It's the hand of God—and I'm as hungry as a wolf. Let's dine first, Uncle Jack."

"I think I've a seal upstairs," said Faxon.

Mr. Lavington sent him a barely perceptible smile. "So sorry to give you the trouble—"

"Oh, I say, don't send him after it now. Let's wait till after dinner!"

Mr. Lavington continued to smile on his guest, and the latter, as if under the faint coercion of the smile, turned from the room and ran upstairs. Having taken the seal from his writing-case he came down again, and once more opened the door of the study. No one was speaking when he entered—they were evidently awaiting his return with the mute impatience of hunger, and he put the seal in Rainer's reach, and stood watching while Mr. Grisben struck a match and held it to one of the candles flanking the inkstand. As the wax descended on the paper Faxon remarked again the strange emaciation, the premature physical weariness, of the hand that held it: he wondered if Mr. Lavington had ever noticed his nephew's hand, and if it were not poignantly visible to him now.

With this thought in his mind, Faxon raised his eyes to look at Mr. Lavington. The great man's gaze rested on Frank Rainer with an expression of untroubled benevolence; and at the same instant Faxon's attention was attracted by the presence in the room of another person, who must have joined the group while he was upstairs searching for the seal. The newcomer was a man of about Mr. Lavington's age and figure, who stood just behind his chair, and who, at the moment when Faxon first saw him, was gazing at young Rainer with an equal intensity of attention. The likeness between the two men—perhaps increased by the fact that the hooded lamps on the table left the figure behind the chair in shadow—struck Faxon the more because of the contrast in their expression. John Lavington, during his nephew's clumsy attempt to drop the wax and apply the seal, continued to fasten on him a look of half-amused affection; while the man behind the chair, so oddly reduplicating the lines of his features and figure, turned on the boy a face of pale hostility.

The impression was so startling that Faxon forgot what was going on about him. He was just dimly aware of young Rainer's exclaiming: "Your turn, Mr. Grisben!" of Mr. Grisben's protesting: "No—no; Mr. Faxon first," and of the pen's being thereupon transferred to his own hand. He received it with a deadly sense of being unable to move, or even to understand what was expected of him, till he became conscious of Mr. Grisben's paternally pointing out the precise spot on which he was to leave his autograph. The effort to fix his attention and steady his hand prolonged the process of signing, and when he stood up—a strange weight of fatigue on all his limbs—the figure behind Mr. Lavington's chair was gone.

Faxon felt an immediate sense of relief. It was puzzling that the man's exit should have been so rapid and noiseless, but the door behind Mr. Lavington was screened by a tapestry hanging, and Faxon concluded that the unknown looker-on had merely had to raise it to pass out. At any rate he was gone, and with his withdrawal the strange weight was lifted. Young Rainer was lighting a cigarette, Mr. Balch inscribing his name at the foot of the document, Mr. Lavington—his eyes no longer on his nephew—examining a strange white-winged orchid in the vase at his elbow. Every thing suddenly seemed to have grown natural and simple again, and Faxon found himself responding with a smile to the affable gesture with which his host declared: "And now, Mr. Faxon, we'll dine."

III

"I wonder how I blundered into the wrong room just now; I thought you told me to take the second door to the left," Faxon said to Frank Rainer as they followed the older men down the gallery.

"So I did; but I probably forgot to tell you which staircase to take. Coming from your bedroom, I ought to have said the fourth door to the right. It's a puzzling house, because my uncle keeps adding to it from year to year. He built this room last summer for his modern pictures."

Young Rainer, pausing to open another door, touched an electric button which sent a circle of light about the walls of a long room hung with canvases of the French impressionist school.

Faxon advanced, attracted by a shimmering Monet, but Rainer laid a hand on his arm.

"He bought that last week. But come along—I'll show you all this after dinner. Or *he* will, rather—he loves it."

"Does he really love things?"

Rainer stared, clearly perplexed at the question. "Rather! Flowers and pictures especially! Haven't you noticed the flowers? I suppose you think his manner's cold; it seems so at first; but he's really awfully keen about things."

Faxon looked quickly at the speaker. "Has your uncle a brother?"

"Brother? No—never had. He and my mother were the only ones."

"Or any relation who—who looks like him? Who might be mistaken for him?"

"Not that I ever heard of. Does he remind you of some one?"

"Yes."

"That's queer. We'll ask him if he's got a double. Come on!"

But another picture had arrested Faxon, and some minutes elapsed before he and his young host reached the dining-room. It was a large room, with the same conventionally handsome furniture and delicately grouped flowers; and Faxon's first glance showed him that only three men were seated about the dining-table. The man who had stood behind Mr. Lavington's chair was not present, and no seat awaited him.

When the young men entered, Mr. Grisben was speaking, and his host, who faced the door, sat looking down at his untouched soup-plate and turning the spoon about in his small dry hand.

"It's pretty late to call them rumours—they were devilish close to facts when we left town this morning," Mr. Grisben was saying, with an unexpected incisiveness of tone.

Mr. Lavington laid down his spoon and smiled interrogatively. "Oh, facts—what *are* facts? Just the way a thing happens to look at a given minute…"

"You haven't heard anything from town?" Mr. Grisben persisted.

"Not a syllable. So you see… Balch, a little more of that *petite marmite*. Mr. Faxon… between Frank and Mr. Grisben, please."

The dinner progressed through a series of complicated courses, ceremoniously dispensed by a prelatical butler attended by three tall footmen, and it was evident that Mr. Lavington took a certain satisfaction in the pageant. That, Faxon reflected, was probably the joint in his armour—that and the flowers. He had changed the subject—not abruptly but firmly—when the young men entered, but Faxon perceived that it still possessed the thoughts of the two elderly visitors, and Mr. Balch presently observed, in a voice that seemed to come from the last survivor down a mine-shaft: "If it *does* come, it will be the biggest crash since '93."

Mr. Lavington looked bored but polite. "Wall Street can stand crashes better than it could then. It's got a robuster constitution."

"Yes; but—"

"Speaking of constitutions," Mr. Grisben intervened: "Frank, are you taking care of yourself?"

A flush rose to young Rainer's cheeks.

"Why, of course! Isn't that what I'm here for?"

"You're here about three days in the month, aren't you? And the rest of the time it's crowded restaurants and hot ballrooms in town. I thought you were to be shipped off to New Mexico?"

"Oh, I've got a new man who says that's rot."

"Well, you don't look as if your new man were right," said Mr. Grisben bluntly.

Faxon saw the lad's colour fade, and the rings of shadow deepen under his gay eyes. At the same moment his uncle turned to him with a renewed intensity of attention. There was such solicitude in Mr. Lavington's gaze that it seemed almost to fling a shield between his nephew and Mr. Grisben's tactless scrutiny.

"We think Frank's a good deal better," he began; "this new doctor—"

The butler, coming up, bent to whisper a word in his ear, and the communication caused a sudden change in Mr. Lavington's expression. His face was naturally so colourless that it seemed not so much to pale as to fade, to dwindle and recede into something blurred and blotted-out. He half rose, sat down again and sent a rigid smile about the table.

"Will you excuse me? The telephone. Peters, go on with the dinner." With small precise steps he walked out of the door which one of the footmen had thrown open.

A momentary silence fell on the group; then Mr. Grisben once more addressed himself to Rainer. "You ought to have gone, my boy; you ought to have gone."

The anxious look returned to the youth's eyes. "My uncle doesn't think so, really."

"You're not a baby, to be always governed by your uncle's opinion. You came of age today, didn't you? Your uncle spoils you… that's what's the matter…"

The thrust evidently went home, for Rainer laughed and looked down with a slight accession of colour.

"But the doctor—"

"Use your common sense, Frank! You had to try twenty doctors to find one to tell you what you wanted to be told."

A look of apprehension overshadowed Rainer's gaiety. "Oh, come—I say!… What would *you* do?" he stammered.

"Pack up and jump on the first train." Mr. Grisben leaned forward and laid his hand kindly on the young man's arm. "Look here: my nephew Jim

Grisben is out there ranching on a big scale. He'll take you in and be glad to have you. You say your new doctor thinks it won't do you any good; but he doesn't pretend to say it will do you harm, does he? Well, then—give it a trial. It'll take you out of hot theatres and night restaurants, anyhow... And all the rest of it... Eh, Balch?"

"Go!" said Mr. Balch hollowly. "Go at *once*," he added, as if a closer look at the youth's face had impressed on him the need of backing up his friend.

Young Rainer had turned ashy-pale. He tried to stiffen his mouth into a smile. "Do I look as bad as all that?"

Mr. Grisben was helping himself to terrapin. "You look like the day after an earthquake," he said.

The terrapin had encircled the table, and been deliberately enjoyed by Mr. Lavington's three visitors (Rainer, Faxon noticed, left his plate untouched) before the door was thrown open to re-admit their host.

Mr. Lavington advanced with an air of recovered composure. He seated himself, picked up his napkin and consulted the gold-monogrammed menu. "No, don't bring back the filet... Some terrapin; yes..." He looked affably about the table. "Sorry to have deserted you, but the storm has played the deuce with the wires, and I had to wait a long time before I could get a good connection. It must be blowing up for a blizzard."

"Uncle Jack," young Rainer broke out, "Mr. Grisben's been lecturing me."

Mr. Lavington was helping himself to terrapin. "Ah—what about?"

"He thinks I ought to have given New Mexico a show."

"I want him to go straight out to my nephew at Santa Paz and stay there till his next birthday." Mr. Lavington signed to the butler to hand the terrapin to Mr. Grisben, who, as he took a second helping, addressed himself again to Rainer. "Jim's in New York now, and going back the day after tomorrow in Olyphant's private car. I'll ask Olyphant to squeeze you in if you'll go. And when you've been out there a week or two, in the saddle all day and sleeping nine hours a night, I suspect you won't think much of the doctor who prescribed New York."

Faxon spoke up, he knew not why. "I was out there once: it's a splendid life. I saw a fellow—oh, a really *bad* case—who'd been simply made over by it."

"It *does* sound jolly," Rainer laughed, a sudden eagerness in his tone.

His uncle looked at him gently. "Perhaps Grisben's right. It's an opportunity—"

Faxon glanced up with a start: the figure dimly perceived in the study was now more visibly and tangibly planted behind Mr. Lavington's chair.

"That's right, Frank: you see your uncle approves. And the trip out there with Olyphant isn't a thing to be missed. So drop a few dozen dinners and be at the Grand Central the day after tomorrow at five."

Mr. Grisben's pleasant grey eye sought corroboration of his host, and Faxon, in a cold anguish of suspense, continued to watch him as he turned his glance on Mr. Lavington. One could not look at Lavington without seeing the presence at his back, and it was clear that, the next minute, some change in Mr. Grisben's expression must give his watcher a clue.

But Mr. Grisben's expression did not change: the gaze he fixed on his host remained unperturbed, and the clue he gave was the startling one of not seeming to see the other figure.

Faxon's first impulse was to look away, to look anywhere else, to resort again to the champagne glass the watchful butler had already brimmed; but some fatal attraction, at war in him with an overwhelming physical resistance, held his eyes upon the spot they feared.

The figure was still standing, more distinctly, and therefore more resemblingly, at Mr. Lavington's back; and while the latter continued to gaze affectionately at his nephew, his counterpart, as before, fixed young Rainer with eyes of deadly menace.

Faxon, with what felt like an actual wrench of the muscles, dragged his own eyes from the sight to scan the other countenances about the table; but not one revealed the least consciousness of what he saw, and a sense of mortal isolation sank upon him.

"It's worth considering, certainly—" he heard Mr. Lavington continue;

and as Rainer's face lit up, the face behind his uncle's chair seemed to gather into its look all the fierce weariness of old unsatisfied hates. That was the thing that, as the minutes laboured by, Faxon was becoming most conscious of. The watcher behind the chair was no longer merely malevolent: he had grown suddenly, unutterably tired. His hatred seemed to well up out of the very depths of balked effort and thwarted hopes, and the fact made him more pitiable, and yet more dire.

Faxon's look reverted to Mr. Lavington, as if to surprise in him a corresponding change. At first none was visible: his pinched smile was screwed to his blank face like a gas-light to a white-washed wall. Then the fixity of the smile became ominous: Faxon saw that its wearer was afraid to let it go. It was evident that Mr. Lavington was unutterably tired too, and the discovery sent a colder current through Faxon's veins. Looking down at his untouched plate, he caught the soliciting twinkle of the champagne glass; but the sight of the wine turned him sick.

"Well, we'll go into the details presently," he heard Mr. Lavington say, still on the question of his nephew's future. "Let's have a cigar first. No—not here, Peters." He turned his smile on Faxon. "When we've had coffee I want to show you my pictures."

"Oh, by the way, Uncle Jack—Mr. Faxon wants to know if you've got a double?"

"A double?" Mr. Lavington, still smiling, continued to address himself to his guest. "Not that I know of. Have you seen one, Mr. Faxon?"

Faxon thought: "My God, if I look up now they'll *both* be looking at me!" To avoid raising his eyes he made as though to lift the glass to his lips; but his hand sank inert, and he looked up. Mr. Lavington's glance was politely bent on him, but with a loosening of the strain about his heart he saw that the figure behind the chair still kept its gaze on Rainer.

"Do you think you've seen my double, Mr. Faxon?"

Would the other face turn if he said yes? Faxon felt a dryness in his throat. "No," he answered.

"Ah? It's possible I've a dozen. I believe I'm extremely usual-looking," Mr. Lavington went on conversationally; and still the other face watched Rainer.

"It was... a mistake... a confusion of memory..." Faxon heard himself stammer. Mr. Lavington pushed back his chair, and as he did so Mr. Grisben suddenly leaned forward.

"Lavington! What have we been thinking of? We haven't drunk Frank's health!"

Mr. Lavington reseated himself. "My dear boy!... Peters, another bottle..." He turned to his nephew. "After such a sin of omission I don't presume to propose the toast myself... but Frank knows... Go ahead, Grisben!"

The boy shone on his uncle. "No, no, Uncle Jack! Mr. Grisben won't mind. Nobody but *you*—today!"

The butler was replenishing the glasses. He filled Mr. Lavington's last, and Mr. Lavington put out his small hand to raise it... As he did so, Faxon looked away.

"Well, then—All the good I've wished you in all the past years... I put it into the prayer that the coming ones may be healthy and happy and many... and *many*, dear boy!"

Faxon saw the hands about him reach out for their glasses. Automatically, he reached for his. His eyes were still on the table, and he repeated to himself with a trembling vehemence: "I won't look up! I won't... I won't..."

His fingers clasped the glass and raised it to the level of his lips. He saw the other hands making the same motion. He heard Mr. Grisben's genial "Hear! Hear!" and Mr. Balch's hollow echo. He said to himself, as the rim of the glass touched his lips: "I won't look up! I swear I won't!—" and he looked.

The glass was so full that it required an extraordinary effort to hold it there, brimming and suspended, during the awful interval before he could trust his hand to lower it again, untouched, to the table. It was this merciful preoccupation which saved him, kept him from crying out, from losing his hold, from slipping down into the bottomless blackness that gaped for him.

As long as the problem of the glass engaged him he felt able to keep his seat, manage his muscles, fit unnoticeably into the group; but as the glass touched the table his last link with safety snapped. He stood up and dashed out of the room.

IV

In the gallery, the instinct of self-preservation helped him to turn back and sign to young Rainer not to follow. He stammered out something about a touch of dizziness, and joining them presently; and the boy nodded sympathetically and drew back.

At the foot of the stairs Faxon ran against a servant. "I should like to telephone to Weymore," he said with dry lips.

"Sorry, sir; wires all down. We've been trying the last hour to get New York again for Mr. Lavington."

Faxon shot on to his room, burst into it, and bolted the door. The lamplight lay on furniture, flowers, books; in the ashes a log still glimmered. He dropped down on the sofa and hid his face. The room was profoundly silent, the whole house was still: nothing about him gave a hint of what was going on, darkly and dumbly, in the room he had flown from, and with the covering of his eyes oblivion and reassurance seemed to fall on him. But they fell for a moment only; then his lids opened again to the monstrous vision. There it was, stamped on his pupils, a part of him forever, an indelible horror burnt into his body and brain. But why into his—just his? Why had he alone been chosen to see what he had seen? What business was it of *his*, in God's name? Any one of the others, thus enlightened, might have exposed the horror and defeated it; but *he*, the one weaponless and defenceless spectator, the one whom none of the others would believe or understand if he attempted to reveal what he knew—*he* alone had been singled out as the victim of this dreadful initiation!

Suddenly he sat up, listening: he had heard a step on the stairs. Some one, no doubt, was coming to see how he was—to urge him, if he felt better, to go down and join the smokers. Cautiously he opened his door; yes, it was young Rainer's step. Faxon looked down the passage, remembered the other stairway and darted to it. All he wanted was to get out of the house. Not another instant would he breathe its abominable air! What business was it of *his*, in God's name?

He reached the opposite end of the lower gallery, and beyond it saw the hall by which he had entered. It was empty, and on a long table he recognised his coat and cap. He got into his coat, unbolted the door, and plunged into the purifying night.

The darkness was deep, and the cold so intense that for an instant it stopped his breathing. Then he perceived that only a thin snow was falling, and resolutely he set his face for flight. The trees along the avenue marked his way as he hastened with long strides over the beaten snow. Gradually, while he walked, the tumult in his brain subsided. The impulse to fly still drove him forward, but he began to feel that he was flying from a terror of his own creating, and that the most urgent reason for escape was the need of hiding his state, of shunning other eyes till he should regain his balance.

He had spent the long hours in the train in fruitless broodings on a discouraging situation, and he remembered how his bitterness had turned to exasperation when he found that the Weymore sleigh was not awaiting him. It was absurd, of course; but, though he had joked with Rainer over Mrs. Culme's forgetfulness, to confess it had cost a pang. That was what his rootless life had brought him to: for lack of a personal stake in things his sensibility was at the mercy of such trifles... Yes; that, and the cold and fatigue, the absence of hope and the haunting sense of starved aptitudes, all these had brought him to the perilous verge over which, once or twice before, his terrified brain had hung.

Why else, in the name of any imaginable logic, human or devilish, should he, a stranger, be singled out for this experience? What could it mean to him, how was he related to it, what bearing had it on his case?... Unless, indeed, it was just because he was a stranger—a stranger everywhere—because he had no personal life, no warm screen of private egotisms to shield him from exposure, that he had developed this abnormal sensitiveness to the vicissitudes of others. The thought pulled him up with a shudder. No! Such a fate was too abominable; all that was strong and sound in him rejected it. A thousand times better regard himself as ill, disorganised, deluded, than as the predestined victim of such warnings!

He reached the gates and paused before the darkened lodge. The wind had risen and was sweeping the snow into his face. The cold had him in its grasp again, and he stood uncertain. Should he put his sanity to the test and go back? He turned and looked down the dark drive to the house. A single ray shone through the trees, evoking a picture of the lights, the flowers, the faces grouped about that fatal room. He turned and plunged out into the road…

He remembered that, about a mile from Overdale, the coachman had pointed out the road to Northridge; and he began to walk in that direction. Once in the road he had the gale in his face, and the wet snow on his moustache and eyelashes instantly hardened to ice. The same ice seemed to be driving a million blades into his throat and lungs, but he pushed on, the vision of the warm room pursuing him.

The snow in the road was deep and uneven. He stumbled across ruts and sank into drifts, and the wind drove against him like a granite cliff. Now and then he stopped, gasping, as if an invisible hand had tightened an iron band about his body; then he started again, stiffening himself against the stealthy penetration of the cold. The snow continued to descend out of a pall of inscrutable darkness, and once or twice he paused, fearing he had missed the road to Northridge; but, seeing no sign of a turn, he ploughed on.

At last, feeling sure that he had walked for more than a mile, he halted and looked back. The act of turning brought immediate relief, first because it put his back to the wind, and then because, far down the road, it showed him the gleam of a lantern. A sleigh was coming—a sleigh that might perhaps give him a lift to the village! Fortified by the hope, he began to walk back toward the light. It came forward very slowly, with unaccountable zigzags and waverings; and even when he was within a few yards of it he could catch no sound of sleigh-bells. Then it paused and became stationary by the roadside, as though carried by a pedestrian who had stopped, exhausted by the cold. The thought made Faxon hasten on, and a moment later he was stooping over a motionless figure huddled against the snow-bank. The lantern had dropped from its bearer's hand, and Faxon, fearfully raising it, threw its light into the face of Frank Rainer.

"Rainer! What on earth are you doing here?"

The boy smiled back through his pallor. "What are *you*, I'd like to know?" he retorted; and, scrambling to his feet with a clutch on Faxon's arm, he added gaily: "Well, I've run you down!"

Faxon stood confounded, his heart sinking. The lad's face was grey.

"What madness—" he began.

"Yes, it *is*. What on earth did you do it for?"

"I? Do what?... Why I... I was just taking a walk... I often walk at night..."

Frank Rainer burst into a laugh. "On such nights? Then you hadn't bolted?"

"Bolted?"

"Because I'd done something to offend you? My uncle thought you had."

Faxon grasped his arm. "Did your uncle send you after me?"

"Well, he gave me an awful rowing for not going up to your room with you when you said you were ill. And when we found you'd gone we were frightened—and he was awfully upset—so I said I'd catch you... You're *not* ill, are you?"

"Ill? No. Never better." Faxon picked up the lantern. "Come; let's go back. It was awfully hot in that dining-room."

"Yes; I hoped it was only that."

They trudged on in silence for a few minutes; then Faxon questioned: "You're not too done up?"

"Oh, no. It's a lot easier with the wind behind us."

"All right. Don't talk any more."

They pushed ahead, walking, in spite of the light that guided them, more slowly than Faxon had walked alone into the gale. The fact of his companion's stumbling against a drift gave Faxon a pretext for saying: "Take hold of my arm," and Rainer obeying, gasped out: "I'm blown!"

"So am I. Who wouldn't be?"

"What a dance you led me! If it hadn't been for one of the servants happening to see you—"

"Yes; all right. And now, won't you kindly shut up?"

Rainer laughed and hung on him. "Oh, the cold doesn't hurt me…"

For the first few minutes after Rainer had overtaken him, anxiety for the lad had been Faxon's only thought. But as each labouring step carried them nearer to the spot he had been fleeing, the reasons for his flight grew more ominous and more insistent. No, he was not ill, he was not distraught and deluded—he was the instrument singled out to warn and save; and here he was, irresistibly driven, dragging the victim back to his doom!

The intensity of the conviction had almost checked his steps. But what could he do or say? At all costs he must get Rainer out of the cold, into the house and into his bed. After that he would act.

The snow-fall was thickening, and as they reached a stretch of the road between open fields the wind took them at an angle, lashing their faces with barbed thongs. Rainer stopped to take breath, and Faxon felt the heavier pressure of his arm.

"When we get to the lodge, can't we telephone to the stable for a sleigh?"

"If they're not all asleep at the lodge."

"Oh, I'll manage. Don't talk!" Faxon ordered; and they plodded on...

At length the lantern ray showed ruts that curved away from the road under tree-darkness.

Faxon's spirits rose. "There's the gate! We'll be there in five minutes."

As he spoke he caught, above the boundary hedge, the gleam of a light at the farther end of the dark avenue. It was the same light that had shone on the scene of which every detail was burnt into his brain; and he felt again its overpowering reality. No—he couldn't let the boy go back!

They were at the lodge at last, and Faxon was hammering on the door. He said to himself: "I'll get him inside first, and make them give him a hot drink. Then I'll see—I'll find an argument..."

There was no answer to his knocking, and after an interval Rainer said: "Look here—we'd better go on."

"No!"

"I can, perfectly—"

"You shan't go to the house, I say!" Faxon redoubled his blows, and at length steps sounded on the stairs. Rainer was leaning against the lintel, and as the door opened the light from the hall flashed on his pale face and fixed eyes. Faxon caught him by the arm and drew him in.

"It *was* cold out there," he sighed; and then, abruptly, as if invisible shears at a single stroke had cut every muscle in his body, he swerved, drooped on Faxon's arm, and seemed to sink into nothing at his feet.

The lodge-keeper and Faxon bent over him, and somehow, between them, lifted him into the kitchen and laid him on a sofa by the stove.

The lodge-keeper, stammering: "I'll ring up the house," dashed out of the room. But Faxon heard the words without heeding them: omens mattered nothing now, beside this woe fulfilled. He knelt down to undo the fur collar about Rainer's throat, and as he did so he felt a warm moisture on his hands. He held them up, and they were red...

THE TRIUMPH OF NIGHT

V

The palms threaded their endless line along the yellow river. The little steamer lay at the wharf, and George Faxon, sitting in the verandah of the wooden hotel, idly watched the coolies carrying the freight across the gang-plank.

He had been looking at such scenes for two months. Nearly five had elapsed since he had descended from the train at Northridge and strained his eyes for the sleigh that was to take him to Weymore: Weymore, which he was never to behold!... Part of the interval—the first part—was still a great grey blur. Even now he could not be quite sure how he had got back to Boston, reached the house of a cousin, and been thence transferred to a quiet room looking out on snow under bare trees. He looked out a long time at the same scene, and finally one day a man he had known at Harvard came to see him and invited him to go out on a business trip to the Malay Peninsula.

"You've had a bad shake-up, and it'll do you no end of good to get away from things."

When the doctor came the next day it turned out that he knew of the plan and approved it. "You ought to be quiet for a year. Just loaf and look at the landscape," he advised.

Faxon felt the first faint stirrings of curiosity.

"What's been the matter with me, anyway?"

"Well, overwork, I suppose. You must have been bottling up for a bad breakdown before you started for New Hampshire last December. And the shock of that poor boy's death did the rest."

Ah, yes—Rainer had died. He remembered...

He started for the East, and gradually, by imperceptible degrees, life crept back into his weary bones and leaden brain. His friend was patient and considerate, and they travelled slowly and talked little. At first Faxon had felt a great shrinking from whatever touched on familiar things. He seldom looked at a newspaper and he never opened a letter without a contraction of the heart. It was not that he had any special cause for apprehension, but merely that a great trail of darkness lay on everything. He had looked too deep down into the abyss… But little by little health and energy returned to him, and with them the common promptings of curiosity. He was beginning to wonder how the world was going, and when, presently, the hotel-keeper told him there were no letters for him in the steamer's mail-bag, he felt a distinct sense of disappointment. His friend had gone into the jungle on a long excursion, and he was lonely, unoccupied and wholesomely bored. He got up and strolled into the stuffy reading-room.

There he found a game of dominoes, a mutilated picture-puzzle, some copies of *Zion's Herald* and a pile of New York and London newspapers.

He began to glance through the papers, and was disappointed to find that they were less recent than he had hoped. Evidently the last numbers had been carried off by luckier travellers. He continued to turn them over, picking out the American ones first. These, as it happened, were the oldest: they dated back to December and January. To Faxon, however, they had all the flavour of novelty, since they covered the precise period during which he had virtually ceased to exist. It had never before occurred to him to wonder what had happened in the world during that interval of obliteration; but now he felt a sudden desire to know.

To prolong the pleasure, he began by sorting the papers chronologically, and as he found and spread out the earliest number, the date at the top of the page entered into his consciousness like a key slipping into a lock. It was the seventeenth of December: the date of the day after his arrival at Northridge. He glanced at the first page and read in blazing characters: "Reported Failure of Opal Cement Company. Lavington's name involved. Gigantic Exposure of Corruption Shakes Wall Street to Its Foundations."

He read on, and when he had finished the first paper he turned to the next. There was a gap of three days, but the Opal Cement "Investigation" still held the centre of the stage. From its complex revelations of greed and ruin his eye wandered to the death notices, and he read: "Rainer. Suddenly, at Northridge, New Hampshire, Francis John, only son of the late…"

His eyes clouded, and he dropped the newspaper and sat for a long time with his face in his hands. When he looked up again he noticed that his gesture had pushed the other papers from the table and scattered them at his feet. The uppermost lay spread out before him, and heavily his eyes began their search again. "John Lavington comes forward with plan for reconstructing Company. Offers to put in ten millions of his own—The proposal under consideration by the District Attorney."

Ten millions… ten millions of his own. But if John Lavington was ruined?… Faxon stood up with a cry. That was it, then—that was what the warning meant! And if he had not fled from it, dashed wildly away from it into the night, he might have broken the spell of iniquity, the powers of darkness might not have prevailed! He caught up the pile of newspapers and began to glance through each in turn for the headline: "Wills Admitted to Probate." In the last of all he found the paragraph he sought, and it stared up at him as if with Rainer's dying eyes.

That—*that* was what he had done! The powers of pity had singled him out to warn and save, and he had closed his ears to their call, and washed his hands of it, and fled. Washed his hands of it! That was the word. It caught him back to the dreadful moment in the lodge when, raising himself up from Rainer's side, he had looked at his hands and seen that they were red…

BEWITCHED

I

THE snow was still falling thickly when Orrin Bosworth, who farmed the land south of Lonetop, drove up in his cutter to Saul Rutledge's gate. He was surprised to see two other cutters ahead of him. From them descended two muffled figures. Bosworth, with increasing surprise, recognised Deacon Hibben, from North Ashmore, and Sylvester Brand, the widower, from the old Bearcliff farm on the way to Lonetop.

It was not often that anybody in Hemlock County entered Saul Rutledge's gate; least of all in the dead of winter, and summoned (as Bosworth, at any rate, had been) by Mrs. Rutledge, who passed, even in that unsocial region, for a woman of cold manners and solitary character. The situation was enough to excite the curiosity of a less imaginative man than Orrin Bosworth.

As he drove in between the broken-down white gateposts topped by fluted urns the two men ahead of him were leading their horses to the adjoining shed. Bosworth followed, and hitched his horse to a post. Then the three tossed off the snow from their shoulders, clapped their numb hands together, and greeted each other.

"Hallo, Deacon."

"Well, well, Orrin—." They shook hands.

"'Day, Bosworth," said Sylvester Brand, with a brief nod. He seldom put any cordiality into his manner, and on this occasion he was still busy about his horse's bridle and blanket.

Orrin Bosworth, the youngest and most communicative of the three, turned back to Deacon Hibben, whose long face, queerly blotched and mouldy-looking, with blinking peering eyes, was yet less forbidding than Brand's heavily-hewn countenance.

"Queer, our all meeting here this way. Mrs. Rutledge sent me a message to come," Bosworth volunteered.

The Deacon nodded. "I got a word from her too—Andy Pond come with it yesterday noon. I hope there's no trouble here—"

He glanced through the thickening fall of snow at the desolate front of the Rutledge house, the more melancholy in its present neglected state because, like the gateposts, it kept traces of former elegance. Bosworth had often wondered how such a house had come to be built in that lonely stretch between North Ashmore and Cold Corners. People said there had once been other houses like it, forming a little township called Ashmore, a sort of mountain colony created by the caprice of an English Royalist officer, one Colonel Ashmore, who had been murdered by the Indians, with all his family, long before the Revolution. This tale was confirmed by the fact that the ruined cellars of several smaller houses were still to be discovered under the wild growth of the adjoining slopes, and that the Communion plate of the moribund Episcopal church of Cold Corners was engraved with the name of Colonel Ashmore, who had given it to the church of Ashmore in the year 1723. Of the church itself no traces remained. Doubtless it had been a modest wooden edifice, built on piles, and the conflagration which had burnt the other houses to the ground's edge had reduced it utterly to ashes. The whole place, even in summer, wore a mournful solitary air, and people wondered why Saul Rutledge's father had gone there to settle.

"I never knew a place," Deacon Hibben said, "as seemed as far away from humanity. And yet it ain't so in miles."

"Miles ain't the only distance," Orrin Bosworth answered; and the two men, followed by Sylvester Brand, walked across the drive to the front door. People in Hemlock County did not usually come and go by their front doors, but all three men seemed to feel that, on an occasion which appeared to be so exceptional, the usual and more familiar approach by the kitchen would not be suitable.

They had judged rightly; the Deacon had hardly lifted the knocker when the door opened and Mrs. Rutledge stood before them.

"Walk right in," she said in her usual dead-level tone; and Bosworth, as he followed the others, thought to himself: "Whatever's happened, she's not going to let it show in her face."

It was doubtful, indeed, if anything unwonted could be made to show in Prudence Rutledge's face, so limited was its scope, so fixed were its features. She was dressed for the occasion in a black calico with white spots, a collar of crochet-lace fastened by a gold brooch, and a grey woollen shawl crossed under her arms and tied at the back. In her small narrow head the only marked prominence was that of the brow projecting roundly over pale spectacled eyes. Her dark hair, parted above this prominence, passed tight and flat over the tips of her ears into a small braided coil at the nape; and her contracted head looked still narrower from being perched on a long hollow neck with cord-like throat-muscles. Her eyes were of a pale cold grey, her complexion was an even white. Her age might have been anywhere from thirty-five to sixty.

The room into which she led the three men had probably been the dining-room of the Ashmore house. It was now used as a front parlour, and a black stove planted on a sheet of zinc stuck out from the delicately fluted panels of an old wooden mantel. A newly-lit fire smouldered reluctantly, and the room was at once close and bitterly cold.

"Andy Pond," Mrs. Rutledge cried to some one at the back of the house, "step out and call Mr. Rutledge. You'll likely find him in the wood-shed, or round the barn somewheres." She rejoined her visitors. "Please suit yourselves to seats," she said.

The three men, with an increasing air of constraint, took the chairs she pointed out, and Mrs. Rutledge sat stiffly down upon a fourth, behind a rickety bead-work table. She glanced from one to the other of her visitors.

"I presume you folks are wondering what it is I asked you to come here for," she said in her dead-level voice. Orrin Bosworth and Deacon Hibben murmured an assent; Sylvester Brand sat silent, his eyes, under their great thicket of eyebrows, fixed on the huge boot-tip swinging before him.

"Well, I allow you didn't expect it was for a party," continued Mrs. Rutledge.

No one ventured to respond to this chill pleasantry, and she continued: "We're in trouble here, and that's the fact. And we need advice—Mr. Rutledge and myself do." She cleared her throat, and added in a lower tone, her pitilessly clear eyes looking straight before her: "There's a spell been cast over Mr. Rutledge."

The Deacon looked up sharply, an incredulous smile pinching his thin lips. "A spell?"

"That's what I said: he's bewitched."

Again the three visitors were silent; then Bosworth, more at ease or less tongue-tied than the others, asked with an attempt at humour: "Do you use the word in the strict Scripture sense, Mrs. Rutledge?"

She glanced at him before replying: "That's how *he* uses it."

The Deacon coughed and cleared his long rattling throat. "Do you care to give us more particulars before your husband joins us?"

Mrs. Rutledge looked down at her clasped hands, as if considering the question. Bosworth noticed that the inner fold of her lids was of the same uniform white as the rest of her skin, so that when she dropped them her rather prominent eyes looked like the sightless orbs of a marble statue. The impression was unpleasing, and he glanced away at the text over the mantelpiece, which read:

The Soul That Sinneth It Shall Die.

"No," she said at length, "I'll wait."

At this moment Sylvester Brand suddenly stood up and pushed back his chair. "I don't know," he said, in his rough bass voice, "as I've got any particular lights on Bible mysteries; and this happens to be the day I was to go down to Starkfield to close a deal with a man."

Mrs. Rutledge lifted one of her long thin hands. Withered and wrinkled by hard work and cold, it was nevertheless of the same leaden white as her face. "You won't be kept long," she said. "Won't you be seated?"

Farmer Brand stood irresolute, his purplish underlip twitching. "The Deacon here—such things is more in his line…"

"I want you should stay," said Mrs. Rutledge quietly; and Brand sat down again.

A silence fell, during which the four persons present seemed all to be listening for the sound of a step; but none was heard, and after a minute or two Mrs. Rutledge began to speak again.

"It's down by that old shack on Lamer's pond; that's where they meet," she said suddenly.

Bosworth, whose eyes were on Sylvester Brand's face, fancied he saw a sort of inner flush darken the farmer's heavy leathern skin. Deacon Hibben leaned forward, a glitter of curiosity in his eyes.

"They—*who*, Mrs. Rutledge?"

"My husband, Saul Rutledge… and her…"

Sylvester Brand again stirred in his seat. "Who do you mean by *her*?" he asked abruptly, as if roused out of some far-off musing.

Mrs. Rutledge's body did not move; she simply revolved her head on her long neck and looked at him.

"Your daughter, Sylvester Brand."

The man staggered to his feet with an explosion of inarticulate sounds. "My—my daughter? What the hell are you talking about? My daughter? It's a damned lie… it's… it's…"

"Your daughter *Ora*, Mr. Brand," said Mrs. Rutledge slowly.

Bosworth felt an icy chill down his spine. Instinctively he turned his eyes away from Brand, and they rested on the mildewed countenance of Deacon Hibben. Between the blotches it had become as white as Mrs. Rutledge's, and the Deacon's eyes burned in the whiteness like live embers among ashes.

Brand gave a laugh: the rusty creaking laugh of one whose springs of mirth are never moved by gaiety. "My daughter *Ora?*" he repeated.

"Yes."

"My *dead* daughter?"

"That's what he says."

"Your husband?"

"That's what Mr. Rutledge says."

Orrin Bosworth listened with a sense of suffocation; he felt as if he were wrestling with long-armed horrors in a dream. He could no longer resist letting his eyes return to Sylvester Brand's face. To his surprise it had resumed a natural imperturbable expression. Brand rose to his feet. "Is that all?" he queried contemptuously.

"All? Ain't it enough? How long is it since you folks seen Saul Rutledge, any of you?" Mrs. Rutledge flew out at them.

Bosworth, it appeared, had not seen him for nearly a year; the Deacon had only run across him once, for a minute, at the North Ashmore post office, the previous autumn, and acknowledged that he wasn't looking any too good then. Brand said nothing, but stood irresolute.

"Well, if you wait a minute you'll see with your own eyes; and he'll tell you with his own words. That's what I've got you here for—to see for yourselves what's come over him. Then you'll talk different," she added, twisting her head abruptly toward Sylvester Brand.

The Deacon raised a lean hand of interrogation.

"Does your husband know we've been sent for on this business, Mrs. Rutledge?"

Mrs. Rutledge signed assent.

"It was with his consent, then—?"

She looked coldly at her questioner. "I guess it had to be," she said. Again Bosworth felt the chill down his spine. He tried to dissipate the sensation by speaking with an affectation of energy.

"Can you tell us, Mrs. Rutledge, how this trouble you speak of shows itself… what makes you think…?"

She looked at him for a moment; then she leaned forward across the rickety bead-work table. A thin smile of disdain narrowed her colourless lips. "I don't think—I know."

"Well—but how?"

She leaned closer, both elbows on the table, her voice dropping. "I seen 'em."

In the ashen light from the veiling of snow beyond the windows the Deacon's little screwed-up eyes seemed to give out red sparks. "Him and the dead?"

"Him and the dead."

"Saul Rutledge and—and Ora Brand?"

"That's so."

Sylvester Brand's chair fell backward with a crash. He was on his feet again, crimson and cursing. "It's a God-damned fiend-begotten lie…"

"Friend Brand… friend Brand…" the Deacon protested.

"Here, let me get out of this. I want to see Saul Rutledge himself, and tell him—"

"Well, here he is," said Mrs. Rutledge.

The outer door had opened; they heard the familiar stamping and shaking of a man who rids his garments of their last snowflakes before penetrating to the sacred precincts of the best parlour. Then Saul Rutledge entered.

II

As he came in he faced the light from the north window, and Bosworth's first thought was that he looked like a drowned man fished out from under the ice—"self-drowned," he added. But the snow-light plays cruel tricks with a man's colour, and even with the shape of his features; it must have been partly that, Bosworth reflected, which transformed Saul Rutledge from the straight muscular fellow he had been a year before into the haggard wretch now before them.

The Deacon sought for a word to ease the horror. "Well, now, Saul—you look's if you'd ought to set right up to the stove. Had a touch of ague, maybe?"

The feeble attempt was unavailing. Rutledge neither moved nor answered. He stood among them silent, incommunicable, like one risen from the dead.

Brand grasped him roughly by the shoulder. "See here, Saul Rutledge, what's this dirty lie your wife tells us you've been putting about?"

Still Rutledge did not move. "It's no lie," he said.

Brand's hand dropped from his shoulder. In spite of the man's rough bullying power he seemed to be undefinably awed by Rutledge's look and tone.

"No lie? You've gone plumb crazy, then, have you?"

Mrs. Rutledge spoke. "My husband's not lying, nor he ain't gone crazy. Don't I tell you I seen 'em?"

Brand laughed again. "Him and the dead?"

"Yes."

"Down by the Lamer pond, you say?"

"Yes."

"And when was that, if I might ask?"

"Day before yesterday."

A silence fell on the strangely assembled group. The Deacon at length broke it to say to Mr. Brand: "Brand, in my opinion we've got to see this thing through."

Brand stood for a moment in speechless contemplation: there was something animal and primitive about him, Bosworth thought, as he hung thus, lowering and dumb, a little foam beading the corners of that heavy purplish underlip. He let himself slowly down into his chair. "I'll see it through."

The two other men and Mrs. Rutledge had remained seated. Saul Rutledge stood before them, like a prisoner at the bar, or rather like a sick man before the physicians who were to heal him. As Bosworth scrutinised that hollow face, so wan under the dark sunburn, so sucked inward and consumed by some hidden fever, there stole over the sound healthy man the thought that perhaps, after all, husband and wife spoke the truth, and that they were all at that moment really standing on the edge of some forbidden mystery. Things that the rational mind would reject without a thought seemed no longer so easy to dispose of as one looked at the actual Saul Rutledge and remembered the man he had been a year before. Yes; as the Deacon said, they would have to see it through…

"Sit down then, Saul; draw up to us, won't you?" the Deacon suggested, trying again for a natural tone.

Mrs. Rutledge pushed a chair forward, and her husband sat down on it. He stretched out his arms and grasped his knees in his brown bony fingers; in that attitude he remained, turning neither his head nor his eyes.

"Well, Saul," the Deacon continued, "your wife says you thought mebbe we could do something to help you through this trouble, whatever it is."

Rutledge's grey eyes widened a little. "No; I didn't think that. It was her idea to try what could be done."

"I presume, though, since you've agreed to our coming, that you don't object to our putting a few questions?"

Rutledge was silent for a moment; then he said with a visible effort: "No; I don't object."

"Well—you've heard what your wife says?"

Rutledge made a slight motion of assent.

"And—what have you got to answer? How do you explain…?"

Mrs. Rutledge intervened. "How can he explain? I seen 'em."

There was a silence; then Bosworth, trying to speak in an easy reassuring tone, queried: "That so, Saul?"

"That's so."

Brand lifted up his brooding head. "You mean to say you... you sit here before us all and say..."

The Deacon's hand again checked him. "Hold on, friend Brand. We're all of us trying for the facts, ain't we?" He turned to Rutledge. "We've heard what Mrs. Rutledge says. What's your answer?"

"I don't know as there's any answer. She found us."

"And you mean to tell me the person with you was... was what you took to be..." the Deacon's thin voice grew thinner: "Ora Brand?"

Saul Rutledge nodded.

"You knew... or thought you knew... you were meeting with the dead?"

Rutledge bent his head again. The snow continued to fall in a steady unwavering sheet against the window, and Bosworth felt as if a winding-sheet were descending from the sky to envelop them all in a common grave.

"Think what you're saying! It's against our religion! Ora... poor child!... died over a year ago. I saw you at her funeral, Saul. How can you make such a statement?"

"What else can he do?" thrust in Mrs. Rutledge.

There was another pause. Bosworth's resources had failed him, and Brand once more sat plunged in dark meditation. The Deacon laid his quivering finger-tips together, and moistened his lips.

"Was the day before yesterday the first time?" he asked.

The movement of Rutledge's head was negative.

"Not the first? Then when..."

"Nigh on a year ago, I reckon."

"God! And you mean to tell us that ever since—?"

"Well... look at him," said his wife. The three men lowered their eyes.

After a moment Bosworth, trying to collect himself, glanced at the Deacon. "Why not ask Saul to make his own statement, if that's what we're here for?"

"That's so," the Deacon assented. He turned to Rutledge. "Will you try and give us your idea… of… of how it began?"

There was another silence. Then Rutledge tightened his grasp on his gaunt knees, and still looking straight ahead, with his curiously clear unseeing gaze: "Well," he said, "I guess it begun away back, afore even I was married to Mrs. Rutledge…" He spoke in a low automatic tone, as if some invisible agent were dictating his words, or even uttering them for him. "You know," he added, "Ora and me was to have been married."

Sylvester Brand lifted his head. "Straighten that statement out first, please," he interjected.

"What I mean is, we kept company. But Ora she was very young. Mr. Brand here he sent her away. She was gone nigh to three years, I guess. When she come back I was married."

"That's right," Brand said, relapsing once more into his sunken attitude.

"And after she came back did you meet her again?" the Deacon continued.

"Alive?" Rutledge questioned.

A perceptible shudder ran through the room.

"Well—of course," said the Deacon nervously.

Rutledge seemed to consider. "Once I did—only once. There was a lot of other people round. At Cold Corners fair it was."

"Did you talk with her then?"

"Only a minute."

"What did she say?"

His voice dropped. "She said she was sick and knew she was going to die, and when she was dead she'd come back to me."

"And what did you answer?"

"Nothing."

"Did you think anything of it at the time?"

"Well, no. Not till I heard she was dead I didn't. After that I thought of it—and I guess she drew me." He moistened his lips.

"Drew you down to that abandoned house by the pond?"

Rutledge made a faint motion of assent, and the Deacon added: "How did you know it was there she wanted you to come?"

"She... just drew me..."

There was a long pause. Bosworth felt, on himself and the other two men, the oppressive weight of the next question to be asked. Mrs. Rutledge opened and closed her narrow lips once or twice, like some beached shellfish gasping for the tide. Rutledge waited.

"Well, now, Saul, won't you go on with what you was telling us?" the Deacon at length suggested.

"That's all. There's nothing else."

The Deacon lowered his voice. "She just draws you?"

"Yes."

"Often?"

"That's as it happens..."

"But if it's always there she draws you, man, haven't you the strength to keep away from the place?"

For the first time, Rutledge wearily turned his head toward his questioner. A spectral smile narrowed his colourless lips. "Ain't any use. She follers after me..."

There was another silence. What more could they ask, then and there? Mrs. Rutledge's presence checked the next question. The Deacon seemed hopelessly to revolve the matter. At length he spoke in a more authoritative tone. "These are forbidden things. You know that, Saul. Have you tried prayer?"

Rutledge shook his head.

"Will you pray with us now?"

Rutledge cast a glance of freezing indifference on his spiritual adviser. "If you folks want to pray, I'm agreeable," he said. But Mrs. Rutledge intervened.

"Prayer ain't any good. In this kind of thing it ain't no manner of use; you know it ain't. I called you here, Deacon, because you remember the last case in this parish. Thirty years ago it was, I guess; but you remember. Lefferts

Nash—did praying help *him*? I was a little girl then, but I used to hear my folks talk of it winter nights. Lefferts Nash and Hannah Cory. They drove a stake through her breast. That's what cured him."

"Oh—" Orrin Bosworth exclaimed.

Sylvester Brand raised his head. "You're speaking of that old story as if this was the same sort of thing?"

"Ain't it? Ain't my husband pining away the same as Lefferts Nash did? The Deacon here knows—"

The Deacon stirred anxiously in his chair. "These are forbidden things," he repeated. "Supposing your husband is quite sincere in thinking himself haunted, as you might say. Well, even then, what proof have we that the… the dead woman… is the spectre of that poor girl?"

"Proof? Don't he say so? Didn't she tell him? Ain't I seen 'em?" Mrs. Rutledge almost screamed.

The three men sat silent, and suddenly the wife burst out: "A stake through the breast! That's the old way; and it's the only way. The Deacon knows it!"

"It's against our religion to disturb the dead."

"Ain't it against your religion to let the living perish as my husband is perishing?" She sprang up with one of her abrupt movements and took the family Bible from the what-not in a corner of the parlour. Putting the book on the table, and moistening a livid finger-tip, she turned the pages rapidly, till she came to one on which she laid her hand like a stony paper-weight. "See here," she said, and read out in her level chanting voice:

"'Thou shalt not suffer a witch to live.'

"That's in Exodus, that's where it is," she added, leaving the book open as if to confirm the statement.

Bosworth continued to glance anxiously from one to the other of the four people about the table. He was younger than any of them, and had had more contact with the modern world; down in Starkfield, in the bar of the Fielding House, he could hear himself laughing with the rest of the men at such old wives' tales. But it was not for nothing that he had been born under the icy shadow of Lonetop, and had shivered and hungered as a lad through the bitter Hemlock County winters. After his parents died, and he had taken hold of the farm himself, he had got more out of it by using improved methods, and by supplying the increasing throng of summer-boarders over Stotesbury way with milk and vegetables. He had been made a selectman of North Ashmore; for so young a man he had a standing in the county. But the roots of the old life were still in him. He could remember, as a little boy, going twice a year with his mother to that bleak hill-farm out beyond Sylvester Brand's, where Mrs. Bosworth's aunt, Cressidora Cheney, had been shut up for years in a cold clean room with iron bars in the windows. When little Orrin first saw Aunt Cressidora she was a small white old woman, whom her sisters used to "make decent" for visitors the day that Orrin and his mother were expected. The child wondered why there were bars to the window. "Like a canary-bird," he said to his mother. The phrase made Mrs. Bosworth reflect. "I do believe they keep Aunt Cressidora too lonesome," she said; and the next time she went up the mountain with the little boy he carried to his great-aunt a canary in a little wooden cage. It was a great excitement; he knew it would make her happy.

The old woman's motionless face lit up when she saw the bird, and her eyes began to glitter. "It belongs to me," she said instantly, stretching her soft bony hand over the cage.

"Of course it does, Aunt Cressy," said Mrs. Bosworth, her eyes filling.

But the bird, startled by the shadow of the old woman's hand, began to flutter and beat its wings distractedly. At the sight, Aunt Cressidora's calm face suddenly became a coil of twitching features. "You she-devil, you!" she cried in a high squealing voice; and thrusting her hand into the cage she dragged out the terrified bird and wrung its neck. She was plucking the hot body, and squealing "she-devil, she-devil!" as they drew little Orrin from the room. On the way down the mountain his mother wept a great deal, and said: "You must never tell anybody that poor Auntie's crazy, or the men would come and take her down to the asylum at Starkfield, and the shame of it would kill us all. Now promise." The child promised.

He remembered the scene now, with its deep fringe of mystery, secrecy and rumour. It seemed related to a great many other things below the surface of his thoughts, things which stole up anew, making him feel that all the old people he had known, and who "believed in these things," might after all be right. Hadn't a witch been burned at North Ashmore? Didn't the summer folk still drive over in jolly buckboard loads to see the meeting-house where the trial had been held, the pond where they had ducked her and she had floated?... Deacon Hibben believed; Bosworth was sure of it. If he didn't, why did people from all over the place come to him when their animals had queer sicknesses, or when there was a child in the family that had to be kept shut up because it fell down flat and foamed? Yes, in spite of his religion, Deacon Hibben *knew*...

And Brand? Well, it came to Bosworth in a flash: that North Ashmore woman who was burned had the name of Brand. The same stock, no doubt; there had been Brands in Hemlock County ever since the white men had come there. And Orrin, when he was a child, remembered hearing his parents say that Sylvester Brand hadn't ever oughter married his own cousin, because of the blood. Yet the couple had had two healthy girls, and when Mrs. Brand pined away and died nobody suggested that anything had been wrong with her mind. And Vanessa and Ora were the handsomest girls anywhere round. Brand knew it, and scrimped and saved all he could to send Ora, the eldest, down to Starkfield to learn book-keeping. "When she's married I'll send you," he used to say to little Venny, who was his favourite. But Ora never married. She was away three years, during which Venny ran wild on the slopes of Lonetop; and when Ora came back she sickened and died—poor girl! Since then Brand had grown more savage and morose. He was a hard-working farmer, but there wasn't much to be got out of those barren Bearcliff acres. He was said to have taken to drink since his wife's death; now and then men ran across him in the "dives" of

Stotesbury. But not often. And between times he laboured hard on his stony acres and did his best for his daughters. In the neglected graveyard of Cold Corners there was a slanting head-stone marked with his wife's name; near it, a year since, he had laid his eldest daughter. And sometimes, at dusk, in the autumn, the village people saw him walk slowly by, turn in between the graves, and stand looking down on the two stones. But he never brought a flower there, or planted a bush; nor Venny either. She was too wild and ignorant...

Mrs. Rutledge repeated: "That's in Exodus."

The three visitors remained silent, turning about their hats in reluctant hands. Rutledge faced them, still with that empty pellucid gaze which frightened Bosworth. What was he seeing?

"Ain't any of you folks got the grit—?" his wife burst out again, half hysterically.

Deacon Hibben held up his hand. "That's no way, Mrs. Rutledge. This ain't a question of having grit. What we want first of all is... proof..."

"That's so," said Bosworth, with an explosion of relief, as if the words had lifted something black and crouching from his breast. Involuntarily the eyes of both men had turned to Brand. He stood there smiling grimly, but did not speak.

"Ain't it so, Brand?" the Deacon prompted him.

"Proof that spooks walk?" the other sneered.

"Well—I presume you want this business settled too?"

The old farmer squared his shoulders. "Yes—I do. But I ain't a sperritualist. How the hell are you going to settle it?"

Deacon Hibben hesitated; then he said, in a low incisive tone: "I don't see but one way—Mrs. Rutledge's."

There was a silence.

"What?" Brand sneered again. "Spying?"

The Deacon's voice sank lower. "If the poor girl *does* walk... her that's your child... wouldn't you be the first to want her laid quiet? We all know there've been such cases… mysterious visitations… Can any one of us here deny it?"

"I seen 'em," Mrs. Rutledge interjected.

There was another heavy pause. Suddenly Brand fixed his gaze on Rutledge. "See here, Saul Rutledge, you've got to clear up this damned calumny, or I'll know why. You say my dead girl comes to you." He laboured with his breath, and then jerked out: "When? You tell me that, and I'll be there."

Rutledge's head drooped a little, and his eyes wandered to the window. "Round about sunset, mostly."

"You know beforehand?"

Rutledge made a sign of assent.

"Well, then—tomorrow, will it be?"

Rutledge made the same sign.

Brand turned to the door. "I'll be there." That was all he said. He strode out between them without another glance or word. Deacon Hibben looked at Mrs. Rutledge. "We'll be there too," he said, as if she had asked him; but she had not spoken, and Bosworth saw that her thin body was trembling all over. He was glad when he and Hibben were out again in the snow.

III

They thought that Brand wanted to be left to himself, and to give him time to unhitch his horse they made a pretence of hanging about in the doorway while Bosworth searched his pockets for a pipe he had no mind to light.

But Brand turned back to them as they lingered. "You'll meet me down by Lamer's pond tomorrow?" he suggested. "I want witnesses. Round about sunset."

They nodded their acquiescence, and he got into his sleigh, gave the horse a cut across the flanks, and drove off under the snow-smothered hemlocks. The other two men went to the shed.

"What do you make of this business, Deacon?" Bosworth asked, to break the silence.

The Deacon shook his head. "The man's a sick man—that's sure. Something's sucking the life clean out of him."

But already, in the biting outer air, Bosworth was getting himself under better control. "Looks to me like a bad case of the ague, as you said."

"Well—ague of the mind, then. It's his brain that's sick."

Bosworth shrugged. "He ain't the first in Hemlock County."

"That's so," the Deacon agreed. "It's a worm in the brain, solitude is."

"Well, we'll know this time tomorrow, maybe," said Bosworth. He scrambled into his sleigh, and was driving off in his turn when he heard his companion calling after him. The Deacon explained that his horse had cast a shoe; would Bosworth drive him down to the forge near North Ashmore, if it wasn't too much out of his way? He didn't want the mare slipping about on the freezing snow, and he could probably get the blacksmith to drive him back and shoe her in Rutledge's shed. Bosworth made room for him under the bearskin, and the two men drove off, pursued by a puzzled whinny from the Deacon's old mare.

The road they took was not the one that Bosworth would have followed to reach his own home. But he did not mind that. The shortest way to the forge passed close by Lamer's pond, and Bosworth, since he was in for the business, was not sorry to look the ground over. They drove on in silence.

The snow had ceased, and a green sunset was spreading upward into the crystal sky. A stinging wind barbed with ice-flakes caught them in the face on the open ridges, but when they dropped down into the hollow by Lamer's pond the air was as soundless and empty as an unswung bell. They jogged along slowly, each thinking his own thoughts.

"That's the house… that tumble-down shack over there, I suppose?" the Deacon said, as the road drew near the edge of the frozen pond.

"Yes: that's the house. A queer hermit-fellow built it years ago, my father used to tell me. Since then I don't believe it's ever been used but by the gipsies."

Bosworth had reined in his horse, and sat looking through pine-trunks purpled by the sunset at the crumbling structure. Twilight already lay under the trees, though day lingered in the open. Between two sharply-patterned pine-boughs he saw the evening star, like a white boat in a sea of green.

His gaze dropped from that fathomless sky and followed the blue-white undulations of the snow. It gave him a curious agitated feeling to think that here, in this icy solitude, in the tumble-down house he had so often passed without heeding it, a dark mystery, too deep for thought, was being enacted. Down that very slope, coming from the graveyard at Cold Corners, the being they called "Ora" must pass toward the pond. His heart began to beat stiflingly. Suddenly he gave an exclamation: "Look!"

He had jumped out of the cutter and was stumbling up the bank toward the slope of snow. On it, turned in the direction of the house by the pond, he had detected a woman's foot-prints; two; then three; then more. The Deacon scrambled out after him, and they stood and stared.

"God—barefoot!" Hibben gasped. "Then it *is*… the dead…"

Bosworth said nothing. But he knew that no live woman would travel with naked feet across that freezing wilderness. Here, then, was the proof the Deacon had asked for—they held it. What should they do with it?

"Supposing we was to drive up nearer—round the turn of the pond, till we get close to the house," the Deacon proposed in a colourless voice. "Mebbe then…"

Postponement was a relief. They got into the sleigh and drove on. Two or three hundred yards farther the road, a mere lane under steep bushy banks, turned sharply to the right, following the bend of the pond. As they rounded the turn they saw Brand's cutter ahead of them. It was empty, the horse tied to a tree-trunk. The two men looked at each other again. This was not Brand's nearest way home.

Evidently he had been actuated by the same impulse which had made them rein in their horse by the pond-side, and then hasten on to the deserted hovel. Had he too discovered those spectral foot-prints? Perhaps it was for that very reason that he had left his cutter and vanished in the direction of the house. Bosworth found himself shivering all over under his bearskin. "I wish to God the dark wasn't coming on," he muttered. He tethered his own horse near Brand's, and without a word he and the Deacon ploughed through the snow, in the track of Brand's huge feet. They had only a few yards to walk to overtake him. He did not hear them following him, and when Bosworth spoke his name, and he stopped short and turned, his heavy face was dim and confused, like a darker blot on the dusk. He looked at them dully, but without surprise.

"I wanted to see the place," he merely said.

The Deacon cleared his throat. "Just take a look… yes… We thought so… But I guess there won't be anything to *see*…" He attempted a chuckle.

The other did not seem to hear him, but laboured on ahead through the pines. The three men came out together in the cleared space before the house. As they emerged from beneath the trees they seemed to have left night behind. The evening star shed a lustre on the speckless snow, and Brand, in that lucid circle, stopped with a jerk, and pointed to the same light foot-prints turned toward the house—the track of a woman in the snow. He stood still, his face working. "Bare feet…" he said.

The Deacon piped up in a quavering voice: "The feet of the dead."

Brand remained motionless. "The feet of the dead," he echoed.

Deacon Hibben laid a frightened hand on his arm. "Come away now, Brand; for the love of God come away."

The father hung there, gazing down at those light tracks on the snow—light as fox or squirrel trails they seemed, on the white immensity. Bosworth thought to himself: "The living couldn't walk so light—not even Ora Brand couldn't have, when she lived…" The cold seemed to have entered into his very marrow. His teeth were chattering.

Brand swung about on them abruptly. "*Now!*" he said, moving on as if to an assault, his head bowed forward on his bull neck.

"Now—now? Not in there?" gasped the Deacon. "What's the use? It was tomorrow he said—." He shook like a leaf.

"It's now," said Brand. He went up to the door of the crazy house, pushed it inward, and meeting with an unexpected resistance, thrust his heavy shoulder against the panel. The door collapsed like a playing-card, and Brand stumbled after it into the darkness of the hut. The others, after a moment's hesitation, followed.

Bosworth was never quite sure in what order the events that succeeded took place. Coming in out of the snow-dazzle, he seemed to be plunging into total blackness. He groped his way across the threshold, caught a sharp splinter of the fallen door in his palm, seemed to see something white and wraithlike surge up out of the darkest corner of the hut, and then heard a revolver shot at his elbow, and a cry—

Brand had turned back, and was staggering past him out into the lingering daylight. The sunset, suddenly flushing through the trees, crimsoned his face like blood. He held a revolver in his hand and looked about him in his stupid way.

"They *do* walk, then," he said and began to laugh. He bent his head to examine his weapon. "Better here than in the churchyard. They shan't dig her up *now*," he shouted out. The two men caught him by the arms, and Bosworth got the revolver away from him.

IV

The next day Bosworth's sister Loretta, who kept house for him, asked him, when he came in for his midday dinner, if he had heard the news.

Bosworth had been sawing wood all the morning, and in spite of the cold and the driving snow, which had begun again in the night, he was covered with an icy sweat, like a man getting over a fever.

"What news?"

"Venny Brand's down sick with pneumonia. The Deacon's been there. I guess she's dying."

Bosworth looked at her with listless eyes. She seemed far off from him, miles away. "Venny Brand?" he echoed.

"You never liked her, Orrin."

"She's a child. I never knew much about her."

"Well," repeated his sister, with the guileless relish of the unimaginative for bad news, "I guess she's dying." After a pause she added: "It'll kill Sylvester Brand, all alone up there."

Bosworth got up and said: "I've got to see to poulticing the grey's fetlock." He walked out into the steadily falling snow.

Venny Brand was buried three days later. The Deacon read the service; Bosworth was one of the pall-bearers. The whole countryside turned out, for the snow had stopped falling, and at any season a funeral offered an opportunity for an outing that was not to be missed. Besides, Venny Brand was young and handsome—at least some people thought her handsome, though she was so swarthy—and her dying like that, so suddenly, had the fascination of tragedy.

"They say her lungs filled right up... Seems she'd had bronchial troubles before... I always said both them girls was frail... Look at Ora, how she took and wasted away! And it's colder'n all outdoors up there to Brand's... Their mother, too, *she* pined away just the same. They don't ever make old bones on the mother's side of the family... There's that young Bedlow over there; they say Venny was engaged to him... Oh, Mrs. Rutledge, excuse *me*... Step right into the pew; there's a seat for you alongside of grandma..."

Mrs. Rutledge was advancing with deliberate step down the narrow aisle of the bleak wooden church. She had on her best bonnet, a monumental structure which no one had seen out of her trunk since old Mrs. Silsee's funeral, three years before. All the women remembered it. Under its perpendicular pile her narrow face, swaying on the long thin neck, seemed whiter than ever; but her air of fretfulness had been composed into a suitable expression of mournful immobility.

"Looks as if the stone-mason had carved her to put atop of Venny's grave," Bosworth thought as she glided past him; and then shivered at his own sepulchral fancy. When she bent over her hymn book her lowered lids reminded him again of marble eyeballs; the bony hands clasping the book were bloodless. Bosworth had never seen such hands since he had seen old Aunt Cressidora Cheney strangle the canary-bird because it fluttered.

The service was over, the coffin of Venny Brand had been lowered into her sister's grave, and the neighbours were slowly dispersing. Bosworth, as pall-bearer, felt obliged to linger and say a word to the stricken father. He waited till Brand had turned from the grave with the Deacon at his side. The three men stood together for a moment; but not one of them spoke. Brand's face was the closed door of a vault, barred with wrinkles like bands of iron.

Finally the Deacon took his hand and said: "The Lord gave—"

Brand nodded and turned away toward the shed where the horses were hitched. Bosworth followed him. "Let me drive along home with you," he suggested.

Brand did not so much as turn his head. "Home? What home?" he said; and the other fell back.

Loretta Bosworth was talking with the other women while the men unblanketed their horses and backed the cutters out into the heavy snow. As Bosworth waited for her, a few feet off, he saw Mrs. Rutledge's tall bonnet lording it above the group. Andy Pond, the Rutledge farm-hand, was backing out the sleigh.

"Saul ain't here today, Mrs. Rutledge, is he?" one of the village elders piped, turning a benevolent old tortoise-head about on a loose neck, and blinking up into Mrs. Rutledge's marble face.

Bosworth heard her measure out her answer in slow incisive words. "No. Mr. Rutledge he ain't here. He would 'a' come for certain, but his aunt Minorca Cummins is being buried down to Stotesbury this very day and he had to go down there. Don't it sometimes seem zif we was all walking right in the Shadow of Death?"

As she walked toward the cutter, in which Andy Pond was already seated, the Deacon went up to her with visible hesitation. Involuntarily Bosworth also moved nearer. He heard the Deacon say: "I'm glad to hear that Saul is able to be up and around."

She turned her small head on her rigid neck, and lifted the lids of marble.

"Yes, I guess he'll sleep quieter now.—And *her* too, maybe, now she don't lay there alone any longer," she added in a low voice, with a sudden twist of her chin toward the fresh black stain in the graveyard snow. She got into the cutter, and said in a clear tone to Andy Pond: "'S long as we're down here I don't know but what I'll just call round and get a box of soap at Hiram Pringle's."

MISS MARY PASK

I

IT was not till the following spring that I plucked up courage to tell Mrs. Bridgeworth what had happened to me that night at Morgat.

In the first place, Mrs. Bridgeworth was in America; and after the night in question I lingered on abroad for several months—not for pleasure, God knows, but because of a nervous collapse supposed to be the result of having taken up my work again too soon after my touch of fever in Egypt. But, in any case, if I had been door to door with Grace Bridgeworth I could not have spoken of the affair before, to her or to any one else; not till I had been rest-cured and built up again at one of those wonderful Swiss sanatoria where they clean the cobwebs out of you. I could not even have written to her—not to save my life. The happenings of that night had to be overlaid with layer upon layer of time and forgetfulness before I could tolerate any return to them.

The beginning was idiotically simple; just the sudden reflex of a New England conscience acting on an enfeebled constitution. I had been painting in Brittany, in lovely but uncertain autumn weather, one day all blue and silver, the next shrieking gales or driving fog. There is a rough little white-washed inn out on the Pointe du Raz, swarmed over by tourists in summer but a sea-washed solitude in autumn; and there I was staying and trying to do waves, when some one said: "You ought to go over to Cape something else, beyond Morgat."

I went, and had a silver-and-blue day there; and on the way back the name of Morgat set up an unexpected association of ideas: Morgat—Grace Bridgeworth—Grace's sister, Mary Pask—"You know my darling Mary has a little place now near Morgat; if you ever go to Brittany do go to see her. She lives such a lonely life—it makes me so unhappy."

That was the way it came about. I had known Mrs. Bridgeworth well for years, but had only a hazy intermittent acquaintance with Mary Pask, her older and unmarried sister. Grace and she were greatly attached to each other, I knew; it had been Grace's chief sorrow, when she married my old friend Horace Bridgeworth, and went to live in New York, that Mary, from whom she had never before been separated, obstinately lingered on in Europe, where the two sisters had been travelling since their mother's death. I never quite understood why Mary Pask refused to join Grace in America. Grace said it was because she was "too artistic"—but, knowing the elder Miss Pask, and the extremely elementary nature of her interest in art, I wondered whether it were not rather because she disliked Horace Bridgeworth. There was a third alternative—more conceivable if one knew Horace—and that was that she may have liked him too much. But that again became untenable (at least I supposed it did) when one knew Miss Pask: Miss Pask with her round flushed face, her innocent bulging eyes, her old-maidish flat decorated with art-tidies, and her vague and timid philanthropy. Aspire to Horace—!

Well, it was all rather puzzling, or would have been if it had been interesting enough to be worth puzzling over. But it was not. Mary Pask was like hundreds of other dowdy old maids, cheerful derelicts content with their innumerable little substitutes for living. Even Grace would not have interested me particularly if she hadn't happened to marry one of my oldest friends, and to be kind to his friends. She was a handsome, capable and rather dull woman, absorbed in her husband and children, and without an ounce of imagination; and between her attachment to her sister and Mary Pask's worship of her there lay the inevitable gulf between the feelings of the sentimentally unemployed and those whose affections are satisfied. But a close intimacy had linked the two sisters before Grace's marriage, and Grace was one of the sweet conscientious women who go on using the language of devotion about people whom they live happily without seeing; so that when she said: "You know it's years since Mary and I have been together—not since little Molly was born. If only she'd come to America! Just think... Molly is six, and has never seen her darling auntie..." when she said this, and added: "If you go to Brittany promise me you'll look up my Mary," I was moved in that dim depth of one where unnecessary obligations are contracted.

And so it came about that, on that silver-and-blue afternoon, the idea "Morgat—Mary Pask—to please Grace" suddenly unlocked the sense of duty in me. Very well: I would chuck a few things into my bag, do my day's painting, go to see Miss Pask when the light faded, and spend the night at the inn at Morgat. To this end I ordered a rickety one-horse vehicle to await me at the inn when I got back from my painting, and in it I started out toward sunset to hunt for Mary Pask...

As suddenly as a pair of hands clapped over one's eyes, the sea-fog shut down on us. A minute before we had been driving over a wide bare upland, our backs turned to a sunset that crimsoned the road ahead; now the densest night enveloped us. No one had been able to tell me exactly where Miss Pask lived; but I thought it likely that I should find out at the fishers' hamlet toward which we were trying to make our way. And I was right... an old man in a doorway said: Yes—over the next rise, and then down a lane to the left that led to the sea; the American lady who always used to dress in white. Oh, *he* knew... near the *Baie des Trépassés*.

"Yes; but how can we see to find it? I don't know the place," grumbled the reluctant boy who was driving me.

"You will when we get there," I remarked.

"Yes—and the horse foundered meantime! I can't risk it, sir; I'll get into trouble with the *patron*."

Finally an opportune argument induced him to get out and lead the stumbling horse, and we continued on our way. We seemed to crawl on for a long time through a wet blackness impenetrable to the glimmer of our only lamp. But now and then the pall lifted or its folds divided; and then our feeble light would drag out of the night some perfectly commonplace object—a white gate, a cow's staring face, a heap of roadside stones—made portentous and incredible by being thus detached from its setting, capriciously thrust at us, and as suddenly withdrawn. After each of these projections the darkness grew three times as thick; and the sense I had had for some time of descending a gradual slope now became that of scrambling down a precipice. I jumped out hurriedly and joined my young driver at the horse's head.

"I can't go on—I won't, sir!" he whimpered.

"Why, see, there's a light over there—just ahead!"

The veil swayed aside, and we beheld two faintly illuminated squares in a low mass that was surely the front of a house.

"Get me as far as that—then you can go back if you like."

The veil dropped again; but the boy had seen the lights and took heart. Certainly there was a house ahead of us; and certainly it must be Miss Pask's, since there could hardly be two in such a desert. Besides, the old man in the hamlet had said: "Near the sea"; and those endless modulations of the ocean's voice, so familiar in every corner of the Breton land that one gets to measure distances by them rather than by visual means, had told me for some time past that we must be making for the shore. The boy continued to lead the horse on without making any answer. The fog had shut in more closely than ever, and our lamp merely showed us the big round drops of wet on the horse's shaggy quarters.

The boy stopped with a jerk. "There's no house—we're going straight down to the sea."

"But you saw those lights, didn't you?"

"I thought I did. But where are they now? The fog's thinner again. Look—I can make out trees ahead. But there are no lights any more."

"Perhaps the people have gone to bed," I suggested jocosely.

"Then hadn't we better turn back, sir?"

"What—two yards from the gate?"

The boy was silent: certainly there was a gate ahead, and presumably, behind the dripping trees, some sort of dwelling. Unless there was just a field and the sea... the sea whose hungry voice I heard asking and asking, close below us. No wonder the place was called the Bay of the Dead! But what could have induced the rosy benevolent Mary Pask to come and bury herself there? Of course the boy wouldn't wait for me... I knew that... the *Baie des Trépassés* indeed! The sea whined down there as if it were feeding-time, and the Furies, its keepers, had forgotten it...

There *was* the gate! My hand had struck against it. I felt along to the latch, undid it, and brushed between wet bushes to the house-front. Not a candle-glint anywhere. If the house were indeed Miss Pask's, she certainly kept early hours...

II

Night and fog were now one, and the darkness as thick as a blanket. I felt vainly about for a bell. At last my hand came in contact with a knocker and I lifted it. The clatter with which it fell sent a prolonged echo through the silence; but for a minute or two nothing else happened.

"There's no one there, I tell you!" the boy called impatiently from the gate.

But there was. I had heard no steps inside, but presently a bolt shot back, and an old woman in a peasant's cap pushed her head out. She had set her candle down on a table behind her, so that her face, aureoled with lacy wings, was in obscurity; but I knew she was old by the stoop of her shoulders and her fumbling movements. The candle-light, which made her invisible, fell full on my face, and she looked at me.

"This is Miss Mary Pask's house?"

"Yes, sir." Her voice—a very old voice—was pleasant enough, unsurprised and even friendly.

"I'll tell her," she added, shuffling off.

"Do you think she'll see me?" I threw after her.

"Oh, why not? The idea!" she almost chuckled. As she retreated I saw that she was wrapped in a shawl and had a cotton umbrella under her arm. Obviously she was going out—perhaps going home for the night. I wondered if Mary Pask lived all alone in her hermitage.

The old woman disappeared with the candle and I was left in total darkness. After an interval I heard a door shut at the back of the house and then a slow clumping of aged *sabots* along the flags outside. The old woman had evidently picked up her *sabots* in the kitchen and left the house. I wondered if she had told Miss Pask of my presence before going, or whether she had just left me there, the butt of some grim practical joke of her own. Certainly there was no sound within doors. The footsteps died out, I heard a gate click—then complete silence closed in again like the fog.

"I wonder—" I began within myself; and at that moment a smothered memory struggled abruptly to the surface of my languid mind.

"But she's *dead*—Mary Pask is *dead!*" I almost screamed it aloud in my amazement.

It was incredible, the tricks my memory had played on me since my fever! I had known for nearly a year that Mary Pask was dead—had died suddenly the previous autumn—and though I had been thinking of her almost continuously for the last two or three days it was only now that the forgotten fact of her death suddenly burst up again to consciousness.

Dead! But hadn't I found Grace Bridgeworth in tears and crape the very day I had gone to bid her goodbye before sailing for Egypt? Hadn't she laid the cable before my eyes, her own streaming with tears while I read: "Sister died suddenly this morning requested burial in garden of house particulars by letter"—with the signature of the American Consul at Brest, a friend of

Bridgeworth's I seemed to recall? I could see the very words of the message printed on the darkness before me.

As I stood there I was a good deal more disturbed by the discovery of the gap in my memory than by the fact of being alone in a pitch-dark house, either empty or else inhabited by strangers. Once before of late I had noted this queer temporary blotting-out of some well-known fact; and here was a second instance of it. Decidedly, I wasn't as well over my illness as the doctors had told me... Well, I would get back to Morgat and lie up there for a day or two, doing nothing, just eating and sleeping...

In my self-absorption I had lost my bearings, and no longer remembered where the door was. I felt in every pocket in turn for a match—but since the doctors had made me give up smoking, why should I have found one?

The failure to find a match increased my sense of irritated helplessness, and I was groping clumsily about the hall among the angles of unseen furniture when a light slanted along the rough-cast wall of the stairs. I followed its direction, and on the landing above me I saw a figure in white shading a candle with one hand and looking down. A chill ran along my spine, for the figure bore a strange resemblance to that of Mary Pask as I used to know her.

"Oh, it's *you!*" she exclaimed in the cracked twittering voice which was at one moment like an old woman's quaver, at another like a boy's falsetto. She came shuffling down in her baggy white garments, with her usual clumsy swaying movements; but I noticed that her steps on the wooden stairs were soundless. Well—they would be, naturally!

I stood without a word, gazing up at the strange vision above me, and saying to myself: "There's nothing there, nothing whatever. It's your digestion, or your eyes, or some damned thing wrong with you somewhere—"

But there was the candle, at any rate; and as it drew nearer, and lit up the place about me, I turned and caught hold of the door-latch. For, remember, I had seen the cable, and Grace in crape...

"Why, what's the matter? I assure you, you don't disturb me!" the white figure twittered; adding, with a faint laugh: "I don't have so many visitors nowadays—"

She had reached the hall, and stood before me, lifting her candle shakily and peering up into my face. "You haven't changed—not as much as I should have thought. But *I* have, haven't I?" she appealed to me with another laugh; and abruptly she laid her hand on my arm. I looked down at the hand, and thought to myself: "*That* can't deceive me."

I have always been a noticer of hands. The key to character that other people seek in the eyes, the mouth, the modelling of the skull, I find in the curve of the nails, the cut of the finger-tips, the way the palm, rosy or sallow, smooth or seamed, swells up from its base. I remembered Mary Pask's hand vividly because it was so like a caricature of herself; round, puffy, pink, yet prematurely old and useless. And there, unmistakably, it lay on my sleeve: but changed and shrivelled—somehow like one of those pale freckled toadstools that the least touch resolves to dust… Well—to dust? Of course…

I looked at the soft wrinkled fingers, with their foolish little oval finger-tips that used to be so innocently and naturally pink, and now were blue under the yellowing nails—and my flesh rose in ridges of fear.

"Come in, come in," she fluted, cocking her white untidy head on one side and rolling her bulging blue eyes at me. The horrible thing was that she still practised the same arts, all the childish wiles of a clumsy capering coquetry. I felt her pull on my sleeve and it drew me in her wake like a steel cable.

The room she led me into was—well, "unchanged" is the term generally used in such cases. For as a rule, after people die, things are tidied up, furniture is sold, remembrances are despatched to the family. But some morbid piety (or Grace's instructions, perhaps) had kept this room looking exactly as I supposed it had in Miss Pask's lifetime. I wasn't in the mood for noting details; but in the faint dabble of moving candle-light I was half aware of bedraggled cushions, odds and ends of copper pots, and a jar holding a faded branch of some late-flowering shrub. A real Mary Pask "interior"!

The white figure flitted spectrally to the chimney-piece, lit two more candles, and set down the third on a table. I hadn't supposed I was superstitious—but those three candles! Hardly knowing what I did, I hurriedly bent and blew one out. Her laugh sounded behind me.

"Three candles—you still mind that sort of thing? I've got beyond all that, you know," she chuckled. "Such a comfort… such a sense of freedom…" A fresh shiver joined the others already coursing over me.

"Come and sit down by me," she entreated, sinking to a sofa. "It's such an age since I've seen a living being!"

Her choice of terms was certainly strange, and as she leaned back on the white slippery sofa and beckoned me with one of those unburied hands my impulse was to turn and run. But her old face, hovering there in the candle-light, with the unnaturally red cheeks like varnished apples and the blue eyes swimming in vague kindliness, seemed to appeal to me against my cowardice, to remind me that, dead or alive, Mary Pask would never harm a fly.

"Do sit down!" she repeated, and I took the other corner of the sofa.

"It's so wonderfully good of you—I suppose Grace asked you to come?" She laughed again—her conversation had always been punctuated by rambling laughter. "It's an event—quite an event! I've had so few visitors since my death, you see."

Another bucketful of cold water ran over me; but I looked at her resolutely, and again the innocence of her face disarmed me.

I cleared my throat and spoke—with a huge panting effort, as if I had been heaving up a grave-stone. "You live here alone?" I brought out.

"Ah, I'm glad to hear your voice—I still remember voices, though I hear so few," she murmured dreamily. "Yes—I live here alone. The old woman you saw goes away at night. She won't stay after dark… she says she can't. Isn't it funny? But it doesn't matter; I like the darkness." She leaned to me with one of her irrelevant smiles. "The dead," she said, "naturally get used to it."

Once more I cleared my throat; but nothing followed.

She continued to gaze at me with confidential blinks. "And Grace? Tell me all about my darling. I wish I could have seen her again… just once." Her laugh came out grotesquely. "When she got the news of my death—were you with her? Was she terribly upset?"

I stumbled to my feet with a meaningless stammer. I couldn't answer—I couldn't go on looking at her.

"Ah, I see… it's too painful," she acquiesced, her eyes brimming, and she turned her shaking head away.

"But after all… I'm glad she was so sorry… It's what I've been longing to be told, and hardly hoped for. Grace forgets…" She stood up too and flitted across the room, wavering nearer and nearer to the door.

"Thank God," I thought, "she's going."

"Do you know this place by daylight?" she asked abruptly.

I shook my head.

"It's very beautiful. But you wouldn't have seen *me* then. You'd have had to take your choice between me and the landscape. I hate the light—it makes my head ache. And so I sleep all day. I was just waking up when you came." She smiled at me with an increasing air of confidence. "Do you know where I usually sleep? Down below there—in the garden!" Her laugh shrilled out again. "There's a shady corner down at the bottom where the sun never bothers one. Sometimes I sleep there till the stars come out."

The phrase about the garden, in the consul's cable, came back to me and I thought: "After all, it's not such an unhappy state. I wonder if she isn't better off than when she was alive?"

Perhaps she was—but I was sure *I* wasn't, in her company. And her way of sidling nearer to the door made me distinctly want to reach it before she did. In a rush of cowardice I strode ahead of her—but a second later she had the latch in her hand and was leaning against the panels, her long white raiment hanging about her like grave-clothes. She drooped her head a little sideways and peered at me under her lashless lids.

"You're not going?" she reproached me.

I dived down in vain for my missing voice, and silently signed that I was.

"Going—going away? Altogether?" Her eyes were still fixed on me, and I saw two tears gather in their corners and run down over the red glistening circles on her cheeks. "Oh, but you mustn't," she said gently. "I'm too lonely…"

I stammered something inarticulate, my eyes on the blue-nailed hand that grasped the latch. Suddenly the window behind us crashed open, and a gust of wind, surging in out of the blackness, extinguished the candle on the nearest chimney-corner. I glanced back nervously to see if the other candle were going out too.

"You don't like the noise of the wind? *I* do. It's all I have to talk to… People don't like me much since I've been dead. Queer, isn't it? The peasants are so superstitious. At times I'm really lonely…" Her voice cracked in a last effort at laughter, and she swayed toward me, one hand still on the latch.

"Lonely, lonely! If you *knew* how lonely! It was a lie when I told you I wasn't! And now you come, and your face looks friendly… and you say you're going to leave me! No—no—no—you shan't! Or else, why did you come? It's cruel… I used to think I knew what loneliness was… after Grace married, you know. Grace thought she was always thinking of me, but she wasn't. She called me 'darling,' but she was thinking of her husband and children. I said to myself then: 'You couldn't be lonelier if you were dead.' But I know better now… There's been no loneliness like this last year's… none! And sometimes I sit here and think: 'If a man came along some day and took a fancy to you?'" She gave another wavering cackle. "Well, such things *have* happened, you know, even after youth's gone… a man who'd had his troubles too. But no one came till tonight… and now you say you're going!" Suddenly she flung herself toward me. "Oh, stay with me, stay with me… just tonight… It's so sweet and quiet here… No one need know… no one will ever come and trouble us."

I ought to have shut the window when the first gust came. I might have known there would soon be another, fiercer one. It came now, slamming back the loose-hinged lattice, filling the room with the noise of the sea and with wet swirls of fog, and dashing the other candle to the floor. The light went out, and I stood there—we stood there—lost to each other in the roaring coiling darkness. My heart seemed to stop beating; I had to fetch up my breath with great heaves that covered me with sweat. The door—the door—well, I knew I had been facing it when the candle went. Something white and wraithlike seemed to melt and crumple up before me in the night, and avoiding the spot where it had sunk away I stumbled around it in a wide circle, got the latch in my hand, caught my foot in a scarf or sleeve, trailing loose and invisible, and freed myself with a jerk from this last obstacle. I had the door open now. As I got into the hall I heard a whimper from the blackness behind me; but I scrambled on to the hall door, dragged it open and bolted out into the night. I slammed the door on that pitiful low whimper, and the fog and wind enveloped me in healing arms.

III

When I was well enough to trust myself to think about it all again I found that a very little thinking got my temperature up, and my heart hammering in my throat. No use… I simply couldn't stand it… for I'd seen Grace Bridgeworth in crape, weeping over the cable, and yet I'd sat and talked with her sister, on the same sofa—her sister who'd been dead a year!

The circle was a vicious one; I couldn't break through it. The fact that I was down with fever the next morning might have explained it; yet I couldn't get away from the clinging reality of the vision. Supposing it *was* a ghost I had been talking to, and not a mere projection of my fever? Supposing something survived of Mary Pask—enough to cry out to me the unuttered loneliness of a lifetime, to express at last what the living woman had always had to keep dumb and hidden? The thought moved me curiously—in my weakness I lay and wept over it. No end of women were like that, I supposed, and perhaps, after death, if they got their chance they tried to use it... Old tales and legends floated through my mind; the bride of Corinth, the mediæval vampire—but what names to attach to the plaintive image of Mary Pask!

My weak mind wandered in and out among these visions and conjectures, and the longer I lived with them the more convinced I became that something *which had been Mary Pask* had talked with me that night... I made up my mind, when I was up again, to drive back to the place (in broad daylight, this time), to hunt out the grave in the garden—that "shady corner where the sun never bothers one"—and appease the poor ghost with a few flowers. But the doctors decided otherwise; and perhaps my weak will unknowingly abetted them. At any rate, I yielded to their insistence that I should be driven straight from my hotel to the train for Paris, and thence transshipped, like a piece of luggage, to the Swiss sanatorium they had in view for me. Of course I meant to come back when I was patched up again... and meanwhile, more and more tenderly, but more intermittently, my thoughts went back from my snow-mountain to that wailing autumn night above the *Baie des Trépassés*, and the revelation of the dead Mary Pask who was so much more real to me than ever the living one had been.

IV

After all, why should I tell Grace Bridgeworth—ever? I had had a glimpse of things that were really no business of hers. If the revelation had been vouchsafed to me, ought I not to bury it in those deepest depths where the inexplicable and the unforgettable sleep together? And besides, what interest could there be to a woman like Grace in a tale she could neither understand nor believe in? She would just set me down as "queer"—and enough people had done that already. My first object, when I finally did get back to New York, was to convince everybody of my complete return to mental and physical soundness; and into this scheme of evidence my experience with Mary Pask did not seem to fit. All things considered, I would hold my tongue.

But after a while the thought of the grave began to trouble me. I wondered if Grace had ever had a proper grave-stone put on it. The queer neglected look of the house gave me the idea that perhaps she had done nothing—had brushed the whole matter aside, to be attended to when she next went abroad. "Grace forgets," I heard the poor ghost quaver… No, decidedly, there could be no harm in putting (tactfully) just that one question about the care of the grave; the more so as I was beginning to reproach myself for not having gone back to see with my own eyes how it was kept…

Grace and Horace welcomed me with all their old friendliness, and I soon slipped into the habit of dropping in on them for a meal when I thought they were likely to be alone. Nevertheless my opportunity didn't come at once—I had to wait for some weeks. And then one evening, when Horace was dining out and I sat alone with Grace, my glance lit on a photograph of her sister—an old faded photograph which seemed to meet my eyes reproachfully.

"By the way, Grace," I began with a jerk, "I don't believe I ever told you: I went down to that little place of… of your sister's the day before I had that bad relapse."

At once her face lit up emotionally. "No, you never told me. How sweet of you to go!" The ready tears overbrimmed her eyes. "I'm *so* glad you did." She lowered her voice and added softly: "And did you see her?"

The question sent one of my old shudders over me. I looked with amazement at Mrs. Bridgeworth's plump face, smiling at me through a veil of painless tears. "I do reproach myself more and more about darling Mary," she added tremulously. "But tell me—tell me everything."

There was a knot in my throat; I felt almost as uncomfortable as I had in Mary Pask's own presence. Yet I had never before noticed anything uncanny about Grace Bridgeworth. I forced my voice up to my lips.

"Everything? Oh, I can't—." I tried to smile.

"But you did see her?"

I managed to nod, still smiling.

Her face grew suddenly haggard—yes, haggard! "And the change was so dreadful that you can't speak of it? Tell me—was that it?"

I shook my head. After all, what had shocked me was that the change was so slight—that between being dead and alive there seemed after all to be so little difference, except that of a mysterious increase in reality. But Grace's eyes were still searching me insistently. "You must tell me," she reiterated. "I know I ought to have gone there long ago—"

"Yes; perhaps you ought." I hesitated. "To see about the grave, at least…"

She sat silent, her eyes still on my face. Her tears had stopped, but her look of solicitude slowly grew into a stare of something like terror. Hesitatingly, almost reluctantly, she stretched out her hand and laid it on mine for an instant. "Dear old friend—" she began.

"Unfortunately," I interrupted, "I couldn't get back myself to see the grave… because I was taken ill the next day…"

"Yes, yes; of course. I know." She paused. "Are you *sure* you went there at all?" she asked abruptly.

"Sure? Good Lord—" It was my turn to stare. "Do you suspect me of not being quite right yet?" I suggested with an uneasy laugh.

"No—no… of course not… but I don't understand."

"Understand what? I went into the house… I saw everything, in fact, *but* her grave…"

"Her grave?" Grace jumped up, clasping her hands on her breast and darting away from me. At the other end of the room she stood and gazed, and then moved slowly back.

"Then, after all—I wonder?" She held her eyes on me, half fearful and half reassured. "Could it be simply that you never heard?"

"Never heard?"

"But it was in all the papers! Don't you ever read them? I meant to write… I thought I *had* written… but I said: 'At any rate he'll see it in the papers.'… You know I'm always lazy about letters…"

"See what in the papers?"

"Why, that she *didn't* die… She isn't dead! There isn't any grave, my dear man! It was only a cataleptic trance… An extraordinary case, the doctors say… But didn't she tell you all about it—if you say you saw her?" She burst into half-hysterical laughter: "Surely she must have told you that she wasn't dead?"

"No," I said slowly, "she didn't tell me that."

We talked about it together for a long time after that—talked on till Horace came back from his men's dinner, after midnight. Grace insisted on going in and out of the whole subject, over and over again. As she kept repeating, it was certainly the only time that poor Mary had ever been in the papers. But though I sat and listened patiently I couldn't get up any real interest in what she said. I felt I should never again be interested in Mary Pask, or in anything concerning her.

THE MOVING FINGER

THE news of Mrs. Grancy's death came to me with the shock of an immense blunder—one of fate's most irretrievable acts of vandalism. It was as though all sorts of renovating forces had been checked by the clogging of that one wheel. Not that Mrs. Grancy contributed any perceptible momentum to the social machine: her unique distinction was that of filling to perfection her special place in the world. So many people are like badly-composed statues, over-lapping their niches at one point and leaving them vacant at another. Mrs. Grancy's niche was her husband's life; and if it be argued that the space was not large enough for its vacancy to leave a very big gap, I can only say that, at the last resort, such dimensions must be determined by finer instruments than any ready-made standard of utility. Ralph Grancy's was in short a kind of disembodied usefulness: one of those constructive influences that, instead of crystallising into definite forms, remain as it were a medium for the development of clear thinking and fine feeling. He faithfully irrigated his own dusty patch of life, and the fruitful moisture stole far beyond his boundaries. If, to carry on the metaphor, Grancy's life was a sedulously-cultivated enclosure, his wife was the flower he had planted in its midst—the embowering tree, rather, which gave him rest and shade at its foot and the wind of dreams in its upper branches.

We had all—his small but devoted band of followers—known a moment when it seemed likely that Grancy would fail us. We had watched him pitted against one stupid obstacle after another—ill-health, poverty, misunderstanding and, worst of all for a man of his texture, his first wife's soft insidious egotism. We had seen him sinking under the leaden embrace of her affection like a swimmer in a drowning clutch; but just as we despaired he had always come to the surface again, blinded, panting, but striking out fiercely for the shore. When at last her death released him it became a question as to how much of the man she had carried with her. Left alone, he revealed numb withered patches, like a tree from which a parasite has been stripped. But gradually he began to put out new leaves; and when he met the lady who was to become his second wife—his one *real* wife, as his friends reckoned—the whole man burst into flower.

The second Mrs. Grancy was past thirty when he married her, and it was clear that she had harvested that crop of middle joy which is rooted in young despair. But if she had lost the surface of eighteen she had kept its inner light; if her cheek lacked the gloss of immaturity her eyes were young with the stored youth of half a lifetime. Grancy had first known her somewhere in the East—I believe she was the sister of one of our consuls out there—and when he brought her home to New York she came among us as a stranger. The idea of Grancy's remarriage had been a shock to us all. After one such calcining most men would have kept out of the fire; but we agreed that he was predestined to sentimental blunders, and we awaited with resignation the embodiment of his latest mistake. Then Mrs. Grancy came—and we understood. She was the most beautiful and the most complete of explanations. We shuffled our defeated omniscience out of sight and gave it hasty burial under a prodigality of welcome. For the first time in years we had Grancy off our minds. "He'll do something great now!" the least sanguine of us prophesied; and our sentimentalist emended: "He *has* done it—in marrying her!"

It was Claydon, the portrait-painter, who risked this hyperbole; and who soon afterward, at the happy husband's request, prepared to defend it in a portrait of Mrs. Grancy. We were all—even Claydon—ready to concede that

Mrs. Grancy's unwontedness was in some degree a matter of environment. Her graces were complementary and it needed the mate's call to reveal the flash of colour beneath her neutral-tinted wings. But if she needed Grancy to interpret her, how much greater was the service she rendered him! Claydon professionally described her as the right frame for him; but if she defined she also enlarged, if she threw the whole into perspective she also cleared new ground, opened fresh vistas, reclaimed whole areas of activity that had run to waste under the harsh husbandry of privation. This interaction of sympathies was not without its visible expression. Claydon was not alone in maintaining that Grancy's presence—or indeed the mere mention of his name—had a perceptible effect on his wife's appearance. It was as though a light were shifted, a curtain drawn back, as though, to borrow another of Claydon's metaphors, Love the indefatigable artist were perpetually seeking a happier "pose" for his model. In this interpretative light Mrs. Grancy acquired the charm which makes some women's faces like a book of which the last page is never turned. There was always something new to read in her eyes. What Claydon read there—or at least such scattered hints of the ritual as reached him through the sanctuary doors—his portrait in due course declared to us. When the picture was exhibited it was at once acclaimed as his masterpiece; but the people who knew Mrs. Grancy smiled and said it was flattered. Claydon, however, had not set out to paint *their* Mrs. Grancy—or ours even—but Ralph's; and Ralph knew his own at a glance. At the first confrontation he saw that Claydon had understood. As for Mrs. Grancy, when the finished picture was shown to her she turned to the painter and said simply: "Ah, you've done me facing the east!"

The picture, then, for all its value, seemed a mere incident in the unfolding of their double destiny, a foot-note to the illuminated text of their lives. It was not till afterward that it acquired the significance of last words spoken on a threshold never to be recrossed. Grancy, a year after his marriage, had given up his town house and carried his bliss an hour's journey away, to a little place among the hills. His various duties and interests brought him frequently to New York, but we necessarily saw him less often than when his house had served as the rallying-point of kindred enthusiasms. It seemed a pity that such an influence should be withdrawn, but we all felt that his long arrears of happiness should be paid in whatever coin he chose. The distance from which the fortunate couple radiated warmth on us was not too great for friendship to traverse; and our conception of a glorified leisure took the form of Sundays spent in the Grancys' library, with its sedative rural outlook, and the portrait of Mrs. Grancy illuminating its studious walls. The picture was at its best in that setting; and we used to accuse Claydon of visiting Mrs. Grancy in order to see her portrait. He met this by declaring that the portrait *was* Mrs. Grancy; and there were moments when the statement seemed unanswerable. One of us, indeed—I think it must have been the novelist—said that Claydon had been saved from falling in love with Mrs. Grancy only by falling in love with his picture of her; and it was noticeable that he, to whom his finished work was no more than the shed husk of future effort, showed a perennial tenderness for this one achievement. We smiled afterward to think how often, when Mrs. Grancy was in the room, her presence reflecting itself in our talk like a gleam of sky in a hurrying current, Claydon, averted from the real woman, would sit as it were listening to the picture. His attitude, at the time, seemed only a part of the unusualness of those picturesque afternoons, when the most familiar combinations of life underwent a magical change. Some human happiness is a landlocked lake; but the Grancys' was an open sea, stretching a buoyant and illimitable surface to the voyaging interests of life. There was room and to spare on those waters for all our separate ventures; and always, beyond the sunset, a mirage of the fortunate isles toward which our prows were bent.

II

It was in Rome that, three years later, I heard of her death. The notice said "suddenly"; I was glad of that. I was glad too—basely perhaps—to be away from Grancy at a time when silence must have seemed obtuse and speech derisive.

I was still in Rome when, a few months afterward, he suddenly arrived there. He had been appointed secretary of legation at Constantinople and was on the way to his post. He had taken the place, he said frankly, "to get away." Our relations with the Porte held out a prospect of hard work, and that, he explained, was what he needed. He could never be satisfied to sit down among the ruins. I saw that, like most of us in moments of extreme moral tension, he was playing a part, behaving as he thought it became a man to behave in the eye of disaster. The instinctive posture of grief is a shuffling compromise between defiance and prostration; and pride feels the need of striking a worthier attitude in face of such a foe. Grancy, by nature musing and retrospective, had chosen the rôle of the man of action, who answers blow for blow and opposes a mailed front to the thrusts of destiny; and the completeness of the equipment testified to his inner weakness. We talked only of what we were not thinking of, and parted, after a few days, with a sense of relief that proved the inadequacy of friendship to perform, in such cases, the office assigned to it by tradition.

Soon afterward my own work called me home, but Grancy remained several years in Europe. International diplomacy kept its promise of giving him work to do, and during the year in which he acted as *chargé d'affaires* he acquitted himself, under trying conditions, with conspicuous zeal and discretion. A political redistribution of matter removed him from office just as he had proved his usefulness to the government; and the following summer I heard that he had come home and was down at his place in the country.

On my return to town I wrote him and his reply came by the next post. He answered as it were in his natural voice, urging me to spend the following

Sunday with him, and suggesting that I should bring down any of the old set who could be persuaded to join me. I thought this a good sign, and yet—shall I own it?—I was vaguely disappointed. Perhaps we are apt to feel that our friends' sorrows should be kept like those historic monuments from which the encroaching ivy is periodically removed.

That very evening at the club I ran across Claydon. I told him of Grancy's invitation and proposed that we should go down together; but he pleaded an engagement. I was sorry, for I had always felt that he and I stood nearer Ralph than the others, and if the old Sundays were to be renewed I should have preferred that we two should spend the first alone with him. I said as much to Claydon and offered to fit my time to his; but he met this by a general refusal.

"I don't want to go to Grancy's," he said bluntly. I waited a moment, but he appended no qualifying clause.

"You've seen him since he came back?" I finally ventured.

Claydon nodded.

"And is he so awfully bad?"

"Bad? No: he's all right."

"All right? How can he be, unless he's changed beyond all recognition?"

"Oh, you'll recognise *him*," said Claydon, with a puzzling deflection of emphasis.

His ambiguity was beginning to exasperate me, and I felt myself shut out from some knowledge to which I had as good a right as he.

"You've been down there already, I suppose?"

"Yes; I've been down there."

"And you've done with each other—the partnership is dissolved?"

"Done with each other? I wish to God we had!" He rose nervously and tossed aside the review from which my approach had diverted him. "Look here," he said, standing before me, "Ralph's the best fellow going and there's nothing under heaven I wouldn't do for him—short of going down there again." And with that he walked out of the room.

Claydon was incalculable enough for me to read a dozen different meanings into his words; but none of my interpretations satisfied me. I determined, at any rate, to seek no farther for a companion; and the next Sunday I travelled down to Grancy's alone. He met me at the station and I saw at once that he had changed since our last meeting. Then he had been in fighting array, but now if he and grief still housed together it was no longer as enemies. Physically the transformation was as marked but less reassuring. If the spirit triumphed the body showed its scars. At five-and-forty he was grey and stooping, with the tired gait of an old man. His serenity, however, was not the resignation of age. I saw that he did not mean to drop out of the game. Almost immediately he began to speak of our old interests; not with an effort, as at our former meeting, but simply and naturally, in the tone of a man whose life has flowed back into its normal channels. I remembered, with a touch of self-reproach, how I had distrusted his reconstructive powers; but my admiration for his reserved force was now tinged by the sense that, after all, such happiness as his ought to have been paid with his last coin. The feeling grew as we neared the house and I found how inextricably his wife was interwoven with my remembrance of the place: how the whole scene was but an extension of that vivid presence.

Within doors nothing was changed, and my hand would have dropped without surprise into her welcoming clasp. It was luncheon-time, and Grancy led me at once to the dining-room, where the walls, the furniture, the very plate and porcelain, seemed a mirror in which a moment since her face had been reflected. I wondered whether Grancy, under the recovered tranquillity of his smile, concealed the same sense of her nearness, saw perpetually between himself and the actual her bright unappeasable ghost. He spoke of her once or twice, in an easy incidental way, and her name seemed to hang in the air after he had uttered it, like a chord that continues to vibrate. If he felt her presence it was evidently as an enveloping medium, the moral atmosphere in which he breathed. I had never before known how completely the dead may survive.

After luncheon we went for a long walk through the autumnal fields and woods, and dusk was falling when we re-entered the house. Grancy led the way to the library, where, at this hour, his wife had always welcomed us back to a bright fire and a cup of tea. The room faced the west, and held a clear light of its own after the rest of the house had grown dark. I remembered how young she had looked in this pale gold light, which irradiated her eyes and hair, or silhouetted her girlish outline as she passed before the windows. Of all the rooms the library was most peculiarly hers; and here I felt that her nearness might take visible shape. Then, all in a moment, as Grancy opened the door, the feeling vanished and a kind of resistance met me on the threshold. I looked about me. Was the room changed? Had some desecrating hand effaced the traces of her presence? No; here too the setting was undisturbed. My feet sank into the same deep-piled Daghestan; the book-shelves took the firelight on the same rows of rich subdued bindings; her armchair stood in its old place near the tea-table; and from the opposite wall her face confronted me.

Her face—but *was* it hers? I moved nearer and stood looking up at the portrait. Grancy's glance had followed mine and I heard him move to my side.

"You see a change in it?" he said.

"What does it mean?" I asked.

"It means—that five years have passed."

"Over *her*?"

"Why not?—Look at me!" He pointed to his grey hair and furrowed temples. "What do you think kept *her* so young? It was happiness! But now—" he looked up at her with infinite tenderness. "I like her better so," he said. "It's what she would have wished."

"Have wished?"

"That we should grow old together. Do you think she would have wanted to be left behind?"

I stood speechless, my gaze travelling from his worn grief-beaten features to the painted face above. It was not furrowed like his; but a veil of years seemed to have descended on it. The bright hair had lost its elasticity, the cheek its clearness, the brow its light: the whole woman had waned.

Grancy laid his hand on my arm. "You don't like it?" he said sadly.

"Like it? I—I've lost her!" I burst out.

"And I've found her," he answered.

"In *that?*" I cried with a reproachful gesture.

"Yes; in that." He swung round on me almost defiantly. "The other had become a sham, a lie! This is the way she would have looked—does look, I mean. Claydon ought to know, oughtn't he?"

I turned suddenly. "Did Claydon do this for you?"

Grancy nodded.

"Since your return?"

"Yes. I sent for him after I'd been back a week—." He turned away and gave a thrust to the smouldering fire. I followed, glad to leave the picture behind me. Grancy threw himself into a chair near the hearth, so that the light fell on his sensitive variable face. He leaned his head back, shading his eyes with his hand, and began to speak.

III

"You fellows knew enough of my early history to guess what my second marriage meant to me. I say guess, because no one could understand—really. I've always had a feminine streak in me, I suppose: the need of a pair of eyes that should see with me, of a pulse that should keep time with mine. Life is a big thing, of course; a magnificent spectacle; but I got so tired of looking at it alone! Still, it's always good to live, and I had plenty of happiness—of the evolved kind. What I'd never had a taste of was the simple inconscient sort that one breathes in like the air…

"Well—I met her. It was like finding the climate in which I was meant to live. You know what she was—how indefinitely she multiplied one's points of contact with life, how she lit up the caverns and bridged the abysses! Well, I swear to you (though I suppose the sense of all that was latent in me) that what I used to think of on my way home at the end of the day, was simply that when I opened this door she'd be sitting over there, with the lamplight falling in a particular way on one little curl in her neck... When Claydon painted her he caught just the look she used to lift to mine when I came in—I've wondered, sometimes, at his knowing how she looked when she and I were alone.—How I rejoiced in that picture! I used to say to her, 'You're my prisoner now—I shall never lose you. If you grew tired of me and left me you'd leave your real self there on the wall!' It was always one of our jokes that she was going to grow tired of me—

"Three years of it—and then she died. It was so sudden that there was no change, no diminution. It was as if she had suddenly become fixed, immovable, like her own portrait: as if Time had ceased at its happiest hour, just as Claydon had thrown down his brush one day and said, 'I can't do better than that.'

"I went away, as you know, and stayed over there five years. I worked as hard as I knew how, and after the first black months a little light stole in on me. From thinking that she would have been interested in what I was doing I came to feel that she *was* interested—that she was there and that she knew. I'm not talking any psychical jargon—I'm simply trying to express the sense I had that an influence so full, so abounding as hers couldn't pass like a spring shower. We had so lived into each other's hearts and minds that the consciousness of what she would have thought and felt illuminated all I did. At first she used to come back shyly, tentatively, as though not sure of finding me; then she stayed longer and longer, till at last she became again the very air I breathed... There were bad moments, of course, when her nearness mocked me with the loss of the real woman; but gradually the distinction between the two was effaced and the mere thought of her grew warm as flesh and blood.

"Then I came home. I landed in the morning and came straight down here. The thought of seeing her portrait possessed me and my heart beat like a lover's as I opened the library door. It was in the afternoon and the room was full of light. It fell on her picture—the picture of a young and radiant woman. She smiled at me coldly across the distance that divided us. I had the feeling that she didn't even recognise me. And then I caught sight of myself in the mirror over there—a grey-haired broken man whom she had never known!

"For a week we two lived together—the strange woman and the strange man. I used to sit night after night and question her smiling face; but no answer ever came. What did she know of me, after all? We were irrevocably separated by the five years of life that lay between us. At times, as I sat here, I almost grew to hate her; for her presence had driven away my gentle ghost, the real wife who had wept, aged, struggled with me during those awful years… It was the worst loneliness I've ever known. Then, gradually, I began to notice a look of sadness in the picture's eyes; a look that seemed to say: 'Don't you see that *I* am lonely too?' And all at once it came over me how she would have hated to be left behind! I remembered her comparing life to a heavy book that could not be read with ease unless two people held it together; and I thought how impatiently her hand would have turned the pages that divided us!—So the idea came to me: 'It's the picture that stands between us; the picture that is dead, and not my wife. To sit in this room is to keep watch beside a corpse.' As this feeling grew on me the portrait became like a beautiful mausoleum in which she had been buried alive: I could hear her beating against the painted walls and crying to me faintly for help…

"One day I found I couldn't stand it any longer and I sent for Claydon. He came down and I told him what I'd been through and what I wanted him to do. At first he refused point-blank to touch the picture. The next morning

I went off for a long tramp, and when I came home I found him sitting here alone. He looked at me sharply for a moment and then he said: 'I've changed my mind; I'll do it.' I arranged one of the north rooms as a studio and he shut himself up there for a day; then he sent for me. The picture stood there as you see it now—it was as though she'd met me on the threshold and taken me in her arms! I tried to thank him, to tell him what it meant to me, but he cut me short.

"'There's an up train at five, isn't there?' he asked. 'I'm booked for a dinner tonight. I shall just have time to make a bolt for the station and you can send my traps after me.' I haven't seen him since.

"I can guess what it cost him to lay hands on his masterpiece; but, after all, to him it was only a picture lost, to me it was my wife regained!"

IV

After that, for ten years or more, I watched the strange spectacle of a life of hopeful and productive effort based on the structure of a dream. There could be no doubt to those who saw Grancy during this period that he drew his strength and courage from the sense of his wife's mystic participation in his task. When I went back to see him a few months later I found the portrait had been removed from the library and placed in a small study upstairs, to which he had transferred his desk and a few books. He told me he always sat there when he was alone, keeping the library for his Sunday visitors. Those who missed the portrait of course made no comment on its absence, and the few who were in his secret respected it. Gradually all his old friends had gathered about him and our Sunday afternoons regained something of their former character; but Claydon never reappeared among us.

As I look back now I see that Grancy must have been failing from the time of his return home. His invincible spirit belied and disguised the signs of weakness that afterward asserted themselves in my remembrance of him. He seemed to have an inexhaustible fund of life to draw on, and more than one of us was a pensioner on his superfluity.

Nevertheless, when I came back one summer from my European holiday and heard that he had been at the point of death, I understood at once that we had believed him well only because he wished us to.

I hastened down to the country and found him midway in a slow convalescence. I felt then that he was lost to us and he read my thought at a glance.

"Ah," he said, "I'm an old man now and no mistake. I suppose we shall have to go half-speed after this; but we shan't need towing just yet!"

The plural pronoun struck me, and involuntarily I looked up at Mrs. Grancy's portrait. Line by line I saw my fear reflected in it. It was the face of a woman *who knows that her husband is dying*. My heart stood still at the thought of what Claydon had done.

Grancy had followed my glance. "Yes, it's changed her," he said quietly. "For months, you know, it was touch and go with me—we had a long fight of it, and it was worse for her than for me." After a pause he added: "Claydon has been very kind; he's so busy nowadays that I seldom see him, but when I sent for him the other day he came down at once."

I was silent and we spoke no more of Grancy's illness; but when I took leave it seemed like shutting him in alone with his death-warrant.

The next time I went down to see him he looked much better. It was a Sunday and he received me in the library, so that I did not see the portrait again. He continued to improve and toward spring we began to feel that, as he had said, he might yet travel a long way without being towed.

One evening, on returning to town after a visit which had confirmed my sense of reassurance, I found Claydon dining alone at the club. He asked me to join him and over the coffee our talk turned to his work.

"If you're not too busy," I said at length, "you ought to make time to go down to Grancy's again."

He looked up quickly. "Why?" he asked.

"Because he's quite well again," I returned with a touch of cruelty. "His wife's prognostications were mistaken."

Claydon stared at me a moment. "Oh, *she* knows," he affirmed with a smile that chilled me.

"You mean to leave the portrait as it is then?" I persisted.

He shrugged his shoulders. "He hasn't sent for me yet!"

A waiter came up with the cigars and Claydon rose and joined another group.

It was just a fortnight later that Grancy's housekeeper telegraphed for me. She met me at the station with the news that he had been "taken bad" and that the doctors were with him. I had to wait for some time in the deserted library before the medical men appeared. They had the baffled manner of empirics who have been superseded by the great Healer; and I lingered only long enough to hear that Grancy was not suffering and that my presence could do him no harm.

I found him seated in his armchair in the little study. He held out his hand with a smile.

"You see she was right after all," he said.

"She?" I repeated, perplexed for the moment.

"My wife." He indicated the picture. "Of course I knew she had no hope from the first. I saw that"—he lowered his voice—"after Claydon had been here. But I wouldn't believe it at first!"

I caught his hands in mine. "For God's sake don't believe it now!" I adjured him.

He shook his head gently. "It's too late," he said. "I might have known that she knew."

"But, Grancy, listen to me," I began; and then I stopped. What could I say that would convince him? There was no common ground of argument on which we could meet; and after all it would be easier for him to die feeling that she *had* known. Strangely enough, I saw that Claydon had missed his mark…

V

Grancy's will named me as one of his executors; and my associate, having other duties on his hands, begged me to assume the task of carrying out our friend's wishes. This placed me under the necessity of informing Claydon that the portrait of Mrs. Grancy had been bequeathed to him; and he replied by the next post that he would send for the picture at once. I was staying in the deserted house when the portrait was taken away; and as the door closed on it I felt that Grancy's presence had vanished too. Was it his turn to follow her now, and could one ghost haunt another?

After that, for a year or two, I heard nothing more of the picture, and though I met Claydon from time to time we had little to say to each other. I had no definable grievance against the man and I tried to remember that he had done a fine thing in sacrificing his best picture to a friend; but my resentment had all the tenacity of unreason.

One day, however, a lady whose portrait he had just finished begged me to go with her to see it. To refuse was impossible, and I went with the less reluctance that I knew I was not the only friend she had invited. The others were all grouped around the easel when I entered, and after contributing my share to the chorus of approval I turned away and began to stroll about the studio. Claydon was something of a collector and his things were generally worth looking at. The studio was a long tapestried room with a curtained archway at one end. The curtains were looped back, showing a smaller apartment, with books and flowers and a few fine bits of bronze and porcelain. The tea-table standing in this inner room proclaimed that it was open to inspection, and I wandered in. A *bleu poudré* vase first attracted me; then I turned to examine a slender bronze Ganymede, and in so doing found myself face to face with Mrs. Grancy's portrait. I stared up at her blankly and she smiled back at me in all the recovered radiance of youth. The artist had effaced every trace of his later touches and the original picture had reappeared. It throned alone on the panelled wall, asserting a brilliant supremacy over its carefully-chosen surroundings. I felt in an instant that the whole room was tributary to it: that Claydon had heaped his treasures at the feet of the woman he loved. Yes—it was the woman he had loved and not the picture; and my instinctive resentment was explained.

Suddenly I felt a hand on my shoulder.

"Ah, how could you?" I cried, turning on him.

"How could I?" he retorted. "How could I *not?* Doesn't she belong to me now?"

I moved away impatiently.

"Wait a moment," he said with a detaining gesture. "The others have gone and I want to say a word to you.—Oh, I know what you've thought of me—I can guess! You think I killed Grancy, I suppose?"

I was startled by his sudden vehemence. "I think you tried to do a cruel thing," I said.

"Ah—what a little way you others see into life!" he murmured. "Sit down a moment—here, where we can look at her—and I'll tell you."

He threw himself on the ottoman beside me and sat gazing up at the picture, with his hands clasped about his knee.

"Pygmalion," he began slowly, "turned his statue into a real woman; *I* turned my real woman into a picture. Small compensation, you think—but you don't know how much of a woman belongs to you after you've painted her!—Well, I made the best of it, at any rate—I gave her the best I had in me; and she gave me in return what such a woman gives by merely being. And after all she rewarded me enough by making me paint as I shall never paint again! There was one side of her, though, that was mine alone, and that was her beauty; for no one else understood it. To Grancy even it was the mere expression of herself—what language is to thought. Even when he saw the picture he didn't guess my secret—he was so sure she was all his! As though a man should think he owned the moon because it was reflected in the pool at his door—

"Well—when he came home and sent for me to change the picture it was like asking me to commit murder. He wanted me to make an old woman of her—of her who had been so divinely, unchangeably young! As if any man who really loved a woman would ask her to sacrifice her youth and beauty for his sake! At first I told him I couldn't do it—but afterward, when he left me alone with the picture, something queer happened. I suppose it was because I was always so confoundedly fond of Grancy that it went against me to refuse what he asked. Anyhow, as I sat looking up at her, she seemed to say, 'I'm not yours but his, and I want you to make me what he wishes.' And so I did it. I could have cut my hand off when the work was done—I daresay he told you I never would go back and look at it. He thought I was too busy—he never understood…

"Well—and then last year he sent for me again—you remember. It was after his illness, and he told me he'd grown twenty years older and that he wanted her to grow older too—he didn't want her to be left behind. The doctors all thought he was going to get well at that time, and he thought so too; and so did I when I first looked at him. But when I turned to the picture—ah, now I don't ask you to believe me; but I swear it was *her* face that told me he was dying, and that she wanted him to know it! She had a message for him and she made me deliver it."

He rose abruptly and walked toward the portrait; then he sat down beside me again.

"Cruel? Yes, it seemed so to me at first; and this time, if I resisted, it was for *his* sake and not for mine. But all the while I felt her eyes drawing me, and gradually she made me understand. If she'd been there in the flesh (she seemed to say) wouldn't she have seen before any of us that he was dying? Wouldn't he have read the news first in her face? And wouldn't it be horrible if now he should discover it instead in strange eyes?—Well—that was what she wanted of me and I did it—I kept them together to the last!" He looked up at the picture again. "But now she belongs to me," he repeated…

MR. JONES

I

Lady Jane Lynke was unlike other people: when she heard that she had inherited Bells, the beautiful old place which had belonged to the Lynkes of Thudeney for something like six hundred years, the fancy took her to go and see it unannounced. She was staying at a friend's nearby, in Kent, and the next morning she borrowed a motor and slipped away alone to Thudeney-Blazes, the adjacent village.

It was a lustrous, motionless day. Autumn bloom lay on the Sussex downs, on the heavy trees of the weald, on streams moving indolently, far off across the marshes. Farther still, Dungeness, a fitful streak, floated on an immaterial sea which was perhaps, after all, only sky.

In the softness Thudeney-Blazes slept: a few aged houses bowed about a duck-pond, a silvery spire, orchards thick with dew. Did Thudeney-Blazes ever wake?

Lady Jane left the motor to the care of the geese on a miniature common, pushed open a white gate into a field (the griffoned portals being padlocked), and struck across the park toward a group of carved chimney-stacks. No one seemed aware of her.

In a dip of the land, the long low house, its ripe brick masonry overhanging a moat deeply sunk about its roots, resembled an aged cedar spreading immemorial red branches. Lady Jane held her breath and gazed.

A silence distilled from years of solitude lay on lawns and gardens. No one had lived at Bells since the last Lord Thudeney, then a penniless younger son, had forsaken it sixty years before to seek his fortune in Canada. And before that, he and his widowed mother, distant poor relations, were housed in one of the lodges, and the great place, even in their day, had been as mute and solitary as the family vault.

Lady Jane, daughter of another branch, to which an earldom and considerable possessions had accrued, had never seen Bells, hardly heard its name. A succession of deaths, and the whim of an old man she had never known, now made her heir to all this beauty; and as she stood and looked she was glad she had come to it from so far, from impressions so remote and different. "It would be dreadful to be used to it—to be thinking already about the state of the roof, or the cost of a heating system."

Till this her thirty-fifth year, Lady Jane had led an active, independent and decided life. One of several daughters, moderately but sufficiently provided for, she had gone early from home, lived in London lodgings, travelled in tropic lands, spent studious summers in Spain and Italy, and written two or three brisk, business-like little books about cities usually dealt with sentimentally. And now, just back from a summer in the south of France, she stood ankle-deep in wet bracken, and gazed at Bells lying there under a September sun that looked like moonlight.

"I shall never leave it!" she ejaculated, her heart swelling as if she had taken the vow to a lover.

She ran down the last slope of the park and entered the faded formality of gardens with clipped yews as ornate as architecture, and holly hedges as solid as walls. Adjoining the house rose a low, deep-buttressed chapel. Its door was ajar, and she thought this of good augury: her forebears were waiting for her. In the porch she remarked fly-blown notices of services, an umbrella stand, a dishevelled door-mat: no doubt the chapel served as the village church. The thought gave her a sense of warmth and neighbourliness. Across the damp flags of the chancel, monuments and brasses showed through a traceried screen. She examined them curiously. Some hailed her with vocal memories, others whispered out of the remote and the unknown: it was a shame to know so little about her own family. But neither Crofts nor Lynkes had ever greatly distinguished themselves; they had gathered substance simply by holding on to what they had, and slowly accumulating privileges and acres. "Mostly by clever marriages," Lady Jane thought with a faint contempt.

At that moment her eyes lit on one of the less ornate monuments: a plain sarcophagus of grey marble niched in the wall and surmounted by the bust of a young man with a fine arrogant head, a Byronic throat and tossed-back curls.

"Peregrine Vincent Theobald Lynke, Baron Clouds, fifteenth Viscount Thudeney of Bells, Lord of the Manors of Thudeney, Thudeney-Blazes, Upper Lynke, Lynke-Linnet—" so it ran, with the usual tedious enumeration of honours, titles, court and county offices, ending with: "Born on May 1st, 1790, perished of the plague at Aleppo in 1828." And underneath, in small cramped characters, as if crowded as an afterthought into an insufficient space: "Also His Wife."

That was all. No name, dates, honours, epithets, for the Viscountess Thudeney. Did she too die of the plague at Aleppo? Or did the "also" imply her actual presence in the sarcophagus which her husband's pride had no doubt prepared for his own last sleep, little guessing that some Syrian drain was to receive him? Lady Jane racked her memory in vain. All she knew was that the death without issue of this Lord Thudeney had caused the property to revert to the Croft-Lynkes, and so, in the end, brought her to the chancel step where, shyly, she knelt a moment, vowing to the dead to carry on their trust.

She passed on to the entrance court, and stood at last at the door of her new home, a blunt tweed figure in heavy mud-stained shoes. She felt as intrusive as a tripper, and her hand hesitated on the door-bell. "I ought to have brought some one with me," she thought; an odd admission on the part of a young woman who, when she was doing her books of travel, had prided herself on forcing single-handed the most closely guarded doors. But those other places, as she looked back, seemed easy and accessible compared to Bells.

She rang, and a tinkle answered, carried on by a flurried echo which seemed to ask what in the world was happening. Lady Jane, through the nearest window, caught the spectral vista of a long room with shrouded furniture. She could not see its farther end, but she had the feeling that someone stationed there might very well be seeing her.

"Just at first," she thought, "I shall have to invite people here—to take the chill off."

She rang again, and the tinkle again prolonged itself; but no one came.

At last she reflected that the care-takers probably lived at the back of the house, and pushing open a door in the court-yard wall she worked her way around to what seemed a stable-yard. Against the purple brick sprawled a neglected magnolia, bearing one late flower as big as a planet. Lady Jane rang at a door marked "Service." This bell, though also languid, had a wakefuller sound, as if it were more used to being rung, and still knew what was likely to follow; and after a delay during which Lady Jane again had the sense of being peered at—from above, through a lowered blind—a bolt shot, and a woman looked out. She was youngish, unhealthy, respectable and frightened; and she blinked at Lady Jane like someone waking out of sleep.

"Oh," said Lady Jane—"do you think I might visit the house?"

"The house?"

"I'm staying near here—I'm interested in old houses. Mightn't I take a look?"

The young woman drew back. "The house isn't shown."

"Oh, but not to—not to—" Jane weighed the case. "You see," she explained, "I know some of the family: the Northumberland branch."

"You're related, madam?"

"Well—distantly, yes." It was exactly what she had not meant to say; but there seemed no other way.

The woman twisted her apron-strings in perplexity. "Come, you know," Lady Jane urged, producing half-a-crown. The woman turned pale.

"I couldn't, madam; not without asking." It was clear that she was sorely tempted.

"Well, ask, won't you?" Lady Jane pressed the tip into a hesitating hand. The young woman shut the door and vanished. She was away so long that the visitor concluded her half-crown had been pocketed, and there was an end; and she began to be angry with herself, which was more often her habit than to be so with others.

"Well, for a fool, Jane, you're a complete one," she grumbled.

A returning footstep, listless, reluctant—the tread of one who was not going to let her in. It began to be rather comic.

The door opened, and the young woman said in her dull sing-song: "Mr. Jones says that no one is allowed to visit the house."

She and Lady Jane looked at each other for a moment, and Lady Jane read the apprehension in the other's eyes.

"Mr. Jones? Oh?—Yes; of course, keep it…" She waved away the woman's hand.

"Thank you, madam." The door closed again, and Lady Jane stood and gazed up at the inexorable face of her old home.

II

"But you didn't get in? You actually came back without so much as a peep?"

Her story was received, that evening at dinner, with mingled mirth and incredulity.

"But, my dear! You mean to say you asked to see the house, and they wouldn't let you? *Who* wouldn't?" Lady Jane's hostess insisted.

"Mr. Jones."

"Mr. Jones?"

"He said no one was allowed to visit it."

"Who on earth is Mr. Jones?"

"The care-taker, I suppose. I didn't see him."

"Didn't see him either? But I never heard such nonsense! Why in the world didn't you insist?"

"Yes; why didn't you?" they all chorused; and she could only answer, a little lamely: "I think I was afraid."

"Afraid? *You*, darling?" There was fresh hilarity. "Of Mr. Jones?"

"I suppose so." She joined in the laugh, yet she knew it was true: she had been afraid.

Edward Stramer, the novelist, an old friend of her family, had been listening with an air of abstraction, his eyes on his empty coffee-cup. Suddenly, as the mistress of the house pushed back her chair, he looked across the table at Lady Jane. "It's odd: I've just remembered something. Once, when I was a youngster, I tried to see Bells; over thirty years ago it must have been." He glanced at his host. "Your mother drove me over. And we were not let in."

There was a certain flatness in this conclusion, and someone remarked that Bells had always been known as harder to get into than any other house thereabouts.

"Yes," said Stramer; "but the point is that we were refused in exactly the same words. Mr. Jones said no one was allowed to visit the house."

"Ah—he was in possession already? Thirty years ago? Unsociable fellow, Jones. Well, Jane, you've got a good watch-dog."

They moved to the drawing-room, and the talk drifted to other topics. But Stramer came and sat down beside Lady Jane. "It is queer, though, that at such a distance of time we should have been given exactly the same answer."

She glanced up at him curiously. "Yes; and you didn't try to force your way in either?"

"Oh, no: it was not possible."

"So I felt," she agreed.

"Well, next week, my dear, I hope we shall see it all, in spite of Mr. Jones," their hostess intervened, catching their last words as she moved toward the piano.

"I wonder if we shall see Mr. Jones," said Stramer.

III

Bells was not nearly as large as it looked; like many old houses it was very narrow, and but one storey high, with servants' rooms in the low attics, and much space wasted in crooked passages and superfluous stairs. If she closed the great saloon, Jane thought, she might live there comfortably with the small staff which was the most she could afford. It was a relief to find the place less important than she had feared.

For already, in that first hour of arrival, she had decided to give up everything else for Bells. Her previous plans and ambitions—except such as might fit in with living there—had fallen from her like a discarded garment, and things she had hardly thought about, or had shrugged away with the hasty subversiveness of youth, were already laying quiet hands on her; all the lives from which her life had issued, with what they bore of example or admonishment. The very shabbiness of the house moved her more than splendours, made it, after its long abandonment, seem full of the careless daily coming and going of people long dead, people to whom it had not been a museum, or a page of history, but cradle, nursery, home, and sometimes, no doubt, a prison. If those marble lips in the chapel could speak! If she could hear some of their comments on the old house which had spread its silent shelter over their sins and sorrows, their follies and submissions! A long tale, to which she was about to add another chapter, subdued and humdrum beside some of those earlier annals, yet probably freer and more varied than the unchronicled lives of the great-aunts and great-grandmothers buried there so completely that they must hardly have known when they passed from their beds to their graves. "Piled up like dead leaves," Jane thought, "layers and layers of them, to preserve something forever budding underneath."

Well, all these piled-up lives had at least preserved the old house in its integrity; and that was worth while. She was satisfied to carry on such a trust.

She sat in the garden looking up at those rosy walls, iridescent with damp and age. She decided which windows should be hers, which rooms given to the friends from Kent who were motoring over, Stramer among them, for a modest house-warming; then she got up and went in.

The hour had come for domestic questions; for she had arrived alone, unsupported even by the old family housemaid her mother had offered her. She preferred to start afresh, convinced that her small household could be staffed from the neighbourhood. Mrs. Clemm, the rosy-cheeked old person who had curtsied her across the threshold, would doubtless know.

Mrs. Clemm, summoned to the library, curtsied again. She wore black silk, gathered and spreading as to skirt, flat and perpendicular as to bodice. On her glossy false front was a black lace cap with ribbons which had faded from violet to ash-colour, and a heavy watch-chain descended from the lava brooch under her crochet collar. Her small round face rested on the collar like a red apple on a white plate: neat, smooth, circular, with a pursed-up mouth, eyes like black seeds, and round ruddy cheeks with the skin so taut that one had to look close to see that it was as wrinkled as a piece of old crackly.

Mrs. Clemm was sure there would be no trouble about servants. She herself could do a little cooking: though her hand might be a bit out. But there was her niece to help; and she was quite of her ladyship's opinion, that there was no need to get in strangers. They were mostly a poor lot; and besides, they might not take to Bells. There were persons who didn't. Mrs. Clemm smiled a sharp little smile, like the scratch of a pin, as she added that she hoped her ladyship wouldn't be one of them.

As for under-servants... well, a boy, perhaps? She had a great-nephew she might send for. But about women—under-housemaids—if her ladyship thought they couldn't manage as they were; well, she really didn't know. Thudeney-Blazes? Oh, she didn't think so... There was more dead than living at Thudeney-Blazes... everyone was leaving there... or in the churchyard... one house after another being shut... death was everywhere, wasn't it, my lady? Mrs. Clemm said it with another of her short sharp smiles, which provoked the appearance of a frosty dimple.

"But my niece Georgiana is a hard worker, my lady; her that let you in the other day..."

"That didn't," Lady Jane corrected.

"Oh, my lady, it was too unfortunate. If only your ladyship had have said... poor Georgiana had ought to have seen; but she never *did* have her wits about her, not for answering the door."

"But she was only obeying orders. She went to ask Mr. Jones."

Mrs. Clemm was silent. Her small hands, wrinkled and resolute, fumbled with the folds of her apron, and her quick eyes made the circuit of the room and then came back to Lady Jane's.

"Just so, my lady; but, as I told her, she'd ought to have know—"

"And who is Mr. Jones?"

Mrs. Clemm's smile snapped out again, deprecating, respectful. "Well, my lady, he's more dead than living, too... if I may say so," was her surprising answer.

"Is he? I'm sorry to hear that; but who is he?"

"Well, my lady, he's... he's my great-uncle, as it were... my grandmother's own brother, as you might say."

"Ah; I see." Lady Jane considered her with growing curiosity. "He must have reached a great age, then."

"Yes, my lady; he has that. Though I'm not," Mrs. Clemm added, the dimple showing, "as old myself as your ladyship might suppose. Living at Bells all these years has been ageing to me; it would be to anybody."

"I suppose so. And yet," Lady Jane continued, "Mr. Jones has survived; has stood it well—as you certainly have?"

"Oh, not as well as I have," Mrs. Clemm interjected, as if resentful of the comparison.

"At any rate, he still mounts guard; mounts it as well as he did thirty years ago."

"Thirty years ago?" Mrs. Clemm echoed, her hands dropping from her apron to her sides.

"Wasn't he here thirty years ago?"

"Oh, yes, my lady; certainly; he's never once been away that I know of."

"What a wonderful record! And what exactly are his duties?"

Mrs. Clemm paused again, her hands still motionless in the folds of her start. Lady Jane noticed that the fingers were tightly clenched, as if to check an involuntary gesture.

"He began as pantry-boy; then footman; then butler, my lady; but it's hard to say, isn't it, what an old servant's duties are, when he's stayed on in the same house so many years?"

"Yes; and that house always empty."

"Just so, my lady. Everything came to depend on him; one thing after another. His late lordship thought the world of him."

"His late lordship? But he was never here! He spent all his life in Canada."

Mrs. Clemm seemed slightly disconcerted. "Certainly, my lady." (Her voice said: "Who are you, to set me right as to the chronicles of Bells?") "But by letter, my lady; I can show you the letters. And there was his lordship before, the sixteenth Viscount. He *did* come here once."

"Ah, did he?" Lady Jane was embarrassed to find how little she knew of them all. She rose from her seat. "They were lucky, all these absentees, to have some one to watch over their interests so faithfully. I should like to see Mr. Jones—to thank him. Will you take me to him now?"

"Now?" Mrs. Clemm moved back a step or two; Lady Jane fancied her cheeks paled a little under their ruddy varnish. "Oh, not today, my lady."

"Why? Isn't he well enough?"

"Not nearly. He's between life and death, as it were," Mrs. Clemm repeated, as if the phrase were the nearest approach she could find to a definition of Mr. Jones's state.

"He wouldn't even know who I was?"

Mrs. Clemm considered a moment. "I don't say *that*, my lady;" her tone implied that to do so might appear disrespectful. "He'd know you, my lady; but you wouldn't know *him*." She broke off and added hastily: "I mean, for what he is: he's in no state for you to see him."

"He's so very ill? Poor man! And is everything possible being done?"

"Oh, everything; and more too, my lady. But perhaps," Mrs. Clemm suggested, with a clink of keys, "this would be a good time for your ladyship to take a look about the house. If your ladyship has no objection, I should like to begin with the linen."

IV

"And Mr. Jones?" Stramer queried, a few days later, as they sat, Lady Jane and the party from Kent, about an improvised tea-table in a recess of one of the great holly-hedges.

The day was as hushed and warm as that on which she had first come to Bells, and Lady Jane looked up with a smile of ownership at the old walls which seemed to smile back, the windows which now looked at her with friendly eyes.

"Mr. Jones? Who's Mr. Jones?" the others asked; only Stramer recalled their former talk.

Lady Jane hesitated. "Mr. Jones is my invisible guardian; or rather, the guardian of Bells."

They remembered then. "Invisible? You don't mean to say you haven't seen him yet?"

"Not yet; perhaps I never shall. He's very old—and very ill, I'm afraid."

"And he still rules here?"

"Oh, absolutely. The fact is," Lady Jane added, "I believe he's the only person left who really knows all about Bells."

"Jane, my *dear*! That big shrub over there against the wall! I verily believe it's *Templetonia retusa*. It *is!* Did any one ever hear of its standing an English winter?" Gardeners all, they dashed off towards the shrub in its sheltered angle. "I shall certainly try it on a south wall at Dipway," cried the hostess from Kent.

Tea over, they moved on to inspect the house. The short autumn day was drawing to a close; but the party had been able to come only for an afternoon, instead of staying over the week-end, and having lingered so long in the gardens they had only time, indoors, to puzzle out what they could through the shadows. Perhaps, Lady Jane thought, it was the best hour to see a house like Bells, so long abandoned, and not yet warmed into new life.

The fire she had had lit in the saloon sent its radiance to meet them, giving the great room an air of expectancy and welcome. The portraits, the Italian cabinets, the shabby armchairs and rugs, all looked as if life had but lately left them; and Lady Jane said to herself: "Perhaps Mrs. Clemm is right in advising me to live here and close the blue parlour."

"My dear, what a fine room! Pity it faces north. Of course you'll have to shut it in winter. It would cost a fortune to heat."

Lady Jane hesitated. "I don't know: I *had* meant to. But there seems to be no other…"

"No other? In all this house?" They laughed; and one of the visitors, going ahead and crossing a panelled anteroom, cried out: "But here! A delicious room; windows south—yes, and west. The warmest of the house. This is perfect."

They followed, and the blue room echoed with exclamations. "Those charming curtains with the parrots… and the blue of that *petit point* firescreen! But, Jane, of course you must live here. Look at this citron-wood desk!"

Lady Jane stood on the threshold. "It seems that the chimney smokes hopelessly."

"Hopelessly? Nonsense! Have you consulted anybody? I'll send you a wonderful man..."

"Besides, if you put in one of those one-pipe heaters... At Dipway..."

Stramer was looking over Lady Jane's shoulder. "What does Mr. Jones say about it?"

"He says no one has ever been able to use this room; not for ages. It was the housekeeper who told me. She's his great-niece, and seems simply to transmit his oracles."

Stramer shrugged. "Well, he's lived at Bells longer than you have. Perhaps he's right."

"How absurd!" one of the ladies cried. "The housekeeper and Mr. Jones probably spend their evenings here, and don't want to be disturbed. Look—ashes on the hearth! What did I tell you?"

Lady Jane echoed the laugh as they turned away. They had still to see the library, damp and dilapidated, the panelled dining-room, the breakfast-parlour, and such bedrooms as had any old furniture left; not many, for the late lords of Bells, at one time or another, had evidently sold most of its removable treasures.

When the visitors came down their motors were waiting. A lamp had been placed in the hall, but the rooms beyond were lit only by the broad clear band of western sky showing through uncurtained casements. On the doorstep one of the ladies exclaimed that she had lost her hand-bag—no, she remembered; she had laid it on the desk in the blue room. Which way was the blue room?

"I'll get it," Jane said, turning back. She heard Stramer following. He asked if he should bring the lamp.

"Oh, no; I can see."

She crossed the threshold of the blue room, guided by the light from its western window; then she stopped. Some one was in the room already; she felt rather than saw another presence. Stramer, behind her, paused also; he did not speak or move. What she saw, or thought she saw, was simply an old man with bent shoulders turning away from the citron-wood desk. Almost before she had received the impression there was no one there; only the slightest stir of the needlework curtain over the farther door. She heard no step or other sound.

"There's the bag," she said, as if the act of speaking, and saying something obvious, were a relief.

In the hall her glance crossed Stramer's, but failed to find there the reflection of what her own had registered.

He shook hands, smiling. "Well, goodbye. I commit you to Mr. Jones's care; only don't let him say that *you're* not shown to visitors."

She smiled: "Come back and try," and then shivered a little as the lights of the last motor vanished beyond the great black hedges.

v

Lady Jane had exulted in her resolve to keep Bells to herself till she and the old house should have had time to make friends. But after a few days she recalled the uneasy feeling which had come over her as she stood on the threshold after her first tentative ring. Yes; she had been right in thinking she would have to have people about her to take the chill off. The house was too old, too mysterious, too much withdrawn into its own secret past, for her poor little present to fit into it without uneasiness.

But it was not a time of year when, among Lady Jane's friends, it was easy to find people free. Her own family were all in the north, and impossible to dislodge. One of her sisters, when invited, simply sent her back a list of shooting-dates; and her mother wrote: "Why not come to us? What can you have to do all alone in that empty house at this time of year? Next summer we're all coming."

Having tried one or two friends with the same result, Lady Jane bethought her of Stramer. He was finishing a novel, she knew, and at such times he liked to settle down somewhere in the country where he could be sure of not being disturbed. Bells was a perfect asylum, and though it was probable that some other friend had anticipated her, and provided the requisite seclusion, Lady Jane decided to invite him. "Do bring your work and stay till it's finished—and don't be in a hurry to finish. I promise that no one shall bother you—" and she added, half-nervously: "Not even Mr. Jones." As she wrote she felt an absurd impulse to blot the words out. "He might not like it," she thought; and the "he" did not refer to Stramer.

Was the solitude already making her superstitious? She thrust the letter into an envelope, and carried it herself to the post-office at Thudeney-Blazes. Two days later a wire from Stramer announced his arrival.

He came on a cold stormy afternoon, just before dinner, and as they went up to dress Lady Jane called after him: "We shall sit in the blue parlour this evening." The housemaid Georgiana was crossing the passage with hot water for the visitor. She stopped and cast a vacant glance at Lady Jane. The latter met it, and said carelessly: 'You hear, Georgiana? The fire in the blue parlour."

While Lady Jane was dressing she heard a knock, and saw Mrs. Clemm's round face just inside the door, like a red apple on a garden wall.

"Is there anything wrong about the saloon, my lady? Georgiana understood—"

"That I want the fire in the blue parlour. Yes. What's wrong with the saloon is that one freezes there."

"But the chimney smokes in the blue parlour."

"Well, we'll give it a trial and if it does I'll send for some one to arrange it."

"Nothing can be done, my lady. Everything has been tried, and—"

Lady Jane swung about suddenly. She had heard Stramer singing a cheerful hunting-song in a cracked voice, in his dressing-room at the other end of the corridor.

"That will do, Mrs. Clemm. I want the fire in the blue parlour."

"Yes, my lady." The door closed on the housekeeper.

"So you decided on the saloon after all?" Stramer said, as Lady Jane led the way there after their brief repast.

"Yes: I hope you won't be frozen. Mr. Jones swears that the chimney in the blue parlour isn't safe; so, until I can fetch the mason over from Strawbridge—"

"Oh, I see." Stramer drew up to the blaze in the great fireplace. "We're very well off here; though heating this room is going to be ruinous. Meanwhile, I note that Mr. Jones still rules."

Lady Jane gave a slight laugh.

"Tell me," Stramer continued, as she bent over the mixing of the Turkish coffee, "what is there about him? I'm getting curious."

Lady Jane laughed again, and heard the embarrassment in her laugh. "So am I."

"Why—you don't mean to say you haven't seen him yet?"

"No. He's still too ill."

"What's the matter with him? What does the doctor say?"

"He won't see the doctor."

"But look here—if things take a worse turn—I don't know; but mightn't you be held to have been negligent?"

"What can I do? Mrs. Clemm says he has a doctor who treats him by correspondence. I don't see that I can interfere."

"Isn't there some one beside Mrs. Clemm whom you can consult?"

She considered: certainly, as yet, she had not made much effort to get into relation with her neighbours. "I expected the vicar to call. But I've enquired: there's no vicar any longer at Thudeney-Blazes. A curate comes from Strawbridge every other Sunday. And the one who comes now is new: nobody about the place seems to know him."

"But I thought the chapel here was in use? It looked so when you showed it to us the other day."

"I thought so too. It used to be the parish church of Lynke-Linnet and Lower-Lynke; but it seems that was years ago. The parishioners objected to coming so far; and there weren't enough of them. Mrs. Clemm says that nearly everybody has died off or left. It's the same at Thudeney-Blazes."

Stramer glanced about the great room, with its circle of warmth and light by the hearth, and the sullen shadows huddled at its farther end, as if hungrily listening. "With this emptiness at the centre, life was bound to cease gradually on the outskirts."

Lady Jane followed his glance. "Yes; it's all wrong. I must try to wake the place up."

"Why not open it to the public? Have a visitors' day?"

She thought a moment. In itself the suggestion was distasteful; she could imagine few things that would bore her more. Yet to do so might be a duty, a first step toward re-establishing relations between the lifeless house and its neighbourhood. Secretly, she felt that even the coming and going of indifferent unknown people would help to take the chill from those rooms, to brush from their walls the dust of too-heavy memories.

"Who's that?" asked Stramer. Lady Jane started in spite of herself and glanced over her shoulder; but he was only looking past her at a portrait which a dart of flame from the hearth had momentarily called from its obscurity.

"That's a Lady Thudeney." She got up and went toward the picture with a lamp. "Might be an Opie, don't you think? It's a strange face, under the smirk of the period."

Stramer took the lamp and held it up. The portrait was that of a young woman in a short-waisted muslin gown caught beneath the breast by a cameo. Between clusters of beribboned curls a long fair oval looked out dumbly, inexpressively, in a stare of frozen beauty. "It's as if the house had been too empty even then," Lady Jane murmured. "I wonder which she was? Oh, I know: it must be 'Also His Wife'."

Stramer stared.

"It's the only name on her monument. The wife of Peregrine Vincent Theobald, who perished of the plague at Aleppo in 1828. Perhaps she was very fond of him, and this was painted when she was an inconsolable widow."

"They didn't dress like that as late as 1828." Stramer holding the lamp closer, deciphered the inscription on the border of the lady's India scarf; *Juliana, Viscountess Thudeney, 1818.* "She must have been inconsolable before his death, then."

Lady Jane smiled. "Let's hope she grew less so after it."

Stramer passed the lamp across the canvas. "Do you see where she was painted? In the blue parlour. Look: the old panelling; and she's leaning on the citron-wood desk. They evidently used the room in winter then." The lamp paused on the background of the picture: a window framing snow-laden paths and hedges in icy perspective.

"Curious," Stramer said—"and rather melancholy: to be painted against that wintry desolation. I wish you could find out more about her. Have you dipped into your archives?"

"No. Mr. Jones—"

"He won't allow that either?"

"Yes; but he's lost the key of the muniment-room. Mrs. Clemm has been trying to get a locksmith."

"Surely the neighbourhood can still produce one?"

"There *was* one at Thudeney-Blazes; but he died the week before I came."

"Of course!"

"Of course?"

"Well, in Mrs. Clemm's hands keys get lost, chimneys smoke, locksmiths die…" Stramer stood, light in hand, looking down the shadowy length of the saloon. "I say, let's go and see what's happening now in the blue parlour."

Lady Jane laughed: a laugh seemed easy with another voice nearby to echo it. "Let's—"

She followed him out of the saloon, across the hall in which a single candle burned on a far-off table, and past the stairway yawning like a black funnel above them. In the doorway of the blue parlour Stramer paused. "Now, then, Mr. Jones!"

It was stupid, but Lady Jane's heart gave a jerk: she hoped the challenge would not evoke the shadowy figure she had half seen that other day.

"Lord, it's cold!" Stramer stood looking about him. "Those ashes are still on the hearth. Well, it's all very queer." He crossed over to the citron-wood desk. "There's where she sat for her picture—and in this very armchair—look!"

"Oh, don't!" Lady Jane exclaimed. The words slipped out unawares.

"Don't—what?"

"Try those drawers—" she wanted to reply; for his hand was stretched toward the desk.

"I'm frozen; I think I'm starting a cold. Do come away," she grumbled, backing toward the door.

Stramer lighted her out without comment. As the lamplight slid along the walls Lady Jane fancied that the needlework curtain over the farther door stirred as it had that other day. But it may have been the wind rising outside...

The saloon seemed like home when they got back to it.

"There *is* no Mr. Jones!"

Stramer proclaimed it triumphantly when they met the next morning. Lady Jane had motored off early to Strawbridge in quest of a mason and a locksmith. The quest had taken longer than she had expected, for everybody in Strawbridge was busy on jobs nearer by, and unaccustomed to the idea of going to Bells, with which the town seemed to have had no communication within living memory. The younger workmen did not even know where the place was, and the best Lady Jane could do was to coax a locksmith's apprentice to come with her, on the understanding that he would be driven back to the nearest station as soon as his job was over. As for the mason, he had merely taken note of her request, and promised half-heartedly to send somebody when he could. "Rather off our beat, though."

She returned, discouraged and somewhat weary, as Stramer was coming downstairs after his morning's work.

"No Mr. Jones?" she echoed.

"Not a trace! I've been trying the old Glamis experiment—situating his room by its window. Luckily the house is smaller…"

Lady Jane smiled. "Is this what you call locking yourself up with your work?"

"I can't work: that's the trouble. Not till this is settled. Bells is a fidgety place."

"Yes," she agreed.

"Well, I wasn't going to be beaten; so I went to try to find the head-gardener."

"But there isn't—"

"No. Mrs. Clemm told me. The head-gardener died last year. That woman positively glows with life whenever she announces a death. Have you noticed?"

Yes: Lady Jane had.

"Well—I said to myself that if there wasn't a head-gardener there must be an underling; at least one. I'd seen somebody in the distance, raking leaves, and I ran him down. Of course he'd never seen Mr. Jones."

"You mean that poor old half-blind Jacob? He couldn't see anybody."

"Perhaps not. At any rate, he told me that Mr. Jones wouldn't let the leaves be buried for leaf-mould—I forget why. Mr. Jones's authority extends even to the gardens."

"Yet you say he doesn't exist!"

"Wait. Jacob is half-blind, but he's been here for years, and knows more about the place than you'd think. I got him talking about the house, and I pointed to one window after another, and he told me each time whose the room was, or had been. But he couldn't situate Mr. Jones."

"I beg your ladyship's pardon—" Mrs. Clemm was on the threshold, cheeks shining, skirt rustling, her eyes like drills. "The locksmith your ladyship brought back; I understand it was for the lock of the muniment-room—"

"Well?"

"He's lost one of his tools, and can't do anything without it. So he's gone. The butcher's boy gave him a lift back."

Lady Jane caught Stramer's faint chuckle. She stood and stared at Mrs. Clemm, and Mrs. Clemm stared back, deferential but unflinching.

"Gone? Very well; I'll motor after him."

"Oh, my lady, it's too late. The butcher's boy had his motor-cycle... Besides, what could he do?"

"Break the lock," exclaimed Lady Jane, exasperated.

"Oh, my lady—" Mrs. Clemm's intonation marked the most respectful incredulity. She waited another moment, and then withdrew, while Lady Jane and Stramer considered each other.

"But this is absurd," Lady Jane declared when they had lunched, waited on, as usual, by the flustered Georgiana. "I'll break in that door myself, if I have to.—Be careful please, Georgiana," she added; "I was speaking of doors, not dishes." For Georgiana had let fall with a crash the dish she was removing from the table. She gathered up the pieces in her tremulous fingers, and vanished. Jane and Stramer returned to the saloon.

"Queer!" the novelist commented.

"Yes." Lady Jane, facing the door, started slightly. Mrs. Clemm was there again; but this time subdued, unrustling, bathed in that odd pallor which enclosed but seemed unable to penetrate the solid crimson of her cheeks.

"I beg pardon, my lady. The key is found." Her hand, as she held it out, trembled like Georgiana's.

VI

"It's not here," Stramer announced, a couple of hours later.

"What isn't?" Lady Jane queried, looking up from a heap of disordered papers. Her eyes blinked at him through the fog of yellow dust raised by her manipulations.

"The clue.—I've got all the 1800 to 1840 papers here; and there's a gap."

She moved over to the table above which he was bending. "A gap?"

"A big one. Nothing between 1815 and 1835. No mention of Peregrine or of Juliana."

They looked at each other across the tossed papers, and suddenly Stramer exclaimed: "Some one has been here before us—just lately."

Lady Jane stared, incredulous, and then followed the direction of his downward pointing hand.

"Do you wear flat heelless shoes?" he questioned. "And of that size? Even my feet are too small to fit into those foot-prints. Luckily there wasn't time to sweep the floor!"

Lady Jane felt a slight chill, a chill of a different and more inward quality than the shock of stuffy coldness which had met them as they entered the unaired attic set apart for the storing of the Thudeney archives.

"But how absurd! Of course when Mrs. Clemm found we were coming up she came—or sent some one—to open the shutters."

"That's not Mrs. Clemm's foot, or the other woman's. She must have sent a man—an old man with a shaky uncertain step. Look how it wanders."

"Mr. Jones, then!" said Lady Jane, half impatiently.

"Mr. Jones. And he got what he wanted, and put it—where?"

"Ah, *that*—! I'm freezing, you know; let's give this up for the present." She rose, and Stramer followed her without protest; the muniment-room was really untenable.

"I must catalogue all this stuff some day, I suppose," Lady Jane continued, as they went down the stairs. "But meanwhile, what do you say to a good tramp, to get the dust out of our lungs?"

He agreed, and turned back to his room to get some letters he wanted to post at Thudeney-Blazes.

Lady Jane went down alone. It was a fine afternoon, and the sun, which had made the dust-clouds of the muniment-room so dazzling, sent a long shaft through the west window of the blue parlour, and across the floor of the hall.

Certainly Georgiana kept the oak floors remarkably well; considering how much else she had to do, it was surp—

Lady Jane stopped as if an unseen hand had jerked her violently back. On the smooth parquet before her she had caught the trace of dusty foot-prints—the prints of broad-soled heelless shoes—making for the blue parlour and crossing its threshold. She stood still with the same inward shiver that she had felt upstairs; then, avoiding the foot-prints, she too stole very softly toward the blue parlour, pushed the door wider, and saw, in the long dazzle of autumn light, as if translucid, edged with the glitter, an old man at the desk.

"Mr. Jones!"

A step came up behind her: Mrs. Clemm with the post-bag. "You called, my lady?"

"I... yes..."

When she turned back to the desk there was no one there.

She faced about on the housekeeper. "Who was that?"

"Where, my lady?"

Lady Jane, without answering, moved toward the needlework curtain, in which she had detected the same faint tremor as before. "Where does that door go to—behind the curtain?"

"Nowhere, my lady. I mean; there is no door."

Mrs. Clemm had followed; her step sounded quick and assured. She lifted up the curtain with a firm hand. Behind it was a rectangle of roughly plastered wall, where an opening had visibly been bricked up.

"When was that done?"

"The wall built up? I couldn't say. I've never known it otherwise," replied the housekeeper.

The two women stood for an instant measuring each other with level eyes; then the housekeeper's were slowly towered, and she let the curtain fall from her hand. "There are a great many things in old houses that nobody knows about," she said.

"There shall be as few as possible in mine," said Lady Jane.

"My lady!" The housekeeper stepped quickly in front of her. "My lady, what are you doing?" she gasped.

Lady Jane had turned back to the desk at which she had just seen—or fancied she had seen—the bending figure of Mr. Jones.

"I am going to look through these drawers," she said.

The housekeeper still stood in pale immobility between her and the desk. "No, my lady—no. You won't do that."

"Because—?"

Mrs. Clemm crumpled up her black silk apron with a despairing gesture. "Because—if you *will*, have it—that's where Mr. Jones keeps his private papers. I know he'd oughtn't to..."

"Ah—then it was Mr. Jones I saw here?"

The housekeeper's arms sank to her sides and her mouth hung open on an unspoken word "You *saw* him?" The question came out in a confused whisper; and before Lady Jane could answer, Mrs. Clemm's arms rose again, stretched before her face as if to fend off a blaze of intolerable light, or some forbidden sight she had long since disciplined herself not to see. Thus screening her eyes she hurried across the hall to the door of the servants' wing.

Lady Jane stood for a moment looking after her; then, with a slightly shaking hand, she opened the desk and hurriedly took out from it all the papers—a small bundle—that it contained. With them she passed back into the saloon.

As she entered it her eye was caught by the portrait of the melancholy lady in the short-waisted gown whom she and Stramer had christened "Also His Wife." The lady's eyes, usually so empty of all awareness save of her own frozen beauty, seemed suddenly waking to an anguished participation in the scene.

"Fudge!" muttered Lady Jane, shaking off the spectral suggestion as she turned to meet Stramer on the threshold.

VII

The missing papers were all there. Stramer and she spread them out hurriedly on a table and at once proceeded to gloat over their find. Not a particularly important one, indeed; in the long history of the Lynkes and Crofts it took up hardly more space than the little handful of documents did, in actual bulk, among the stacks of the muniment-room. But the fact that these papers filled a gap in the chronicles of the house, and situated the sad-faced beauty as veritably the wife of the Peregrine Vincent Theobald Lynke who had "perished of the plague at Aleppo in 1828"—this was a discovery sufficiently exciting to whet amateur appetites, and to put out of Lady Jane's mind the strange incident which had attended the opening of the cabinet.

For a while she and Stramer sat silently and methodically going through their respective piles of correspondence; but presently Lady Jane, after glancing over one of the yellowing pages, uttered a startled exclamation.

"How strange! Mr. Jones again—always Mr. Jones!"

Stramer looked up from the papers he was sorting. "You too? I've got a lot of letters here addressed to a Mr. Jones by Peregrine Vincent, who seems to have been always disporting himself abroad, and chronically in want of money. Gambling debts, apparently... ah and women... a dirty record altogether..."

"Yes? My letter is not written to a Mr. Jones; but it's about one. Listen." Lady Jane began to read. "'Bells, February 20th, 1826...' (It's from poor 'Also His Wife' to her husband.) 'My dear Lord, Acknowledging as I ever do the burden of the sad impediment which denies me the happiness of being more frequently in your company, I yet fail to conceive how anything in my state obliges that close seclusion in which Mr. Jones persists—and by your express orders, so he declares—in confining me. Surely, my lord, had you found it possible to spend more time with me since the day of our marriage, you would yourself have seen it to be unnecessary to put this restraint upon me. It is true, alas, that my unhappy infirmity denies me the happiness to speak with you, or to hear the accents of the voice I should love above all others could it but reach me; but, my dear husband, I would have you consider that my mind is in no way affected by this obstacle, but goes out to you, as my heart does, in a perpetual eagerness of attention, and that to sit in this great house alone, day after day, month after month, deprived of your company, and debarred also from any intercourse but that of the servants you have chosen to put about me, is a fate more cruel than I deserve and more painful than I can bear. I have entreated Mr. Jones, since he seems all-powerful with you, to represent this to you, and to transmit this my last request—for should I fail I am resolved to make no other—that you should consent to my making the acquaintance of a few of your friends and neighbours, among whom I cannot but think there must be some kind hearts that would take pity on my unhappy situation, and afford me such companionship as would give me more courage to bear your continual absence...'"

Lady Jane folded up the letter. "Deaf and dumb—ah, poor creature! That explains the look—"

"And this explains the marriage," Stramer continued unfolding a stiff parchment document. "Here are the Viscountess Thudeney's marriage settlements. She appears to have been a Miss Portallo, daughter of Obadiah Portallo Esqre, of Purflew Castle, Caermarthenshire, and Bombay House, Twickenham, East India merchant, senior member of the banking house of Portallo and Prest—and so on and so on. And the figures run up into hundreds of thousands."

"It's rather ghastly—putting the two things together. All the millions and—imprisonment in the blue parlour. I suppose her Viscount had to have the money, and was ashamed to have it known how he had got it…" Lady Jane shivered. "Think of it—day after day, winter after winter, year after year… speechless, soundless, alone… under Mr. Jones's guardianship. Let me see: what year were they married?"

"In 1817."

"And only a year later that portrait was painted. And she had the frozen look already."

Stramer mused: "Yes; it's grim enough. But the strangest figure in the whole case is still—Mr. Jones."

"Mr. Jones—yes. Her keeper," Lady Jane mused "I suppose he must have been this one's ancestor. The office seems to have been hereditary at Bells."

"Well—I don't know."

Stramer's voice was so odd that Lady Jane looked up at him with a stare of surprise. "What if it were the same one?" suggested Stramer with a queer smile.

"The same?" Lady Jane laughed. "You're not good at figures are you? If poor Lady Thudeney's Mr. Jones were alive now he'd be—"

"I didn't say ours was alive now," said Stramer.

"Oh—why, what…?" she faltered.

But Stramer did not answer; his eyes had been arrested by the precipitate opening of the door behind his hostess, and the entry of Georgiana, a livid, dishevelled Georgiana, more than usually bereft of her faculties, and gasping out something inarticulate.

"Oh, my lady—it's my aunt—she won't answer me," Georgiana stammered in a voice of terror.

Lady Jane uttered an impatient exclamation. "Answer you? Why—what do you want her to answer?"

"Only whether she's alive, my lady," said Georgiana with streaming eyes.

Lady Jane continued to look at her severely. "Alive? Alive? Why on earth shouldn't she be?"

"She might as well be dead—by the way she just lies there."

"Your aunt dead? I saw her alive enough in the blue parlour half an hour ago," Lady Jane returned. She was growing rather *blasé* with regard to Georgiana's panics; but suddenly she felt this to be of a different nature from any of the others. "Where is it your aunt's lying?"

"In her own bedroom, on her bed," the other wailed, "and won't say why."

Lady Jane got to her feet, pushing aside the heaped-up papers, and hastening to the door with Stramer in her wake.

As they went up the stairs she realised that she had seen the housekeeper's bedroom only once, on the day of her first obligatory round of inspection, when she had taken possession of Bells. She did not even remember very clearly where it was, but followed Georgiana down the passage and through a door which communicated, rather surprisingly, with a narrow walled-in staircase that was unfamiliar to her. At its top she and Stramer found themselves on a small landing upon which two doors opened. Through the confusion of her mind Lady Jane noticed that these rooms, with their special staircase leading down to what had always been called his lordship's suite, must obviously have been occupied by his lordship's confidential servants. In one of them, presumably, had been lodged the original Mr. Jones, the Mr. Jones of the yellow letters, the letters purloined by Lady Jane. As she crossed the threshold, Lady Jane remembered the housekeeper's attempt to prevent her touching the contents of the desk.

Mrs. Clemm's room, like herself, was neat, glossy and extremely cold. Only Mrs. Clemm herself was no longer like Mrs. Clemm. The red-apple glaze had barely faded from her cheeks, and not a lock was disarranged in the unnatural lustre of her false front; even her cap ribbons hung symmetrically along either cheek. But death had happened to her, and had made her into someone else. At first glance it was impossible to say if the unspeakable horror in her wide-open eyes were only the reflection of that change, or of the agent by whom it had come. Lady Jane, shuddering, paused a moment while Stramer went up to the bed.

"Her hand is warm still—but no pulse." He glanced about the room. "A glass anywhere?" The cowering Georgiana took a hand-glass from the neat chest of drawers, and Stramer held it over the housekeeper's drawn-back lip…

"She's dead," he pronounced.

"Oh, poor thing! But how—?" Lady Jane drew near, and was kneeling down, taking the inanimate hand in hers, when Stramer touched her on the arm, and then silently raised a finger of warning. Georgiana was crouching in the farther corner of the room, her face buried in her lifted arms.

"Look here," Stramer whispered. He pointed to Mrs. Clemm's throat, and Lady Jane, bending over, distinctly saw a circle of red marks on it—the marks of recent bruises. She looked again into the awful eyes.

"She's been strangled," Stramer whispered.

Lady Jane, with a shiver of fear, drew down the housekeeper's lids. Georgiana, her face hidden, was still sobbing convulsively in the corner. There seemed, in the air of the cold orderly room, something that forbade wonderment and silenced conjecture. Lady Jane and Stramer stood and looked at each other without speaking. At length Stramer crossed over to Georgiana, and touched her on the shoulder. She appeared unaware of the touch, and he grasped her shoulder and shook it. "Where is Mr. Jones?" he asked.

The girl looked up, her face blurred and distorted with weeping, her eyes dilated as if with the vision of some latent terror. "Oh, sir, she's not really dead, is she?"

Stramer repeated his question in a loud authoritative tone; and slowly she echoed it in a scarce-heard whisper. "Mr. Jones—?"

"Get up, my girl, and send him here to us at once, or tell us where to find him."

Georgiana, moved by the old habit of obedience, struggled to her feet and stood unsteadily, her heaving shoulders braced against the wall. Stramer asked her sharply if she had not heard what he had said.

"Oh, poor thing, she's so upset—" Lady Jane intervened compassionately. "Tell me, Georgiana: where shall we find Mr. Jones?"

The girl turned to her with eyes as fixed as the dead woman's. "You won't find him anywhere," she slowly said.

"Why not?"

"Because he's not here."

"Not here? Where is he, then?" Stramer broke in.

Georgiana did not seem to notice the interruption. She continued to stare at Lady Jane with Mrs. Clemm's awful eyes. "He's in his grave in the churchyard—these years and years he is. Long before ever I was born… my aunt hadn't ever seen him herself, not since she was a tiny child… That's the terror of it… that's why she always had to do what he told her to… because you couldn't ever answer him back…" Her horrific gaze turned from Lady Jane to the stony face and fast-glazing pupils of the dead woman. "You hadn't ought to have meddled with his papers, my lady… That's what he's punished her for… When it came to those papers he wouldn't ever listen to human reason… he wouldn't…" Then, flinging her arms above her head, Georgiana straightened herself to her full height before falling in a swoon at Stramer's feet.

THE END

POMEGRANATE SEED

I

CHARLOTTE Ashby paused on her doorstep. Dark had descended on the brilliancy of the March afternoon, and the grinding rasping street life of the city was at its highest. She turned her back on it, standing for a moment in the old-fashioned, marble-flagged vestibule before she inserted her key in the lock. The sash curtains drawn across the panes of the inner door softened the light within to a warm blur through which no details showed. It was the hour when, in the first months of her marriage to Kenneth Ashby, she had most liked to return to that quiet house in a street long since deserted by business and fashion. The contrast between the soulless roar of New York, its devouring blaze of lights, the oppression of its congested traffic, congested houses, lives, minds and this veiled sanctuary she called home, always stirred her profoundly. In the very heart of the hurricane she had found her tiny islet—or thought she had. And now, in the last months, everything was changed, and she always wavered on the doorstep and had to force herself to enter.

While she stood there she called up the scene within: the hall hung with old prints, the ladder-like stairs, and on the left her husband's long shabby library, full of books and pipes and worn armchairs inviting to meditation. How she had loved that room! Then, upstairs, her own drawing-room, in which, since the death of Kenneth's first wife, neither furniture nor hangings had been changed, because there had never been money enough, but which Charlotte had made her own by moving furniture about and adding more books, another lamp, a table for the new reviews. Even on the occasion of her only visit to the first Mrs. Ashby—a distant, self-centred woman, whom she had known very slightly—she had looked about her with an innocent envy, feeling it to be exactly the drawing-room she would have liked for herself; and now for more than a year it had been hers to deal with as she chose—the room to which she hastened back at dusk on winter days, where she sat reading by the fire, or answering notes at the pleasant roomy desk, or going over her stepchildren's copy books, till she heard her husband's step.

Sometimes friends dropped in; sometimes—oftener—she was alone; and she liked that best, since it was another way of being with Kenneth, thinking over what he had said when they parted in the morning, imagining what he would say when he sprang up the stairs, found her by herself and caught her to him.

Now, instead of this, she thought of one thing only—the letter she might or might not find on the hall table. Until she had made sure whether or not it was there, her mind had no room for anything else. The letter was always the same—a square greyish envelope with "Kenneth Ashby, Esquire," written on it in bold but faint characters. From the first it had struck Charlotte as peculiar that anyone who wrote such a firm hand should trace the letters so lightly; the address was always written as though there were not enough ink in the pen, or the writer's wrist were too weak to bear upon it. Another curious thing was that, in spite of its masculine curves, the writing was so visibly feminine. Some hands are sexless, some masculine, at first glance; the writing on the grey envelope, for all its strength and assurance, was without doubt a woman's. The envelope never bore anything but the recipient's name; no stamp, no address. The letter was presumably delivered by hand—but by whose? No doubt it was slipped into the letter box, whence the parlourmaid, when she closed the shutters and lit the lights, probably extracted it. At any rate, it was always in the evening, after dark, that Charlotte saw it lying there. She thought of the letter in the singular, as "it," because, though there had been several since her marriage—seven, to be exact—they were so alike in appearance that they had become merged in one another in her mind, become one letter, become "it."

The first had come the day after their return from their honeymoon—a journey prolonged to the West Indies, from which they had returned to New York after an absence of more than two months. Re-entering the house with her husband, late on that first evening—they had dined at his mother's—she had seen, alone on the hall table, the grey envelope. Her eye fell on it before Kenneth's, and her first thought was: "Why, I've seen that writing before," but where she could not recall. The memory was just definite enough for her to identify the script whenever it looked up at her faintly from the same pale envelope; but on that first day she would have thought no more of the letter if when her husband's glance lit on it, she had not chanced to be looking at him. It all happened in a flash—his seeing the letter, putting out his hand for it, raising it to his short-sighted eyes to decipher the faint writing, and then abruptly withdrawing the arm he had slipped through Charlotte's, and moving away to the hanging light, his back turned to her. She had waited—waited for a sound, an exclamation; waited for him to open the letter; but he had slipped it into his pocket without a word and followed her into the library. And there they had sat down by the fire and lit their cigarettes, and he had remained silent, his head thrown back broodingly against the armchair, his eyes fixed on the hearth, and presently had passed his hand over his forehead and said: "Wasn't it unusually hot at my mother's tonight? I've got a splitting head. Mind if I take myself off to bed?"

That was the first time. Since then Charlotte had never been present when he had received the letter. It usually came before he got home from his office, and she had to go upstairs and leave it lying there. But even if she had not seen it, she would have known it had come by the change in his face when he joined her—which, on those evenings, he seldom did before they met for dinner. Evidently, whatever the letter contained, he wanted to be by himself to deal with it; and when he reappeared he looked years older, looked emptied of life and courage, and hardly conscious of her presence. Sometimes he was silent for the rest of the evening; and if he spoke, it was usually to hint some criticism of her household arrangements, suggest some change in the domestic administration, to ask, a little nervously, if she didn't think Joyce's nursery governess was rather young and flighty, or if she herself always saw to it that Peter—whose throat was delicate—was properly wrapped up when he went to school. At such times Charlotte would remember the friendly warnings she had received when she became engaged to Kenneth Ashby: "Marrying a heartbroken widower! Isn't that rather risky? You know Elsie Ashby absolutely dominated him;" and how she had jokingly replied: "He may be glad of a little liberty for a change." And in this respect she had been right. She had needed no one to tell her, during the first months, that her husband was perfectly happy with her. When they came back from their protracted honeymoon the same friends said: "What have you done to Kenneth? He looks twenty years younger"; and this time she answered with careless joy: "I suppose I've got him out of his groove."

But what she noticed after the grey letters began to come was not so much his nervous tentative faultfinding—which always seemed to be uttered against his will—as the look in his eyes when he joined her after receiving one of the letters. The look was not unloving, not even indifferent; it was the look of a man who had been so far away from ordinary events that when he returns to familiar things they seem strange. She minded that more than the faultfinding.

Though she had been sure from the first that the handwriting on the grey envelope was a woman's, it was long before she associated the mysterious letters with any sentimental secret. She was too sure of her husband's love, too confident of filling his life, for such an idea to occur to her. It seemed far more likely that the letters—which certainly did not appear to cause him any sentimental pleasure—were addressed to the busy lawyer than to the private person. Probably they were from some tiresome client—women, he had often told her, were nearly always tiresome as clients—who did not want her letters opened by his secretary and therefore had them carried to his house. Yes; but in that case the unknown female must be unusually troublesome, judging from the effect her letters produced. Then again, though his professional discretion was exemplary, it was odd that he had never uttered an impatient comment, never remarked to Charlotte, in a moment of expansion, that there was a nuisance of a woman who kept badgering him about a case that had gone against her. He had made more than one semi-confidence of the kind—of course without giving names or details; but concerning this mysterious correspondent his lips were sealed.

There was another possibility: what is euphemistically called an "old entanglement." Charlotte Ashby was a sophisticated woman. She had few illusions about the intricacies of the human heart; she knew that there were often old entanglements. But when she had married Kenneth Ashby, her friends, instead of hinting at such a possibility, had said: "You've got your work cut out for you. Marrying a Don Juan is a sinecure to it. Kenneth's never looked at another woman since he first saw Elsie Corder. During all the years of their marriage he was more like an unhappy lover than a comfortably contented husband. He'll never let you move an armchair or change the place of a lamp; and whatever you venture to do, he'll mentally compare with what Elsie would have done in your place."

Except for an occasional nervous mistrust as to her ability to manage the children—a mistrust gradually dispelled by her good humour and the children's obvious fondness for her—none of these forebodings had come true. The desolate widower, of whom his nearest friends said that only his absorbing professional interests had kept him from suicide after his first wife's death, had fallen in love, two years later, with Charlotte Gorse, and after an impetuous wooing had married her and carried her off on a tropical honeymoon. And ever since he had been as tender and lover-like as during those first radiant weeks. Before asking her to marry him he had spoken to her frankly of his great love for his first wife and his despair after her sudden death; but even then he had assumed no stricken attitude, or implied that life offered no possibility of renewal. He had been perfectly simple and natural, and had confessed to Charlotte that from the beginning he had hoped the future held new gifts for him. And when, after their marriage, they returned to the house where his twelve years with his first wife had been spent, he had told Charlotte at once that he was sorry he couldn't afford to do the place over for her, but that he knew every woman had her own views about furniture and all sorts of household arrangements a man would never notice, and had begged her to make any changes she saw fit without bothering to consult him. As a result, she made as few as possible; but his way of beginning their new life in the old setting was so frank and unembarrassed that it put her immediately at her ease, and she was almost sorry to find that the portrait of Elsie Ashby, which used to hang over the desk in his library, had been transferred in their absence to the children's nursery. Knowing herself to be the indirect cause of this banishment, she spoke of it to her husband; but he answered: "Oh, I thought they ought to grow up with her looking down on them." The answer moved Charlotte, and satisfied her; and as time went by she had to confess that she felt more at home in her house, more at ease and in confidence with her husband, since that long, coldly beautiful face on the library wall no longer followed her with guarded eyes. It was as if Kenneth's love had penetrated to the secret she hardly acknowledged to her own heart—her passionate need to feel herself the sovereign even of his past.

With all this stored-up happiness to sustain her, it was curious that she had lately found herself yielding to a nervous apprehension. But there the apprehension was; and on this particular afternoon—perhaps because she was more tired than usual, or because of the trouble of finding a new cook or, for some other ridiculously trivial reason, moral or physical—she found herself unable to react against the feeling. Latchkey in hand, she looked back down the silent street to the whirl and illumination of the great thoroughfare beyond, and up at the sky already aflare with the city's nocturnal life. "Outside there," she thought, "sky-scrapers, advertisements, telephones, wireless, aeroplanes, movies, motors, and all the rest of the twentieth century; and on the other side of the door something I can't explain, can't relate to them. Something as old as the world, as mysterious as life... Nonsense! What am I worrying about? There hasn't been a letter for three months now—not since the day we came back from the country after Christmas... Queer that they always seem to come after our holidays!... Why should I imagine there's going to be one tonight!"

No reason why, but that was the worst of it—one of the worsts!—that there were days when she would stand there cold and shivering with the premonition of something inexplicable, intolerable, to be faced on the other side of the curtained panes; and when she opened the door and went in, there would be nothing; and on other days when she felt the same premonitory chill, it was justified by the sight of the grey envelope. So that ever since the last had come she had taken to feeling cold and premonitory every evening, because she never opened the door without thinking the letter might be there.

Well, she'd had enough of it; that was certain. She couldn't go on like that. If her husband turned white and had a headache on the days when the letter came, he seemed to recover afterward; but she couldn't. With her the strain had become chronic, and the reason was not far to seek. Her husband knew from whom the letter came and what was in it; he was prepared beforehand for whatever he had to deal with, and master of the situation, however bad; whereas she was shut out in the dark with her conjectures.

"I can't stand it! I can't stand it another day!" she exclaimed aloud, as she put her key in the lock. She turned the key and went in; and there, on the table, lay the letter.

II

She was almost glad of the sight. It seemed to justify everything, to put a seal of definiteness on the whole blurred business. A letter for her husband; a letter from a woman—no doubt another vulgar case of "old entanglement". What a fool she had been ever to doubt it, to rack her brains for less obvious explanations! She took up the envelope with a steady, contemptuous hand, looked closely at the faint letters, held it against the light and just discerned the outline of the folded sheet within. She knew that now she would have no peace till she found out what was written on that sheet.

Her husband had not come in; he seldom got back from his office before half-past six or seven, and it was not yet six. She would have time to take the letter up to the drawing-room, hold it over the teakettle which at that hour always simmered by the fire in expectation of her return, solve the mystery and replace the letter where she had found it. No one would be the wiser, and her gnawing uncertainty would be over. The alternative, of course, was to question her husband; but to do that seemed even more difficult. She weighed the letter between thumb and finger, looked at it again under the light, started up the stairs with the envelope—and came down again and laid it on the table.

"No, I evidently can't," she said, disappointed.

What should she do, then? She couldn't go up alone to that warm welcoming room, pour out her tea, look over her correspondence, glance at a book or review—not with that letter lying below and the knowledge that in a little while her husband would come in, open it and turn into the library alone, as he always did on the days when the grey envelope came.

Suddenly she decided. She would wait in the library and see for herself; see what happened between him and the letter when they thought themselves unobserved. She wondered the idea had never occurred to her before.

By leaving the door ajar, and sitting in the corner behind it, she could watch him unseen… Well, then, she would watch him! She drew a chair into the corner, sat down, her eyes on the crack, and waited.

As far as she could remember, it was the first time she had ever tried to surprise another person's secret, but she was conscious of no compunction. She simply felt as if she were fighting her way through a stifling fog that she must at all costs get out of.

At length she heard Kenneth's latchkey and jumped up. The impulse to rush out and meet him had nearly made her forget why she was there; but she remembered in time and sat down again. From her post she covered the whole range of his movements—saw him enter the hall, draw the key from the door and take off his hat and overcoat. Then he turned to throw his gloves on the hall table, and at that moment he saw the envelope. The light was full on his face, and what Charlotte first noted there was a look of surprise. Evidently he had not expected the letter—had not thought of the possibility of its being there that day. But though he had not expected it, now that he saw it he knew well enough what it contained. He did not open it immediately, but stood motionless, the colour slowly ebbing from his face. Apparently he could not make up his mind to touch it; but at length he put out his hand, opened the envelope, and moved with it to the light. In doing so he turned his back on Charlotte, and she saw only his bent head and slightly stooping shoulders. Apparently all the writing was on one page, for he did not turn the sheet but continued to stare at it for so long that he must have reread it a dozen times—or so it seemed to the woman breathlessly watching him. At length she saw him move; he raised the letter still closer to his eyes, as though he had not fully deciphered it. Then he lowered his head, and she saw his lips touch the sheet.

"Kenneth!" she exclaimed, and went out into the hall.

The letter clutched in his hand, her husband turned and looked at her. "Where were you?" he said, in a low bewildered voice, like a man waked out of his sleep.

"In the library, waiting for you." She tried to steady her voice: "What's the matter! What's in that letter? You look ghastly."

Her agitation seemed to calm him, and he instantly put the envelope into his pocket with a slight laugh. "Ghastly? I'm sorry. I've had a hard day in the office—one or two complicated cases. I look dog-tired, I suppose."

"You didn't look tired when you came in. It was only when you opened that letter—"

He had followed her into the library, and they stood gazing at each other. Charlotte noticed how quickly he had regained his self-control; his profession had trained him to rapid mastery of face and voice. She saw at once that she would be at a disadvantage in any attempt to surprise his secret, but at the same moment she lost all desire to manœuvre, to trick him into betraying anything he wanted to conceal. Her wish was still to penetrate the mystery, but only that she might help him to bear the burden it implied. "Even if it *is* another woman," she thought.

"Kenneth," she said, her heart beating excitedly, "I waited here on purpose to see you come in. I wanted to watch you while you opened that letter."

His face, which had paled, turned to dark red; then it paled again. "That letter? Why especially that letter?"

"Because I've noticed that whenever one of those letters comes it seems to have such a strange effect on you."

A line of anger she had never seen before came out between his eyes, and she said to herself: "The upper part of his face is too narrow; this is the first time I ever noticed it."

She heard him continue, in the cool and faintly ironic tone of the prosecuting lawyer making a point: "Ah; so you're in the habit of watching people open their letters when they don't know you're there?"

"Not in the habit. I never did such a thing before. But I had to find out what she writes to you, at regular intervals, in those grey envelopes."

He weighed this for a moment; then: "The intervals have not been regular," he said.

"Oh, I daresay you've kept a better account of the dates than I have," she retorted, her magnanimity vanishing at his tone. "All I know is that every time that woman writes to you—"

"Why do you assume it's a woman?"

"It's a woman's writing. Do you deny it?"

He smiled. "No, I don't deny it. I asked only because the writing is generally supposed to look more like a man's."

Charlotte passed this over impatiently. "And this woman—what does she write to you about?"

Again he seemed to consider a moment. "About business."

"Legal business?"

"In a way, yes. Business in general"

"You look after her affairs for her?"

"Yes."

"You've looked after them for a long time?"

"Yes. A very long time."

"Kenneth, dearest, won't you tell me who she is?"

"No. I can't." He paused, and brought out, as if with a certain hesitation: "Professional secrecy."

The blood rushed from Charlotte's heart to her temples. "Don't say that—don't!"

"Why not?"

"Because I saw you kiss the letter."

The effect of the words was so disconcerting that she instantly repented having spoken them. Her husband, who had submitted to her cross-questioning with a sort of contemptuous composure, as though he were humouring an unreasonable child, turned on her a face of terror and distress. For a minute he seemed unable to speak; then, collecting himself with an effort, he stammered out. "The writing is very faint; you must have seen me holding the letter close to my eyes to try to decipher it."

"No; I saw you kissing it." He was silent. "Didn't I see you kissing it?"

He sank back into indifference. "Perhaps."

"Kenneth! You stand there and say that—to me?"

"What possible difference can it make to you? The letter is on business, as I told you. Do you suppose I'd lie about it? The writer is a very old friend whom I haven't seen for a long time."

"Men don't kiss business letters, even from women who are very old friends, unless they have been their lovers, and still regret them."

He shrugged his shoulders slightly and turned away, as if he considered the discussion at an end and were faintly disgusted at the turn it had taken.

"Kenneth!" Charlotte moved toward him and caught hold of his arm.

He paused with a look of weariness and laid his hand over hers. "Won't you believe me?" he asked gently.

"How can I? I've watched these letters come to you—for months now they've been coming. Ever since we came back from the West Indies—one of them greeted me the very day we arrived. And after each one of them I see their mysterious effect on you, I see you disturbed, unhappy, as if someone were trying to estrange you from me."

"No, dear; not that. Never!"

She drew back and looked at him with passionate entreaty. "Well, then, prove it to me, darling. It's so easy!"

He forced a smile. "It's not easy to prove anything to a woman who's once taken an idea into her head."

"You've only got to show me the letter."

His hand slipped from hers and he drew back and shook his head.

"You won't?"

"I can't."

"Then the woman who wrote it is your mistress."

"No, dear. No."

"Not now, perhaps. I suppose she's trying to get you back, and you're struggling, our of pity for me. My poor Kenneth!"

"I swear to you she never was my mistress."

Charlotte felt the tears rushing to her eyes. "Ah, that's worse, then—that's hopeless! The prudent ones are the kind that keep their hold on a man. We all know that." She lifted her hands and hid her face in them.

Her husband remained silent; he offered neither consolation nor denial, and at length, wiping away her tears, she raised her eyes almost timidly to his.

"Kenneth, think! We've been married such a short time. Imagine what you're making me suffer. You say you can't show me this letter. You refuse even to explain it."

"I've told you the letter is on business. I will swear to that, too."

"A man will swear to anything to screen a woman. If you want me to believe you, at least tell me her name. If you'll do that, I promise you I won't ask to see the letter."

There was a long interval of suspense, during which she felt her heart beating against her ribs in quick admonitory knocks, as it warning her of the danger she was incurring.

"I can't," he said at length.

"Not even her name?"

"No."

"You can't tell me anything more?"

"No."

Again a pause; this time they seemed both to have reached the end of their arguments and to be helplessly facing each other across a baffling waste of incomprehension.

Charlotte stood breathing rapidly, her hands against her breast. She felt as if she had run a hard race and missed the goal. She had meant to move her husband and had succeeded only in irritating him; and this error of reckoning seemed to change him into a stranger, a mysterious incomprehensible being whom no argument or entreaty of hers could reach. The curious thing was that she was aware in him of no hostility or even impatience, but only of a remoteness, an inaccessibility, far more difficult to overcome. She felt herself excluded, ignored, blotted out of his life. But after a moment or two, looking at him more calmly, she saw that he was suffering as much as she was. His distant guarded face was drawn with pain; the coming of the grey envelope, though it always cast a shadow, had never marked him as deeply as this discussion with his wife.

Charlotte took heart; perhaps, after all, she had not spent her last shaft. She drew nearer and once more laid her hand on his arm. "Poor Kenneth! If you knew how sorry I am for you—"

She thought he winced slightly at this expression of sympathy, but he took her hand and pressed it.

"I can think of nothing worse than to be incapable of loving long," she continued; "to feel the beauty of a great love and to be too unstable to bear its burden."

He turned on her a look of wistful reproach. "Oh, don't say that of me. Unstable!"

She felt herself at last on the right tack, and her voice trembled with excitement as she went on: "Then what about me and this other woman? Haven't you already forgotten Elsie twice within a year?"

She seldom pronounced his first wife's name; it did not come naturally to her tongue. She flung it out now as if she were flinging some dangerous explosive into the open space between them, and drew back a step, waiting to hear the mine go off.

Her husband did not move; his expression grew sadder, but showed no resentment. "I have never forgotten Elsie," he said.

Charlotte could not repress a faint laugh. "Then, you poor dear, between the three of us—"

"There are not—" he began; and then broke off and put his hand to his forehead.

"Not what?"

"I'm sorry; I don't believe I know what I'm saying. I've got a blinding headache." He looked wan and furrowed enough for the statement to be true, but she was exasperated by his evasion.

"Ah, yes; the grey-envelope headache!"

She saw the surprise in his eyes. "I'd forgotten how closely I've been watched," he said coldly. "If you'll excuse me, I think I'll go up and try an hour in the dark, to see if I can get rid of this neuralgia."

She wavered; then she said, with desperate resolution; "I'm sorry your head aches. But before you go I want to say that sooner or later this question must be settled between us. Someone is trying to separate us, and I don't care what it costs me to find out who it is." She looked him steadily in the eyes. "If it costs me your love, I don't care! If I can't have your confidence I don't want anything from you."

He still looked at her wistfully. "Give me time"

"Time for what? It's only a word to say."

"Time to show you that you haven't lost my love or my confidence."

"Well, I'm waiting."

He turned toward the door, and then glanced back hesitatingly. "Oh, do wait, my love," he said, and went out of the room.

She heard his tired step on the stairs and the closing of his bedroom door above. Then she dropped into a chair and buried her face in her folded arms. Her first movement was one of compunction; she seemed to herself to have been hard, unhuman, unimaginative. "Think of telling him that I didn't care if my insistence cost me his love! The lying rubbish!" She started up to follow him and unsay the meaningless words. But she was checked by a reflection. He had had his way, after all; he had eluded all attacks on his secret, and now he was shut up alone in his room, reading that other woman's letter.

III

She was still reflecting on this when the surprised parlour-maid came in and found her. No, Charlotte said, she wasn't going to dress for dinner;

Mr. Ashby didn't want to dine. He was very tired and had gone up to his room to rest; later she would have something brought on a tray to the drawing-room. She mounted the stairs to her bedroom. Her dinner dress was lying on the bed, and at the sight the quiet routine of her daily life took hold of her and she began to feel as if the strange talk she had just had with her husband must have taken place in another world, between two beings who were not Charlotte Gorse and Kenneth Ashby, but phantoms projected by her fevered imagination. She recalled the year since her marriage—her husband's constant devotion; his persistent, almost too insistent tenderness; the feeling he had given her at times of being too eagerly dependent on her, too searchingly close to her, as if there were not air enough between her soul and his. It seemed preposterous, as she recalled all this, that a few moments ago she should have been accusing him of an intrigue with another woman! But, then, what—

Again she was moved by the impulse to go up to him, beg his pardon and try to laugh away the misunderstanding. But she was restrained by the fear of forcing herself upon his privacy. He was troubled and unhappy, oppressed by some grief or fear; and he had shown her that he wanted to fight out his battle alone. It would be wiser, as well as more generous, to respect his wish. Only, how strange, how unbearable, to be there, in the next room to his, and feel herself at the other end of the world! In her nervous agitation she almost regretted not having had the courage to open the letter and put it back on the hall table before he came in. At least she would have known what his secret was, and the bogy might have been laid. For she was beginning now to think of the mystery as something conscious, malevolent: a secret persecution before which he quailed, yet from which he could not free himself. Once or twice in his evasive eyes she thought she had detected a desire for help, an impulse of confession, instantly restrained and suppressed. It was as if he felt she could have helped him if she had known, and yet had been unable to tell her!

There flashed through her mind the idea of going to his mother. She was very fond of old Mrs. Ashby, a firm-fleshed, clear-eyed old lady, with an astringent bluntness of speech which responded to the forthright and simple in Charlotte's own nature. There had been a tacit bond between them ever since the day when Mrs. Ashby senior, coming to lunch for the first time with her new daughter-in-law, had been received by Charlotte downstairs in the library, and glancing up at the empty wall above her son's desk, had remarked laconically: "Elsie gone, eh?" adding, at Charlotte's murmured explanation: "Nonsense. Don't have her back. Two's company." Charlotte, at this reading of her thoughts, could hardly refrain from exchanging a smile of complicity with her mother-in-law; and it seemed to her now that Mrs. Ashby's almost uncanny directness might pierce to the core of this new mystery. But here again she hesitated, for the idea almost suggested a betrayal. What right had she to call in anyone, even so close a relation, to surprise a secret which her husband was trying to keep from her? "Perhaps, by and by, he'll talk to his mother of his own accord," she thought, and then ended: "But what does it matter? He and I must settle it between us."

She was still brooding over the problem when there was a knock on the door and her husband came in. He was dressed for dinner and seemed surprised to see her sitting there, with her evening dress lying unheeded on the bed.

"Aren't you coming down?"

"I thought you were not well and had gone to bed," she faltered.

He forced a smile. "I'm not particularly well, but we'd better go down." His face, though still drawn, looked calmer than when he had fled upstairs an hour earlier.

"There it is; he knows what's in the letter and has fought his battle out again, whatever it is," she reflected, "while I'm still in darkness." She rang and gave a hurried order that dinner should be served as soon as possible—just a short meal, whatever could be got ready quickly, as both she and Mr. Ashby were rather tired and not very hungry.

Dinner was announced, and they sat down to it. At first neither seemed able to find a word to say; then Ashby began to make conversation with an assumption of case that was more oppressive than his silence. "How tired he is! How terribly overtired!" Charlotte said to herself, pursuing her own thoughts while he rambled on about municipal politics, aviation, an exhibition of modern French painting, the health of an old aunt and the installing of the automatic telephone. "Good heavens, how tired he is!"

When they dined alone they usually went into the library after dinner, and Charlotte curled herself up on the divan with her knitting while he settled down in his armchair under the lamp and lit a pipe. But this evening, by tacit agreement, they avoided the room in which their strange talk had taken place, and went up to Charlotte's drawing-room.

They sat down near the fire, and Charlotte said: "Your pipe?" after he had put down his hardly tasted coffee.

He shook his head. "No, not tonight."

"You must go to bed early; you look terribly tired. I'm sure they overwork you at the office."

"I suppose we all overwork at times."

She rose and stood before him with sudden resolution. "Well, I'm not going to have you use up your strength slaving in that way. It's absurd. I can see you're ill." She bent over him and laid her hand on his forehead. "My poor old Kenneth. Prepare to be taken away soon on a long holiday."

He looked up at her, startled. "A holiday?"

"Certainly. Didn't you know I was going to carry you off at Easter? We're going to start in a fortnight on a month's voyage to somewhere or other. On any one of the big cruising steamers." She paused and bent closer, touching his forehead with her lips. "I'm tired, too, Kenneth."

He seemed to pay no heed to her last words, but sat, his hands on his knees, his head drawn back a little from her caress, and looked up at her with a stare of apprehension. "Again? My dear, we can't; I can't possibly go away."

"I don't know why you say 'again,' Kenneth; we haven't taken a real holiday this year."

"At Christmas we spent a week with the children in the country."

"Yes, but this time I mean away from the children, from servants, from the house. From everything that's familiar and fatiguing. Your mother will love to have Joyce and Peter with her."

He frowned and slowly shook his head. "No, dear; I can't leave them with my mother."

"Why, Kenneth, how absurd! She adores them. You didn't hesitate to leave them with her for over two months when we went to the West Indies."

He drew a deep breath and stood up uneasily. "That was different."

"Different? Why?"

"I mean, at that time I didn't realise"—He broke off as if to choose his words and then went on: "My mother adores the children, as you say. But she isn't always very judicious. Grandmothers always spoil children. And she sometimes talks before them without thinking." He turned to his wife with an almost pitiful gesture of entreaty. "Don't ask me to, dear."

Charlotte mused. It was true that the elder Mrs. Ashby had a fearless tongue, but she was the last woman in the world to say or hint anything before her grandchildren at which the most scrupulous parent could take offence. Charlotte looked at her husband in perplexity.

"I don't understand."

He continued to turn on her the same troubled and entreating gaze. "Don't try to," he muttered.

"Not try to?"

"Not now—not yet." He put up his hands and pressed them against his temples. "Can't you see that there's no use in insisting? I can't go away, no matter how much I might want to."

Charlotte still scrutinised him gravely. "The question is, do you want to?"

He returned her gaze for a moment; then his lips began to tremble, and he said, hardly above his breath: "I want—anything you want."

"And yet—"

"Don't ask me. I can't leave—I can't!"

"You mean that you can't go away out of reach of those letters!"

Her husband had been standing before her in an uneasy, half-hesitating attitude; now he turned abruptly away and walked once or twice up and down the length of the room, his head bent, his eyes fixed on the carpet.

Charlotte felt her resentfulness rising with her fears. "It's that," she persisted. "Why not admit it? You can't live without them."

He continued his troubled pacing of the room; then he stopped short, dropped into a chair and covered his face with his hands. From the shaking of his shoulders, Charlotte saw that he was weeping. She had never seen a man cry, except her father after her mother's death, when she was a little girl; and she remembered still how the sight had frightened her. She was frightened now; she felt that her husband was being dragged away from her into some mysterious bondage, and that she must use up her last atom of strength in the struggle for his freedom, and for hers.

"Kenneth—Kenneth!" she pleaded, kneeling down beside him. "Won't you listen to me? Won't you try to see what I'm suffering? I'm not unreasonable, darling; really not. I don't suppose I should ever have noticed the letters if it hadn't been for their effect on you. It's not my way to pry into other people's affairs; and even if the effect had been different—yes, yes; listen to me—if I'd seen that the letters made you happy, that you were watching eagerly for them, counting the days between their coming, that you wanted them, that they gave you something I haven't known how to give—why, Kenneth, I don't say I shouldn't have suffered from that, too; but it would have been in a different way, and I should have had the courage to hide what I felt, and the hope that some day you'd come to feel about me as you did about the writer of the letters. But what I can't bear is to see how you dread them, how they make you suffer, and yet how you can't live without them and won't go away lest you should miss one during your absence. Or perhaps," she added, her voice breaking into a cry of accusation—"perhaps it's because she's actually forbidden you to leave. Kenneth, you must answer me! Is that the reason? Is it because she's forbidden you that you won't go away with me?"

She continued to kneel at his side, and raising her hands, she drew his gently down. She was ashamed of her persistence, ashamed of uncovering that baffled disordered face, yet resolved that no such scruples should arrest her. His eyes were lowered, the muscles of his face quivered; she was making him suffer even more than she suffered herself. Yet this no longer restrained her.

"Kenneth, is it that? She won't let us go away together?"

Still he did not speak or turn his eyes to her; and a sense of defeat swept over her. After all, she thought, the struggle was a losing one. "You needn't answer. I see I'm right," she said.

Suddenly, as she rose, he turned and drew her down again. His hands caught hers and pressed them so tightly that she felt her rings cutting into her flesh. There was something frightened, convulsive in his hold; it was the clutch of a man who felt himself slipping over a precipice. He was staring up at her now as if salvation lay in the face she bent above him. "Of course we'll go away together. We'll go wherever you want," he said in a low confused voice; and putting his arm about her, he drew her close and pressed his lips on hers.

IV

Charlotte had said to herself: "I shall sleep tonight," but instead she sat before her fire into the small hours, listening for any sound that came from her husband's room. But he, at any rate, seemed to be resting after the tumult of the evening. Once or twice she stole to the door and in the faint light that came in from the street through his open window she saw him stretched out in heavy sleep—the sleep of weakness and exhaustion. "He's ill," she thought—"he's undoubtedly ill. And it's not overwork; it's this mysterious persecution."

She drew a breath of relief. She had fought through the weary fight and the victory was hers—at least for the moment. If only they could have started at once—started for anywhere! She knew it would be useless to ask him to leave before the holidays; and meanwhile the secret influence—as to which she was still so completely in the dark—would continue to work against her, and she would have to renew the struggle day after day till they started on their journey. But after that everything would be different. If once she could get her husband away under other skies, and all to herself, she never doubted her power to release him from the evil spell he was under. Lulled to quiet by the thought, she, too, slept at last.

When she woke, it was long past her usual hour, and she sat up in bed surprised and vexed at having overslept herself. She always liked to be down to share her husband's breakfast by the library fire; but a glance at the clock made it clear that he must have started long since for his office. To make sure, she jumped out of bed and went into his room; but it was empty. No doubt he had looked in on her before leaving, seen that she still slept, and gone downstairs without disturbing her; and their relations were sufficiently lover-like for her to regret having missed their morning hour.

She rang and asked if Mr. Ashby had already gone. Yes, nearly an hour ago, the maid said. He had given orders that Mrs. Ashby should not be waked and that the children should not come to her till she sent for them… Yes, he had gone up to the nursery himself to give the order. All this sounded usual enough; and Charlotte hardly knew why she asked: "And did Mr. Ashby leave no other message?"

Yes, the maid said, he did; she was so sorry she'd forgotten. He'd told her, just as he was leaving, to say to Mrs. Ashby that he was going to see about their passages, and would she please be ready to sail tomorrow?

Charlotte echoed the woman's "tomorrow," and sat staring at her incredulously. "Tomorrow—you're sure he said to sail tomorrow?"

"Oh, ever so sure, ma'am. I don't know how I could have forgotten to mention it."

"Well, it doesn't matter. Draw my bath, please." Charlotte sprang up, dashed through her dressing, and caught herself singing at her image in the glass as she sat brushing her hair. It made her feel young again to have scored such a victory. The other woman vanished to a speck on the horizon, as this one, who ruled the foreground, smiled back at the reflection of her lips and eyes. He loved her, then—he loved her as passionately as ever. He had divined what she had suffered, had understood that their happiness depended on their getting away at once, and finding each other again after yesterday's desperate groping in the fog. The nature of the influence that had come between them did not much matter to Charlotte now; she had faced the phantom and dispelled it. "Courage—that's the secret! If only people who are in love weren't always so afraid of risking their happiness by looking it in the eyes." As she brushed back her light abundant hair it waved electrically above her head, like the palms of victory. Ah, well, some women knew how to manage men, and some didn't—and only the fair—she gaily paraphrased—deserve the brave! Certainly she was looking very pretty.

The morning danced along like a cockleshell on a bright sea—such a sea as they would soon be speeding over. She ordered a particularly good dinner, saw the children off to their classes, had her trunks brought down, consulted with the maid about getting out summer clothes—for of course they would be heading for heat and sunshine—and wondered if she oughtn't to take Kenneth's flannel suits out of camphor. "But how absurd," she reflected, "that I don't yet know where we're going!" She looked at the clock, saw that it was close on noon, and decided to call him up at his office. There was a slight delay; then she heard his secretary's voice saying that Mr. Ashby had looked in for a moment early, and left again almost immediately... Oh, very well; Charlotte would ring up later. How soon was he likely to be back? The secretary answered that she couldn't tell; all they knew in the office was that when he left he had said he was in a hurry because he had to go out of town.

Out of town! Charlotte hung up the receiver and sat blankly gazing into new darkness. Why had he gone out of town? And where had he gone? And of all days, why should he have chosen the eve of their suddenly planned departure? She felt a faint shiver of apprehension. Of course he had gone to see that woman—no doubt to get her permission to leave. He was as completely in bondage as that; and Charlotte had been fatuous enough to see the palms of victory on her forehead. She burst into a laugh and, walking across the room, sat down again before her mirror. What a different face she saw! The smile on her pale lips seemed to mock the rosy vision of the other Charlotte. But gradually her colour crept back. After all, she had a right to claim the victory, since her husband was doing what she wanted, not what the other woman exacted of him. It was natural enough, in view of his abrupt decision to leave the next day, that he should have arrangements to make, business matters to wind up; it was not even necessary to suppose that his mysterious trip was a visit to the writer of the letters. He might simply have gone to see a client who lived out of town. Of course they would not tell Charlotte at the office; the secretary had hesitated before imparting even such meagre information as the fact of Mr. Ashby's absence. Meanwhile, she would go on with her joyful preparations, content to learn later in the day to what particular island of the blest she was to be carried.

The hours wore on, or rather were swept forward on a rush of eager preparations. At last the entrance of the maid who came to draw the curtains roused Charlotte from her labours, and she saw to her surprise that the clock marked five. And she did not yet know where they were going the next day! She rang up her husband's office and was told that Mr. Ashby had not been there since the early morning. She asked for his partner, but the partner could add nothing to her information, for he himself, his suburban train having been behind time, had reached the office after Ashby had come and gone. Charlotte stood perplexed; then she decided to telephone to her mother-in-law. Of course Kenneth, on the eve of a month's absence, must have gone to see his mother. The mere fact that the children—in spite of his vague objections—would certainly have to be left with old Mrs. Ashby, made it obvious that he would have all sorts of matters to decide with her.

At another time Charlotte might have felt a little hurt at being excluded from their conference, but nothing mattered now but that she had won the day, that her husband was still hers and not another woman's. Gaily she called up Mrs. Ashby, heard her friendly voice, and began: "Well, did Kenneth's news surprise you? What do you think of our elopement?"

Almost instantly, before Mrs. Ashby could answer, Charlotte knew what her reply would be. Mrs. Ashby had not seen her son, she had had no word from him and did not know what her daughter-in-law meant. Charlotte stood silent in the intensity of her surprise. "But then, where *has* he been?" she thought. Then, recovering herself, she explained their sudden decision to Mrs. Ashby, and in doing so, gradually regained her own self-confidence, her conviction that nothing could ever again come between Kenneth and herself. Mrs. Ashby took the news calmly and approvingly. She, too, had thought that Kenneth looked worried and overtired, and she agreed with her daughter-in-law that in such cases change was the surest remedy, "I'm always so glad when he gets away. Elsie hated travelling; she was always finding pretexts to prevent his going anywhere. With you, thank goodness, it's different." Nor was Mrs. Ashby surprised at his not having had time to let her know of his departure. He must have been in a rush from the moment the decision was taken; but no doubt he'd drop in before dinner. Five minutes' talk was really all they needed. "I hope you'll gradually cure Kenneth of his mania for going over and over a question that could be settled in a dozen words. He never used to be like that, and if he carried the habit into his professional work he'd soon lose all his clients… Yes, do come in for a minute, dear, if you have time; no doubt he'll turn up while you're here." The tonic ring of Mrs. Ashby's voice echoed on reassuringly in the silent room while Charlotte continued her preparations.

Toward seven the telephone rang, and she darted to it. Now she would know! But it was only from the conscientious secretary, to say that Mr. Ashby hadn't been back, or sent any word, and before the office closed she thought she ought to let Mrs. Ashby know. "Oh, that's all right. Thanks a lot!" Charlotte called out cheerfully, and hung up the receiver with a trembling hand. But perhaps by this time, she reflected, he was at his mother's. She shut her drawers and cupboards, put on her hat and coat and called up to the nursery that she was going out for a minute to see the children's grandmother.

Mrs. Ashby lived nearby, and during her brief walk through the cold spring dusk Charlotte imagined that every advancing figure was her husband's. But she did not meet him on the way, and when she entered the house she found her mother-in-law alone. Kenneth had neither telephoned nor come. Old Mrs. Ashby sat by her bright fire, her knitting needles flashing steadily through her active old hands, and her mere bodily presence gave reassurance to Charlotte. Yes, it was certainly odd that Kenneth had gone off for the whole day without letting any of them know; but, after all, it was to be expected. A busy lawyer held so many threads in his hands that any sudden change of plan would oblige him to make all sorts of unforeseen arrangements and adjustments. He might have gone to see some client in the suburbs and been detained there; his mother remembered his telling her that he had charge of the legal business of a queer old recluse somewhere in New Jersey, who was immensely rich but too mean to have a telephone. Very likely Kenneth had been stranded there.

But Charlotte felt her nervousness gaining on her. When Mrs. Ashby asked her at what hour they were sailing the next day and she had to say she didn't know—that Kenneth had simply sent her word he was going to take their passages—the uttering of the words again brought home to her the strangeness of the situation. Even Mrs. Ashby conceded that it was odd; but she immediately added that it only showed what a rush he was in.

"But, mother, its nearly eight o'clock! He must realise that I've got to know when we're starting tomorrow."

"Oh, the boat probably doesn't sail till evening. Sometimes they have to wait till midnight for the tide. Kenneth's probably counting on that. After all, he has a level head."

Charlotte stood up. "It's not that. Something has happened to him."

Mrs. Ashby took off her spectacles and rolled up her knitting. "If you begin to let yourself imagine things—"

"Aren't you in the least anxious?"

"I never am till I have to be. I wish you'd ring for dinner, my dear. You'll stay and dine? He's sure to drop in here on his way home."

Charlotte called up her own house. No, the maid said, Mr. Ashby hadn't come in and hadn't telephoned. She would tell him as soon as he came that Mrs. Ashby was dining at his mother's. Charlotte followed her mother-in-law into the dining-room and sat with parched throat before her empty plate, while Mrs. Ashby dealt calmly and efficiently with a short but carefully prepared repast. "You'd better eat something, child, or you'll be as bad as Kenneth... Yes, a little more asparagus, please, Jane."

She insisted on Charlotte's drinking a glass of sherry and nibbling a bit of toast; then they returned to the drawing-room, where the fire had been made up, and the cushions in Mrs. Ashby's armchair shaken out and smoothed. How safe and familiar it all looked; and out there, somewhere in the uncertainty and mystery of the night, lurked the answer to the two women's conjectures, like an indistinguishable figure prowling on the threshold.

At last Charlotte got up and said: "I'd better go back. At this hour Kenneth will certainly go straight home."

Mrs. Ashby smiled indulgently. "It's not very late, my dear. It doesn't take two sparrows long to dine."

"It's after nine." Charlotte bent down to kiss her. "The fact is, I can't keep still."

Mrs. Ashby pushed aside her work and rested her two hands on the arms of her chair. "I'm going with you," she said, helping herself up.

Charlotte protested that it was too late, that it was not necessary, that she would call up as soon as Kenneth came in, but Mrs. Ashby had already rung for her maid. She was slightly lame, and stood resting on her stick while her wraps were brought. "If Mr. Kenneth turns up, tell him he'll find me at his own house," she instructed the maid as the two women got into the taxi which had been summoned. During the short drive Charlotte gave thanks that she was not returning home alone. There was something warm and substantial in the mere fact of Mrs. Ashby's nearness, something that corresponded with the clearness of her eyes and the texture of her fresh, firm complexion. As the taxi drew up she laid her hand encouragingly on Charlotte's. "You'll see; there'll be a message."

The door opened at Charlotte's ring and the two entered. Charlotte's heart beat excitedly; the stimulus of her mother-in-law's confidence was beginning to flow through her veins.

"You'll see—you'll see," Mrs. Ashby repeated.

The maid who opened the door said no, Mr. Ashby had not come in, and there had been no message from him.

"You're sure the telephone's not out of order?" his mother suggested; and the maid said, well, it certainly wasn't half an hour ago; but she'd just go and ring up to make sure. She disappeared, and Charlotte turned to take off her hat and cloak. As she did so her eyes lit on the hall table, and there lay a grey envelope, her husband's name faintly traced on it. "Oh!" she cried out, suddenly aware that for the first time in months she had entered her house without wondering if one of the grey letters would be there.

"What is it, my dear?" Mrs. Ashby asked with a glance of surprise.

Charlotte did not answer. She took up the envelope and stood staring at it as if she could force her gaze to penetrate to what was within. Then an idea occurred to her. She turned and held out the envelope to her mother-in-law.

"Do you know that writing?" she asked.

Mrs. Ashby took the letter. She had to feel with her other hand for her eyeglasses, and when she had adjusted them she lifted the envelope to the light. "Why!" she exclaimed; and then stopped. Charlotte noticed that the letter shook in her usually firm hand. "But this is addressed to Kenneth,"

Mrs. Ashby said at length, in a low voice. Her tone seemed to imply that she felt her daughter-in-law's question to be slightly indiscreet.

"Yes, but no matter," Charlotte spoke with sudden decision. "I want to know—do you know the writing?"

Mrs. Ashby handed back the letter. "No," she said distinctly.

The two women had turned into the library. Charlotte switched on the electric light and shut the door. She still held the envelope in her hand.

"I'm going to open it," she announced.

She caught her mother-in-law's startled glance. "But, dearest—a letter not addressed to you? My dear, you can't!"

"As if I cared about that—now!" She continued to look intently at Mrs. Ashby. "This letter may tell me where Kenneth is."

Mrs. Ashby's glossy bloom was effaced by a quick pallor; her firm cheeks seemed to shrink and wither. "Why should it? What makes you believe—It can't possibly—"

Charlotte held her eyes steadily on that altered face. "Ah, then you *do* know the writing?" she flashed back.

"Know the writing? How should I? With all my son's correspondents… What I do know is—" Mrs. Ashby broke off and looked at her daughter-in-law entreatingly, almost timidly.

Charlotte caught her by the wrist, "Mother! What do you know? Tell me! You must!"

"That I don't believe any good ever came of a woman's opening her husband's letters behind his back."

The words sounded to Charlotte's irritated ears as flat as a phrase culled from a book of moral axioms. She laughed impatiently and dropped her mother-in-law's wrist. "Is that all? No good can come of this letter, opened or unopened. I know that well enough. But whatever ill comes, I mean to find out what's in it." Her hands had been trembling as they held the envelope, but now they grew firm, and her voice also. She still gazed intently at Mrs. Ashby. "This is the ninth letter addressed in the same hand that has come for Kenneth since we've been married. Always these same grey envelopes. I've kept count of them because after each one he has been like a man who has had some dreadful shock. It takes him hours to shake off their effect. I've told him so. I've told him I must know from whom they come, because I can see they're killing him. He won't answer my questions; he says he can't tell me anything about the letters; but last night he promised to go away with me—to get away from them."

Mrs. Ashby, with shaking steps, had gone to one of the armchairs and sat down in it, her head drooping forward on her breast. "Ah", she murmured.

"So now you understand—"

"Did he tell you it was to get away from them?"

"He said, to get away—to get away. He was sobbing so that he could hardly speak. But I told him I knew that was why."

"And what did he say?"

"He took me in his arms and said he'd go wherever I wanted."

"Ah, thank God!" said Mrs. Ashby. There was a silence, during which she continued to sit with bowed head and eyes averted from her daughter-in-law. At last she looked up and spoke. "Are you sure there have been as many as nine?"

"Perfectly. This is the ninth. I've kept count."

"And he has absolutely refused to explain?"

"Absolutely."

Mrs. Ashby spoke through pale contracted lips. "When did they begin to come? Do you remember?"

Charlotte laughed again. "Remember? The first one came the night we got back from our honeymoon."

"All that time?" Mrs. Ashby lifted her head and spoke with sudden energy. "Then—yes, open it."

The words were so unexpected that Charlotte felt the blood in her temples, and her hands began to tremble again. She tried to slip her finger under the flap of the envelope, but it was so tightly stuck that she had to hunt on her husband's writing table for his ivory letter-opener. As she pushed about the familiar objects his own hands had so lately touched, they sent through her the icy chill emanating from the little personal effects of someone newly dead. In the deep silence of the room the tearing of the paper as she slit the envelope sounded like a human cry. She drew out the sheet and carried it to the lamp.

"Well?" Mrs. Ashby asked below her breath.

Charlotte did not move or answer. She was bending over the page with wrinkled brows, holding it nearer and nearer to the light. Her sight must be blurred, or else dazzled by the reflection of the lamplight on the smooth surface of the paper, for, strain her eyes as she would, she could discern only a few faint strokes, so faint and faltering as to be nearly undecipherable.

"I can't make it out," she said.

"What do you mean, dear?"

"The writing's too indistinct... Wait."

She went back to the table and, sitting down close to Kenneth's reading lamp, slipped the letter under a magnifying glass. All this time she was aware that her mother-in-law was watching her intently.

"Well?" Mrs. Ashby breathed.

"Well, it's no clearer. I can't read it."

"You mean the paper is an absolute blank?"

"No, not quite. There is writing on it. I can make out something like 'mine'—oh, and 'come.' It might be come."

Mrs. Ashby stood up abruptly. Her face was even paler than before. She advanced to the table and, resting her two hands on it, drew a deep breath. "Let me see," she said, as if forcing herself to a hateful effort.

Charlotte felt the contagion of her whiteness. "She knows," she thought. She pushed the letter across the table. Her mother-in-law lowered her head over it in silence, but without touching it with her pale wrinkled hands.

Charlotte stood watching her as she herself, when she had tried to read the letter, had been watched by Mrs. Ashby. The latter fumbled for her glasses, held them to her eyes, and bent still closer to the outspread page, in order, as it seemed, to avoid touching it. The light of the lamp fell directly on her old face, and Charlotte reflected what depths of the unknown may lurk under the clearest and most candid lineaments. She had never seen her mother-in-law's features express any but simple and sound emotions—cordiality, amusement, a kindly sympathy; now and again a flash of wholesome anger. Now they seemed to wear a look of fear and hatred, of incredulous dismay and almost cringing defiance. It was as if the spirits warring within her had distorted her face to their own likeness. At length she raised her head. "I can't—I can't," she said in a voice of childish distress.

"You can't make it out either?"

She shook her head, and Charlotte saw two tears roll down her cheeks.

"Familiar as the writing is to you?" Charlotte insisted with twitching lips.

Mrs. Ashby did not take up the challenge. "I can make out nothing—nothing."

"But you do know the writing?"

Mrs. Ashby lifted her head timidly; her anxious eyes stole with a glance of apprehension around the quiet familiar room. "How can I tell? I was startled at first…"

"Startled by the resemblance?"

"Well, I thought—"

"You'd better say it out, mother! You knew at once it was *her* writing?"

"Oh, wait, my dear—wait."

"Wait for what?"

Mrs. Ashby looked up; her eyes, travelling slowly past Charlotte, were lifted to the blank wall behind her son's writing table.

Charlotte, following the glance, burst into a shrill laugh of accusation. "I needn't wait any longer! You've answered me now! You're looking straight at the wall where her picture used to hang!"

Mrs. Ashby lifted her hand with a murmur of warning. "Sh-h."

"Oh, you needn't imagine that anything can ever frighten me again!" Charlotte cried.

Her mother-in-law still leaned against the table. Her lips moved plaintively. "But we're going mad—we're both going mad. We both know such things are impossible."

Her daughter-in-law looked at her with a pitying stare. "I've known for a long time now that everything was possible."

"Even this?"

"Yes, exactly this."

"But this letter—after all, there's nothing in this letter—"

"Perhaps there would be to him. How can I tell? I remember his saying to me once that if you were used to a handwriting the faintest stroke of it became legible. Now I see what he meant. He *was* used to it."

"But the few strokes that I can make out are so pale. No one could possibly read that letter."

Charlotte laughed again. "I suppose everything's pale about a ghost," she said stridently.

"Oh, my child—my child—don't say it!"

"Why shouldn't I say it, when even the bare walls cry it out? What difference does it make if her letters are illegible to you and me? If even you can see her face on that blank wall, why shouldn't he read her writing on this blank paper? Don't you see that she's everywhere in this house, and the closer to him because to everyone else she's become invisible?" Charlotte dropped into a chair and covered her face with her hands. A turmoil of sobbing shook her from head to foot. At length a touch on her shoulder made her look up, and she saw her mother-in-law bending over her. Mrs. Ashby's face seemed to have grown still smaller and more wasted, but it had resumed its usual quiet look. Through all her tossing anguish, Charlotte felt the impact of that resolute spirit.

"Tomorrow—tomorrow. You'll see. There'll be some explanation tomorrow."

Charlotte cut her short. "An explanation? Who's going to give it, I wonder?"

Mrs. Ashby drew back and straightened herself heroically. "Kenneth himself will," she cried out in a strong voice. Charlotte said nothing, and the old woman went on: "But meanwhile we must act; we must notify the police. Now, without a moment's delay. We must do everything—everything."

Charlotte stood up slowly and stiffly; her joints felt as cramped as an old woman's. "Exactly as if we thought it could do any good to do anything?"

Resolutely Mrs. Ashby cried: "Yes!" and Charlotte went up to the telephone and unhooked the receiver.

THE FULLNESS OF LIFE

I

For hours she had lain in a kind of gentle torpor, not unlike that sweet lassitude which masters one in the hush of a midsummer noon, when the heat seems to have silenced the very birds and insects, and, lying sunk in the tasselled meadowgrasses, one looks up through a level roofing of maple-leaves at the vast, shadowless, and unsuggestive blue. Now and then, at ever-lengthening intervals, a flash of pain darted through her, like the ripple of sheet-lightning across such a midsummer sky; but it was too transitory to shake her stupor, that calm, delicious, bottomless stupor into which she felt herself sinking more and more deeply, without a disturbing impulse of resistance, an effort of reattachment to the vanishing edges of consciousness.

The resistance, the effort, had known their hour of violence; but now they were at an end. Through her mind, long harried by grotesque visions, fragmentary images of the life that she was leaving, tormenting lines of verse, obstinate presentiments of pictures once beheld, indistinct impressions of rivers, towers, and cupolas, gathered in the length of journeys half forgotten—through her mind there now only moved a few primal sensations of colourless well-being; a vague satisfaction in the thought that she had swallowed her noxious last draught of medicine... and that she should never again hear the creaking of her husband's boots—those horrible boots—and that no one would come to bother her about the next day's dinner... or the butcher's book...

At last even these dim sensations spent themselves in the thickening obscurity which enveloped her; a dusk now filled with pale geometric roses, circling softly, interminably before her, now darkened to a uniform blue-blackness, the hue of a summer night without stars. And into this darkness she felt herself sinking, sinking, with the gentle sense of security of one upheld from beneath. Like a tepid tide it rose around her, gliding ever higher and higher, folding in its velvety embrace her relaxed and tired body, now submerging her breast and shoulders, now creeping gradually, with soft inexorableness, over her throat to her chin, to her ears, to her mouth... Ah, now it was rising too high; the impulse to struggle was renewed;... her mouth was full;... she was choking... Help!

"It is all over," said the nurse, drawing down the eyelids with official composure.

The clock struck three. They remembered it afterwards. Someone opened the window and let in a blast of that strange, neutral air which walks the earth between darkness and dawn; someone else led the husband into another room. He walked vaguely, like a blind man, on his creaking boots.

II

She stood, as it seemed, on a threshold, yet no tangible gateway was in front of her. Only a wide vista of light, mild yet penetrating as the gathered glimmer of innumerable stars, expanded gradually before her eyes, in blissful contrast to the cavernous darkness from which she had of late emerged.

She stepped forward, not frightened, but hesitating, and as her eyes began to grow more familiar with the melting depths of light about her, she distinguished the outlines of landscape, at first swimming in the opaline uncertainty of Shelley's vaporous creations, then gradually resolved into distincter shape—the vast unrolling of a sunlit plain, aërial forms of mountains, and presently the silver crescent of a river in the valley, and a blue stencilling of trees along its curve—something suggestive in its ineffable hue of an azure background of Leonardo's, strange, enchanting, mysterious, leading on the eye and the imagination into regions of fabulous delight. As she gazed, her heart beat with a soft and rapturous surprise; so exquisite a promise she read in the summons of that hyaline distance.

"And so death is not the end after all," in sheer gladness she heard herself exclaiming aloud. "I always knew that it couldn't be. I believed in Darwin, of course. I do still; but then Darwin himself said that he wasn't sure about the soul—at least, I think he did—and Wallace was a spiritualist; and then there was St. George Mivart—"

Her gaze lost itself in the ethereal remoteness of the mountains.

"How beautiful! How satisfying!" she murmured. "Perhaps now I shall really know what it is to live."

As she spoke she felt a sudden thickening of her heartbeats, and looking up she was aware that before her stood the Spirit of Life.

"Have you never really known what it is to live?" the Spirit of Life asked her.

"I have never known," she replied, "that fullness of life which we all feel ourselves capable of knowing; though my life has not been without scattered hints of it, like the scent of earth which comes to one sometimes far out at sea."

"And what do you call the fullness of life?" the Spirit asked again.

"Oh, I can't tell you, if you don't know," she said, almost reproachfully. "Many words are supposed to define it—love and sympathy are those in commonest use, but I am not even sure that they are the right ones, and so few people really know what they mean."

"You were married," said the Spirit, "yet you did not find the fullness of life in your marriage?"

"Oh, dear, no," she replied, with an indulgent scorn, "my marriage was a very incomplete affair."

"And yet you were fond of your husband?"

"You have hit upon the exact word; I was fond of him, yes, just as I was fond of my grandmother, and the house that I was born in, and my old nurse. Oh, I was fond of him, and we were counted a very happy couple. But I have sometimes thought that a woman's nature is like a great house full of rooms: there is the hall, through which everyone passes in going in and out; the drawing-room, where one receives formal visits; the sitting-room, where the members of the family come and go as they list; but beyond that, far beyond, are other rooms, the handles of whose doors perhaps are never turned; no one knows the way to them, no one knows whither they lead; and in the innermost room, the holy of holies, the soul sits alone and waits for a footstep that never comes."

"And your husband", asked the Spirit, after a pause, "never got beyond the family sitting-room?"

"Never," she returned, impatiently; "and the worst of it was that he was quite content to remain there. He thought it perfectly beautiful, and sometimes, when he was admiring its commonplace furniture, insignificant as the chairs and tables of a hotel parlour, I felt like crying out to him: 'Fool, will you never guess that close at hand are rooms full of treasures and wonders, such as the eye of man hath not seen, rooms that no step has crossed, but that might be yours to live in, could you but find the handle of the door?'"

"Then," the Spirit continued, "those moments of which you lately spoke, which seemed to come to you like scattered hints of the fullness of life, were not shared with your husband?"

"Oh, no—never. He was different. His boots creaked, and he always slammed the door when he went out, and he never read anything but railway novels and the sporting advertisements in the papers—and—and, in short, we never understood each other in the least."

"To what influence, then, did you owe those exquisite sensations?"

"I can hardly tell. Sometimes to the perfume of a flower; sometimes to a verse of Dante or of Shakespeare; sometimes to a picture or a sunset, or to one of those calm days at sea, when one seems to be lying in the hollow of a blue pearl; sometimes, but rarely, to a word spoken by someone who chanced to give utterance, at the right moment, to what I felt but could not express."

"Someone whom you loved?" asked the Spirit.

"I never loved anyone, in that way," she said, rather sadly, "nor was I thinking of any one person when I spoke, but of two or three who, by touching for an instant upon a certain chord of my being, had called forth a single note of that strange melody which seemed sleeping in my soul. It has seldom happened, however, that I have owed such feelings to people; and no one ever gave me a moment of such happiness as it was my lot to feel one evening in the Church of Orsanmichele, in Florence."

"Tell me about it," said the Spirit.

"It was near sunset on a rainy spring afternoon in Easter week. The clouds had vanished, dispersed by a sudden wind, and as we entered the church the fiery panes of the high windows shone out like lamps through the dusk. A priest was at the high altar, his white cope a livid spot in the incense-laden obscurity, the light of the candles flickering up and down like fireflies about his head; a few people knelt nearby. We stole behind them and sat down on a bench close to the tabernacle of Orcagna.

"Strange to say, though Florence was not new to me, I had never been in the church before; and in that magical light I saw for the first time the inlaid steps, the fluted columns, the sculptured bas-reliefs and canopy of the marvellous shrine. The marble, worn and mellowed by the subtle hand of time, took on an unspeakable rosy hue, suggestive in some remote way of honey-coloured columns of the Parthenon, but more mystic, more complex, a colour not born of the sun's inveterate kiss, but made of cryptal twilight, and the flame of candles upon martyrs' tombs, and gleams of sunset through symbolic panes of chrysoprase and ruby; such a light as illumines the missals in the library of Siena, or burns like a hidden fire through the Madonna of Gian Bellini in the Church of the Redeemer, at Venice; the light of the Middle Ages, richer, more solemn, more significant than the limpid sunshine of Greece.

"The church was silent, but for the wail of the priest and the occasional scraping of a chair against the floor, and as I sat there bathed in that light, absorbed in rapt contemplation of the marble miracle which rose before me, cunningly wrought as a casket of ivory and enriched with jewel-like incrustations and tarnished gleams of gold, I felt myself borne onward along a mighty current whose source seemed to be in the very beginning of things, and whose tremendous waters gathered as they went all the mingled streams of human passion and endeavour. Life in all its varied manifestations of beauty and strangeness seemed weaving a rhythmical dance around me as I moved, and wherever the spirit of man had passed I knew that my foot had once been familiar.

"As I gazed, the mediæval bosses of the tabernacle of Orcagna seemed to melt and flow into their primal forms, so that the folded lotus of the Nile and the Greek acanthus were braided with the runic knots and fish-tailed monsters of the North, and all the plastic terror and beauty born of man's hand from the Ganges to the Baltic quivered and mingled in Orcagna's apotheosis of Mary. And so the river bore me on, past the alien face of antique civilisations and the familiar wonders of Greece, till I swam upon the fiercely rushing tide of the Middle Ages, with its swirling eddies of passion, its heaven-reflecting pools of poetry and art; I heard the rhythmic blow of the craftsmen's hammers in the goldsmiths' workshops and on the walls of churches, the party-cries of armed factions in the narrow streets, the organ-roll of Dante's verse, the crackle of the faggots around Arnold of Brescia, the twitter of the swallows to which St. Francis preached, the laughter of the ladies listening on the hillside to the quips of the Decameron, while plague-struck Florence howled beneath them—all this and much more I heard, joined in strange unison with voices earlier and more remote, fierce, passionate, or tender, yet subdued to such awful harmony that I thought of the song that the morning stars sang together and felt as though it were sounding in my ears. My heart beat to suffocation, the tears burned my lids, the joy, the mystery of it seemed too intolerable to be borne. I could not understand even then the words of the song; but I knew that if there had been someone at my side who could have heard it with me, we might have found the key to it together.

"I turned to my husband, who was sitting beside me in an attitude of patient dejection, gazing into the bottom of his hat; but at that moment he rose, and stretching his stiffened legs, said, mildly: 'Hadn't we better be going? There doesn't seem to be much to see here, and you know the table d'hôte dinner is at half-past six o'clock.' "

Her recital ended, there was an interval of silence; then the Spirit of Life said: "There is a compensation in store for such needs as you have expressed."

"Oh, then you *do* understand?" she exclaimed. "Tell me what compensation, I entreat you!"

"It is ordained", the Spirit answered, "that every soul which seeks in vain on earth for a kindred soul to whom it can lay bare its inmost being shall find that soul here and be united to it for eternity."

A glad cry broke from her lips.

"Ah, shall I find him at last?" she cried, exultant.

"He is here," said the Spirit of Life.

She looked up and saw that a man stood near whose soul (for in that unwonted light she seemed to see his soul more clearly than his face) drew her towards him with an invincible force.

"Are you really he?" she murmured.

"I am he," he answered.

She laid her hand in his and drew him towards the parapet which overhung the valley.

"Shall we go down together," she asked him, "into that marvellous country; shall we see it together, as if with the selfsame eyes, and tell each other in the same words all that we think and feel?"

"So", he replied, "have I hoped and dreamed."

"What?" she asked, with rising joy. "Then you, too, have looked for me?"

"All my life."

"How wonderful! And did you never, never find anyone in the other world who understood you?"

"Not wholly—not as you and I understand each other."

"Then you feel it, too? Oh, I am happy," she sighed.

They stood, hand in hand, looking down over the parapet upon the shimmering landscape which stretched forth beneath them into sapphirine space, and the Spirit of Life, who kept watch near the threshold, heard now and then a floating fragment of their talk blown backwards like the stray swallows which the wind sometimes separates from their migratory tribe.

"Did you never feel at sunset—"

"Ah, yes; but I never heard anyone else say so. Did you?"

"Do you remember that line in the third canto of the 'Inferno'?"

"Ah, that line—my favourite always. Is it possible—"

"You know the stooping Victory in the frieze of the Nike Apteros?"

"You mean the one who is tying her sandal? Then you have noticed, too, that all Botticelli and Mantegna are dormant in those flying folds of her drapery?"

"After a storm in autumn have you never seen—"

"Yes, it is curious how certain flowers suggest certain painters—the perfume of the carnation, Leonardo; that of the rose Titian; the tuberose, Crivelli—"

"I never supposed that anyone else had noticed it."

"Have you never thought—"

"Oh, yes, often and often; but I never dreamed that anyone else had."

"But surely you must have felt—"

"Oh, yes, yes; and you, too—"

"How beautiful! How strange—"

Their voices rose and fell, like the murmur of two fountains answering each other across a garden full of flowers. At length, with a certain tender impatience, he turned to her and said: "Love, why should we linger here? All eternity lies before us. Let us go down into that beautiful country together and make a home for ourselves on some blue hill above the shining river."

As he spoke, the hand she had forgotten in his was suddenly withdrawn, and he felt that a cloud was passing over the radiance of her soul.

"A home," she repeated, slowly, "a home for you and me to live in for all eternity?"

"Why not, love? Am I not the soul that yours has sought?"

"Y-yes—yes, I know—but, don't you see, home would not be like home to me, unless—"

"Unless?" he wonderingly repeated.

She did not answer, but she thought to herself, with an impulse of whimsical inconsistency, "Unless you slammed the door and wore creaking boots."

But he had recovered his hold upon her hand, and by imperceptible degrees was leading her towards the shining steps which descended to the valley.

"Come, O my soul's soul," he passionately implored; "why delay a moment? Surely you feel, as I do, that eternity itself is too short to hold such bliss as ours. It seems to me that I can see our home already. Have I not always seen it in my dreams? It is white, love, is it not, with polished columns, and a sculptured cornice against the blue? Groves of laurel and oleander and thickets of roses surround it; but from the terrace where we walk at sunset, the eye looks out over woodlands and cool meadows where, deep-bowered under ancient boughs, a stream goes delicately towards the river. Indoors our favourite pictures hang upon the walls and the rooms are lined with books. Think, dear, at last we shall have time to read them all. With which shall we begin? Come, help me to choose. Shall it be 'Faust' or the *Vita Nuova*, the 'Tempest' or 'Les Caprices de Marianne,' or the thirty-first canto of the *Paradise*, or 'Epipsychidion' or 'Lycidas'? Tell me, dear, which one?"

As he spoke he saw the answer trembling joyously upon her lips; but it died in the ensuing silence, and she stood motionless, resisting the persuasion of his hand.

"What is it?" he entreated.

"Wait a moment," she said, with a strange hesitation in her voice. "Tell me first, are you quite sure of yourself? Is there no one on earth whom you sometimes remember?"

"Not since I have seen you," he replied; for, being a man, he had indeed forgotten.

Still she stood motionless, and he saw that the shadow deepened on her soul.

"Surely, love," he rebuked her, "it was not that which troubled you? For my part I have walked through Lethe. The past has melted like a cloud before the moon. I never lived until I saw you."

She made no answer to his pleadings, but at length, rousing herself with a visible effort, she turned away from him and moved towards the Spirit of Life, who still stood near the threshold.

"I want to ask you a question," she said, in a troubled voice.

"Ask," said the Spirit.

"A little while ago," she began, slowly, "you told me that every soul which has not found a kindred soul on earth is destined to find one here."

"And have you not found one?" asked the Spirit.

"Yes; but will it be so with my husband's soul also?"

"No," answered the Spirit of Life, "for your husband imagined that he had found his soul's mate on earth in you; and for such delusions eternity itself contains no cure."

She gave a little cry. Was it of disappointment or triumph?

"Then—then what will happen to him when he comes here?"

"That I cannot tell you. Some field of activity and happiness he will doubtless find, in due measure to his capacity for being active and happy."

She interrupted, almost angrily: "He will never be happy without me."

"Do not be too sure of that," said the Spirit.

She took no notice of this, and the Spirit continued: "He will not understand you here any better than he did on earth."

"No matter," she said; "I shall be the only sufferer, for he always thought that he understood me."

"His boots will creak just as much as ever—"

"No matter."

"And he will slam the door—"

"Very likely."

"And continue to read railway novels—"

She interposed, impatiently: "Many men do worse than that."

"But you said just now", said the Spirit, "that you did not love him."

"True," she answered, simply; "but don't you understand that I shouldn't feel at home without him? It is all very well for a week or two—but for eternity! After all, I never minded the creaking of his boots, except when my head ached, and I don't suppose it will ache *here*; and he was always so sorry when he had slammed the door, only he never *could* remember not to. Besides, no one else would know how to look after him, he is so helpless. His inkstand would never be filled, and he would always be out of stamps and visiting-cards. He would never remember to have his umbrella recovered, or to ask the price of anything before he bought it. Why, he wouldn't even know what novels to read. I always had to choose the kind he liked, with a murder or a forgery and a successful detective."

She turned abruptly to her kindred soul, who stood listening with a mien of wonder and dismay.

"Don't you see", she said, "that I can't possibly go with you?"

"But what do you intend to do?" asked the Spirit of Life.

"What do I intend to do?" she returned, indignantly. "Why, I mean to wait for my husband, of course. If he had come here first *he* would have waited for me for years and years; and it would break his heart not to find me here when he comes." She pointed with a contemptuous gesture to the magic vision of hill and vale sloping away to the translucent mountains. "He wouldn't give a fig for all that," she said, "if he didn't find me here."

"But consider," warned the Spirit, "that you are now choosing for eternity. It is a solemn moment."

"Choosing!" she said, with a half-sad smile. "Do you still keep up here that old fiction about choosing? I should have thought that *you* knew better than that. How can I help myself? He will expect to find me here when he comes, and he would never believe you if you told him that I had gone away with someone else—never, never."

"So be it," said the Spirit. "Here, as on earth, each one must decide for himself."

She turned to her kindred soul and looked at him gently, almost wistfully. "I am sorry," she said. "I should have liked to talk with you again; but you will understand, I know, and I dare say you will find someone else a great deal cleverer—"

And without pausing to hear his answer she waved him a swift farewell and turned back towards the threshold.

"Will my husband come soon?" she asked the Spirit of Life.

"That you are not destined to know," the Spirit replied.

"No matter," she said, cheerfully; "I have all eternity to wait in."

And still seated alone on the threshold, she listens for the creaking of his boots.